HEAVEN

THE BOOK OF LEO AND ELISE

By

LOWELL NEKKO

This is a work of fiction in which all events and characters in this book are completely imaginary. Any resemblance to actual people is entirely coincidental.

No parts of this book may be copied, distributed, or published in any form without permission from the copyright holder.

This work and derivatives cannot be used to train machine learning models without the permission of the copyright holder.

Cover art by Lowell Nekko
Cityscape graphic courtesy of Vecteezy.com

nekkobooks.com
New York

CONTENTS

ARRIVAL

Leo rolled in bed, begging for a few extra minutes of sleep, but the sharp sunrays cut through the defense of his eyelids and forced him to surrender to the new day. He frowned and peeled his eyes open. The space looked familiar. Acutely familiar, in fact. Leo blinked, his molars still showing, propped himself up, and gazed around. If he didn't know better, he'd say that he had traveled back in space and time. He was in his room from the days when *The Wall* was still topping the charts. A gentle breeze animated the sheer curtains drawn over the balcony's open doors and an elderly woman was sitting on the ottoman he'd had back then, looking at him.

"Mom?!" Leo mumbled.

"Good morning," she said softly and smiled. She was as he had carved her into his mind on the day she died, only healthy and with her hair dye obliterating all traces of silver. Even her voice was the same! Or his memory was not serving him particularly well.

"Come," she continued. "We are waiting for you."

Leo sat on the edge and lingered there, trying to make sense of the scene. The last thing he remembered was a sharp pain in his chest and darkness dropping down like the lid of a dumpster, only without the clank. The pain was gone now, and he was feeling unusually energized. Was he hallucinating under the influence of some drug? The visions in his dreams were always smudged and chaotic, like animated abstract paintings, with each hazy shape and blob of color representing someone or something. Often there wasn't even color—it was all in shades of gray. Maybe fifty? He never counted them; he couldn't. It was like watching a malfunctioning analogue TV set. But not now, the visuals were crystal clear, upgraded to 8K and in 3D.

"Come," his mom repeated and got up. Leo followed. He looked at his old desk. He'd built it himself from sheets of plywood he expropriated from the stack Mr. Toro, the next-door neighbor, had kept for ages in their storage unit in the basement. Leo liked making things. His eyes moved next to the dream catcher pinned over the headboard from that trip to Niagara Falls in the summer of '79. And the *Star Wars* poster hanging on the wall above the nightstand.

His mom opened the door and stepped into the hallway. Leo glided his finger down the glossy paper of the poster. Later in life he would have a friend whose nickname was Jabba the Hutt.

He pushed the silly memory away and hurried after her. At the end of the hallway was the half-lite kitchen door with the Open/Closed sign he once installed on it for fun still hanging there. Midway to the left was the living room. A cat showed briefly at the threshold, then pulled back inside. *Fluffy?* Leo thought . . . *or Ginger?* Ah, they both looked alike, he'd have to sniff their butts to tell them apart. He glanced into the room and saw the white wallpaper, the beige wall-to-wall carpet, and the set of very old but sturdy armchairs his father left behind. The animal had disappeared. The kitchen door made its weird crackling sound and drew his attention. His mother stood by it, waiting for him to enter first.

"Wait for a sec . . ." Leo said. He wanted to see his face. There had always been a mirror in the bathroom. But the bathroom door was missing, now just a smooth surface. Was it bricked up for some reason? Leo was even more confused. He knocked on the wall—it didn't sound hollow, then stepped into the kitchen. It was the version with pink cabinets and sky-blue tiles. His mom's parents, Vivian and Nicholas, sat beside the small table. Vivian was sipping tea from an old hand-crafted porcelain cup she never actually used—the china set was just for display—and Nick was petting Fluffy, who had loafed on his thigh. A beer bottle stood on the table next to him. Both smiled and rose to greet him. The cat slipped to the floor and glanced at the humans with contempt.

"Mirror, mirror, where are you?" Leo murmured, scanning the kitchen. *Nah, we never had one in here. Wait!* There was a mirror in his mother's room adjacent to the kitchen, on her dresser! He turned around and opened the door. It wasn't her room. It was his. The one he was dwelling in before his great-grandmother passed, and he took over her space making this one available for other occupants.

"There aren't any," his grandmother said. "Come, sit, have some tea or coffee. Tell us how you've been. Your mom was last, and it's been twenty years."

Leo looked past her through the kitchen window, trying to see what it was like outside, but the leafy trees were in the way. He sighed and sat down. Should he be happy to see them? They could not be real. What brought them back and why?

"Here," his mom said and pushed a steaming mug toward him. "You can have a cigarette, if you want. It will do you no harm now."

"But isn't he too young to smoke?" Nick asked.

"He's sixty, er, eighty."

"Yeah, sure, I keep forgetting," Nick replied, his tone calm, and sat back in his chair. Fluffy walked to Leo's mom and rubbed at her legs. Leo bent down and petted the animal. The cat looked up and winced. From day one, their relationship was strained for whatever reason a feline might have to dislike a human. Maybe he smelled like a banana.

"Leo," his grandma said, "you are not dreaming."

Leo sat upright and looked at her, then at his mom, then at Nick. *Not dreaming?* Maybe not, considering how barely coherent his dreams always were, but this place couldn't be real either. He was living far from his childhood home, very far. Unless . . .

"Am I dead?"

"Yes," his mom said and laid her hands on his shoulders. Then she stroked what was left of his hair. Somehow it felt as if he still had a full mane. He raised hand in a bid to confirm but stopped halfway and slapped his thigh instead. "Great! Just great!"

"And you?" He squinted. "Are you zombies?"

"What do you think? Could it be otherwise?" Nick asked with a chuckle.

"I don't know. It feels so unreal . . ."

"Unreal?" Nick's deep voice thundered. "It felt very real to me when I arrived. That's what tipped me off. Frankly I didn't expect it to be like this. I expected angels and choruses. And to meet God. Or Satan and raging fires. And I was relieved to find neither. Being broiled is excruciating but so is singing praises to no end. I know, I was a choir boy . . ."

It began to dawn on Leo that the experience was gratifying. The light was bright but not blinding, the air was fresh, and the coffee smelled nice and tasted great unlike the decaf shit forced upon him by his hypertension. His body felt strong and buoyant, and he was glad to be sharing the room with them despite his doubts.

"Hi, Leo!" a voice called from behind him. He turned sideways and traced the source. A woman in her forties with an old-fashioned hairstyle and similarly ancient dress was standing in the door frame.

"Babette?" Leo inquired with hesitation. He remembered well the old photograph of his great-grandmother, from which this woman seemed to have materialized. But how? His great-grandmother was ninety years old when she passed away.

"My favorite in-law!" Nick exclaimed mockingly but received no reprimand. Leo turned to check him then back to that woman. And there she was—the granny he remembered with her paper-thin, spotty wrinkled skin and her silver hair, rolled in a bun. Leo squeezed his eyes shut then opened them again. She was still there, still old. Suddenly it became difficult to breathe, his heart started pounding, and he felt an urge to escape from the friendly crowd. He stood up resolutely and announced, "I'm going out!"

"Sure," his mom said. "We can walk the dog."

"No, I want to be alone!" Leo laid his hands on his great-grand-mother's shoulders, hugged her briefly, then squeezed himself past her toward the exit.

"I understand . . ." His mother followed him with her gaze, sighed, and sat in the chair he'd just vacated.

Leo opened the apartment door and examined the space in front of him. The elevator cage was there on the left, the walls—painted the same pale-yellow color he'd always known. He closed the door behind him, pushed the elevator button, and soon heard the hum of the mo-tor, accompanied by the faint scent of hot grease. As the cabin top emerged, Leo changed his mind and decided to take the stairs.

Upon reaching them, he gripped the handrail tightly and carefully extended his left foot forward—his legs were not what they used to be. Then he realized that, so far, he had no trouble walking. He low-ered the foot on the first step below, then tried the other one. His joints felt well-oiled, and his muscles were springy. Leo took a few more steps down while still clutching the handrail, then relaxed his grip and proceeded at a steady pace. Then faster. And faster. He started skipping steps, then leaped over several of them just as he used to do in his youth. The momentum threw him at the entrance door. He pushed it open with both hands and came to a stop on the sidewalk. *Wow!*

The street was deserted. The sun was already high, the weather balmy, the air fresh. The shade from the trees dulled the spears of the sunrays before they could reach his eyes. In his childhood, the air of-ten stank of rotting garbage and vehicular exhaust.

The French restaurant was still across the street, emitting clanking kitchen noises and muffled conversations.

Interesting . . . Leo crossed and looked inside. The tables were dressed in red tablecloths with salt and pepper dispensers ready to salute the patrons, but there was not a soul in sight. Leo wanted to explore further, when a high-pitched meow sounded nearby. A black kitten was standing on the sill of a basement window, looking at him, as if unsure whether to stay or run.

"Inky?" Leo murmured, a distant memory surfacing in his mind. He squatted and tried to pet the tiny animal. "Is that you, boy?"

"No, this is Schmo," said another familiar voice. "You have finally arrived, I see . . ."

Leo gasped and twisted his neck. "Steve!"

Stephen had died in 2020 from COVID. They'd first met on day one in school but became friends later. They were then separated briefly for their military training. After that they went on to attend the same university. All these years together turned them into best friends. By the look of it, truly forever, if this was the afterlife. Later, they drifted apart when Leo had moved overseas but went wild for a night each time Leo visited the motherland. Until, one day, Leo got a text from a mutual friend saying that Steve was gone.

"Yes, sir!" the other man said with glee and helped him rise to his feet.

They hugged.

"Long time no see, eh?" Steve said.

"Yes, but how did you know I was—"

"Here? It will come to you eventually; it is not easy to find words to describe it. Come, let's get some drinks, it's the tradition, no?"

Steve lifted the little animal from the sill and slid it in his pocket like a stuffed toy.

"You're gonna squash him!" objected Leo.

"Nah, he's all right. Let's go, I'm thirsty."

"What about 'Le Chienne'?" suggested Leo.

"The bitch? What bitch?"

"The restaurant. Right here," Leo said impatiently, pointing at the entrance, where the name of the establishment was spelled out clearly.

Steve looked puzzled. "This ain't a restaurant. Last time I recall it was an art gallery, but now it's closed . . ." Steve paused. "Ah, I see . . ."

"You see what?"

"Later," the other man replied. "Yeah, let's give it a try. I'm curious . . ."

Leo pulled the door, but it stayed shut. *That's strange—just a minute ago it was wide open. When did they lock it?* He shook it, then pressed his palms against the glass and peeked inside. The tables were still there, still expecting patrons.

"Well, I guess I'm not welcome here," said Steve. "It must be past my time."

I don't understand, thought Leo. He wanted answers, but he was afraid to ask the questions. Was he really dead? Or somewhere in a coma on life support and the sensory deprivation had sent some parts of his brain into overdrive? How could he tell?

I have no face! he realized, as no discernible reflection appeared in the glass. He sighed. *Whatever, it is still exciting!*

"Hey, Steve!" Leo called. "Why aren't there any cars around? Don't people drive here?"

"People? Do you see any? No people, no cars. Makes perfect sense, no?"

Indeed, there weren't any people either. That was, beside the two of them and his folks upstairs.

"I have a car," continued Steve. "Hey, that's a good idea, let's take a ride!"

"How?"

"Follow me!" his friend said and walked toward the intersection, while petting the kitten with a finger. When they turned the corner, a yellow Lamborghini with both doors up waited for them. It was a very old model, yet still looked slick. The quintessential Italian sports car and very representative of Steve's passion.

"Wanna drive?" Steve offered politely.

"Nope, you take it. I don't know the place, do I?"

"I guess you are right. Looks can be deceiving."

They climbed in. Steve revved the engine, then drove carefully over the uneven granite pavers until they reached the smooth asphalt of Linden Boulevard. Leo silently examined the surroundings. Neither people nor vehicles were anywhere to be seen. The buildings seemed to match his memories of them. But something was amiss. He narrowed his eyes, trying to spot the difference.

Graffiti! There was no graffiti! Ah, how he hated it! He recognized the art form aspect and there were some cool pieces, Banksy and Lady Pink works coming to mind, but most graffiti were just the doodles of talentless vandals, putting a lot of unwelcome strain on his optic nerves.

"There is no graffiti," he said.

"What? Ah, yes, I hate it too." Steve made a right turn and headed toward the cross-river tunnel.

"So, tell me, have you heard of the girls lately?" Steve asked, referring probably to his two daughters. "Pickie joined the club quite some time ago, no news since then."

"Sorry mate, no idea. I haven't seen them since you passed and that was not yesterday." It was becoming increasingly natural for Leo to casually refer to someone's death. "They are still here . . . erm, I mean there . . . I suppose . . . and I was in Johannesburg."

"Did you get murdered there?"

"No, revisiting old places . . . on vacation. The city of gold is now a dump." Leo sighed. "I knew that, but I couldn't help seeing it with my own eyes. It is sad . . . anyway, I haven't been home for a couple of years, and you never introduced me to your wife, remember? So, what I know is what others may share, and it hasn't been much."

"I get it. And what about you? You had a son, right? How's he?" Steve asked.

"Eric's doing fine, thanks. Did you forget that I remarried, and I have a daughter too?"

"Ah, yeah, it slipped my mind, sorry."

Leo threw a grumpy glance at his friend but then mellowed. Ah, the curse of distance. He himself had forgotten what Steve called his offspring.

"Her name's Abigail." He reminded. "It's laughable, but she's young enough to be my grandchild. But men do stupid things in their fifties. She's married. To a girl."

Steve glanced at Leo. "You are joking, right?"

"No, why would I be? You've heard of lesbians, have you not?"

"Sure . . . and you are OK with it? I mean, it must have been bad when she confessed, right? Did you kick her out?"

Leo frowned.

"I am perfectly OK, and I *did not* kick her out. Susan, Abi's wife was dating Eric in those days, but then Abi flew over to visit her grandma and the two, er, Abi and Susi, discovered each other, unfortunately to Eric's detriment. He was gracious though—still loves his sister and when Susi asked him to be the father of her child he agreed. I don't know if they slept together, or he donated sperm. Anyway . . . He is alone, though. And lonely, going through girlfriends and never finding the one to keep. I sometimes worry that Susi leaving him for a girl, for his own sister, might have scarred him in some way."

"I get it," Steve said. "Times change, and I am glad it didn't hurt. What about Abi's mom? News about Beatrice?"

"Bea—no idea. Liz—she was pushing for a kid, and I succumbed. She's much younger after all, never been a mom, her wish was understandable, and Abigail Lily Annette Elizabeth Hackensack was made." Leo laughed.

"That's a mouthful. Her mom's not royalty by any chance, is she?"

"Nah, we liked the sound of it but when it came time to fill out forms it became a problem. Luckily, there aren't many of this kind left to fill. D'you remember the ones with the squares, one for each letter . . ."

"Yeah." Steve chuckled. "Did you glue two of them together?"

Leo did not reply. He was looking out and wondering where all the traffic signs had gone. There were no signs and no other cars, besides the one they were riding in. Strange world.

He turned to his friend. "What do you make out of this place?"

"It is the afterlife, for sure. And it is weird, but you will get used to it."

"I would have expected the afterlife to be much more crowded, overpopulated, in fact. With all the people dying over the millennia."

"Maybe it is crowded, but we just can't see and interact with others. We can see only people we have emotional connections with. I guess it must be a positive one. I can't remember seeing anyone I've disliked." Steve got onto the freeway, switched to manual, and pushed the pedal to the floor. "Wow, I love it!" he exclaimed as the acceleration fused them with the seats.

"Where are we going?" Leo asked.

"No idea. In this world you never know."

Leo looked at the speedometer. Steve was grinning and occasionally biting his lips while tapping the gear paddles with his fingertips, as if playing a tune. The needle approached the 350 kph mark. Each time Steve entered a bend, the tires screeched, leaving black trails and streaks of smoke behind, and Leo was thrust sharply to the left or right.

Steve was exhilarated, but being tossed around like a hot potato brought Leo zero joy. This car was fun to drive, not so much to ride, especially with a maniac like his friend behind the wheel. He couldn't help wondering what would happen if Steve was unable to keep the monster on the road and they slammed into the barrier. Would they die again? Or would he awaken in the real world? As a kid, he had that reoccurring dream where something sinister and scary was chasing him and, to escape, he had to jump from a high floor and wake up before hitting the ground.

"Steve, what would happen if we crashed?!" Leo shouted, trying to overpower the wind noise and engine's roar. The driver did not react. Leo leaned closer to his friend and shouted in his ear, "Hey, Steve!"

"What?" Steve shouted back, eyes still firmly on the road.

"Please crash!" Leo barked and jerked the steering wheel. Steve lost his grip. The car lurched violently and became airborne.

YOU ONLY DIE TWICE

Leo flipped his eyes open and tried to bring the human silhouette casting a shadow over him into focus.

"Silly boy. You only die twice," Annette said softly, and stepped back.

Leo sat up. He had returned to his room. His mother was her usual patient self.

"Come," she said, "we are still waiting. Will you please at least pretend to be jolly for seeing us?"

"Are you real?" he retorted.

"In a way. You don't have to be angry."

"I guess you are right." He checked his teeth with his tongue—they were all accounted for. The damn implants had cost a small fortune. "Whatever this place may be, I kind of feel good about it, to be honest. I just crashed Steve's car . . ." he added with a sense of guilt. "Will he be OK? He was inside too."

"Steve Gasfart?"

"Yep!" Leo giggled loudly.

"You seem proud of the accomplishment . . ."

"No, not that; you said 'Gasfart'."

"So?" His mother nudged her shoulders up and pouted.

"This is how we mock him. His real surname is 'Haaspert'."

"Oh!" The woman blushed but recovered quickly. "You are fine, aren't you? Same applies to him. These are the rules here. You only die twice. At least this is what we think . . ."

"What do you mean by 'twice'?"

"You'll understand," Annette said and beckoned him to follow. This time they took a left and entered the living room. Vivian, Nick, and Babs were there. Fluffy emerged from behind the curtain, sat, and began grooming himself. Leo slumped into the unoccupied armchair and tilted his head upward staring at the ceiling. His mom pulled a stool.

"Leo, don't you get it yet?" his grandmother asked. "This is all it's about—getting back together for a while. Then we drift away."

Leo looked at her. Memories of the days he spent with her climbing the mountains and eating porridge in the cable car flooded his mind. And Granny Babs throwing anything in sight at Mr. Geber, the neighbor from the second floor, who was chasing Leo through the yard for daring to pick an apple. There was an apple tree on the common property, which for some reason Geber had assumed belonged to him alone and guarded jealously. Walter Geber was a senile old man, so this was in a way normal.

Leo could not recall if she scored a hit, so he went on, "Babs, do you remember throwing stuff at old Walter, when he went ballistic about the apple I 'stole'? Did you manage to hit him?"

Babette smiled and said, "I don't think so. I was throwing laundry pegs, so even if I did, he wouldn't have noticed. But you outran him anyway."

"So, you weren't really helping, were you?" Leo laughed and so did the others.

The doorbell chimed, yet nobody moved. They just turned their heads toward the foyer.

A man, Uncle George, filled the door frame. "Hello! How's it going? Leo, you OK?". He was as energetic as Leo could recall.

Leo rose and exchanged the customary hugs with his uncle. "Getting acclimated." He smiled, then peeked into the foyer over George's shoulder and asked, "Where's Miriam? She must be here somewhere, mustn't she?"

The mood changed.

"Not all people end up here," Nick said. "She didn't make it." He continued in a quiet voice as if talking to himself, "Maybe we didn't love her enough . . ."

Miriam was Leo's aunt, his mother's younger sister. She was a colorful character and a talented singer, but sadly, also an addict. Leo remembered mostly her bright side, but he was aware of her antics as well. Her violent screaming sessions, her empty promises, her thievery. Her stints in rehab had cost small fortunes, only for her to relapse soon after checking out. She joined a band in the late '60s and started getting high on heroin and LSD and anything else she could inject, ingest, and sniff like probably everybody else doing art at that time. She neither made it big, nor did she join her idols Jim and Janice in the 27 Club. She muddled on instead, making life miserable for herself and those around her for another twenty-seven years until one day she overdosed. George was incredibly patient and loving and tried his best to help her. He divorced her eventually but pushed for custody of their two kids and did a great job as a single dad. An early pattern was beginning to emerge for Leo about this world and its inhabitants.

"We're all here now, so let's feast," Vivian clapped her hands and rose to her feet surprisingly vivaciously for her seventy-nine years of age. Leo turned in his chair and glanced at the dining table behind him. It was already laid out with steam coming out of the many pots. How did he not notice it when he entered the room? And how did it end up here in the first place? Leo looked around, gasping in surprise. The room was different. It now belonged to an even earlier time of his life, featuring beige walls, dark brown, velvet curtains, the Ficus in the corner, and the large dining table surrounded by leather uphol-stered chairs. Amazing! These transformations were growing on him. He wished he knew how it all worked. Figuring it out was something he could occupy himself with in the days to come.

They each chose a place around the table. Nick picked up the still hot boule, broke it quickly into pieces, and handed them out. Leo took his and saw something wrapped in foil embedded in the crumb. He dug it up with fingers. It was a coin. Leo remembered—this was Christmas boule. His maternal lineage was Eastern Orthodox, and they kept some of its customs.

Leo smiled. He recalled the festive mood of those early winter eve-nings when Babette and Vivian were making the Coin bread and other scrumptious stuff as the holidays drew nearer. He was an only child, and they always rigged the Christmas Eve draw so he ended up with the coin. He looked at the other dishes on the table. There was his great-grandmother's handmade poultry pie. He loved it. They had a range cooker in the apartment. Babette, however, always used the services of a nearby bakery for her pies and pastries. She said that the pies tasted much better when baked in a wood-fired oven. She never baked one in their electric oven for him to compare, but what she was producing was delicious and he didn't dispute her claim; he simply didn't care.

He spotted homemade chocolate mousse. Something he hadn't tasted for over a decade after he developed diabetes in his late 60s. Also, his mother's chicken fingers and her whitefish soup. It was a col-lection of signature dishes, each having been withdrawn from his menu with the passing of its cook. The smells sent his mind to a point in time when the memories converged. He stayed there for a mo-ment, then returned to the present.

"Mom, what did you mean by 'you only die twice'? You deflected my question, really . . ."

"Well, to get here you must die, right?"

"Still debatable," Leo said. "I may be somewhere in a coma, imag-ining you all."

"I understand your hesitation. You were always a skeptic. I talk from experience," she replied. "When I got here, I met Granddad Marcus and Granddad Peter and Mother Vesna and even my goldfish. But I can't see them anymore. They disappeared. I can't bring them back no matter what."

"Yeah," Nick added. "Same here. This life is not forever. Well, I don't know that for sure. The point is we no longer have contact with prior generations. Which, I guess counts as 'not forever.' They were here, then not so much, then one day they disappeared altogether. Maybe they've moved on, the way we all did when we migrated here from old Earth."

Leo turned toward his great-grandmother. "Babs, you were very observant. Did you meet God?"

"No, but I met Mom and Dad and Sheela and Valentine and Marcus and Vivian and your mom and you," Babette said softly, her face lighting up. "That makes me very glad."

"I am sure it was He who granted me these wishes and this time," she added and traced the cross.

"Maybe it was Him indeed," Nick said. "Maybe one day we'll know. Cheers now . . ."

"So, this is what you meant by 'you only die twice'. One comes here and then one fades away. Interesting . . ." Leo said, then attacked the food with gusto. He'd had to endure so many dietary restrictions in the fading years of his life—but was now, at last, free to pig out.

DAD

The next morning, Leo woke up alone. The door was ajar, and the aroma of freshly brewed coffee had found its way into his room, tickling his nostrils. Leo sat on the edge and searched the room for his clothes, then realized he already had them on. Did he go to bed fully dressed? Seemed he had drunk a bit too much, for no recall of the late evening was forthcoming. Sleeping like that would not have been comfortable, yet he didn't have the feeling that this was the case. He wasn't perspiring and no garment was creased and unsightly.

He pulled up his sleeves and inspected his forearms. He could see them clearly, unlike in his dreams. He remembered the character of Don Juan from Carlos Castañeda's books and how Don Juan was saying that controlling dreams meant being able to see one's hands. Maybe he was dreaming after all and had somehow acquired this important skill. He looked at his hands and fanned his fingers. He was eighty-one and these limbs did not belong to him, certainly not to a person that old. They looked—how could he put it—ageless. He again grew desperate to find a mirror. The one in the foyer was gone, the bathroom was missing too, and he ended up in his other room.

Where do people here poop and pee? Maybe he should try finding a bathroom again. Yesterday he'd stuffed himself, and drank, yet his bowels hadn't moved at all. Was he constipated? What if the urge came? These thoughts faded away, and he found himself standing in front of an apartment door. The little brass plaque read "Hackensack." He pushed the button of the doorbell, wondering how he'd traveled there.

"A dead man walking," his father said from behind him.

Leo briskly pivoted around on his heels. "Hi, Dad! I'm here."

"Obviously. Come in."

Leo dropped all pretense of comprehending. The door was right in front of him, now it was behind?! Why? Maybe Richard would explain. He followed his father and almost bumped his head on the frame, ducking just before his skull kissed the wood. He had forgotten how unusually low it was.

The room he stepped into was white, with the old wall units still there but painted in the same color as the walls. This made the space feel larger. The couch was new. This is how he remembered the room from his last visit, after his father died. *I wonder what he is seeing?* Leo thought.

"Hey, Dad, what color are the walls?"

"White."

"And the wall units?"

"Also white. Your stepmom didn't change much."

"I see . . . Will I see her?" Leo asked. "And Granddad and Mom? A chance to get to know them, no?"

"Jessica—for sure. But your grandparents—no, they already drifted away. Anyway, tell me, how's your brother? No one beside you has joined recently, and we are eager for some news."

As usual his half-brother Carl was the star, but Leo let it slide. He no longer cared after all these years. "If this is the afterlife, people die every day. Are the gates this tight?"

"Just think—who did you see?"

Leo quickly returned to the original question: "He's doing just fine for his age, I heard. He found God, though, and your good great kids are driven mad from his incessant preaching. They asked me to try to talk some sense into him, but it was hopeless. I don't know why the Holy Alcohol possessed him; he was a reasonable man."

"You shouldn't be so deriding. Belief helps people meet the end of earthly life. After all, nobody knows what awaits, and that breeds fear—the fear of ceasing to exist. Did you ever anticipate this place? If you did, would the fear of dying not have been mitigated to a great degree? Turning to God is his way of dealing with his dread."

"I agree, but he's not even seventy and it can get annoying very quickly when the devotee starts proselytizing aggressively. You did not insist that your musings about the afterlife were the undeniable and only truth, nor did you try to save us from your god. He's a hard-core born-again Christian now, a missionary for the Faith."

"A zealot you say . . . If so, he may not make it here one day," Richard responded thoughtfully.

"How's that?" Leo asked, but before he got an answer, the door opened and his stepmother entered the room.

"Hello, darling!" She extended arms in embrace. "Did it hurt? How's Carl? Seen him recently? What about the kids?"

"Slow down . . ." Leo said. "I'll tell you all I know."

"I was just telling Dad that Carl found Jesus and became a royal pain to be around. Is there any way to message him that hell does not exist, and we are all doing just fine?"

"I am not so sure," Richard said.

"About what, a way to message him?"

"No, about hell. Or both rather. There is no way to send a message back from here, that I know of. Maybe there is, just that we are unaware. Same with hell—how can we be sure? We didn't know anything about this realm, yet we are here. So, there may be a hell somewhere out there, a place where other people end up in."

"Right!" Leo was surprised by the way his father said it. He usually chastised people for not seeing it all themselves. The answer was right there, but the interlocutors were too dumb, distracted, in love, whatever, so they missed what should have been obvious. He had always known better, and it had driven him and Leo apart. His dad was not a bad man and smart too, but his attitude toward others was often condescending and overly paternalistic. And he had the awful habit of answering each question with a question of his own. That simple unimposing explanation was a change for him. Maybe this was what Leo wanted his dad to be like, and his mind was indulging him. As his dad said, who knew? What tests could be performed to determine exactly what was going on? Leo decided to push his luck, worrying that old Richard might resurface.

"Dad, what do you think of this place?"

"What about it?"

"I mean, am I really dead and my consciousness somehow survived and ended up here? Or am I still alive and dreaming?"

"How do you know that you existed elsewhere in the first place? Did you forget Plato, Rene Descartes? It could have been the same—another simulation or whatever. I have banged my head with these questions for what seems like decades now, and I am afraid I have no answers. It could be either way, or neither way."

"What seems like decades," Leo repeated. "The perception of time here is not the same as before, is that what you are saying?"

"Yes. How old were you?"

"Eighty-one."

"So, there is thirty-plus year difference between my earthly demise and yours and it does feel like this. But on the other hand, I do not have thirty years' worth of memories of this place. It is as if time passes much faster when we are idle, so we can't grow bored."

"Is that a plus? Lieutenant Dunbar said that if you want to live forever, you must be bored," Leo said, quoting from his old literary favorite, *Catch 22*.

"You could spend a very long time here and you would probably agree that eternal life would suck. There is a limit to what we can do and comprehend."

Holy poop, I'm enjoying a conversation with my dad for once. Leo removed his shoes under the table and wiggled his toes, trying to remember when he had put these socks on. Then his thought returned to his father. They used to almost always end up hostile toward each other when they were alive. Richard would have objected to Lieutenant Dunbar's allusion, and Leo would have been annoyed by his dad's insistence on being clinical in his speech. To Leo, these had not been leisurely conversations. He was sitting exams that required precise answers with no room to improvise and crack a joke. Maybe this was Richard bringing work home—he was a tenured professor, after all.

"What about people who are not interested in doing anything at all? I had friends like that."

"Most people do have something they like spending time on. Maybe all. I bet your friends did."

Leo considered the statement for a moment, "Damn, you are right again! Yes, they did, of course. What a dummy I am," he said self-deprecatingly.

"Indeed!" His father cracked a laugh too and nudged his brows up.

"Come, let's have some food." Leo's stepmother invited them after the air took the scent of roasted meat. He had no favorite dish she was the master of, and he wondered what exactly would be on the menu. Eating was something that seemed unchanged—he had a feast at home, now more. And still no bowel movements. The men stood up and headed to the dining room. His dad's pad had one of these—still a luxury for most people. Leo saw the bathroom door and his chance to find a mirror. And maybe poop!

"Gonna wash my hands," he said, hurriedly opening the door and stepping inside. The room was dark. He shut his eyes, trying to remember where the light switch was, and slipped into a void.

ON THE FOURTH DAY

Shit, Leo thought, when he found himself under the linens in his room. This place was determined to keep him from looking at his face. And was it yesterday that he met with his dad or just now? He got out of bed and headed for the kitchen, this time paying no attention to his attire. His mom was playing Solitaire.

"Where are the others?" Leo asked.

"Viv and Nick are back at their place and Grandma is in her room."

"But I just came out of there and she wasn't," Leo disagreed.

"Ah . . . I see. So, this is how it works . . ."

Before it was his, it belonged to his great-grandmother. He turned back and approached the room quietly. He put his hand on the door handle and slowly pushed it down until he heard the latch click. The door went ajar with a shy screech. Leo peeked inside. It was *his* room. He closed the door, then tried again. Same result. He then opened it quickly. Still no Babs. Leo closed the door yet again and paused, thinking . . .

"You must knock!" his mom shouted from the kitchen.

He obeyed.

"Come in," He heard Babette saying.

Leo hesitated. What if it didn't work again? He pushed down on the handle. The door swung a quarter open. Leo inserted his head in the gap and looked inside the room. His great-grandmother was sitting in her bed, book in hand. It was either from the rows of books lined up on the wall shelf above her or from the lot on the rolling table parked beside the bed. Babette had had difficulty moving in the last years of her life, so things got rearranged for easy access. The room was mostly as he remembered, yet something felt askew.

"Hi, sweetie." She put the book aside. "Come in, come in."

Leo took the invite, stepped in and pushed the door shut. He moved his gaze around trying to find something out of place. The spare bed was there, against the other wall. The antique, hand-carved wardrobe he later destroyed in a fit of stupidity was there too, serving also as a headboard, which his great-grandmother's stack of pillows rested against. Her rocking chair was in place, as was the treasured icon of The Virgin Mary with the Infant his great-grandmother prayed under every day. The Persian rug, which fell victim to one of his many cats years later, was also present, covering the polished wooden floor. Leo turned his attention to the books on the shelf.

"Gran, do these ever change?"

"Ah, yes, they do," she answered. "But I find some of the new stories strange."

"Like what?"

"Like women loving women for example. And stories of witches doing good."

"But you still read them, seems . . ."

"Yes, the stories are entertaining, and hate is what's bad, not love, even when the love is twisted."

"Do you know that they can get married now? The lesbians I mean. And the gays."

"The gays? Who are these?"

"Homosexual men."

"Ah, the pederasts. Well, times change. I lived a long life, and I saw lots of changes. They used to put them in jail. Now you say pederasts can marry. To whom? Other men?"

Leo nodded. Babette blessed herself, kissed the crucifix she wore, and rolled her eyes.

"Do you know that your great-great-granddaughter is a lesbian? She's married to another girl."

Babette's gaze darkened. "I wouldn't say I'm happy, but I would have stood by her side even in my time. Is she a good girl?"

"What exactly constitutes 'good' in your view?"

"Well, is she a good person? Someone worth loving? Not like Miriam."

"Absolutely!" Leo said. "But why are you holding Aunt Miriam as a benchmark for goodness? She was a drug addict, and drugs change personality. And shouldn't love be unconditional?"

Babette thought for a while, flicking her eyes like a panicked mouse, obviously processing something internally, perhaps a contradiction. From Leo's perspective, the Bible was full of these—love thy neighbor unless she happens to be queer.

Babette finally spoke, "No, not a benchmark, just an example. Miriam was selfish. She knew she was hurting the people around her, people who loved her dearly, yet made no effort to repair herself. There are recovered addicts, aren't there? Her bandmates—they had normal lives as far as I know. You have no idea how patient your grandparents and George were. No judging, anyone can fall into a trap, just helping hands. But she . . . Never mind, I am beginning to judge."

"So, you are not seeing these people as sinners, deserving God's wrath?"

"I never did. They are sick and shall be helped, not judged and jailed. If God disapproves of them, He alone will take care."

"They are not sick, Grandma. Maybe in your time they were considered sick, but not anymore."

"I think that they are ill; something's not screwed right somewhere," insisted Babette. "But a good Christian, a good person, would care for the sick. Like Jesus in His time. Illness makes us afraid, and this is perhaps why so many people fear and hate them. They are afraid of contagion. But Jesus walked amongst the lepers and healed them!"

Leo sighed, however, understood the viewpoint. He wished that more people would share it. He was prepared to make the concession to the pastors that homosexuality was a birth defect for as long as that made his daughter's life easier. But then they would try to "heal" her . . . Damn! People born with heterochromia are not considered abominations. Why should homosexuality be treated any differently? People are born gay, and people are born psychopaths. Yet, the latter—a clear and present danger—are constantly voted and promoted to leadership positions while some jurisdictions once more made being queer a criminal offense. Abigail had to move twice since California turned red.

"Grandma, please don't call gay men pederasts. It is nasty and offensive. Gays are consenting adult males, not sexual predators, and perhaps the best friends a girl can have."

Babette raised her eyebrows.

"I should find a woman of my generation to explain," Leo said. Then it dawned on him—his great-grandmother was not wearing her eyeglasses, nor were there any in sight!

"Grandma, what do you see now?" Leo shoved two fingers in her face. In the past she struggled with the count.

She smiled and said, "I see my boy."

"What boy?"

"The one I remember."

"You mean me when I was fourteen?"

"Yes. I wish I could see you as a grown-up, but it is hard to master quickly. It takes some time."

"What do you mean?"

"Here we see what we remember. I passed when you were fourteen. Your grandfather died when you were only seven. Your mom—when you were in your late fifties, right? So, this is what we see and hear. A teen, a boy, a grown-up man. When you start to see yourself, then you can show yourself to others at any age you wish. For as long as you can find a face to look at in the mirror . . ."

Leo wasn't sure that he understood. Perhaps she meant to say to find a mirror to look at his face in.

"I can't find a single mirror in this world, so how am I supposed to look at me?"

"Seek inside you. Remember," Babette said and faded away. Leo was sitting in his own room now, his head spinning violently.

"Hey, Gran, wait!" he called out, but she was gone. He stepped in the hallway and shut the door, then knocked repeatedly. No answer came. He opened the door and saw his space again, not hers.

"What's going on?" He marched in the kitchen and demanded from his mother. "Grandma's gone. I can't get into her room anymore."

"So, it has started . . ." Annette said with a sad tone.

"What has started?"

"The drift."

What the fuck . . . Leo thought angrily, then went to the range and poured himself some coffee. When he turned around, his mom was gone. He sat in the chair she was occupying just a second ago, slurped, and began to ponder whether to curse the weirdness of this place or to rejoice.

ELISE

Find a mirror. This is what Grandma said, right? But where? Each time he tried, something odd happened. Well, maybe not an oddity here, but not helpful either. The reflections in the glass were distorted beyond recognition. There were no cars on the streets to try their chrome parts. He forgot to check out Steve's mirrors. Steve—Leo hadn't yet apologized for his actions.

He unsuccessfully tried to "teleport" to Steve's place. Interestingly, he managed it when he visited his dad, and he didn't even have to think of it or step outside. He imagined Steve, then his place . . . nothing. There had to be a way, but he figured that, as a novice, he was yet to find it out. For the time being, he was going to do it the old-world way. Leo pulled the apartment door shut and headed down the old terrazzo stairs. The street looked the same—bright and inviting, but still devoid of people and cars. And birds?

Now that he thought about it, he hadn't heard any chirping and cooing. He stood still and listened. The sounds made their way hesitantly at first, then gained confidence. The street livened with sparrows flitting from branch to branch on the lookout for sneaky stray cats, and the occasional pigeon walking clumsily on the ground in search of seeds and crumbs. He thought that he could hear the distant hiss and hum of moving cars. A sliver of white smoke rose from the restaurant's vent stack. And the same faint unintelligible voices he heard before.

Maybe Steve will show up again, Leo thought. *Mirror . . . inside the restaurant, the restrooms had mirrors!* Leo walked in and looked around. Still no people, but there were plates, some empty, others still untouched. And cups and glasses too. Leo was unable to recall where the restrooms were. The restaurant was occupying an old building with several disjoined dining halls and a garden.

Leo ran his gaze in a circle in a bid to find someone to get directions from, but the place was empty. Yeah, this seemed to be the norm around here. He moved from hall to hall. There was once a bar, where patrons waited to be seated. It had mirrored shelves. But it was missing now. Apparently, this place hated bars. And restrooms.

Leo left the restaurant and headed up the street. Steve's place was quite a distance away, but without buses or trams to hop on he was compelled to walk, and he had nothing else to do anyway. He hadn't seen much of the city, of *this* city. It looked familiar, yet glaringly different at the same time. Noises, but no people, no graffiti, no cars. He turned around the corner and halted his advance pursing his lips. He was on Steve's street. He performed an ultra-clumsy moonwalk and looked to his left. It was not his street. He looked straight on again— Steve's street.

Leo made a full turn on his heels. He was standing on another street, the one he should have been on when he made the left. It seemed that this place could somehow read his intentions and transform itself to fit. That would explain the lack of vehicles—no need for them. But then there's still that distant noise . . .

Leo pivoted in a half-circle again, his eyesight blurring briefly. When his vision cleared, he was standing in front of Steve's door. *Wow!* Cool, yet also annoying. He would appreciate more control over these twists. Like just stepping out of and into somewhere . . .

Anyway, maybe that was something else to learn how to perform. He poked the doorbell button. The buzzer sounded, but there was no response. He rang again, then again, this time continuously. Perhaps his friend had become hard on hearing. Leo reached for his phone, but of course it wasn't there. No phones allowed either. *What do those addicted to their devices do here?* Leo asked himself. *And what happens to smart implants?*

He hung at the door for another minute or so, wondering what to do next, then descended the stairs. He didn't want to go straight back home. Maybe just look around, see what's old and new? Leo left Steve's neighborhood and made a right onto the main thoroughfare. In the old world it was loaded with traffic, but here it was quiet. All city noises were muted, as if coming from afar. The tram tracks were not rusty though, noted Leo. Normally they would be, when disused.

Storefronts lined the boulevard. Electronic billboards cycled through their ads, and the occasional pharmacy's green cross sign was flashing even in the daylight. *The billboards seem out of place in this low-tech world,* Leo pouted. He walked past a small café. The outdoor tables were covered with checkered tablecloths, held in place with metal clips. The sugar dispensers were acting as paperweights for the menus. Leo decided to run a test. He pulled a chair, sat down, took a menu, and flipped through it. Chocolate cake, almond cake, hazelnut parfait, Parisian kiss.

All yummy, but an espresso shot would suffice. Leo turned around to check if somebody would approach to take his order. Nobody did. Leo faced the table again and there it was: the espresso he wanted, and the glass of ice-cold water a respectful establishment would serve alongside the brew.

He was beginning to get a grasp on the workings of this place. *What else can I wish for and make suddenly appear?* Leo wondered. He paged through the menu again and checked the items.

There were no listed prices. Leo took a sip from the cup and relaxed in the chair. If it was him generating all these visions, it wasn't bad. He congratulated himself. Quite exciting, actually! If it was a real place, another realm he never thought existed, still fine. Maybe a little lonely, but clean and quiet, and the food and drink were more than decent and also, free. Leo nudged his mouth into a smile, returned the empty cup to the table, and continued his stroll.

Soon the river came into view. Seemed a tad too soon. Steve's place was almost an hour's walk away from it and Leo hadn't been on the move for that long. But this was not the same city, after all.

Just before the bridge Leo turned left. This way led to downtown. In the newer parts of the city, parks and playgrounds along the river were interspersed with luxury apartment buildings where factories once stood. Some industrial carcasses appeared intact but were no longer housing machines, being converted into trendy lofts and shopping malls. There should have been barges and small boats floating nonstop up and down the river day and night, but he saw none. Only house boats moored along the riverbanks.

Leo sat on a swing and looked at the scenery. He remembered the distant days when he used to hang around late at night on the playgrounds with his friends. He recalled his first cigarette, and how he got drunk for the first time and threw up in the river. The factories were still operational, and the river was polluted. In winter, the smoke from the chimney stacks cooled down quickly and settled near the surface, mixing with the vehicular exhaust and stinking up the entire place on days with no wind. That changed over time. Leo was living abroad, and each visit home was commemorated with at least one more defunct factory. Fortunately, this was not a sign of decay, but rather of a transformation. The industries moved to the periphery and became environmentally conscious.

When Leo got closer to downtown the scenery changed. The river was squeezed between two boulevards—one on each bank. The boulevards were flanked by residential and office buildings. In the nineties, the City laid bike lanes, however, these were missing here. Leo presumed that either this place had no bikes, or the lack of cars made dedicated bike lanes unnecessary. But then why car lanes?

Maybe there were cars, just that he couldn't see them, same as people. Yeah, right—Steve had a car and said something to this effect.

He reached another bridge, turned right, and began to cross. When he got to the middle, Leo stopped, leaned against the stone balustrade, and looked over. The river at this spot was deep, yet he could see fish swimming—so clear was the water. When was the last time he saw it like that? Lately it had gotten much cleaner indeed, but he could not recall seeing it this clear, and with fish. The fish were certainly present though, because there were anglers with their gear hanging around, some in pairs, conversing, smoking—later vaping—and drinking beer.

Leo climbed on the balustrade and crossed the spans between the lampposts, balancing precariously on the narrow surface with spread arms. At the last one, he jumped and landed elegantly on the sidewalk. Extraordinary achievement for someone of his age! His bones would have shattered in the other world. He wasn't eighty-one here—there was no way! In his idiot years, he did the walk to show off in the wee hours of the mornings, when there was no sane adult to start yelling that he might fall and break his neck or drown. Today he was emboldened by the knowledge that he was now safe. And he didn't spit in the water this time around. Over the years, he'd become civilized.

His old school was nearby, so perhaps he should check it out. The traffic lights at the intersection were green. Leo glanced at the lights in the opposite direction—also green. With no traffic, that made sense, too. He crossed confidently and soon afterward was standing in front of the pompous edifice, thinking of the past. The building looked the same—the glazed blue bricks, the arched windows, the grand staircase. Each year on opening day the street was closed to cars until noon, allowing a ceremony to take place.

The prestigious school was desired by many parents for their kids, and he'd had to undergo a screening test. He'd been a ten-year-old kid with recently divorced parents and little confidence in his math and language skills, but, as it turned out, they were not bad at all, and he was admitted. Graduates from the school proceeded to study at top universities across Europe and sometimes overseas, mostly in the States. Usually, they ended up holding well-paying corporate jobs. Leo followed this path for almost a decade, then veered off.

"Hi, Leo," rang a greeting in a long-lost voice. A voice that made his heart race. Was it even still the same?

"Lizzy?" Leo slowly turned around, and his eyes grew wider. The teenaged girl behind him was displaying a glowing smile. Her name

29

was Elise, and she was his first big love. She had been killed in a horrific accident many years ago, their fairytale cut short in a very painful way. He'd been devastated when she passed.

His face turned red and his heart—or whatever he had now—pounded loudly. He wanted to take her in his arms and hold her tightly, kiss every part of her body and shed a sea of joyful tears. Time had turned her into a legend, and Leo had no idea what to actually do. Maybe her feelings toward him were never this intense, or maybe his own were now amplified. Too much time had passed, to be sure. He lifted his arm and caressed her cheek, saying nothing. Elise placed her hand over his and closed her eyes.

"How have you been?" Elise asked quietly, her eyes still shut.

"Well, I lived a life. Grew up, got married, then again ... two kids ..." He stopped. It wasn't right to talk about an old man's life to someone who had died so young. "Sorry, that was insensitive."

"Not at all," Elise said and looked at him. "I'd love to hear your solo story. Then we can try to write our own, I hope. Let's go." She pulled him by the sleeve.

"Where to?"

"You'll see."

They climbed the grand staircase and went inside the building. The interior matched his memories of ancient times, even though it had most certainly been modernized. Elise ran up the stairs, Leo tagging mindlessly along. She continued going up after the last floor, then Leo guessed their destination.

He hurried past the girl, opened the attic door, and pulled her into the full of stale air space. Leo pushed her back against the wall, ignoring the dense spider webs, his heart racing even faster, then let go. Elise locked her hands behind his neck, pulled him closer, and tilted her head up. They kissed. Just like all these years ago, when they were truly young. Or rather, when *he* was young, as Elise never grew old.

The kiss was laced with passion—it went deep and lasted long. His burning desire for this girl, having retreated to the deepest crevices of his mind after the sad event, surged to the surface with considerable force and took over.

They'd never had intercourse before she passed away. He'd been a horny seventeen-year-old with zero experience in lovemaking. She'd been younger, also clueless and too afraid to cross the line. There was no sex ed in those days—the topic was taboo—so they were left to their own devices.

But that was in another world. Leo ran his hands up her thighs, pulling the long black skirt up, then held her by the waist as they kissed briefly. She unbuttoned his trousers, pulled the zipper down, and slid her small hand into his undies. Leo gasped, found her lips, and she parted them to let his tongue in. She tasted good! Incredibly good! Leo rubbed her breasts, wondering if her nipples were still making bulges on her clothes; they were so firm now. She split his shirt open and ran her tongue up his chest, then across as if blessing him with it, then undid his button and got rid of her underwear.

He reached down and helped her straddle him. The girl was panting, chasing his gaze through half-open eyes. She welcomed him inside her and clenched her teeth. Leo took a deep breath. He was ecstatic! He didn't consider for a second that he was supposed to be dysfunctional and old. They leaned against the wall and started swaying, her legs wrapped tightly around his hips. His engorged member slid effortlessly in and out. Their tongues played with each other, then parted reluctantly to allow in more air. The sensation was overwhelming, indescribable! Pure delight!

When she started shaking in his arms and moaning loudly, he was on the verge of firing the gun. Her breathing quivered; he felt shivers in his groin. The accumulated pleasure burst into thousands of gleeful shards. Elise was now crying. Her body twitched a few times, then the tense muscles relaxed. Leo lingered before letting her feet touch the floor, then clutched her in his arms. She ran her tongue slowly over his chest, cuddled into him and listened to his heart.

"I told you that it would be nice!" Leo breathed out.

'Nice' was such a weak word. This was perhaps the loudest bang in his existence! He just made love to HER!

Elise traced a circle around his nipple with her fingertip and said softly, "But you never made a move back then, you were all bark and no bite. I didn't know what to do. You were also still a virgin. Lots of complications . . ."

She gently freed herself from his embrace. "But not anymore!" She giggled and briefly rubbed his still unsettled instrument, then pulled her skirt down and began dusting it off with both hands. Then she returned to him, rose on her toes and they kissed again. And again. And again.

Damn, she tastes so good! Leo licked his lips, breathed in, and finally zipped up, leaving his shirt untucked like he had in those long-gone days, to the annoyance and constant reprimands of the school staff.

Then he stomped in place, suddenly confused, only now feeling the full impact of what just took place.

"Wow, we actually did it! And we are dead!" His voice trembled.

"You sounded so calm and reassuring a second ago." She tilted her head and smiled again. "What gave?"

"What didn't?" Leo was staring at her unbelievingly, "You . . . here . . . sorry, I am in a bit of a shock."

"I understand." The girl slowly tucked his shirt back into his trousers, rubbing against his torso when she reached behind. Her nipples were still making the bulges he observed. Leo felt tickling in his loins again but chose not to indulge. Instead, he opened the attic door and inspected the surroundings.

Elise pushed him unceremoniously from behind. "Nobody's here, not until I wish it to be so."

"Are you saying that unless you wish to be alone there's always someone to say 'Hi' to?" Leo's experience so far pointed in the opposite direction.

"Er, I mean there aren't usually any other ghosts around. Nobody to hide from. And we are not school kids anymore, are we?"

"Ghosts? Other ones? You're not helping . . ."

"Well, what are we? When you meet somebody here, it is certainly a ghost. Someone who used to be alive. What are such things called?"

"Zombies," Leo said and made way for her. They descended to the ground floor and stepped outside. Leo decided to reenact another moment from their past. He led her to the nearby back alley and started kissing her, reaching into her mouth and tracing her lips. She giggled, then pushed him away just as she used to do back in the days, when he went overboard.

"Wanna cigarette?" Elise offered a pack she pulled from her pocket.

"No, thanks. I quit almost half a century ago."

"You won't get cancer here."

"Yeah, I kind of know, you only die twice, right?"

"Not sure what you mean," said Elise, then cursed. "Ah, crap, I dropped my bag upstairs. Hold this." She pushed the cigarette into his hand and ran toward the school. Leo sniffed it from afar and the world around him spun.

*
**

"Thank you!" his mom said and took the cigarette from him.

"Huh? Seriously . . ." Leo muttered, looking around. He was back at home, leaning against the living room wall.

"You jumped just now, did you not?" Annette puffed out a ring.

"No, I was outside and standing. Now I am still standing but at home!"

"We call it jumping. You see, time here, if such a thing exists at all, isn't linear. You are doing one thing, then you find yourself someplace else, then eventually you may go back to where you were and carry on. This place gives you experiences, not a life. Not the life as we knew it, that is. So, we get to experience weird stuff."

She drew again from the cigarette and made another ring, "I'm glad that you lived."

"You know, I met Elise again. She didn't."

"Good . . . I mean that you met her. She's a nice girl, moved here too early. I wonder what she'd say if she could see you now. The aged you . . ."

Now that she mentioned it, Leo thought that his mom did look younger.

"Probably 'Ew!'"

"No. Old age has value. It means you saw a lot and had experiences she would never have."

"What if these experiences were painful? What if you want to forget it all? Me, you—we've been fortunate."

Annette thought for a while, then nodded in agreement. "I see your point. But it's hard to find someone with such life experience to talk to. Maybe even impossible."

"Mom, what age are you projecting outward now?"

"About fiftyish, I suppose?"

"Why?"

"Because I don't want to shock you if I look twenty-seven."

"Then just be you. I mean, don't project anything. Let me see the mother I remember."

"Ew!"

Leo laughed.

"Did you try it, by the way?" Annette continued. "It takes some time to learn. I am eager to see you as a kid, but this is something up to you."

"Grandma said I had to find a mirror, but so far, I found none. The bathroom is missing, and I don't see any mirrors in your room either . . ."

"Go ask again. She'll be glad to spend more time with you, as she doesn't have much of it left."

"Is she dying for a second time?"

"I'm afraid she is . . ." His mother sighed and extinguished the cigarette.

Leo went to his great-grandmother's door and knocked politely. "Come in!"

Leo entered. Babette was sitting in the rocking chair, holding another book, with Ginger purring in her lap. Two pairs of eyes trained on him.

"Sweetie, come, sit." Babette waved her hand while Ginger abandoned his cozy spot and came to deposit his scent on Leo. "How are you settling in? You shall tell me more about your life—the other one."

"Well, things are weird, but I think . . . I like them this way. How did you adapt? I have watched films and read stories and there's tech that delivers similar experiences now. It is . . . it is like living in a movie, but your time was different."

"God gave me only what I needed, and what I could exist with. He made it easy."

"But none of this is in the Bible." Leo gestured around. "How did you know it was Him?"

"The knowledge comes from your heart. I believe that it was God and His angels who built this place for us. Yes, it isn't in the Holy Book, but there are many other things the Bible doesn't mention explicitly. I was taken by surprise, indeed, but what would life be like if there were no surprises?"

"Poor Godfrey," Leo said oozing sarcasm. Babette furrowed her eyebrows, then appeared to realize the implications of what she had just said. Apparently, she decided not to pursue the subject further.

"So, tell me more about you, Eric, and Abi?" she inquired.

"Sure, but may I ask you to first shed some more light on how to do the age projections?"

The now-young woman in front of him gave a smile. "Of course, sweetie."

Leo jerked backward, then realized it was still Babette and relaxed his grip on the ottoman.

"How did you do that?"

"It's easy once you get used, but it takes some time. Like learning to ride a bicycle. Hard at first, then second nature." Babette leaned nearer and said, "First, you must find a mirror."

"I have been trying to, but the closest I've gotten to seeing my face was in blurry reflections in some piece of glass here and there."

"No, no. Not this kind of mirror. You must imagine one. And when you look at it, you will project out the image you see."

Leo closed his eyes and tried to follow the instructions. But all he could think of, all that he could imagine, was Elise, now and back when they were alive. The joy he'd felt when they were together, the fear of rejection that preceded it, the reluctance to confess his love, and the euphoria when it was reciprocated. The overwhelming sadness and despair when he heard the news, the closed-casket funeral. The desire of the flesh, finally satisfied . . .

He opened his eyes and tried to brush these thoughts aside and concentrate on the task at hand. He took a deep breath and shut them again. No luck this time either. Yeah, he could see something like a mirror in the dark, but it was her reflection in it, not his. Frailness possessed his physique for a moment. Leo moaned in frustration and lifted his eyelids. He was no longer in Babette's room!

IN THE OPEN

He was sitting on a bench in the small riverside park, near Elise's place—legs outstretched, arms resting on his lap. Was he slipping in and out of a coma, and entering different dreams with each "in"? This would explain these so-called jumps. Leo lifted his gaze. The sun was low, but not quite yet ready to retire for the night, causing shadows to stretch into infinity. His heart skipped a beat when he sensed her presence next to him. He turned his head.

"Where in South Africa?" Elise asked.

"Where? What?" Leo had no idea what she was talking about.

"Did you just jump? Like you were in another place, and you blinked, and you found yourself in a different place?"

Leo nodded.

"Ah, it happens, don't worry."

"I am not. Mother told me time isn't linear here."

"That's a way to put it, yes. You were telling me what happened to you after I died. You took Industrial Design at Neue Polytechnic and got a job at BMW and they sent you overseas."

"Yes, to Rosslyn. It is near Pretoria, the capital. They had a plant in Rosslyn. They closed it down. I went there in '95. Then I moved to Toyota, and in '97 they sent me to the headquarters in Japan."

"Wow!" Elise exclaimed. "You've seen so much! Tell me!"

"The Japanese—their work culture is insane. You belong to the company. In return it is a lifetime tenure, perfect job security. But it was their so-called lost decade. The economy was in shambles, and young people were struggling to get jobs. I was oddly lucky, as they are fiercely nationalistic. I liked drawing cars, fantasizing. Seemed, too, that somebody of importance saw my sketches on the office wall. Next thing I knew, it was, 'Mr. Hackensack, would you like to see Nippon?' I was excited, ecstatic even, but then reality hit hard. The Japanese are very hierarchical and rigid. Middle managers are far worse. Someone barely older than you could boss you around with impunity, and I was at the bottom of the design division and a foreign guy. I spoke no Japanese. People took credit for my work . . ."

Leo continued with his little rant, while Elise gobbled up the story with her eyes open wide. Leo's mouth felt dry from all the talking—he kept licking his lips. A drinking fountain caught his eye. He walked to it, drank, and returned to the bench. Elise was looking at the ground, tracing arches with her heels.

"You know, I wish I had a proper life," she said in a quiet, somewhat sad voice. "You get great perks here, and you have no worries. However, it is not the same. It should be a continuation of one's previous existence. But to me, it is almost everything I know."

Elise took his arm and cuddled into him. The warmth of her body stirred his emotions. He wanted to correct the past and make her happy, but that was impossible. Best case scenario was some sort of simulation this place might come up with. He looked at the bright orange disk and squinted. The sun was flirting with the rooftops across the river.

Elise rolled over, sat on his lap, and placed her hands on his shoulders. Her body shielded him from the rays of the tired star. Her gaze found his eyes:

"Don't be sad for me," she said, then leaned forward. Their lips made contact, then her tongue reached inside his mouth.

She had no taste to speak of, really, yet tasting her felt so good. Bittersweet. Suddenly, he felt guilty. He was on the ninth cloud with Elise in his arms. He had a normal life and now this one, while hers was cut short and all she had was this strange place. If she was even real. Maybe she had nothing at all.

"I want you," Elise whispered, and, in one swift motion, sent her blouse to meet the ground.

"Here?" Leo jerked his head back.

"It doesn't matter. Nobody will see us even if we want to be seen. We are ghosts, remember?" she said, pulling up his shirt.

"Ghosts aren't stealthy . . ." mumbled Leo, offering no resistance. His heart was pounding in anticipation, his mind torn between desire and taboo.

Elise kicked off her panties and jumped back on his lap, giving him a mere instant to unzip. Her light skirt floated in the air, then slowly settled down. Her kiss lingered. His hands traveled up and down her spine. He tried to pinch her nipples, but she was too close, and he didn't want to push her away, not for any reason.

"Relax, feel, adapt . . ." she whispered in his ear then let his dick glide inside her and leaned back emitting a loud huff.

Leo looked her in the eyes and moved his lips in a silent promise, "Of course."

She smiled and rocked her hips, slowly at first, holding his hands. Leo wanted to pull a nipple into his mouth. Wrestling out his hands might put her off and he suppressed the desire, moving his gaze up instead. Elise was looking at him, her head tilted backward, eyelids half-shut, her mouth ajar, the corners nudged up into a faint smile. Leo was done observing. He emptied his mind and leisurely lifted his arms. Hers followed. Her face came closer, much closer, and her breasts rubbed against his chest. Leo tilted his head to the side and ran his tongue over her lips. She intercepted it with hers. The senses flared up, the hearts were pounding, and the sways were getting stronger and stronger, throwing flashes, until it all exploded into a medley of sensations, all of them good. She collapsed on his chest panting, then after a while crawled up and rested her head on his shoulder. Leo embraced her and started twirling her hair around his fingers. His mind was still blank—he let his senses do the work and they did not disappoint. He hoped that it was the same for her.

Suddenly, she caught her breath, wriggled free, sat up straight, and asked, "Would you walk me home?"

"Sure!" Leo bit his lips—did she not like it, why the rush?

"Then let's go." She let her feet touch the ground, dismounted, and stretched with arms up in the air. She then found her shoes and slipped her feet inside. Leo also rose, diligently zipped up, and put his shirt back on. A moment of silence followed.

"Well?" he said.

"What?"

"Aren't you going to get dressed?"

"No," came the unexpected answer. Leo's jaw dropped.

"I like feeling the flow of air with my skin," Elise explained. "Don't you?" She glided her index finger over the tiny hairs of his forearm.

"Okay . . ."

They walked down the footpath. Leo felt embarrassed with this half-naked girl next to him. He was trying to get this new reality sink in while constantly glancing nervously around in search of, well, not really peeping toms, since if they were seen it would be their own fault.

"Lizzy . . ." He tried to appeal to her sense of modesty, his face looking as if it were carved out from the flesh of a ripe watermelon.

"Relaaax! Nobody's here! You wouldn't be worried if we were in-doors, yes?" Elise said, grabbing his wrists and pushing his palms against her breasts. She moved closer and rose on her toes with the intention to kiss, then glanced over his shoulder and announced cheerfully, "Ah, there's another bench!"

"Fuck . . ." Leo let out involuntarily.

"Precisely!"

When they finally arrived at her home, it was already dark. The street-lights were on, but the lush crowns of the trees were casting almost impenetrable shadows. Leo was bare chested. His shirt was gone and his zipper broke, leaving him with only the button to keep his trousers up.

Elise had abandoned all her clothes along the way except for shoes. She pulled the door open and stood still on the threshold for a moment. Leo studied her seductive shape, and his no-longer-shy dick promptly popped out through the gaping flier. When she turned to say goodbye, he took the initiative this time around and silenced her with a kiss. She responded, leaning on his arms and pulling him into the dark foyer. Inside she tugged at his ears, emitted a soft moan, ran her hands down his torso, and undid the button. Leo held her rear and pulled up. She bounced and wrapped her legs around his hips, then swayed until his private part found its way inside her. It glided in with ease and settled comfortably into the warm space. He gulped and moved closer to the wall. Elise pulled herself higher and drove the tip of her tongue into his ear, holding her breath, then nibbled on the lobe. It was Leo's time to rock.

"We would have needed a lot of condoms in the other world," Elise mused when the song was over.

He chuckled. Feeling her body intertwined with his gave him so much pleasure! Even when they stood still. Leo lightly nipped her neck and released her from his hold. Elise took his hand and led him to the door, not allowing him to turn around. He got the message and obeyed. She motioned him still and whispered in his ear, "Good night." Then pushed him gently out and let the door close.

Leo checked his surroundings. He wasn't on the street. The faint light was revealing familiar objects: a staircase, an elevator cage . . . He pushed the button. The cabin was waiting, the bulb inside lit up. He hopped in, performed the ascent to the fourth floor, snuck into the apartment, removed his shoes, and quietly made it in the dark to his room—the old habit kicked in automatically.

THE BOY

When he woke up in the morning, Leo itched to rush straight back to his reacquainted girlfriend. He inflated his lungs and paused, reining in the urge. Her hormones, or whatever ghosts had, raged fiercely and he was tempted to succumb to their call, but he knew better—howling fires consumed their fuel quickly, though maybe not in this realm. However, Leo was reluctant to leave the fate of this relationship to such a chance. He wanted it to last!

He pounded his fists on the mattress, determined to stay true to his intentions and sat on the edge. A scratching noise drew his attention. He stretched his arm and pushed the door handle. The latch clicked, and a ball of fur rushed in. Sylvester jumped in the bed, wagging his tail with such a force as if it were a biting pest he wanted very much to get rid of.

"Hello, Sly!" Leo affectionately hugged the dog and received a slobbering response. Ginger left the room full of disgust.

"I am taking him out for a walk," Annette said from the threshold. "Wanna come?"

"Okay." Leo rose to his feet and looked around for his clothes.

"You are already dressed."

Dressed indeed. He lost his shirt last night and afterward went to bed naked. In the hallway he slipped his shoes on. They took a ride down in the old elevator. When Leo opened the front door, Sylvester pulled his leash and hurried to the nearest tree, but just sniffed it and moved on. It seemed animals also had no need to defecate. That was a relief, as he had dealt with probably tons of pet waste in his other life.

"I am meeting with some friends," Annette said. "Simone, Charlie, Danielle, and Willi Hildebrandt."

"Who's Willi?"

"A classmate. You met him once or twice, I think."

"Doesn't ring a bell."

"D'you remember when you drew a dick on the wall with my lipstick when you were four?"

"I kind of do. I've told the story many times. Maybe you planted the memory. I don't really know. And it wasn't a dick!"

"Well, the drawing resembled one according to those present, but whatever . . . that was Willi's place. We were watching a socker game in the living room, and you were supposed to be napping. Who would have known . . ." Annette said with a chuckle and threw her son a glance.

The son was now unsure who planted what. He had a vague memory of finding his mom's purse and using the lipstick to draw, but the penis was his own teenage addition aiming to make the story funny, or so he thought. He twitched his mouth.

The dog was zigzagging the sidewalk, exploring the scents as dogs usually do. They arrived at the intersection with Linden Boulevard and turned right. Shortly after this, they crossed the bridge and entered Old Town. The narrow cobblestone streets were lined with stores selling souvenirs, books, old toys, period clothing, and all other sorts of primarily tourist merchandise, interspersed with cafés and small restaurants. The doors were open, inviting passers-by to pop in.

"Mom, this is weird, isn't it?"

"What exactly?"

"Look at all these shops and places. They appear as if everybody's still here. But there are no people beside the two of us."

"Are we people?" Annette smiled, then, in a more serious tone, added, "I am sure that there are others, just that we can't see them, we are not exceptional. There are people who love their small stores and cafés, so this world will give them something to enjoy. There are people who like acquiring silly stuff, and there is something for them too. We are meeting in a bistro; somebody has to run it."

"We had to make a living in the old world . . ."

"True, here there is no such imperative, but if you love doing something, there is no prohibition either," Annette countered.

"People love watching porn on the internet. How would they do this here?"

"Here they can practice it!" His mother giggled. Leo ran a hand through his hair thinking, *Maybe she has a point.*

They turned into a side street. It widened almost immediately and morphed into a small plaza. There was the bistro. The entrance was flanked by six cast iron tables—three on each side, all with parasols overhead. Two tables were pulled close together. Dr. Charles, Simone, and Danielle were already seated around them.

"Hey, Ann!" came the greetings. "Leo! Welcome! How are you!"

Simone rose from her chair and gave him a light hug. Danielle remained seated, sending an air kiss instead. Dr. Charles, who was occupying the nearest chair, leaned forward and lazily extended arm for a handshake.

"No complaints, thanks!" Leo said and tried to move the empty chair next to Charles. The chair did not budge. The others guffawed.

"What?" Leo looked at them and furrowed his eyebrows.

"Willi's sitting there. He's probably two meters tall and weighs a ton," Charles explained.

"You can't see him, can you?" asked Simone.

Leo shook his head.

"He can. He said you were strong for a toddler."

Everybody except himself laughed again. Leo scratched the arm holding the backrest, still mystified.

"Now brace for a change!" Simone said, and the old, overweight lady morphed into a still plump thirty-something. In Leo's eyes, she appeared leaner than he remembered, as she'd been outright fat in the old life. Or maybe his memory was inaccurate. Human memories are not photographs. Perhaps this is how she remembered herself. What he initially saw was pretty much on spot, though.

"Do you have to do that?" Dr. Charles asked with a bored look on his face. "You are so self-conscious."

Leo tried to dislodge another chair and, when it moved, he patted the seat, just in case. Another round of loud laughter ensued. He ignored it and sat.

"I can, so why not?" said Simone. "You should do that too. I don't want to look at your drooping faces all the time. You should have died young. Old age is ugly, and I was never beautiful to start with—"

"I met a close friend recently," Leo interrupted. "She died very young, and she can never look old. That made her sad."

Simone looked down and said in a calm voice, "I sympathize, but would anything change for her, if we didn't take advantage of this thing? I was fat almost my entire life, and I cannot make myself look slim no matter what. But at least I can make myself look young. Huh?" She turned her head toward the empty chair, "Willi's saying she probably has something else to fall back on. Something we regulars lack."

Leo missed the magic moment when all the food and drinks appeared: cheeseburgers, paninis, baskets with french fries, and ice-cold beers. Leo took a bite from the nearest burger. It was good—the patty was juicy, loaded with spices. He put it back on the plate and licked his fingers.

"Cheers!" The doctor lifted his glass, then addressed Leo, "And very welcome!"

"Cheers!" came the joint reply. Leo was staring at the empty chair. He was trying to catch any movement of the glass or the panini. He was expecting them to float through the air, held by an invisible hand, but he was disappointed—nothing moved.

He turned to Annette. "Mom, is Willi still here?"

"Mmm," she confirmed, her mouth full.

"And is he drinking?"

She swallowed the bite and said, "Affirmative. He's doing it right now."

"Interesting . . .". He gasped and moved back. She had changed to a younger version of herself too. He took a deep breath and pictured himself as a young boy with his mom crouching, buttoning up his winter coat. For this was the memory her altered look unearthed from his mind.

"Hey, look who's here!" Simone clapped excitedly. "This is what I mean, follow his lead! Hi, sweetie!"

Leo swung his gaze around, trying to catch a glimpse of the new-comer. There was nobody new that he could see.

"Another friend of yours I don't remember?" he asked his mom.

"No, it's you!" she said, "Ah, my little boy!" She outstretched her arm and shuffled his hair. "You transformed."

"Ugh . . . But how? I couldn't have . . ."

"Probably you had some intense vision of yourself. That does it," Annette explained.

"Now you no longer can drink!" The doctor reached and pulled Leo's glass away. Leo tried to intervene, but his arms were too short now. Charles pushed the glass back with a grin. Leo grabbed it with both hands and chugged the brew. Then burped. There was another burst of laughter at his expense.

"What now?" he scolded. "Am I not allowed to have a drink?"

The others were getting short of breath.

"Sorry, mate, it is so funny seeing a kid so angry and so fond of a glass of beer! Your face is red . . ." Charles squeezed the explanation in between his outbursts.

"I remember I was once sitting in a bistro near home," Danielle began. "There was a young family with baby in a stroller. The waiter brought them beer. The dad proceeded to offer some to the kid. The mom objected. 'Why not?' asked the dad. I thought the mother would say 'Because it is alcohol' or something, but she said, 'Because it is too cold.'"

"Dany . . ." Simone pouted. "That story's tired."

"Sorry . . . maybe Leo hasn't heard it?"

"Has something new happened to you guys?" Leo asked, choosing not to take sides, but the story was indeed very old.

"Er," Charles swallowed a laugh, "new things happen, but are mostly quite personal. Also, you are a friend's kid and we still self-censor, even though we know that you are old. At least this is what I do."

"Same here," Simone agreed. "It would take some time for us to adjust, but your appearance right now is not helping." She giggled again.

"And how do I deal with this? The appearance I mean," Leo asked.

"It will wear off," Charles said.

"When?"

"In a day or so. I don't know exactly; I haven't timed it," the good doctor said. He was a medical doctor, as was Leo's mom. Leo wondered why everybody used his professional title to refer to him, but not Annette's. "Dr. Ann" sounded just as good. Leo had this and many other questions for these people, but they seemed engaged in their conversations, and his appearance triggered a bout of laughter each time someone looked at him.

"I'm going home with Sly," Leo announced, glancing at Willi's spot. The plate was empty, and the glass was only half full.

"Sure. There is a shortcut—" Annette began.

"I know, and I'm not tired," Leo cut in, standing up. "Bye, everybody."

"Bye!" "Bye, see you!" they guffawed.

Jerks! He untied Sylvester's leash from his mother's chair. The dog wagged his tail and put his paws on the table, where Leo's burger was. Leo arched over, took the remaining patty, and threw it to Sylvester. The dog scooped it up and chewed it noisily, then they headed home.

As he walked downhill on the old cobblestones, Leo's thoughts returned to Elise. His desire for her was immense, but he was content that he was managing to stay away; being an eight-year-old boy now certainly helped. He closed his eyes and tried to imagine himself as the teen he was when he and the girl met first, tripped on the uneven pavement and almost plummeted. Sylvester, startled by the sudden motion, ran. The leash, wrapped around Leo's wrist, yanked him forward just as he regained his balance, and this time he fell. Luckily for him Sly was a small dog.

Leo got up, inspected his arms for bruises, and shrugged after finding none. A distant hum drew his attention, and he began to speculate how this might work as he continued his descent to New Town.

DREAMWORLD

In the morning, Leo stepped out of his room, closing the door behind him before reentering, seeking admittance first.

"Grandma, how old am I now?"

"Fourteen."

It seemed he had reverted, but he wanted to double-check. He pivoted, and was about to leave his great-grandmother's room to find Ann, but Babette continued, "Why, what happened?"

"Yesterday I became eight. I wanted to know how old I looked now."

"Ah, I see, so you found your mirror?"

"No, it was involuntary. Seems Mom dragged me along when she transformed."

"That would be something new to me," the old woman said. "Never heard of such a thing happening before."

"There's always a first time. By the way, why do you almost always look old?"

Babette leaned back in the chair. "Is there any reason why I shall transform for you? You always knew me old. I was seventy-five when you were born."

"Well, no, not really. Just that I was curious."

"Besides, my bachelors are all gone."

"What bachelors?"

"Leo, look at me," Babette said.

Leo complied. He saw a good-looking young woman, with somewhat sharp features and long black braided hair.

"I was young once too. We had our crushes and sweethearts. We also tried to impress them. And they us. So many souls were lost to war . . ." The young woman's expression darkened. She'd lived through two world wars and certainly knew many people who had not made it.

"Did they not come here?" Leo asked.

"Some had, but their stay had been short, I was told."

"But why?"

"I don't know." Babette sighed. "Marcus is also long gone now. But he was here with me for many years."

Marcus was Leo's great-grandfather. He had passed away before Leo was born. Leo had no memory of him in the flesh. There were a few old, faded photographs in the family album, taken at different times during his lifetime. A young man in soldier's uniform. Another one in his mid-thirties with a thin mustache and wearing a fedora, looking like a 1930s movie star. He was never in the movies; he was a chartered accountant. Ah, the wedding photo. And another one taken shortly before his death, of a bald old man, still wearing a mustache but this time a large bushy one as if to recompense for the shiny scalp. Funny how Leo could picture so well a guy he had never seen alive, but he was unable to see a clear image of himself.

"Grandma, what do you see now?"

"Ah, stop it. Still teen you. You should have come here yesterday; I'd have loved to lay eyes on you as a young boy."

Leo ignored the remark. "You said that I shall see my face in a mirror. I still can't, but somehow, I can visualize Granddad Marcus in detail from all the photos that we had. So, I was thinking, maybe I projected him."

Babette appeared intrigued by the proposition for a moment but ultimately dismissed it. "Not possible. We can do only ourselves. Can you imagine the confusion if it were otherwise?"

She had a point. He thought of all the confusion down below on Earth (assuming they were up in heaven) caused by the deep fakes.

"Gonna see Mother," Leo announced, standing up. He immediately sat down again with blurred vision and a dizzy head. When it cleared, he sucked his lip glancing around—he was alone and in his room.

Babette had disappeared. Leo's heart sank. He was going to miss her. He didn't want her to be gone. What was this drift, anyway?

He cautiously lifted his rear off the ottoman fearing another swirl and took a step toward the hallway. When nothing happened, he proceeded confidently forward.

"Mom, what do you see?" Leo asked from the living room door. Annette was watching television. Television!? He didn't know they had it here. She looked at him and said, "An old bald fart."

"Rude. Besides I was never bald," murmured Leo, his attention drawn by the television set. "There is TV here?"

"Yes, why not?"

"Then there shall be smart devices and computers too, but so far I have seen nothing of the kind."

"Come to think of it, I haven't seen any either."

Leo tried to see a picture on the screen, but the sharp angle he was looking at hampered the attempt—the screen appeared dark. He joined Annette on the couch and stared at the box. Still nothing. Leo tensed his brow.

"Is the TV on?"

"Yes."

"What are you watching?"

"*Midsomer Murders*, why?"

From this vantage point, the screen displayed some signs of life—blurred blobs of dull color, some of them floating, others flashing, sometimes doing both. Then the brightness gradually increased, turning the disjoined smudges into crisp moving pictures. *Aha, that's how you watch television 'round here.* Leo took a mental note.

"Are there any newscasts?"

"Haven't watched any. But many of the movies are new, I mean post-death, so you can form some idea of what is going on. But films are fiction after all." She shrugged. "It is up to new arrivals like you to set the record straight."

Something else was bothering Leo. Then it dawned on him: the TV set had a flat screen. It couldn't be from the eighties. Now that he was paying more attention, the living room itself was different. The dining table and the chairs were gone, and the walls were painted white.

Leo went back to his bedroom. It had changed too. He had a boombox when he was in school, now he saw his hi-fi system. The ottomans were gone, replaced by two chairs he had himself designed and built. They were cool to look at, though not at all comfortable, probably better suited for planters. The walls had changed to a terracotta color.

Leo squatted in front of the cabinet and began perusing his music collection: Genesis, Floyd, Deep Purple, Renaissance, Kansas, Queen, Rammstein . . . Hang on, Rammstein? So out of time. The band wasn't even an idea in the eighties. Did they ever release a record on vinyl? He had no idea and no internet. Leo went quickly through the rest and found more anachronisms. He shook head in amusement, then retrieved *Mutter* and placed the record on the turntable.

"Nun, liebe Kinder, gebt fein Acht . . ." issued from the loudspeakers in Lindemann's familiar voice. *Sounds right*, Leo nodded, then continued, *Why is this place so averse to tech? Have management not heard of streaming?*

An idea formed into his mind—finding a public library—but there was a more pressing issue at hand. He had to talk to Elise about their relationship—the need to take the heat down a notch or two for the sake of durability. Leo stopped the music, put his shoes on, and ran down to the street. When they were alive, he would often buy cheap flowers—a carnation or a bunch of daisies—and push the purchase into her hand when they met. She always kissed him, on the cheek initially, then started pecking his lips. He craved a rerun. There was a flower shop two streets down near the corner, but it opened much later. His memories of the eighties were very foggy when it came to flower shops. Why was he so bad at remembering these places?

He frantically searched his mind for directions. *Ah, yes, there was the one on Latto . . .* He tripped and waved arms to restore his balance. His left hand punched a wall. Leo cursed and looked up. A five-story apartment building he didn't want to see anymore after a certain event engulfed his sight. His emotions now were mixed. For years on end, he avoided this section of the street. Time and him living over-seas eventually changed that—the anguish was no longer felt. Now it was bittersweet, mostly sweet.

Leo pulled open the front door and climbed the stairs to the third floor, taking two steps at a time. Elise's apartment was the middle one. Before he could ring the bell, the door swung open. Elise was right there. She grabbed his hand, crossed his lips, ushered him into her room, and carefully closed the door.

"Lizzy . . ." Leo tried to speak, but she hushed him again.

She pulled a nearby chair, climbed on it, and began pulling his shirt up.

"What a—"

She urged him to be quiet, stepped down, moved the chair aside, and undid the button of his trousers. He produced a faint smile. She unzipped the trousers and pulled them down. He dropped his arms in an impulse to resist, but she blocked the move.

"Up!" Elise commanded. Leo giggled, as the order could be refer-ring equally to multiple parts of his anatomy. She squatted, pushed the trousers and his undies all the way down, and tapped his ankles until he shook the garments off. Then she took a few steps back and inspected the result. Amusement, arousal, and embarrassment ran through him all at the same time.

Elise nodded silently in approval and approached again. Her cupped hand weighed his scrotum. Chills ran up his spine, and he took a deep breath as the arousal advanced. She moved to his side, wrapped one arm around his waist, rubbed her cheek on his chest, and seized his source of pleasure with her free hand. Leo liked her little game—he started swaying his hips while she kept her hand still.

"Good boy!" Elise said seriously and made him crack a laugh. She kept alternating her grip as he swayed, sending waves of delight to his brain. At some point, she took over the action and started moving her hand along the shaft in long steady strokes. Leo tried not to pant; he opened his mouth wide, shut his eyes, and breathed slowly, savoring the thrill.

The embarrassment returned when he finished on the carpet. Elise seemed unfazed. She kept pumping for a while, then released her hold, swirled in front, rose on her toes, pecked his lips, and said quietly, "Did you like it?"

Leo closed his arms around her and whispered back, "Yes, I did."

"Then it is your turn now."

Leo looked around, thinking. His gaze came across the wide concrete windowsill. He took her hand, led her there, and helped her sit on it. The baggy shirt traveled over her head and landed on the floor. She had no underwear. He breathed hot air on her breasts and traced circles with his tongue around her nipples, then drew each in his mouth and held it there, sucking and nibbling until the nipple stiffened and the areola shrank. Elise moaned. Her breaths became more frequent and impatient, and he saw goose bumps appear on the surface of her skin. Leo glanced at her. She licked her lips.

Leo kneeled, maneuvered her legs apart, and ran his tongue along the creases at the roots, then dragged it slowly up and down over the labia. Elise buried her fingers in the hair of his nineteen-year-old self, then leaned on the glass and wrapped her legs around his neck. He kissed her thighs and dipped his tongue, targeting her sweet spot. The girl moaned and quivered each time the two tips met. Leo rocked his head slowly, his tongue protruding as far as it could go. His hands traveled along her thighs, then converged on the vulva; his fingers gently pulled the labia apart, opening more room for his vibrating tongue. She gave a low moan and swayed her hips. Leo pinched two fingers, glided them inside her, and rolled them around, pushing on the walls while the tip of his tongue continued fluttering over the clitoris.

He pulled them out and probed her ring with the lubricated fingertip; she gasped and twisted her torso, then slammed her palms against the glass. He kept going—on and on—joyful that he was delivering delight. She pinched her nipples and rocked, rubbing her vulva on his face until a tremor of excitement accompanied by a loud gasp signaled the arrival of her climax. Elise pushed his head against her crotch and the rocking came gradually to a halt.

She wiped the corners of her eyes, smiled and tugged at his ears, "*Tack! Det var häftigt!*"

"Huh?" Leo nibbled on her thigh and stood up before she could pat his head in revenge.

"Thank you! That was great!" Elise repeated, this time in a language he could understand. She sat back on the windowsill and dangled her legs.

"What language was that?"

"Swedish. I was interested. Wanted to read *Pippi Longstocking* in the original language and learned quite a lot."

"How did you learn? There is no internet here."

"Ah, the magical internet again." She rolled her eyes. "I went to a library. There are books, and a language lab with tapes."

Library . . . thought Leo. He wanted to find one, yes! But the reason he wanted that evaded him right now. Still, paying a visit sounded like a good idea.

"Shall we take a walk?" Leo proposed.

"Sure. Come, I'll show you something," Elise said, then jumped to the floor and went to the imposing wardrobe at the opposite corner of her room. Leo's curiosity kicked in. Elise pulled both doors open and turned around. "Come on in!"

Leo's jaw dropped. He pushed it up with his thumb, pouted, and stepped inside. Elise giggled and pulled his hand. The wardrobe was a portal to yet another world. Instead of garments, he saw a field of lush green grass interspersed with patches of clovers. There were lots of flowers too. Colorful butterflies flapped their wings and tried to land on him, then swerved away just before touchdown.

The sky was bright blue, not a cloud in sight. A short distance away was the edge of a forest, and he could hear the buzz of bees and the splashing of water. Elise led the way. They reached the beginning of a forest path. Ferns and unusually large red-capped mushrooms occupied the spaces between the tree trunks. A large fluffy rabbit crossed the path and disappeared amongst the fern leaves.

"Sorry, it is probably very childish," Elise apologized.

Leo glanced at her with narrowed eyes. "What is childish?"

"This place."

"And what is this place?"

"A toy." The girl faced him and made a visor with her hand, shielding her eyes. "I created it," she added. Then turned around and stepped onto the path. Leo followed.

"How did you do that?"

"Dunno. Once upon a time I was reading lots of fairy tales, and I was trying to picture the world the stories were set in. Like with all the colors, the unicorns, fairies, and gnomes. I could imagine pieces of it—a meadow, a forest, a lake or a stream. Then, with time, I could join all these fragments into larger and larger parts."

They arrived at a waterfall. It wasn't big, but the rumble nevertheless drowned her words. She decided to forgo a shouting match with the falling waters and take a shower in them instead. Leo dipped his toe in the lake and frowned. He disliked cold water, but Elise seemed to enjoy it. She was swirling under the cascade with hands held over her head. She waved at him to join her. He shook his head and sat on a nearby rock. He appreciated the warmth of the stone underneath his buttocks. She respected his choice and left him alone, occupying herself instead with attempts to move under the largest cascade, however, the waters were hitting way too hard. She abandoned the try and dove into the whirlpool.

Leo sprang up. His instinct for danger was still strong. Elise reappeared on the surface toward the center of the lake and swam on her back for a while then dove again. She resurfaced closer to the shore, floated to the shallow waters, stood up, and walked toward him. The scene reminded him of *The Birth of Venus*. Venus was the goddess of love, and he was in love—they were in love. Peculiar emotion for two ghosts.

Elise stepped on the shore, smiled at him, and squeezed the water from her hair. Desire began to build up in him. Before it could manifest, he ran past Elise and plunged into the cold lake. That did the trick. She turned around and gave him a puzzled look.

"You didn't finish the story of creation," Leo said, squatting on the bottom not far from her.

"Ah, yes." Elise took his spot on the warm rock. "Then the parts combined, and when that happened, I could make this world materialize."

"Materialize by just thinking about it?"

"Mmm." She nodded. "Something like that. Initially I had to concentrate and keep thinking about it."

"And now?"

"Now it is like riding a bike; I do it subconsciously."

"Amazing!" Leo said, remembering the ability Simone mentioned. Maybe that was it? "A VR of your own making without the need of a headset!"

"What's VR?"

"Stands for 'virtual reality.' Computer tech, a big thing in the old world. Mostly for gamers. You wear special goggles, which project stereoscopic images. You can interact with the environment—move around, do things, meet other people. They are called avatars. I mean, you are not seeing the actual people, rather a computer-generated image the users chose to represent them, usually nothing like the real person. A world of dreams for some, a nightmare for others."

The cold became too much for him. He got up and walked out of the water. "Shall we go back?"

"Sure!" she nodded.

Leo continued to talk about virtual reality on their way to the clover field. When they reached it, Leo glanced at the large wardrobe. It looked so small and lonely, standing there in the open and with no other pieces of furniture around.

"I dislike the tech a lot," Leo concluded. "It is a refuge from reality for many and has become a shithole with all the creeps, user tracking, targeted advertising and e-commerce. I'd rather people try to fix the real world. May I?" he inquired, indicating that he wanted to open the doors.

"Yeah," Elise said. She appeared distracted, probably still considering the story she had just heard. Leo swung the doors open, and they stepped into her room.

"What's with this wardrobe?" Leo asked, nodding at the thing.

"Ah, it is just for the effect. I've seen such portals in the movies. Not an original idea. I also needed something to take garments from."

"Take garments from?"

"Yeah, haven't you noticed how things work here?"

"Ah, I see." He thought of his own closet, which was always stocked with a variety of clothes. "I wonder what the imagined world of a teenage boy would be like," Leo said while shutting the doors. "Dungeons and dragons perhaps?"

"Yes, what else?"

"Or maybe not," Leo objected. "That's a stereotype. People are different. Mine would be Space—", he continued while getting dressed.

"Sorry, what I said was dumb."

"Who cares! We all do that. I am starving. Can you conjure up some food?" His stomach gurgled in agreement.

"Pizza?"

"Great!"

Elise left the room.

Leo waited, but after some time it appeared that she was not coming back. He went to the door and opened it with no hurry. The hallway was dimly lit and looked familiar. Leo looked over his shoulder and concluded he was in his room. His stomach gurgled again. Leo huffed out a breath. *What efficient metabolism we have here! Eating, drinking, but no waste of any kind!* He was compelled to search for food now.

REMINISCENCE

Leo was again staring at his room's ceiling. Something about yesterday was bothering him, but he could not put his finger on it. He climbed out of bed and headed for the kitchen, attracted by the smell of coffee, which they always consumed large quantities of. He had to speak to his dad about this place and pose the questions he had.

Leo poured himself a cup. Annette wasn't there, but her pack of cigarettes and lighter were next to the unfinished crossword puzzle she liked entertaining herself with.

Leo quit smoking a very long time ago. He couldn't help lighting up because he enjoyed it. Eventually his fingers turned yellow, and he could not stop coughing. He was stinking like an overflowing ashtray, which, as a smoker, he didn't care much about. But the cough and snoring bothered him, as he was waking up in the middle of the night from his own rumble. Quitting was a sensible thing to do.

But—as he was told on several occasions—smoking here allegedly did no harm. Probably because it was also an illusion. Still, he hesitated but eventually cast his worries aside. He took a cigarette and lit it. The taste seemed to be the same and he didn't choke on the smoke. He inhaled and felt dizzy for a moment. He blew the smoke out through his nose and drew again. The dizziness returned. He shut his eyes and stood still.

*
**

When he dared to look around, he found himself in the alley behind his old school. Elise said, "Thanks!" and took the already half-burnt cigarette from his hand. She pulled on it, then put it out and dropped the butt in the nearby storm drain. She held a small red purse with a golden chain strap. It looked out of place with her school uniform.

"What made you wear this?" Leo asked, nodding at her.

"This?" Elise looked down, inspecting her clothes. "Seems appropriate for the occasion, no?" Gleaming, she added, "And what about you?"

Leo checked his own clothes and chuckled. He was also wearing his old school uniform. He was sure that he did not start the day this way.

"You were wearing something else, weren't you? You know, before we met," Leo asked and pointed at the little red purse.

"Yes."

"What was it?"

"Er, blue jeans and white blouse."

"You wore trousers only in winter," Leo remarked.

"That's not true. But close enough," the girl said with another grin.

Leo moved his gaze, not knowing what to do next.

"Where to?" he asked.

"Walk and talk?"

"Sure!" He smiled. Old feelings, having made their way to the surface, were getting ready to take another shot at life.

Elise took his hand. "So, you were shocked when you arrived here, you said?"

"Mmm. Who wouldn't be? Some people expect to see ol' Godfrey, others a bunch of virgins or the guts of a volcano . . . I mean—hell."

"And you?"

"I . . . nothing. Nothing at all. No afterlife for me."

"I don't remember what my expectations were," Elise said, "I didn't think of death back then."

"That is normal, you were seventeen—"

"Eighteen!"

Leo sighed. Did a few days matter?

"But that aside, how do you feel now?"

Leo stopped and looked her in the eyes, "Jolly! And confused . . . ." He resumed the walk, voicing his thoughts, "What is this place? Is it real, a dream, or a simulation? How did we end up here? Where's the other dead folk? Who is guarding the gates? Were they pearly?"

"My grandma insists it's purgatory!" Elise said hurriedly.

"I wish I could know for sure. Maybe this is just my mind making it all up, and, in reality, I am lying comatose in some darn hospital. But I don't want that or else you and everybody else I met would be nothing more than some neurons firing. The visions may be just a gift from a dying brain . . ."

"Or maybe it is real. I have been here for decades. I certainly have independent thoughts. I'm not a figment of your imagination." Elise pursed her lips.

"Perhaps . . . but can you prove that you are not?" Leo's mind was racing, trying in vain to make sense of it all.

"Hey, wake up!" Elise shook his arm. "Aren't you happy to see me?"

Leo looked at her and slowed his mind down. She was wearing blue jeans and a knitted blouse. When did she change?

"I must go now," Elise said. "And you take some rest, you need it, I can tell. It can be dizzying here in the early days. See ya."

She pecked him on the cheek and then turned and ran. Leo put his hands in his pockets and spun around. He was standing in front of his apartment building. He shrugged, retrieved a hand, pulled the door open, and called the elevator. His mind again went into the new reality absorption mode, questions popping everywhere. Leo removed his shoes in the foyer, felt the terrazzo under his feet, and dropped face down in bed. It was indeed overwhelming. He was getting dizzy, as if sinking in a vortex of insane ideas. He searched for a stable enough thought to hold on to so he could stay afloat.

Elise . . . This ghost from his distant past he just met in this strange world, she was the anchor and the distraction he needed. He delved into this remote era. Their story had started in school, where it also ended just three years later. He was in the tenth grade when she joined the prestigious gymnasium. She was a transfer student; he never bothered to ask from where. Maybe he could do it now? Anyway, she was about two years younger. He was born in March, and her birthday was in late December, around Christmas. She was always complaining that she was getting only one gift per annum, when all the other kids were getting two.

Turned out that they resided in the same neighborhood. Leo caught a glimpse of her at the school year's opening ceremony, then on a regular basis, when riding in the tram. He quickly grew attracted to the slim girl with bushy dark blonde hair and large hazel eyes. He liked other girls too, but this one felt special. He was a shy and insecure teen fearing rejection and had no idea what to say or how to make himself likable.

He kept playing out different scenarios in his mind, until one day he got off the tram just before her, took a deep breath, turned around and threw a palm in the air. The tram floors back then were high. He did not expect her to take his hand; best case scenario in his mind was for her not to scoff. However, to his surprise, she grabbed it without hesitation.

"Thanks!" she said cheerfully and smiled.

"You are welcome," mumbled Leo in response.

Both remained still for a moment, then she realized that they were standing in the way of the other disembarking passengers and pulled him by the sleeve. "Let's go!"

"I am Leo Hans." Leo introduced himself.

"Elise Sinclair."

"Oh," Leo exclaimed with a mild surprise. "Are you Scottish?"

"A quarter—my granddad was occupation force. Well, one of them, I mean the grandfathers . . ."

Leo thought it impolite to inquire further, and for a while they walked in silence. Until he finally found the courage to speak again. "Seems we live near each other. I keep seeing you in the tram."

"Yes," she confirmed without giving details. Suddenly, she asked him, "Don't you have a crush on some girl?"

He blushed. *Is it that obvious?* He mumbled in response, "Why are you asking this?"

"I am two grades down."

Indeed, there was a phenomenon that, up to a certain age, boys and maybe girls, too, had no eyes for anybody younger or older than themselves. In years prior, he had a crush on Wasilla, a girl from his own class, and it was not different for anybody else. And since he had a crush on Wasilla, he would have hardly noticed little Elise, even if she were around. Wasilla had been considered a strange name. Her family were migrants from the East, he could recall. Russia maybe?

The next day after school, Leo hurried to catch the tram back home without looking around. It wasn't that he did not want to meet the girl again, but he wanted to avoid giving his keen interest in her away this early.

The morning after that, Leo rode the tram alone. She wasn't in the car, at least he didn't see her. He disembarked and initiated the short walk from the tram stop to the school.

"Hey, you!" a voice called from behind him. Leo stopped and turned around.

"Why didn't you wait for me yesterday?" Elise demanded.

"Well . . ." Leo began, trying not to look indignant, "I didn't want to stalk you."

"Stalk me?!" she said, looking genuinely puzzled. "We go the same way anyway. We can keep each other company. Riding on the tram for almost half an hour is boring, and nobody else seems to be sharing this route."

Leo's aspirations took a hit. He was hoping that Elise liked him too and was not just seeing him as a travel companion. But he was perhaps reading into it too much. Maybe he should lower his expectations and be content with her being friendly.

They continued to ride the tram together, to talk about school, about the past, and sometimes about their plans for the future. She wanted to study architecture. Both liked cats and shared their lives with a member of the feline species. Leo had Fluffy in those days, and

Elise's cat was named Joleen. Fluffy was, well, a fluffy, half-breed Persian they got from one of Leo's mother's friends. Joleen had been literally picked from the street.

After procrastinating for months, Leo eventually asked Elise out on a date. *Flashdance* had just premiered, and the girls seemed to like the flick. So, he went ahead with the proposal. Elise accepted. He was elated.

He still remembered her outfit on that first date—a short white skirt, red sandals, and a red sleeveless blouse. It stuck, because these colors appeared on a plethora of national flags and because he could catch a glimpse of her tits through the large armholes. She wasn't wearing a bra, which he later discovered was her signature style along with the shoes. He couldn't remember her ever wearing high heels. Other girls usually climbed on stilettos on their first dates, but not her, despite her not being tall.

When their relationship deepened, he dared ask her about the bra. "My boobs are small; they don't need support," she answered. Later, she also admitted to trying to make a feminist statement and challenge the strict conservative dress code of their school. "Free the Nipple" sort of thing. Naïve perhaps, but she was still a child. She even looked younger than her peers.

On this first date, she had put on some makeup and lipstick and large hoops dangled from her ears—something also disallowed under the dress code. She had obviously tried to style her hair, one of the many only partially successful shots at it, as Leo was going to discover. In his eyes, though, she looked lovely.

His own outfit was lost to time. Almost certainly a pair of blue jeans and sneakers. He had an off-white linen shirt with two large breast pockets he liked wearing in those days. Yes, he recalled ironing it before the date. He'd even shaved! He himself had some quirks when it came to dressing—he wore his shirts over his trousers, not tucked in. Back then he had no idea that this style would become mainstream years later. He also often wore suspenders. Wow, they were both pioneers, come to think of it!

They found themselves in agreement on skipping the Coke and popcorn ritual and went straight to the theater. The movie wasn't bad. Leo scoffed at the idea of a woman welder. It wasn't a thing in their homeland, and he was also pretty sure the legs of the dancer at the audition did not belong to Jennifer Beals. Years later he was proven right—the dancer was a lady called Marine Jahan, who went uncredited for her work in this film, but Elise was not around to hear his triumphant "I told you so!"

After their first date, they began spending more and more time together. They studied at each other's places, often with her 'taking inspiration' from his old assignments—that is to say, outright copying them. He disapproved of the practice, but this kept her near him, and he chose to look the other way. They took long walks along the river holding hands or playing hide-and-seek, usually with her hiding behind the trunks of large trees and him pretending to be unaware of her location.

One thing they had not yet done was kiss properly. One afternoon, Leo had a free period after lunch—the teacher had called in sick—and Elise decided to skip class and stay with him. They joined a group of his classmates in the nearby backstreet alley, where students routinely congregated to smoke cigarettes and drink bad coffee in plastic cups and, sometimes, beer from cans, purchased illegally from the nearby pub.

It was very hot outside. Leo had left his jacket in the classroom, but Elise was wearing her blazer. When she took it off, the thin shirt below was wet from the perspiration and, as usual, she wore no bra. A guy, Gunther or something, started picking on her. Leo was not in a mood to argue with a bully and pulled her away. They went back to the school building. Leo neither wanted Elise nor himself sniffed by a member of staff, for they had just smoked, so they hid in the attic. Certainly, a poor choice considering the weather, and he began to perspire too. It was comical, in a way, and he remembered how he got turned on looking at her nipples through the wet shirt. Maybe this is what gave him the courage to pull her close and kiss her lips. Which she parted promptly.

*
**

"Hey, wake up!" Elise rubbed his cheek with her palm.

Leo flicked his eyes open. He was lying on his back. He tried to sit but couldn't, something pulled his arms back. He turned his head—his hands were secured to the bedframe with padded handcuffs. Elise had straddled him, his penis still inside her and still erect. She wore a black leather collar around her neck with a thick rope hanging down from a ring attached to it.

"I've raised a kangaroo inside my skull. It hopped."

"I see. Get used to this, jumps happen, more often when you are new. Anyway, when did you come from?" she asked and flashed a cute snarl.

"The eighties. I was reminiscing."

"About what?"

"You and me. When we first spoke, our first date, first kiss . . . no first fuck though; you were the iron maiden back then." Leo chuckled. Indeed, at some point in their relationship he began pestering her with suggestions, then went on trying to convince her to open to sex. It was probably amusing to watch them in those days—he was a salivating dog, and she was an out of reach bundle of delicious bones and meat. That was, until the day her brother called to tell him that she was dead. Leo's heart almost stopped beating when he processed the words, and he was horrified. This memory was very vivid too.

"What happened?" he managed to ask.

"Hit and run," sobbed her brother in response. "It was absolutely awful, her skull cracked open . . ."

Leo could not hold back his tears, nor did he want to, and cried a great deal on this day and many others after that. The Gunther guy mocked him for the sobbing and his puffy eyes. Eventually, Leo pounced on him and beat the hell out of the large dude. That made him a hero in the eyes of his fed-up classmates, but he didn't want this newfound fame. He was heartbroken and wanted his little Lizzy back! Considering it now, he would still have been heartbroken, even if he'd known that they would meet again.

Her words pulled him from the depths of these bygone days. "I wanted it pretty much as well, but I was afraid. You know, getting pregnant and stuff . . . I thought that maybe I would do it when I turn eighteen, but you know what happened." She leaned forward and raised her rear, her nipples tickled his chest, they exchanged saliva and then she started swirling faster. He climaxed, however, she did not stop until she also had her burst of pleasure. She splayed over him like a jellyfish and did not move until her breathing normalized.

"People start at fifteen, even less. The age of consent is sixteen," Leo said.

"Does it matter now?" She rolled to the side, reached for the keys, and uncuffed him. "Now is your turn," she added and handed him the cuffs.

Leo sat in bed, thinking what to do. He still had no recollection of the trip to this place, but he had no doubts why they were here, for it had toys. He kneeled, reached for the book on the stool next to the bed, and paged through it. His expression changed to intrigued and he silently read a passage.

"That is interesting." Leo closed the book, put it back on the stool, and commanded, "Face away from me and bring your hands behind!"

Elise adjusted her position as ordered. Leo cuffed her, threaded the rope from the collar between her legs, pulled it up, then pushed it in her hands. Elise twitched and took a deep breath. Her body stiffened a bit. Leo came close to her cheek and whispered, "Liz, if we were alive, in the old world, you know, would you still be having this kind of fun?"

She did not respond immediately. Then said, "I don't know. Depends, probably not, not with my mindset. I wouldn't have the confidence and trust. I would be worried that I might be hurt or found out and ridiculed and called a whore."

"Even by me?" he asked, gently pinching her nipples.

"Yes, ah, no, sorry . . ." she sounded distracted and confused.

"That's OK, I understand. I was there, and I never gathered the courage to try anything with toys." He had guessed her answer right.

Ah, he loved this realm.

RESENTMENT

Leo remembered that he still owed Steve an apology, but he didn't know how to reach him. Maybe Elise could help, as she'd been here for much longer. She had created a new reality, so, surely, she knew how to find people. She knew Steve. Back then, Leo even suspected Steve of having a crush on his girlfriend.

He left home and at the second intersection turned right. The street was lined with trees. Most streets were. Old Town was an exception—there the streets were winding and narrow. But once outside the old fortress and into the newer parts, the green crowns provided shade for the people crisscrossing the city on foot. The foliage often converged over the narrower streets, and the footpaths sometimes wound in the medians between the traffic lanes. He loved strolling along those paths late at night, when traffic was almost nonexistent. The two of them often did it in the past.

He thought of his adventures in the other world. The States and South Africa were not like this. Very few streets with trees, often in the median, far from the sidewalks if there were sidewalks at all. These countries had car-centric cultures. Nobody cared for pedestrians.

Leo walked past a flower shop. Flower shop! He'd tried to find one before. He climbed the two steps and entered. The air was cool and fragrant with competing scents. He looked around. Price no longer mattered, as everything in this world was free. Wow, communism! In his school days he had to count the pennies and usually bought carnations. Sometimes he splashed out on more expensive species, like chrysanthemums and roses. However, he preferred to keep his allowance for more practical stuff.

Speaking of which, he remembered colleagues in South Africa telling him a story about attending a birthday party in Windhoek. They had brought a bouquet for the lady and the locals snubbed them, as explained later, because the flowers were not food, at least not for humans. In his youth, Leo would have cracked a racist joke. But then he changed. Years before Abi was even born, let alone her coming out as queer. He was glad he did. He shuddered at the thought that he otherwise might have shunned his kid.

Leo picked a bouquet, then reconsidered and put it back in the bucket. Why should he get Elise flowers? He spent a fortune on a bunch of black roses for her funeral and she wasn't even in a state to be impressed by his largesse. He left the store thinking of some other gift. But what else did she like? To his surprise, he had no idea. Cats, yes, but pets were not the best gift. Food? He could think of nothing special, and food in this world was served on a person's whim. It would probably mean something when cooked fresh. He still didn't know what her favorite dishes were, though, nor he would have the time to prepare anything even if he wasn't clueless.

Elise's place was just around the corner. The street he was on was lined with horse chestnuts. The fruits were not ripe yet, still in their spiky shells. Leo climbed on the nearby retaining wall, leaped, and managed to grab hold of a branch with some fruits. It flexed under his weight. Leo landed on the pavement, pulled it down and snapped off the tip.

Elise was waiting by the apartment's door. He handed her the 'gift'. She looked at it with miscomprehension.

"What's this? The ingredients for some magic potion?"

Leo balanced on the edge of the bed and explained. She sat next to him, still holding the branch. "Thank you!" She kissed him on the cheek.

"You remember Steve, don't you?" Leo asked.

She nodded.

"I did something stupid, and I must apologize, but I can't find him. Can you perhaps help?"

Elise nodded again, then left the room and returned with a vase. She dropped the branch in it and placed it on the windowsill. Leo was looking around, trying hard to remember what her room in the old world was like, but he drew a blank.

"Was this room always like that?"

"More or less."

"And you lived here for sixty years?"

"No, I've switched pads." Elise paused, then changed the subject. "Would you pick an outfit for me, please?"

Leo arched his eyebrows, unable to interpret the request, but agreed nevertheless "Sure!"

He nudged up to his feet, but she pulled him back. "Just look at me and think of something."

"Aw!" Leo shifted a bit further and inspected her. "Would you please stand?"

She complied, walking to the large wardrobe and placing hands on her waist while grinning. Then after a long pause, she asked, "Are you done?"

"Mmm" He nodded. "I think so."

Elise opened the wardrobe and guffawed. "Come!" She waved him over.

He rose and approached. She gestured at him to look inside. The wardrobe was empty except for a pair of red stilettos. Leo blushed. He did indeed imagine her naked, but she used to prank him in the past, so he had no way of knowing if this wasn't her doing. He tittered, then decided to confess what he was thinking, and why he'd run unexpectedly into the lake the other day.

"No need to stress, I am raunchy too," Elise said quietly, while looking down. Then she shut the wardrobe doors and commanded, "Try again!"

Leo dipped his head. This time he produced some garments: a black laced skirt and a blouse made of two wide red silk ribbons, joined together by a multitude of beaded threads.

She inspected them and nodded approvingly, "Not bad. Maybe you should have become a fashion designer, not industrial." She slipped out of her gown and put Leo's garments on. "What's this?" she hissed with furrowed brows, after checking the wardrobe again. Leo giggled as Elise revealed the long, thin monkey tail in her hand.

"OK, your call!" She lifted the skirt and strapped the faux tail underneath. "But I am not wearing these shoes."

Leo shrugged.

They went down and onto the street. Leo looked at her, prompting her to take the lead. She caught his gaze, sighed quietly, and took his hand. They walked in a completely different direction than what Leo expected, but he refrained from questioning her. He looked at the cityscape, trying to match it to his memories and was mostly succeeding or this is what he believed. He never knew every street and alley to begin with.

Elise took a shortcut through one of these—a back alley between four office blocks. When they emerged from it at the other end, they almost bumped into their friend.

"Er, hi Steve!" she greeted and let go of Leo's hand.

"Isn't it that pretty little cabbage-head herself!" Steve called with excitement and embraced her with his long arms. "Where have you been?"

"Ah, good, you can see each other," Leo said. "I was worried."

"Sure, why not?" Steve asked.

"Is some sort of emotional connection required for this to be the case?"

"I believe so, yes."

"Sooo?"

Steve burst into laughter, "You dummy! I was so in love with her back then, but you got to the honeypot first."

"Don't call me 'honeypot'!" Elise protested.

"Ah, I see. You never shared this with me."

"What would the point have been? Making you jealous?" Steve said.

"*You* making *me* jealous?" teased Leo. "Anyway, how does it come you only meet now? You both have been here for ages."

The smiles disappeared. Elise looked down, her toe tracing a half-arch on the sidewalk, her hands clutched behind her back. If the tail were real, its tip would certainly be flicking from side to side.

"We have," she said, still looking down, her face turning red.

"Oh!" Leo exclaimed, suddenly feeling resentful. The joke was on him, for Stephen could make him jealous, very jealous.

"Sorry I didn't tell you," Elise continued. "I didn't know how without hurting you."

Leo clenched his teeth and took a deep breath. He wasn't sure whether he needed to breathe here, but it was a reflex he carried over from the land of the living. Then he stretched his mouth into a tortured smile, "That's fine, you have been here for decades, and this is a completely different lifetime. If it can be called that . . ."

"Listen, mate!" Steve said. "Liz is totally into you. The moment you showed up she disappeared. She was with you all this time, wasn't she? And she didn't want me around, I could sense this much. She's been reminiscing your time together and wondering if she would see you again, hopefully not very soon, if you get my dr . . . er, what I mean . . ."

"That is fine, guys." Leo managed to rein in his resentment. "I still possess my earthly emotions, but on a rational level I understand, and I also have no right to object. Please don't worry."

"You understand? Do you understand this existence?" Steve asked, his tone turning serious. "Because I don't."

Leo reached into his pocket and pulled out a pack of cigarettes. He extended his hand in offer toward Steve, but then remembered what he'd died from, and retracted it with a guilty face.

"Gimme one," Steve said. "You can't get cancer here."

"Cancer? I heard it was COVID."

"Both. I had lung cancer too, and the COVID infection made my condition worse and hastened the demise."

Leo drew slowly then exhaled and turned to Steve. "I have always held you both very close to my heart. You are one of my best friends, if not the best. Lizzy is one of my big loves, if not the biggest. I love my grandparents, I love my mother. In a way I love my dad too. We didn't meet eye to eye when he was alive, but I grant him that he wasn't a bad man, only incompatible. I love my cats. And I got to see you all. This is how I understand this place."

Elise took his and Steve's hands and led them in a random direction. They walked in silence for some time. Then Elise turned to Steve and said, "Sorry, Steve, I don't think I can see you alone anymore."

"You can!" Leo insisted. "Of course you can. Polyamory is a thing nowadays, and you are not my property. You are free to do whatever you want. Who knows, we can have a threesome one of these days!"

"OK, I will consider the offer," Elise agreed. "But I still feel bad about not telling you."

Leo pulled her closer, pushed her chin up and sought her lips. "Liz, you were eighteen when you died. I am . . . I was eighty-one. I had other girlfriends and two wives. Who am I to judge you or deny you anything!" He did not realize it at this very moment, but it later dawned on him that, one day, all the ladies he spoke of would show up.

She looked him in the eyes and caressed his cheek. "I love you. I always did, I always will . . . Right now, I want to be with you and only you. That may change, yes, but . . . Where's Steve?"

They spun around. Steve was gone.

"Hang on for a minute," the girl said and closed her eyes. Then she opened them wide, took his hand, and once more led the way. They crossed the street and turned left at the next corner, then left again into a passageway.

At the other end was a cozy courtyard, with tables covered in bright blue tablecloths. Steve was sitting there, legs stretched and crossed, sharing company with a glass of Uzo and a large plate of Greek salad.

"How did you do this?" Leo asked. He'd tried to find his friend and failed.

"It will come to you soon," Elise said. "You get to feel the person you want to see, and if the desire is mutual, the city itself will morph and kind of drag you to the right spot. Steve didn't really want to run away. He just wanted to make room for us to sort ourselves, so it was easy."

"Uzo?" Steve asked with a grin and lifted his glass.

"Sorry, Steve!" Elise said.

Leo's brows went up in confusion as to why she was continuing to apologize. Then he remembered that apologizing was what he wanted to do all along. "I am sorry too, mate."

"What for?" Steve laughed. "Stealing Lizzy?"

"Crashing the car."

"No problem at all! You ended up in bed, I presume?"

Leo nodded.

"Well, so did I and the car—in the garage."

"You don't have a garage at your place," Leo said.

"I do, I moved. Didn't Lizzy tell"—he stopped abruptly, then cleared his throat and finished his sentence "—you? Well, obviously not."

"You lived together, didn't you?" Leo guessed. The resentment returned, accompanied by shame. These two had done nothing wrong, he had no right to feel this way. Apparently, the experience with his first wife had left a deeper scar than he thought. He reached for the glass, which had appeared in front of him, downed it, and coughed. Then said, "Sorry."

Elise looked tense. If she could sense his conflicting emotions, what would she do? Usher him away, considering that she was the instigator? He lit another cigarette, drew from it, exhaled the smoke, and said, "I humbly ask for forgiveness. My bitterness is unjustified and wrong! Shall we get something to eat?"

"Will you wait for me here? I will be back soon," Elise said, then sprang up and ventured into the restaurant.

"Cut her some slack, man," said Steve. "She's been alone for over three decades."

"I know and I am not blaming any of you. I think Beatrice influenced me in a bad way, and it showed."

"Probably," Steve said thoughtfully. "She was a bitch. But a hot one!"

Leo chuckled. Then looked around. "I wonder where she went."

"She'd try to do something for you for sure."

"Gonna find her . . ." Leo rose from the chair and walked to the restaurant door. It seemed there were other, invisible, patrons. He heard clanking coming from the kitchen and headed that way. Elise had donned an apron and was chopping onions. A large pot was boiling on the stove. She didn't notice him. She checked the pot, removed it from the flame, and emptied the contents in a colander in the sink.

Leo approached quietly and placed his hands on her shoulders. She gasped, dropped the pot, and turned around.

"Ah." She sighed with relief when she saw him. "You scared me."

"What are you up to?"

"You mentioned a freshly cooked meal this afternoon, and a man's love goes via his stomach, doesn't it?"

"Not always. You have a direct line to mine." Leo embraced her. She snuck her arms behind his back and clutched them together. There they stood silent and still, savoring each other. Until Leo asked without emotion, "What were you making?"

"Spaghetti with salami and tomato sauce."

Leo let go of her and checked the space. Another apron was hanging on the wall. He walked to it and put it on, "Shall I lend you a hand?"

Elise smiled. "Sure, come here!"

"One sec, let me call Steve in before he disappears again."

Elise nodded.

Steve was already on his fourth or fifth large Uzo and his speech was slurred. "Na-ah, man . . . I'm hoot here, just 'ring the food."

When they returned with the plates however, he was gone.

"Is he home?" Leo asked.

"For sure," Elise said calmly, and slurped a spaghetti mouthful.

COSPLAY

It was another nice, mild, sunny day, getting on his nerves. So far, all days here were alike—sunny and sunny with scattered clouds. This irked Leo. Some rain and even snow would break the monotony that had built up.

"Liz, does it ever rain here?"

"Mmm," she confirmed while pushing him from behind up the steep narrow street in Old Town.

"Snow too?"

"Mmm." She gave up and stepped back. He almost tumbled, being suddenly denied the support of her arms.

"Well, that's a relief," Leo said and chased her. She evaded him and ran into a nearby store. When Leo also went inside, she was nowhere to be seen. The store was selling vintage stuff, mostly items of clothing, but he also saw some broadswords and medieval shields. A wooden mannequin was clad in baroque attire and sported a feathered hat.

Leo looked behind the counter, but the girl wasn't there. Another game of hide-and-seek. They hadn't played one for over sixty years. He took the hat from the mannequin and donned it himself, then checked behind the heavy drape in the corner of the store. Drawing a blank, Leo shifted to the middle and slowly scanned the room for any traces—movement or otherwise. He felt a presence, but he could see no one.

His eye, however, caught something out of place—one of the wooden panels behind the counter had a doorknob. He went and turned it. The panel was a hidden door; it creaked and gave way, revealing narrow stairs leading up. Leo checked behind his back, then began to climb as quietly as possible.

The stairs were old and could not help the occasional squeak under his weight. He emerged in a corridor. At the bottom there was a small stained-glass window, letting some light in. There were several doors on both sides and on the left the stairs extended to the next floor. He halted and considered which way to go—check the rooms or continue up—when he heard a thud coming from upstairs. *Must be her*, he thought and followed the sound trail. His true age spoke—he was already bored with the game and wanted to corner Elise as soon as possible.

The next floor was very similar to the previous: a corridor with doors on both sides and a small window at the end. The stairs continued to the next level, this time on his right. He found that unusual but in old buildings anything was possible. He had to pick a direction again. There were no hints this time, and he made a random choice—up.

The stairs ended on a narrow platform with a single door. Leo pushed the handle and the door creaked open. The space behind it was the attic, dusty and with nothing else inside but spider webs and pigeon droppings. He could hear the cooing of the birds but couldn't see where they were hiding in the dim light coming in through the dirty rooftop aperture. Leo looked at the undisturbed dust on the floor; it seemed he made a wrong turn this time. He shut the door behind him and headed down.

The first two rooms on the left contained cardboard boxes stacked to the ceiling. There was nowhere for her to hide except behind the doors. He checked and then proceeded to the third. This room had shelves and hooks on the walls. On the shelves all sorts of objects were collecting dust—porcelain figurines, some spooky-looking dolls, encrusted jewelry boxes, old clocks. There was a telescope with brass knobs standing on a wooden tripod. Leo went to it, bowed and looked through the eyepiece. As expected, he saw only the out-of-focus ceiling of the room. The dust got into his nostrils, and he sneezed.

The door he opened next revealed a workshop—workbenches along one wall and cabinets along the other. Various tools were lying on the workbenches. In one corner there was a small electric stove with a pot, emitting a foul smell. Leo approached to investigate. A can of bone glue was floating in the water. Leo knew the stuff from his childhood—his father used it to fix things until modern, more convenient adhesives had replaced it. But this was an antiques shop, so they probably used it on purpose.

Leo dipped his finger in the water and gasped. The water was hot. The disturbance shook the can causing ripples on the surface of the glue—it was in liquid state. Someone had to be around, as the feeling of being watched was still present. He turned swiftly and scanned the space. Nothing there, but he heard noise again. He stepped outside, closed the door behind him, and proceeded to the next.

This door resisted at first but gave in when he pushed harder. On the other side there was a pile of what looked like velvet curtains like the one downstairs. Seemed they were stacked behind the door and had crumbled to the floor. Probably the thud he heard. The room smelled of old fabric. Vintage garments were hanging beneath shelves on the walls and on clothing rails. The shelves were occupied by hat boxes of varying dimensions.

Somebody was definitely in this room! Leo could hear shuffling emanating from the far corner and followed the trail. Elise was wearing a period dress and twisting her neck in a vain attempt to capture a glimpse of her back. The dress was way too big for her, and she looked like a kitten in a mitten. Leo couldn't suppress his chuckle.

She lifted her gaze and chirped, "Look at all this stuff—let's cosplay!"

"Mm, why not, seems fun," Leo agreed. "Are there any garments for the gentleman?"

"I think it's on the other side." She wriggled out of the dress from the top end, returned it to the hanger, and began browsing the other dresses on the rail.

Leo went in the direction she indicated and indeed found male attire. He noticed that the rails were labeled by what appeared to be period and size—XVII, XVIII, XIX, S, M, L, etcetera. "The stuff is labeled, let's go with the eighteenth, shall we?" he shouted across the room. He chose a shirt, a pair of breeches, and a coat. His vague recollection also suggested that he should get a vest as well. He already had a hat. Also socks and shoes. He checked around but saw none of these.

Leo reunited with Elise. She was standing in the middle of the aisle, wearing only a pair of pink drawers. She was holding the piece up with hand, trying to figure how to keep it there. He threw his costume over the rail and said, "Here, turn around."

She complied. He pulled up and tied the two ribbons together. Then, unwilling to resist, he reached for her bare breasts from behind and nibbled on her neck. He felt her shiver and kissed her again. He then reached down and undid the knot.

"No, not now . . ." Elise stopped his advance.

He swore silently but stepped back and tied the ribbons again, "Okay." In a minute he was mostly ready, short of only socks and shoes. She was, however, struggling with her corset—the laces were on the back. He dutifully lent a hand while thinking that it seemed impossible for a woman from that time to get dressed without help. Probably only the wealthy ones, though, but then they had servants. Leo took a stack of boxes from the shelf and dumped them on the floor. Elise examined the contents. She settled for a hat decorated with blue silk ribbons and a giant feather, dwarfing his by a long shot.

Both were still barefoot. They split and searched the room for foot-wear—however, it contained none. Leo collected their clothes. The couple walked out and descended the narrow stairs to the lower floor.

Three of the rooms there were under key and lock, but the fourth door yielded. The room held the footwear they were seeking, and knights' armor hung on stands. Elise lifted the heavy dress up and clumsily put on a pair of stockings. Leo's task was easier. He put the socks on, buttoned the breeches, and slipped into the shoes. Elise again chose a pair of almost flat shoes that took her some time to find.

"Why do you hate high heels?" Leo saw his chance to ask at last.

"When I was little, I often played with my mom's shoes. One day I stepped the wrong way and sprained both ankles. The doctor told Mom that I had torn tendons. It hurt a lot. I couldn't walk for weeks. I fear that it may happen again and could be worse since I am bigger now."

"But you are also dead," Leo noted.

She sighed and selected another pair with somewhat higher heels.

On their way out she picked up a faux pearl necklace from the store window. Leo chose a cane. They looked at each other and burst into laughter. Leo held the door open for Elise then followed her on the street. He turned around and tried to catch a glimpse of himself in the glass. The costume he could see, but his face was indistinct, just a shivering dark blob.

He pulled Elise back. "Come, check us out." She stepped next to him—the dress was recognizable, her reflected face though was an-other dark smudge on the glass. Still, Leo grew emotional at the sight of the two figures standing next to each other. He wiped his eye with his knuckle. They were together and they were both dead. Who could have ever thought? Elise, clearly forlorn too, sobbed and buried her face in his chest.

"Sorry," Leo said, "I didn't mean to kill the fun. I just remembered the two of us when we were still alive and young. And I kind of felt sad. This place is not real. I am afraid that you are just a dream . . ."

He held her tightly in his arms, unwilling to let go. Elise was sob-bing and not uttering a word.

"You are going to stain my shirt!" Leo tried to crack a joke with a still tight throat.

"Look!" Elise maneuvered out of his embrace, lifted hand and spat on her palm. The saliva stayed there for maybe a minute then slowly dissipated in the air. "We are ghosts, I told you! But I assure you that

I am real. In the sense that I am not a dream of yours." Then she pulled his coat. "Let's go!"

He discarded as much of the sadness as he could and offered her his arm. She curtsied and locked hers with it.

"Why are you always trying to see yourself?" Elise asked. "I gave up on that long time ago."

"I don't understand why this place is so much against that."

"Dunno." She shrugged. "But think. What would you see if you could? Yourself at ten, at thirty, at sixty? Your dead mask? I don't wanna see myself with a cracked skull and covered with blood and brain . . . Besides, existence is much easier this way. You don't worry if you have acne or not. You simply can't see it and you eventually forget that it is there. Although I am sure that many people had it. I wonder if they still do when projecting . . ."

"Sorry, I lost you," Leo said.

"The acne I'm talking about."

"Ah. You don't have acne. You were lucky, you never did. But we can ask around. I met my mom's friends recently. I will quiz them the next time."

"Don't!" objected Elise. "What if they suddenly remember and start projecting it? People tend to suppress unpleasant memories, and battling acne certainly qualifies. Projection involves memories."

"What wise words from an eighteen-year-old!" He praised her quite sincerely.

"Leo, not you, too!"

"Not what?"

"Forgetting that I'm eighty years old. That is eight-o! Appearances are misleading. It is true, that time here isn't linear nor regular, and experiences differ wildly between the two worlds, but it counts, nevertheless. I am old!"

"Sorry." Leo downcast his eyes. "I meant no insult."

"I know!" she replied cheerfully and did a pirouette. The skirt expanded and rose up to reveal her calves and the funny-looking red velvet shoes. She came out of the spin and said, "I want you to paint me!"

"Paint you? Ah, I get it, maybe then you will see your face!" Leo liked the idea.

"No, no, it won't work. I want you to paint my body."

"How do you know it won't . . . what? Paint your body?"

"Yes!" She placed her hands on his shoulders and commandeered him to pivot. There was a poster for a fashion show, featuring faceless models in body paint.

"Ah, OK, I can try. But I have no body paint. Do you want me to use regular tempera? I still have some at home. It will crack and peel though once dry."

"No, we will find proper paint. By the way, where are our clothes?"

Leo looked at his empty hands. He'd taken the clothes with him when they left the store.

"Seems I've dropped them somewhere along the way. We shall go back to find them and return the costumes."

"Agreed. This place is forgiving, and clothes are just another illusion, but I try to not get spoiled."

"What do you mean clothes are an illusion?"

"Like everything else. It looks real, but can it be? I saw a film once, *The Matrix*, where people—"

"I've seen it too."

"Yes, sure, so isn't it like the Matrix? Space folds, time isn't linear, and we are supposed to be dead."

Leo would normally agree, but his mind became preoccupied with something else. How had she seen *The Matrix*? The first movie came out in the late nineties, maybe 1999.

"When did you see this movie?"

"Ages ago. Before Steve came. What's bothering you?"

"I am surprised you've seen it here," Leo replied.

Elise thought for a moment, then said slowly, "I think I know the answer, but how did you know it was here?"

"Otherwise, we would have seen it together," Leo said without flinching, as if it were the sole option. "Anyway, let's go find our stuff."

"Not necessary."

"Why so? Oh . . ."

Elise was wearing her own clothes. He looked at himself. He was doing the same. In a way. The period attire was gone. Whoever or whatever created this VR was good!

"Come, let's go find body paint." Leo recalled that there was a large art supplies store just outside Old Town near the northern gate and suggested it. The city was less helpful this time around, and they had to cover quite a distance. Maybe five kilometers, even more.

The conversation died at some point, and they walked the remainder of the trip in silence. Leo spotted a flower stall, went to it, and picked a large white dahlia. He bowed and extended his hand. The girl curtsied and took the flower, broke the stem and tucked the blossom in her hair. The dahlia was too big and dislodged soon. She tried again without success.

"I think I gave you trouble with this thing." Leo chuckled and used her hair clip to keep the flower in place. As a result, her hair began to fall over her eyes.

"I shouldn't have tried this. Anyway . . ." She transferred the blossom to her hand and held it there.

By the time they reached the store, the sun was busy setting. The automatic door opened with a faint buzz and let them in. He hadn't been to one of these for ages. He retired as an animator and special effects specialist, but all work was done digitally. Even sketches and storyboards were done on tablets, and whatever little art supplies they used were ordered online and delivered to the studio.

The store was probably long gone from the other world, yet still existed here. It was huge, spanning over two large floors. The air carried scents of oil paints and turpentine. Another bout of nostalgia for days long gone hit Leo. Smells are often a strong catalyst for recall, retrieving and organizing memories from the deepest crevices of a person's mind. Apparently even in allegedly dead people.

As expected, nobody was in attendance. Leo began worrying that it would take days to locate a niche item amongst the enormous lot. "We shall split and search for the paint, me here and you—on the upper level"

"That would not be necessary." Elise pointed to something behind him. A plastic bag carrying the store logo was waiting on the counter. Leo looked inside and shrugged. It contained the merchandise they came for and more—a brochure and some brushes too. He turned, moved his gaze across the spacious interior, and bowed.

"Why did you do that?"

"How do you thank someone or something you cannot directly interact with?"

"Oh, I see . . ." She also turned and bowed deeply to the expanse of the store. "Thank you!" she said in a loud and clear voice. Leo huffed.

The automatic door performed its function again. The couple stepped outside and headed home. The sensation of being observed returned to Leo. "Do you feel as if somebody is watching?"

"Mmm," confirmed Elise, "but I have grown used to it. Sometimes you feel a presence, but solitude is all there is most of the time. It drove me crazy."

"How?" Leo asked.

She did not elaborate, just accelerated the pace of her steps.

"Hey!" He caught up with her. Tears were running down her cheeks. "What is it?" Leo tried to wipe them with his palm. She shoved his hand aside and sank into the foyer of her apartment building without saying goodbye. *Must have really sucked to be alone for thirty freaking years!* Leo thought and felt deep sorrow for his friend. What she had gone through was cruel and unusual punishment that she definitely did not deserve! What was this damn place after all? He heard enough of it bringing loved ones together, and he loved her dearly, but the price she paid to deliver the happiness he was rolling into now was also a large burden on his heart.

He heard hurried steps behind him and turned.

Elise stepped out and tilted her head. "I forgot to say good night!"

Leo dropped the bag on the pavement and gathered her into his arms. Their lips met, then their tongues, rolling and chasing each other, their owners oblivious of everything.

THE BEAR

Leo picked up a box of what would have been called handmade chocolates from what would have been called a specialist store, in what would have been the Old Town. On the surface, it made no sense to walk for over an hour to pick merchandise one could find in a drawer at home. But he wanted something just a tad special. On his way back, the overcast sky produced a drizzle, which interrupted his thoughts and forced him to hurry up. He was hoping for a spatial twist or something, but the city retained its shape.

When he arrived at Elise's place, the drizzle had turned into heavy rain. Leo pulled the front door open, jumped inside, and sighed in relief. He climbed the stairs to the third floor, the usual two steps at a time. Elise was already waiting by the open door. She gave him no chance to speak, just hung around his neck from the moment he crossed the threshold. Leo flexed his knees to force her feet onto the floor, but she folded her legs and left him no choice but to carry her to her room. She then tried to cling to him but inadvertently dug into his chest with her elbows. Leo grunted in pain. The girl returned to the floor and apologized.

"What are you, a koala?" Leo asked.

"No, I'm a cat. Meow!" Elise took a swipe at him with a clawed hand.

"Then you won't eat these." Leo pulled the box from the soggy paper bag and inspected it for damage. "They are not recommended for felines."

"I'm a special cat!"

"Nope. No sweets for cats!"

Elise abandoned the impersonation. She stretched her neck up and pecked him. "Thank you!"

"For what?" Leo smiled. "You could wish for these any time."

"No, it doesn't work this way. Haven't you noticed that whatever you find in the cupboard is generic and always open, like, if it's chocolates, it would be just some no-name box and half of them would already be gone? We can't simply wish stuff into existence. You couldn't, right? You had to go to a store; that's why you are wet. This place meets needs, it doesn't grant wishes."

Leo dwelled on her words for a moment. She had a point, but then he wished her outfit into existence the other day. He brought that up.

"It was a need. I had to wear something, OK!"

Leo guffawed. "You?"

"Hiss!" She became an upset feline again. But what she claimed was not invalid. When it started raining, he wished that it would stop, but to no avail. Neither did the trip get any shorter. There was no need, only a desire. Even the fairy-tale world she dreamt into existence did not follow her will. From his observations, all she could do was to invoke and terminate it. Speaking of which . . .

"Shall we share the chocolates with your pet bears? They can eat sweets," Leo proposed.

"Yes, why not?" Elise agreed and opened the wardrobe doors.

The sky in her world was cloudless again. The local sun seemed to have just sunk behind the mountain range. The grass was the usual bright green. Leo removed his shoes and socks and left them in the room.

"I'm not gonna make you vacuum the grass," Elise said.

"I like walking barefoot."

"Then why aren't you? It makes no difference if it's here or in dreamworld."

"Habit, I guess," Leo murmured.

They passed through the portal. The grass felt soft and springy, and there were no thorns and bugs. Leo enjoyed the sensation; it was like getting a light massage as he walked. He wondered what his version would be like if he ever dreamt one into being. He was not a big fan of nature. It may be stunning from a distance, but up close it poked, pierced, burned, bit, stung, and whatnot. She'd lived in a big city where nature was seen only from afar—the mountain range with snowcapped peaks—and often idealized the landscape she'd had no chance to get to know firsthand. She went on vacations in the countryside, and they also had school trips, but these were short uneventful encounters. Still, his version would be comfy too. He liked comfort.

"You know, we should perhaps hang out more often with Steve. You two spent, how long . . . years together, did you not?"

"Sure," she agreed. "But it is precisely the time we spent together—you are a novelty, you see." She smiled, then continued seriously, "Also he had feelings for me, and he grew a lot on me too. But when you showed up, I wanted you, and only you. It is selfish, I know, but I couldn't help it. I ran to you, and I didn't look back. That almost certainly hurt him, hurt his ego, I wouldn't want to be rubbing salt . . ."

Leo cuddled up to her with an arm around her shoulder. "Liz, my exes may show up some day, you know. I had feelings for them too."

"I would grow bored by then," she said cheerfully. "That's why I want all of you now! While I still can be selfish. And I am an ex too, right? The very first one."

"Yep," Leo confirmed and pulled her even closer. She wriggled out a bit. He tried to put a few broad strokes on an alternative history, where she didn't die. She would certainly be a different person, but how different? Would they have stayed together? Probably not. No matter how much he was in love with her in those days, he did not consider marriage and a lifetime commitment. Not at nineteen, anyway. But then they had classmates who got married and some never divorced.

"Hey, where are you!" She clapped her hands in his face.

"Sorry!"

"Well, I don't mind. OK, I do, just a little bit." She pinched two fingers.

"I can't stop thinking about this existence," Leo said, unwilling to reveal his true thoughts. "How we could set up a test."

"Like?" asked Elise.

"Like what it is—a simulation, a hallucination or a real place with strange properties. I don't know how to start. I'm no scientist. Father is."

"Then go see him."

"I am planning to, but I've been very busy lately," Leo said, trying to provoke a question.

"Mmm," was all she said.

*
**

By the time they arrived at the small log house the sun had set. There were no lost clouds in the sky to reflect the dying rays to the ground, and the forest was dark. Or perhaps her dreamworld was flat. The temperature had dropped too; it was getting chilly outside. They went indoors. The interior was faintly illuminated by the scattered remnants of light coming in through the small windows. Leo spotted a gas lamp on the fireplace mantel. He lit it with his pocket lighter and checked the fireplace. It was ready. He started the fire. He was impressed—she dreamt up a complete two-bedroom off-grid house with running water, channeled in from the nearby stream and a kerosene stove. But no electricity. Maybe that's why it felt so cozy. Probably she had no idea how to route electric wires.

Leo lit a second lamp he found on a hook behind the door and brought it to Elise. She was brewing coffee in a beaten-up stovetop maker. When it was ready, she filled up two porcelain mugs and took them to the upside-down wooden crate that served as a table. Leo unwrapped the box and scouted for a plate or a tray, then changed his mind and just removed the lid. He helped himself to a piece and delivered the rest to the crate. He added more wood to the fireplace and plopped on the couch.

The couch was covered with a thick wool blanket. It was rough to the touch and felt damp, just like in the old world. The fire hadn't yet emitted enough heat to overcome the cold. Elise took another blanket from the stack beside the couch, sat next to Leo, pulled it over them, and curled up. Leo reached from underneath to the crate to distribute the mugs.

"Don't you have something stronger here?"

She shook her head. "No alcohol. I have bears for pets. I would be asking for trouble if I let them get drunk."

"Did you try your own fairy tale or base everything on classic stories?"

"I am writing mine now," Elise said, and moved closer.

Leo left his mug on the crate, took a chocolate from the box, and balanced it on her tongue. She pulled it into her mouth and bounced it around until the piece fully melted, then licked her lips and begged with eyes for more. Leo fed her another piece then ate one himself. The fire grew hotter and pushed the dampness and the cold away.

After a while, they heard scratching on the door. Leo stood up and went to open it. The large brown animal entered with a grunt. Leo closed the door behind it and went to the fireplace to add another log. The bear approached the couch and sniffed Elise. She sat on the edge and buried her hands in the dense fur. The bear sniffed her again, then sat. Elise plucked another chocolate from the box and placed it on her palm. The bear sniffed it too, carefully scooped it into its mouth, and began munching.

Elise hugged the animal again. "Kyle, how are you, my friend? Where's the family?"

The bear repeated the grunt as if trying to answer the question. Kyle was the male bear. Elise had named the sow Ruby and the cub was Splash because of his alleged propensity to splash water and mud when crossing streams or stepping in puddles. Almost classic Goldilocks, just that the bears neither lived in the house, nor could they talk. They were just animated life-sized toys.

"You know, I used to play a lot with them in the past," Elise said with a grain of nostalgia in her voice, while rubbing the animal behind the ears. "I transformed into a little girl, ran around naked, and cuddled with the bears. It felt good. I guess that's why I am a bit of an exhibitionist," she said, admitting to her predisposition to shed her clothes.

Then she sprang up and did exactly that. But instead of the bear she came to Leo, who was squatting on the floor in front of the fireplace and climbed up onto his shoulders. Leo staggered to his feet, grunting. He sought his balance and stood erect upon finding it.

Elise thudded her head against the ceiling beam and cried out, "Ouch!"

Leo squatted promptly and set her down. "How bad is it?"

"Just a small bump," the girl said while rubbing the spot with one hand. The other hand reached to unzip Leo's trousers.

Leo had never had sex under the watchful eyes of a large brown bear. But there is always a first. At one point the animal approached, which made Leo apprehensive, but Elise grabbed it by the ears and kept going.

PETER

Leo woke up in his own bed. Yesterday's adventure felt like a wet dream. And it probably was quite close to that. A dreamt-up bear in a dreamt-up house in a dreamt-up world in a place that itself was probably just a dream. He lifted the cover and gave himself a quick glance. He was naked. He dropped back the cover and looked at the ceiling. He had lost track of the days. And time in general. He wanted to talk to his dad again, right? Forget Elise! Well, not forever of course, only for today. He would try to think of his father and avoid distractions.

Annette was smoking and playing Solitaire again.

"Mom," Leo began, "have you met Father? I mean here?"

"Yes, I have."

"What happened?"

She sighed. "I was truly in love with him when we got married, but then you know what happened." Annette was referring to the growing disagreements and the divorce that followed. Leo was only ten, yet already had a strained relationship with his father. But when Richard moved out and later remarried, Leo nevertheless felt abandoned. Eventually he grew out of it.

"He seems changed now," Leo said.

"He is. We all are," Annette confirmed.

"I see . . . OK, I'm off, I will try to meet him."

"I'll help," Annette said.

Leo wondered what exactly she meant by that, probably something connected with the way encounters worked around here. He took the stairs again. He was full of energy. And questions.

Elise was waiting outside. She was wearing denim shorts and sandals, a tight shirt featuring a stylized Jacob sheep print and a wide-brimmed straw hat.

"Hi!" Leo greeted her and scratched his head.

"You wanted to see me!" Elise's voice rang.

"Well . . ." Leo gazed down. "I did", he admitted, "but I want to do other stuff too and I was trying not to think about you."

"Can't we do this other stuff together?"

"I suppose so . . . I want to talk to my father."

"Then there we shall go," Elise said, and chose a random direction.

"It's the other way."

"Okay." She pivoted on her heels.

"What's with the hat?" Leo said in passing.

"Is something wrong with it?" Elise raised her hands to take it off.

"No, no, it fits you well. Just that I haven't seen you wear such a hat before—you know, flying saucer sized and made of straw. Only beanies in winter and the uniform beret at school."

"People change. Even here," the girl said, her tone serious. "I thought it would go well with the rest of the outfit. Too bad I cannot confirm that."

"It does indeed, rest assured. Especially with your hair . . ." Leo tried to be serious too but cracked and laughed—she reminded him of a little witch, save for the style of the hat. It should have been pointed and black. Elise furrowed her eyebrows.

They walked in silence for a while, then Leo spoke, this time with a grave tone, "Dad doesn't know you. So, you would not be visible to him and neither he to you. It would be awkward."

"I'm used to this, don't worry."

After a few turns, the street they ended on widened and transformed into a four-lane boulevard. The city had lent a hand again. Richard's apartment was very close. The couple entered the foyer and Leo called the elevator. In the other life, it had a concierge; here, the desk was missing. The elevator took them nine floors up. Richard was waiting by the open door. When Leo approached, he made room for him to pass.

"Hi Dad! I am . . ."

Elise hushed him before he could say "not alone." "Don't tell!" She took the flying saucer off her head and went in first.

Richard didn't react to her presence. When Leo entered, he calmly shut the door and followed them into the living room. Jessica greeted Leo from the kitchen.

Elise positioned herself in the middle of the space and looked around. Leo was curious about what she was seeing, as she'd never been in this room before. He almost blurted out the question, but remembered that she didn't want her presence revealed and turned to his father instead, "Dad, is everything OK here?"

"Have you experienced something else so far?"

"You mean that everything is OK, I get it."

"Why did you disappear?" Richard asked and sat in the armchair.

"Why do you want to know?" The son tried to give the father a taste of his own medicine.

"Why would a father not be interested in his son's affairs?"

Is he playing a game or was it old Richard talking? wondered Leo. When he was a young boy, his dad would often drive him to tears with what felt like cruel interrogations about even the most basic things. When Leo sought permission to go out to play, his dad would ask why, then where, then what, then with who, then probably names and addresses if by that time Leo had not already given up and gone sobbing back to his room.

After the divorce, and when his dad remarried, Leo began suspecting Richard of tormenting him on purpose, trying to get rid of his older son. When he wised up a bit in his twenties, Leo started to detect answers hidden in each follow-up question, but he was nevertheless annoyed, and the damage was already done. He overreacted easily, which in turn made his father angry, until they completely lost the ability to conduct a normal conversation.

"I went to the bathroom searching for a mirror and I ended up back home." Leo changed his approach.

Elise, having completed the inspection of the room, sat next to him on the couch. She threw the hat to the far end, turned in Richard's direction and stuck her tongue out. Leo glanced at her, baffled.

"Did you not notice that you've never had to relieve yourself?" his dad asked. Leo rolled his eyes. This question probably translated to, "We have no bathroom here."

"The door was where it was in the other flat, the real one, and I even went inside," he insisted.

Richard relaxed in the chair and sank in thought. Leo caught more movement to his right and looked at Elise. Her thumbs were stuck in her ears, and she was wiggling her fingers. Leo elbowed her while pretending to be stretching.

"Ouch!" she exclaimed loudly and pursed her lips. Leo glanced at his dad. There was no indication that Richard heard anything.

The older old man turned his gaze at him and asked, "Can you describe what exactly happened?"

Leo was about to succumb to his anger, but Elise somehow sensed it and quickly placed her hand on his thigh. He took a deep breath, exhaled, and began recounting the event—him opening the door, reaching for the light switch, and falling into the void.

His stepmom, Jessica, entered the room carrying a tray with three cups of espresso, sugar, and some snacks. She put the tray on the low table, pushed it toward Leo and his dad, took a cup for herself, and sat in the other armchair. Leo reached for his cup, but Elise beat him to it. Leo stuttered, as he saw the cup replicate itself when Elise took it from the tray. One cup departed from the table in her hand and the other remained. Leo picked it up and took a sip.

"Something wrong?" Richard asked.

"Ah, Dad, please stop asking questions!" Leo snapped. "I am tired of this shtick!"

"It is not a gimmick; I am being serious. I always was. Asking questions makes people think about the answer and nudging them toward it is better than just delivering the information."

"I get it, but you went too far," Leo said with regret.

"Sorry." Richard looked down, then back into Leo's eyes. "In retrospect, I think that I did, but unfortunately even here, with all of this place's peculiarities, there is no way to go back in time and change . . ."—*ahem*, he cleared his throat—"change that."

Elise had thumbed her nose now. Leo was on the brink of erupting. He stepped on her toe. She pulled her foot from underneath and kicked him in revenge. He kept a straight face.

"We did travel back in time, in a way," Leo said. "We are interacting with people from our past, my room is from the 1980s, and this entire place is still wholly analogue."

"It is not."

"Are you saying it has computers?" Leo was animated by the notion.

His father ignored the question. "As to your seeing things that should not be there, I cannot rule that out, even though I am not aware of it ever occurring in the past. However, I am . . . , *ahem*, a certain very recent development is making me think that it does happen indeed."

"What recent development are you talking about?"

"Are you sure you don't have something else to tell me?"

"Dad!" Leo begged.

"Okay, okay, I can see her!" Richard threw his hands in the air, then turned toward Elise. "Hi there, my name is Rich Hackensack. And you are?"

"You can?" Leo was stunned, his mouth agape.

Elise froze, then gave herself a massive facepalm, wailed, and buried head in her hands. "Oh no! I am so stupid! Oh no!"

"Elise. This is Elise," Leo answered for her, puzzled by her reaction.

"The girl you cried your heart out for?"

Leo nodded.

"I am sorry, Rich," Elise apologized, having partially regained her composure. "I should have realized that if I could see you, that applied to you too. I'm so dumb!" She dropped her head, her face turning bright red.

"So, your behavior would be somehow justified if I couldn't see you?"

"No! I'm sorry!" She was ready to burst into tears from the embarrassment.

"Don't beat yourself up too much about it," Richard assured light-heartedly. "You are still a kid. If I didn't know better, I'd think you were my granddaughter, Abigail."

Leo's dad had died before Abi was born, so how did he know about her? *Jessica or Annette must have told him.*

Elise sighed. "Rich, I am octogenarian, I just happened to die young."

"Ah, my bad! Of course you are. But you would agree that you did not conduct yourself in accordance with your true age, wouldn't you?"

"No contest on this." She pulled her hat closer and began to rub the brim between her fingers.

"But how does it come you can see each other?" Leo asked.

Richard did not answer immediately. "I don't know, Son, I don't know. This world has ways of keeping its secrets. It is in fact quite hostile to research. I tried . . . we tried, me and Professor Shodey and two other friends, to set up experiments but nothing worked. The results were wildly inconsistent, outright crazy. All that I can say is that this world is nothing like the one we left behind, but that's painfully obvious, why saying it . . . As to you, my best guess is that you two have a very strong emotional connection, and you somehow leak the images to others."

"But if it were a leak, should it not stop working if one of us departs?"

"We haven't tested this hypothesis, have we?" Richard said, his tone frustrated. "Anyway, I don't know even how age projection works. The inference is that we are not seeing with our eyes, but the exact mechanism is unknown. It is a challenge. Maybe this world *is* a simulation, and we are fed computer-generated sensory input."

"But wouldn't that imply that our brains were harvested while still intact and stored somewhere?"

"My brain was smashed," Elise said.

Richard turned to Leo and laughed. "Now you are the one asking questions."

Jessica howled from somewhere in the hallway. She had quietly left the living room a few minutes earlier, probably in boredom or indignation, as she had been ignored.

"That can't be good!" Richard catapulted from his chair and rushed out with Elise and Leo following close behind. Jessica was standing in the doorframe of the bedroom at the bottom of the hallway, tears running down her face. Richard walked to her side and peeked into the room. His expression darkened. Leo kept a respectful distance; Elise stood beside him clutching his arm with both hands.

Richard walked back to them. "Your nephew's here," he announced with anguish.

Leo's head spun violently like never before, and in the next moment he was standing on the sidewalk of a street with Elise still beside him, still clutching his arm. He lost his balance and plummeted to the ground, dragging Elise down with him. They sat still for a while waiting for the dizziness to subside. Elise recovered first and helped him to stagger to his feet.

"What the hell was that?" Leo asked, bewildered.

"They sent us away. They didn't want us there."

"How's that?"

"Emotions here manifest in more ways than in the other life. Richard and your stepmom, they sent us away. They were distressed and wanted to be alone. It was certainly involuntary. They will apologize the next time."

"In theory, they should be happy to see Peter, but they were obviously not. Probably—"

"It has to do with age. You don't want to see your kids here now, do you?"

"Well, we don't know what speed the time runs at here relative to the old world. But I understand. Assuming the same speed, he must have met his demise at the age of forty. Not quite a ripe age to die. I think I get it now . . ." Leo said, thoughtfully, then abruptly changed the subject, "May I ask you something personal?"

"Depends, but go ahead." Elise gave him a nod.

"That day when we went for the first time to your dreamworld, remember?"

"I do, yes."

"In the evening when we came back, you left the room and never returned. And I took the express ride home."

Elise nodded in confirmation.

"Was it you that sent me away?"

Elise repeated the head gesture. "Sorry, I didn't mean to be rude. I felt quite strongly that I wanted to be alone indeed."

"Nothing wrong with that," Leo said. "I was just curious." He placed his arm around her shoulders and drew her close.

"Leo, do you hate your stepbrother, Carl? Any axes to grind?"

"Nope. We were even close, but in the last few years he turned to Jesus and his efforts at saving my soul became excessive, so I stepped back a bit. But other than that, no, Carl and I were just fine. Why?"

"OK, did you hate your nephew Peter then?"

Leo wondered where she was going with this enquiry. "No, not at all. He was a cute kid and turned up a very decent man. Penny, his sister, she's stiff and often condescending, but Peter, I'd say I like him more."

"Then if we are all figments of your imagination, why did you imagine him dying? Why? Your father was distressed, and your stepmother was obviously in a lot of pain. Why did you do this to them?"

Leo listened attentively, then began considering the argument. Maybe she was on to something here. He didn't hate his father; he harbored no resentment toward Jessica, as he didn't care who his father was with.

The flying saucer took off on account of a gust of wind and flew across the street. She ran to catch it. Leo spotted a couple of tables in the shadow of the trees lining the street. His mouth was dry; maybe the tables belonged to some establishment, and he could get something to drink. He turned and called Elise, pointing at the tables. She had just caught her runaway garment and walked back, not showing much care for the poor thing. The hat was torn. Elise found a rubbish bin and stuffed it in with a serious expression on her face. The hat was larger in diameter than the bin itself and resisted.

"There goes my good old summoned-this-morning hat," she said feigning.

Leo did not read her right and offered reassurance. "You can easily get another."

She looked at him while still bent down with both hands in the rubbish bin and said, "I know."

COLD AND GAY

Leo snapped his eyes open expecting to see the ceiling of his room, as was the norm, but today it was different. He propped himself up and scanned the space. He was in what looked like a hotel room. Heavy curtains adorned the floor-to-ceiling windows or perhaps sliding doors. He could not make out which they were from his position. There was a loveseat, two armchairs, and a rectangular coffee table in front of the window. A double desk was affixed to the wall on his side of the king-size bed he was in. On the opposite wall was the obligatory luggage rack and a minibar.

Last night Leo and Elise bounced the idea of visiting Köennendorf, a popular resort town in the mountains, about two hours' drive away. People flocked to it all year round—in winter because of the ski slopes and in summer because of the majestic glacial lake on the shores of which the town stood. Then they split up and went home. This morning, he woke up in a hotel. Apparently, they had traveled overnight.

His girl was still fast asleep next to him. He slipped out of bed quietly and tiptoed to the window. It was a sliding door, as he suspected, leading to a large private balcony. The sky was overcast. The mountains were covered in snow. What a world. Yesterday, it was spring in the city. But the snow lasted much longer in the mountains, and he had absolutely no idea what the season was. He supposedly died in November, and he'd been here for a couple of months now, so, if seasons carried over, it should be winter indeed. But he had never experienced it in the city. A perpetual late spring had by all accounts taken hold of the weather there. It rained sometimes but never snowed and the temperature was always mild.

He dropped the curtain and turned his attention to the rest of the room. On the left facing him was a short passage leading to the room's door. Pretty typical layout. He treaded softly to the door and opened it—only a slight click was heard before it yielded. It revealed a normal hotel corridor with numbered doors on both sides. Leo glanced down. The door had no lock, just a regular door lever, no keyhole, card reader or NFC sensor. Leo shrugged. With only the two of them what were locks needed for indeed.

Leo closed the door, biting his tongue, and faced the room. On his left there was a pair of sliders. He pushed one open. It revealed a shelf with extra pillows and duvets. On the underside there was a rod with hangers. On two of them, ski suits hung suspended. Leo sniffed a faint smell of refreshener. He closed the slider and opened the other. More hangers, two pairs of gloves, two beanie hats, and two thick, knitted scarves. On the floor were two pairs of boots. Seems they came well prepared. He had zero recollection of ever getting ready for the trip; time must have flowed strangely again. Leo squatted and inspected the boots. One pair appeared to be the right size for him. He tried it on—a perfect fit. He wrapped his neck in a scarf and put a beanie on.

Elise moved on the bed. Leo peered around the corner and his gaze crossed with hers.

"'Morning!" Elise said, smiling and still sleepy.

"'Morning to you too," Leo greeted back and stepped into the room.

"Nice outfit!" She nodded at him.

Leo looked down and could not help his guffaw. He was completely naked save for the boots, the scarf, and the beanie. To top this appearance, he was getting aroused.

"Come closer," Elise said and rose just enough to let the duvet slide off and reveal her bare breasts. He took a step in her direction.

"Closer."

He inched toward her some more.

"Closer," she said again.

One more step and his crotch was almost in her face. Elise slowly breathed in, "Mm, the smell of ripe fruit . . ." She pushed the bed sheet, sat on the edge, held his dick between her thumb and index finger and ran her tongue along.

Leo twitched, his heartbeat accelerating. "What fruit?'

"A banana . . ." She ran her tongue again. "Absolutely! It even has the same shape." She shook it.

Leo gasped and murmured, "No wonder Fluffy doesn't like me . . ."

"But I do." She licked the glans. "I wanna eat it . . ."

"Whatever, just please don't peel it!"

Elise chuckled and drew the penis slowly deep into her mouth, while rolling her tongue over the corona. Leo shivered despite the beanie and the thick scarf. She reversed the motion, while sucking, then repeated, leisurely taking her time. She traced again the shaft with her tongue and sucked on the glans.

Leo started panting. His forearms were covered in goose bumps, but his body remained still. Elise probed the opening with the tip of her tongue, then pulled it again into her mouth and slowly rocked her upper body, her lips gliding over the shaft. Leo gently swept his hands over her hair, careful not to interfere. She rolled her tongue again, sending sparks through his loins and up his spine.

Leo edged out when he felt that the geyser was about to erupt, but she bit lightly to keep him still. His heart was in his throat. He clenched his teeth, moaned, and glided his hands over her shoulders then in a second, he was done. Elise continued for a while, then let him pull out and ran her tongue over her lips. Leo crouched and kissed her, sharing the taste. Then he kneeled and tried to go further down in a bid for a payback, but Elise stopped him and breathed in his ear, "Later, I want to stay tense."

She took the beanie from his head and donned it herself, then got up, walked to the closet, peeked inside, and growled.

"What is it?"

"There's nothing in here."

Leo walked to the closet. "There are some gloves." He took a pair off the hook.

Elise pulled it from his hand and slapped his backside. "There's nothing to wear besides ski suits and boots."

"OK, then we'll sit and think something into existence. Like you made me do that one time." He returned to the bed, sat on the edge, and closed his eyes. He heard the sliding door slamming, then the mattress next to him sank under Elise's weight. He quickly opened his eyes wide. "Hey, what if the suits also disappear?"

"Why?"

"Because I am still picturing you naked!" He giggled. She pushed him on his back and sat on top. "So, how do I force you to do otherwise? Exhaust you perhaps?"

He grabbed her waist, plunged her over him, and pulled her nipple inside his mouth. His tongue rolled around it. He could feel it firming; she gasped. He switched to the other—no favorites were allowed. He moved his hand between her legs to find if she was wet. But he was not back in business yet. He pushed her further up and tried to make her sit on his face.

Elise refused. "Not now, I am serious. You know what I mean—don't eat all the food at once. Besides, if we continue like that, we'll never get to the slopes. Is that not why we came?"

Leo turned his head and growled. He nipped her thigh, pushed her out of the way, and hopped to his feet with a grin. "Sure! Let's go!"

The air outside was apparently starving—the cold bit immediately into their cheeks—and also carried the scent of burned wood. Some chimneys were belching smoke. The roofs wore thick white caps; the eaves were adorned with icicles hanging from the gutters. Elise switched to child mode and began dancing and scooping snow and spreading it around. Leo rolled a snowball and threw it at her. He missed and bent down to collect snow for another when the counter-attack came. A skirmish ensued but subsided quickly after he caught her and restricted her movement with a tight hug. They rolled in the snow, and she instinctively transformed into a kid. Until he absent-mindedly tried a French kiss. Elise reverted and pinched his cheeks.

"Mm, sorry." Leo helped her to get off the snowy ground, red-faced.

She clung to his gloved hand. "Which way now?"

Leo pointed. "I think the slopes are over there. Let's go!"

"I have not skied for ages. Doing it alone is boring," the girl confessed after a while.

Leo thought of Steve, but remembered that the guy didn't ski at all and made a confession of his own: "Same here. I haven't skied since my divorce, even earlier—last time I did was before I left for South Africa. I hope I will not embarrass myself too much today."

"Do you still care?"

He glanced at her, smiling. "Less and less."

There was as usual no soul in sight, but the equipment rental shack was open, and the lifts were operational. The slopes were covered in trails. It was eerie—there was that feeling that the place was crowded. What kind of magic was that? Two sets of skis and ski boots were waiting on the counter along with a locker key. *Wow!* The boot change did not take long, and soon they stepped out. Leo blinked rapidly in mis-apprehension—they were standing at the top of the course!

"After you, Fräulein!" Leo winked. Elise stuck her tongue out at him, then pushed off. He let her put some distance between them before following suit. As he had gained enough speed and moved in first place the clouds dispersed, revealing the sun. The brightness of the reflected light blinded him; he lost balance and fell. Elise zipped past him. He rolled to his side and scrambled on his feet. *Gonna catch you!* He snorted and chased after her anew. He had forgotten what fun skiing could be! Notwithstanding the numerous falls.

He tumbled again and again, sometimes face down before reaching the bottom of the run. He was never particularly skilled, but he didn't mind; he was doing it for fun and even the professional skiers were not immune to scooping up large amounts of snow with their mouths.

Ordinarily he was cautious, but here, there were just the two of them. No one to smash into, no kids to run over. He went for even more speed in a bid to catch up with Elise, however, had lost sight of her while tumbling. He turned around to check if he had not overtaken her without noticing or maybe she had fallen and needed help. She had come to a halt some distance downhill, waving at him. Leo looked behind him. The slope there was ascending. Weird, what made him think he had reached the end? He glided down and came to a stop beside her.

Elise's cheeks were red and wet from the melted snow. Snowflakes were clinging to her eyelashes. "Cool shit, skiing!"

"Yep, it is! I had forgotten that. Though it is different without the crowds around. Much better!" Leo cleaned his runny nose with the back of his glove.

"Ew! Gross . . ."

"May I borrow your handkerchief?" Leo snapped.

"Double ew!"

"Tissues by any chance?"

She shook her head.

"Then don't criticize!"

"Fair enough."

The ski run seemed endless. Each time they thought that they'd reached the end, there was more. Eventually, Elise, fatigued, stuck the poles in the snow, plopped down on her back, and spread her arms. Leo braked next to her, panting.

"Are you thinking what I'm thinking?" he asked.

She swayed her head and puffed—the space was folding to create an endless run for them to enjoy. Nice touch, if they sought to save money on the lift fare; otherwise, exhausting, even boring. The lift ride up provided time to rest. Also, how would they know where the tea rooms were—up or down? All they wanted now was a hot beverage and some rest. *How can we tell the management about this*? Leo wondered. He released the clasps, stepped off the skis and set them upright in the snow.

Elise released the clasps while still lying on her back. Leo offered a hand to help her up. The skis, no longer constrained, began to roll. Leo let go of the hand he held and tried to stop the runaways. She fell back and cursed. Leo glanced to and fro, wondering which way to go. By the time he made up his mind and chose to catch the skis, their paths had diverged, and the damn planks had gained speed.

"Leave them," Elise said, and got up on her own. Leo waved farewell to the speeding skis.

"This place deserves it!" Elise grunted and gestured the skis away, "Go!"

Leo let out a laugh.

They walked across the piste back to the rental shack. When they started, the building was at the bottom of the slope, then, while they were inside, it moved to the top, now it was here—somewhere in between. These spatial twists were disorienting; he started feeling dizzy. *Where is our hotel now?* he thought. They were both wet and tired and not inclined to chase hospitality establishments around. Leo dropped the load on the counter and looked around—at the corner, he spotted a vending machine.

"Here." Elise had fetched their boots from the locker.

He checked inside and shook them just in case. Nothing fell. Leo changed and went to the machine; it was dispensing snacks. He pushed the button twice for two chocolate bars.

Elise bit off a piece and held it out with her teeth.

He got the message—he leaned and transferred it into his mouth, pushed it to his cheek, and kissed the girl. "Thanks!" Then he fed her one in return and shivered—the cold was beginning to get to him. Some steaming tea and a hot shower would be great. "Can't they add a bathroom for such occasions? No loo, just bathtub."

"There's probably a pool," Elise said, and snorted—her nose was getting runny too. "We can go there."

Leo rubbed his forehead with pinched fingers thinking how to get back to the hotel. The shack had moved; he had no idea where they were. He grunted in frustration and opened his eyes. At the end of the counter, he saw a stack of brochures featuring a map. He leaned and snatched a few—they might come in handy. He stuffed them in his pocket, chewed and swallowed the last piece of chocolate, and held the door open for his lady. Apparently, time had folded too—the sun was gone and the floodlights of the piste were on. Large snowflakes began to fall from the sky. This world was never noisy; the dampening effect of the snow made it even quieter. It was beautiful though—the black sky sprinkling the earth with water crystals, which reflected and refracted the man-made light on their way down, then piled up without a sound. Romantic as it may be, Leo was not a fan of the snow—having to shovel it had put him off.

Elise soured his mood further with a question, "Where to now? I'm thirsty and I am getting very cold. Brrr . . ."

"Not a clue. We'll just follow this path; it will surely take us to town. And we will get something hot to drink along the way."

They reached the town, but not the hotel. The stores, to his surprise, were closed. The restaurants and pubs too. He bit his lip and sank in thought. They were thirsty, tired, wet, and freezing. They needed drink and shelter. This place catered for human needs; therefore, something had to be wrong. Was the world exacting revenge for the abandoned skis? Or pissed with them for complaining about the morphing of the slopes? At the next locked restaurant door, Leo pulled a brochure, unfolded it, and exposed it to the light streaming through the glass.

There's the bottom of the main run, he noted. The rental shack was there too. And the hotel! "Pugh Inn" was its name, now he remembered. So, they shall take this road here—he pointed at a line on the map.

Elise was shivering. He wouldn't normally hesitate to give her his coat, but he was wearing nothing else. However, the gentleman in him could not resist and he unzipped it.

She violently shook head in denial and said with chattering teeth, "No, you'll freeze!"

He pulled her close and wrapped the coat around her.

"We'll keep each other warm like this. Trouble is, it is difficult to walk."

She kissed his bare chest and nodded.

A few minutes passed, and the couple attempted to find the road to the hotel by following the signs. The signs, however, were unreliable if not outright misleading—instead of getting closer to downtown, they had moved farther away. Leo's anger was ready to leave the confines of his chest and pour out as a stream of vile curses. They took another rest, sharing warmth. It was not easy to get their bearings in the darkness, and there were fewer and fewer lights to assist them. Elise became lethargic and could barely move her feet. Leo was on the verge of panicking. What was going on? It was not supposed to be like this. Was heaven freezing over? Leo's own teeth had begun to chatter.

He looked around. The lane they were on was surrounded by big pine trees in between which were nestled chalets. He couldn't see any lights in the windows, just the porch lamps. He dragged Elise to the closest one, removed his glove and knocked on the door. There was no response. He knocked louder and yelled, still getting no reaction. He lifted the exhausted girl and carried her to the next chalet. He had grown desperate and unceremoniously kicked the door. It did not give in, even after a second more powerful use of brute force.

Leo was already very tired. The freezing temperature had drained him out of energy. He put Elise's feet on the ground and helped her sit down on the flat wooden bench adjacent to the front door. He then decided to try the knob. To his surprise, the door swung open. Leo reached for the light switch. The first lever turned the porch illumination off, but the second activated the indoor lights. He lifted Elise, brought her inside, and put her on the couch. She was shivering uncontrollably. He took off his coat, covered her with it, then turned around trying to find the kitchen; there should be a kettle and maybe tea. Even plain hot water would suffice.

A vaguely familiar man was standing in the doorframe of what was probably a bedroom.

"Shit!" Leo jerked. He had become accustomed to seeing no other people apart from the few well-known faces. Seeing another person in such an unexpected setting spooked him.

The man also appeared shocked. He looked at Leo, then the girl without making a sound. Then he said, "Lizzy?"

Elise wearily opened her eyes and took a moment to focus on the man's face, "Dad?"

Leo's jaw almost hit the floor.

The man turned to him and announced, "I remember you! You are that kid, Lizzy's boyfriend from school—"

"Yes, sir, that would be me indeed, but can we now get something hot for Liz to drink? You don't have a bathtub by any chance?"

"Yes, yes . . .", her father said. "The kitchen's over there." He pointed. "I'll bring dry clothes and blankets."

He sank into the room. Leo thought that he heard him mumbling something. He also remembered the man. They were not on good terms back then. The father grew to tolerate him but was overprotective and aggressive at the beginning. Their first meeting ended up with Dad pushing Leo out of the apartment and throwing Leo's shoes at him. Leo had been with Elise, assisting her with her assignment, when the old man returned from work and went ballistic. This wasn't Leo's first visit to his girlfriend's place, but it was his initiation with her dad. She hadn't seemed to expect her father to react so angrily and had been flabbergasted. Leo was promptly thrown out before she could utter a word.

Leo made tea in a tall mug and brought it to the coffee table. Elise's father was back with blankets, a red cotton shirt, a sweater, and a pair of long ski socks. Leo undressed Elise not thinking much of the father's presence.

The father looked at her, then at Leo's bare chest, then her again. "Why are you naked? You haven't—"

"There were only these ski suits in the hotel room," Leo answered while helping the shivering Elise put the shirt on.

"Yes, but where is your underwear?" insisted the father.

"We were naked, OK? Get over it!" Leo was no longer the easy-to-intimidate seventeen-year-old. He completed the clothes change with the socks. He pulled them up then lifted Elise's legs on the couch and wrapped her in the blankets. Her color was beginning to return.

"Take this," Elise wheezed out and pushed the corner of a blanket in his hand. "You need it too."

"I'll fetch more!" Her father jumped into action. Leo sat next to the girl and handed her the steaming mug. Her palms lingered over the hand holding it. The girl . . . Leo was thinking of Elise as a girl. Her dad had thrown him back in time and he realized how long ago it was. Literally a lifetime ago.

Elise's father summoned him to the present. He dumped another blanket and a load of clothes on the coffee table and asked, "What happened? Why are you here?"

Leo briefed him on the events while changing. He wanted to ask the same question, but chose not to, as that was something for Elise to do. Her father sat in the armchair opposite the couch and fixed his gaze on his daughter. Leo could sense the man's tension; maybe also saw tears. Elise had fallen asleep. Leo released the mug from her grip and took a gulp. The tea was lukewarm, and he was still feeling cold. He stood, went to the thermostat and cranked it up.

"Do you have brandy or something?" he asked the host.

"You should not be . . ." the father began, then seemed to realize that Leo's appearance was misleading. "In the cabinet, there's some Metaxa."

Leo found the bottle, mixed a generous dose with the remaining tea, and sat on the couch at Elise's feet. A half-full packet of cigarettes, probably the father's, drew his attention—he pulled a stick and lit it.

"I must prepare for tomorrow. I will have some explaining to do." Elise's father sighed and rose slowly. Leo remained silent. "There's another room if you want . . ."

"No, I'm good here. Just gonna light the fireplace."

"That's fine," said the other man. He stepped into the bedroom, threw one last glance at his daughter from the threshold, then quietly closed the door.

The brandy didn't make Leo sleepy; he was overexcited. He checked on Elise, then went to the fireplace. It was stacked, ready to go. He tried lighting it with the cigarette lighter, but the flame failed to reach the ball of wrapping paper behind the logs. Maybe some brandy? Leo fetched the bottle and sprinkled some in the fireplace. No luck with that either. Leo looked around him, then remembered the useless brochures he took from the ski rental shack. He went to the coat lying on the floor behind the couch and removed them from the pocket. He shaped one into a V, lit one end, and pushed it close to the kindling. The sticks caught fire and relayed it to the paper ball. It returned the courtesy and set more wood alight. Success at last!

Leo lifted the mug from the floor and relocated to the armchair. Elise was sleeping across the table, twitching occasionally. Leo had questions—what was her dad doing here? And what the hell happened today? But he had to wait for the answers. For some of them, he didn't think he'd get an explanation from management any time soon, if ever.

His thoughts returned to his friend. Yeah, was she a girl. No, of course not, she had existed for a very long time in this world alone. And nearly twenty years in the other. She just looked like one. And most of the time behaved as such. Weird. Was it somehow related to her appearance?

Leo's stomach gurgled. He went to the kitchenette and checked the cabinets. There was a fresh baguette. He broke it in half and took a bite. Where did all the food go? He ate and drank but nothing came out of him ever. Not counting the semen, of course, but was it even semen? He made a mental note to check it; there were microscopes in his old school and maybe these existed in this world as well. The rub was that it dissipated soon after ejaculation, so he'd have to produce a sample in the lab.

He found liverwurst and cheese in the fridge. Great. He made himself a light breakfast and returned to the fireplace to eat it. Elise rolled in her sleep and pushed the blankets on the floor. Leo left the empty plate on the table and went to fix that, then looked at the door. The dawn was getting closer, the color of the sky was changing from dark blue to subdued pink. Leo took the cigarette pack, wrapped himself in his blanket, and went outside.

The cold air nibbled his cheeks again. He lit another cigarette and tried to puff rings, but what came out of his mouth was a cloud of water vapor with some bluish streaks. Memories from a previous lifetime flooded his mind. Him, standing on the verandah of a chalet, smoking, and waiting for the sun to rise. Elise, sleeping in another room with girls from her class. He'd been constantly scanning the footpaths, on the alert for supervising staff. He had not supposed to have been awake that early, let alone smoking. Steve had gotten seriously drunk that night, and his friends had to hide him during the head count. Did Leo want to go back to those times? And relive his other life? Save Elise? Never marry Bea? If he had no memories of the future, what would the point be? If he had memories of the future, but no power to change it, that would be a nightmare. Probably on par with hell. Then, if he was dead indeed and ended up here, where did people like his Aunt Miriam go to? What about Hitler, Mao, Putin, Pol Pot? And the many other giant assholes?

The sunrays were no longer held back by the mountain and pierced his eyes. He blinked and looked to the side. It felt like the start of a beautiful winter day, but Elise's father had some explaining to do as he himself had said, so who knew what might lie ahead. Did this sun have sunspots? Leo returned indoors and turned the kettle on.

"Hi!" Elise had opened one eye and followed his movement in the room.

"Are you a pirate now?" he asked.

"No, why?"

"You have only one eye open."

She pushed her hand out from underneath the blanket and rubbed the other eye. "That better?"

"Sure." He smiled. "Are you feeling all right?"

"Yeah." She sat and checked her outfit. "Where's Dad?"

Leo pointed to the bedroom.

"I wonder what's he doing here", she said quietly. "He's not alone for sure, but not with Mom either. Otherwise, she'd still be fussing. Duh, they still treat me as a child!"

"He said he was going to explain."

"OK." She nodded.

Leo pushed the mug in her hands. "There's brandy, if you want."

She waved hand in refusal and slurped from the mug. Leo went back to the kitchenette, sliced the remaining half of the baguette, and threw the slices on a plate along with some cheese. He saw a cube of butter on the countertop and added that too. He took a table knife from the drawer and dumped the load in front of her.

"Thanks!" She grabbed a slice and stuffed it into her mouth.

Leo reached for a cigarette but changed his mind and just sat back and watched her eat. Why did they eat?

The door behind him made a screeching sound, and Leo turned on his chair to check it out. Elise's dad emerged, clad in dark-gray trousers and a white shirt. On his feet he wore black shoes. Kind of formal for the place, as only the necktie was missing.

"'Morning!" he greeted.

"'Morning!" answered the couple almost simultaneously.

The father went to the kitchenette and turned the kettle on. Then he reached inside the cabinet, where Leo had found the bottle of Greek brandy.

"Here!" Leo lifted the bottle from the floor and passed it to the other man, searching his archives for a name to attach to the face. Nothing. But now was not the moment to inquire.

The father added some to his tea, then lifted the bottle and took a gulp.

"Dad, what's going on?" Elise asked, perhaps sensing that he wanted to talk, but didn't know where to start from.

Her father went back to the bedroom door and peeked inside. Leo thought that he saw for a split second the father waving his hand as if calling someone.

"Uncle Boris!" Elise exclaimed and her eyes widened. Leo couldn't see anyone. He grabbed his coat and the smokes and headed out.

"Stay, boy!" barked Dad, then softened his tone. "I want you to be with her; she may need you."

Wow, how dramatic! Leo did not correct the father's age perception. He dropped the coat back in the armchair and obediently sat next to Elise. It seemed as if she was fixated on someone or something on her father's right side and maybe talking. She did not look perturbed though. She then turned to Leo and said, "Dad is gay."

"Oh, I see . . ." Leo shrugged and then added, "No Boris."

"He's with Uncle Boris, a very old friend of his—"

"Me and Boris, we've been together from before," the father said, addressing both. "We met again in this life."

"Does Mom know?" The father shook his head. "No, I never had the courage to tell her. It will devastate her."

"I think you should," Elise said. Her father dropped his head. Elise's gaze moved to the same spot to his right, then she continued, "I'm fine, I don't mind. But I think that you two should come clean and tell Mom. Promise?"

"Promise," her dad mumbled.

"Then we are all good!" she said cheerfully, stood up and stretched.

Her father approached her and gave her a heartfelt embrace. Then, he turned to Leo and said with trembling voice, "Eh, boy, she's golden. What a lucky man you are."

"She died over sixty years ago, and I spent my life mourning. What kind of luck is that?" Leo answered angrily.

"Sorry, my mind's a bit foggy right now," the father apologized. "Of course, you are old. And she is too. But you didn't have to hide your feelings, neither back then nor now."

"Then come clean! You still can do it," Elise intervened and hugged her dad again.

Her father moved as if trying to pull someone else in the embrace and sighed. Leo stood silent and detached. He started to wonder again what exactly made them come here.

THE PAINT JOB

Leo sat in his bed, stretched his legs, and flexed his toes. He glanced at the sky, now showing a piece of itself through a gap in the drawn in curtains. Cloudy. Change! Good, too much sun could get on the nerves. He rose to his feet, took two steps forward, and pivoted to the right. Time for morning coffee. Leo opened the door and gasped. Elise stood there in her nightgown, holding up paintbrushes in both hands. Leo took a step back.

She walked in and announced, "I want you to paint me. Today!" She pushed the door behind her closed with her foot.

Leo scratched his neck and asked, "Why?" He wasn't really in the mood. He laid hands on her shoulders, nudging her out of his way and opening the door again. He checked if it led to the right place, then dragged his feet down the hallway toward the kitchen. Elise followed.

"The show's today," she said.

"What show?"

"The body paint show, at the Glass Eye theater."

Ah, the one where she came up with the idea, recalled Leo.

"Hi, Annette."

"Hi, Liz."

Leo halted his advance and turned back. His mom was combing her hair in her room, facing its open door in front of which Elise had just passed.

"You two know each other?"

His mother pursed her lips and squeezed out a short, "Yes."

"How?"

"You introduced us, don't you remember?" Annette snapped.

"Yeah, but have you seen each other here?"

"And yes. We exist nearby and you are a strong connection. Elise is fun to be around. I understand why you were so heartbroken."

"Ah, OK." Leo proceeded to the stove and checked the coffee maker. It was full. Leo grabbed two mugs from the cup holder and poured, without consulting Elise if she wanted some. He then put the mugs on the table and sat. Elise joined him, laid the brushes down, and pushed them toward him.

"OK, I'll try," he agreed. "But bear in mind I haven't done it before and there is no internet so I can't find help online."

"I am sure you will manage. Have you got a design in mind? I would like something in dark blue or green."

"Why these?"

"Because I hate pink, and I am also naturally pink. Well, kind of."

Leo rolled his wrist. "So, you hate this kitchen then."

"Why would I?" Elise asked.

"'Cause it's pink."

She thought for a second. "I see . . ."

"What?" Leo insisted.

"No pink."

He got it. He'd painted the cabinets in this color after her death; therefore, she had no memory of its pink days. She was probably seeing the colors from before the renovation. How the hell did this work? His curiosity was stirred again; he was eager to find out, but there were no clues, and he had to do other work now, "OK, no pink. Let's go to my room and put some ideas on paper."

The two headed back, mugs and brushes in hands. Leo noticed his mother narrowing her eyes as they walked past her door.

Leo sat behind his desk and pulled a sketch pad from the drawer. Interesting how well it had held. The sheets were still strong and white after all these years. He knew of course that it was not an original sixty-year-old sketch pad, but the thought was entertaining. He pulled his equally "mature" crayons out, removed the lid, chose the light gray color, and began drawing. First ovals, then he joined the ovals with curved strokes to produce the outlines of a woman's body. He had drawn a lot of characters in his time as visual effects artist; this ought to help. There was a Godzilla anime—one of many—which he'd worked on. It had cute tribal characters with painted bodies, which might work. He added the details to his sketch and pushed it toward Elise, who was sitting on the chair across the desk.

She twitched her lips. "Interesting design but it has too much beige and black. Resembles a patch of leopard skin, stretched to fit a human."

The Avengers! thought Leo. That stupid series had a blue character. Leo remembered the actress's name—Karen Gillan—but not the character's. Whatever. She was blue. And Elise wouldn't know it, as the film was from the noughties. He quickly produced another outline, switched the crayon, and filled most of the interior with blue. Then he added yellow, red, bright green, and even some pink, tore off the page and slid it across the desk.

"This one's nice!" Elise said. "Even the pink, works well, so I will give it a pass. This design reminds me of Nebula."

"Which nebula? I am not conversant in astronomy."

"She's a character from a superhero movie I saw once. *Guardians of the Galaxy.*"

Ah, she's seen that one too. Maybe he was mixing the flicks, but how did she see it? But didn't his mother say that it was possible?

"Don't tell me you liked it," Leo said with contempt.

"I did, actually," she said to his surprise.

Leo decided to change the subject. "OK, missy, let's do it then." He reached down and pulled the bag from the bottom shelf, retrieved the box with the paint, and unsealed it. He grunted approvingly when he found a guide inside. Elise couldn't wait—she moved the chair to the middle of the room, climbed on top, and slipped out of her nightgown.

Leo glanced at her. "Not so fast, I need to read the instructions first."

"Okay." Elise stepped off the chair and quietly sat down.

Leo put the booklet aside and checked the contents of the box. There were eight jars of paint. He took one out and inspected it. Then said, "Lizzy, we will have to change the plan."

"Why?"

"There's not enough paint for a full body. We would need at least four blue jars and there's only one. So maybe—"

"Don't worry, we have enough," Elise interrupted. "Just do it."

Leo concurred silently. She had been here longer, and he'd already seen for himself how things tended to work in the realm. A bottomless jar of paint was certainly a possibility. He took a bed sheet out of his wardrobe and spread it on the floor. Then he motioned her to stand, moved the chair in the middle, and tapped the seat. She climbed back. He opened the jar, dipped a small paintbrush in it, and with confident strokes outlined the design. He then took one of the large brushes he found in the bag alongside the paint and initiated laying the main color. Elise began giggling wildly when the brush entered her butt crack.

The door opened. Annette filled the doorframe, inspected the scene, and called Leo over with her finger. He carefully placed the jar and brush on his desk and joined his mother in the hallway. Elise twisted her neck, trying to catch a glimpse of his mom. Annette avoided crossing eyes with her and closed the door.

"You pervert! You have no shame!" Annette hissed, full of rage as soon as the latch clicked. "She could be your daughter! What the hell do you think you are doing?"

"But Mom, she asked for it . . . and she's not a kid," Leo protested.

"Oh, yeah?" Annette said, fuming. "She's just a teen and you are over sixty! Just look at your bloody self!"

Leo obediently shut his eyes and painted on the canvas of his mind the sixty-year-old himself with Elise perched on top of a chair. He saw nothing wrong with the picture—a model and an artist creating art. Yes, she was naked, but so what? There were plenty of nudes in art. It's not like they were banging or something! His mom should have seen them in the log house with the bear! He clicked his tongue and smiled.

Then he replaced Elise with his daughter, Abigail, as the model. That made him uncomfortable, and if he were faced with this situation, he would perhaps excuse himself. That said, he still saw nothing patently scandalous, but his mother belonged to a different generation.

"She is not my daughter and she's almost as old as me, Mom," he said calmly. "But OK, I will try to talk her out of this." He retraced his steps.

"And you are?" Elise inquired, still standing on the chair with her hands up for fear of smudging the wet paint.

"Drop it, Liz!" Leo said.

"Oh, a more mature, Mr. Hackensack," she said. She beckoned him. "Come here, let me see . . ."

"See what? Ah . . ." It dawned on him. "Did I transform?"

"Yep, you did."

"And how old am I now?"

"Mid-fifties would be my guess? You've aged well."

"Not quite right but close enough. I was sixty-one when Mother passed."

"Was it her?" Elise nodded her head at him.

Leo sucked in his lips then popped them. "She called me a pervert. I think I understand the trigger of her emotions. She is seeing a sixty-year-old man and a teen girl. She knows that it is a romantic relationship, and she suspects that it includes sex. And when you add it all together, it could look inappropriate indeed."

"Let me talk to her."

Before he could stop her, Elise jumped from the chair and ran out of the room. A second later she was knocking on Annette's door. Leo followed at a distance.

"Ann, may I talk to you please?"

The door opened and Elise disappeared inside the room. Leo leaned against the wall of the hallway.

"Ann, Leo's not a pervert. If somebody is, then it is me. I like getting naked all the time, and I like doing wild stuff. And I see a teen boy, not your grown-up son." She paused, and Leo heard a lighter clicking. He came closer to the door and peeked through the gap. Elise had borrowed a cigarette from his mother, and the latter was standing by the window with her arms crossed and still sporting a mean face.

"Damn it, I am getting tired of everybody forgetting that I am old!" Elise slipped out of view, leaving a trail of blue smoke behind.

"You behave like a kid. Look at yourself." Annette pointed with a nod.

"So, what, are you jealous?"

Leo's mother scoffed.

"Well maybe you should be, it is fun!" Elise said with venom. She sounded like a different person now. She came back into sight and flicked the cigarette over the ashtray, sitting on the odd-looking without its mirror dresser. "Maybe you would feel differently if I appeared older, but you know the rules here; I can't look old even if I wanted to. And believe me, many times I wished that I could."

Annette remained silent. Elise flipped the cigarette again, drew on it one last time, and squashed the butt in the ashtray.

"Are you two having sex?" Leo's mother asked.

Leo banged the door completely open and stomped into the room. "What business of yours is that?"

Elise held her palm up, tilting her head. "Yes, we are. And I don't care how old he may look. If appearances bother you, please get over it. Or come watch porn!"

Leo knew his mother well and didn't like the overly calm expression on her face—it meant an impending storm. "Come, Lizzy, let's not escalate. I'm gonna walk you home."

Elise bowed deeply and turned to leave the room.

Annette raised a hand, her brow still furrowed. "Wait!"

Elise stopped, hesitated for a moment, then turned around.

"Leo, my apologies for sticking my nose where it did not belong." She then addressed Elise. "And you, Liz, forgive me for forgetting your age. I did indeed let forward appearances drive my emotions. So, do whatever you want." Then she muttered something.

Leo caught just the last few words: " . . . I myself like much older men."

"Thank you!" Elise said.

"Mom, how is Babs?" Leo asked unexpectedly.

"I don't know. Go find out yourself."

Yeah, with a blue girl in tow. What if Babs also saw? thought Leo. Babette will have to wait.

When they returned to his room, he sat behind his desk with hands in his lap. "Sorry, Liz, but we won't make it to the show. Frankly, I can't continue right now."

"No worries, there's another one coming. Will you walk me home?" She reached for her gown and put it on.

"Sure, but can't you just teleport? The way you came today?" He didn't want to go out.

"No, I don't get to choose. The city decides. And our emotions. I can tell you don't want me to go, because otherwise I'd not be here. So, we will have to do it the old-fashioned way."

"Do you want to go?"

She took a moment to respond, "No, not really."

"Then stay. I'll try to sketch you for a change."

Elise curled up in his armchair, and he felt her eyes examining his older self. He took the pad and started drawing, glancing at her often. Whenever their eyes met, he paused and smiled.

"Why are you smiling?"

"I don't know, I'm not trying to draw a caricature, if that's what you think."

"A caricature would be fine too, if it resembles me."

Leo continued for a while, then suddenly cursed, dropped the sketch pad on the desk and shoved it aside. "It is not working. I can't get your face right!"

Elise got up and approached the desk. She turned the pad toward her and checked out the drawing. A girl, curled up in an armchair, with eraser smudges where the head was supposed to be.

"Not your fault." She came to his side of the desk and tried to straddle his lap, but he grabbed his knees. "I meant what I said to your mom; I don't care how old you look."

Leo relaxed a bit and allowed her to sit.

"Maybe I can paint you!" She giggled and reached over for the paint. He stood still. Elise opened the jar, dipped the brush, and made several strokes with it across his cheeks. She changed the color and began painting what felt like dots. Then more strokes with another color.

"What am I now?" he asked, when she left the jar on the desk and stood up to check her work from a distance.

"A scarecrow."

"Thanks!"

Elise returned to the armchair and sat. She then rose again, walked to the open balcony door, and leaned against the rail. Leo was doodling on his pad. Elise went to the chair in the middle of the room and began circling it, pinning the top rail with her index finger. Leo lifted eyes from the sketch pad and looked at her. It appeared to him she had gotten bored.

"Let's play games!" she said, confirming his suspicion.

"What games?"

"Cards, we can play cards. You have a deck, right?"

"Yeah, somewhere here . . ." Leo started checking the drawers. She snuck behind him. Leo sensed the approach and turned sharply in anticipation of some prank. She grabbed his head with both hands, tilted it up, leaned forward, and delivered a smooch.

"No, not now please . . ." Leo wriggled out.

"Not now what?" she asked, looking genuinely confused, "I . . . I just wanted to let you know that I still love you." She pinched his ears. "You've aged well, you know. You look better than before."

"I, erm, I thought that . . . erm, you wanted sex . . ." stuttered Leo.

"I didn't. But maybe this is what *you* wanted?" she said sharply.

Leo did not repudiate the allegation. She was right. His worries resurfaced, but he felt that the moment wasn't apt for a talk. "You gave me a smooch. What do you expect me to think?" he said instead.

Elise took the deck of cards from his hand, dragged the chair to the coffee table, straddled it backward, and crossed her arms on the backrest.

"Take the armchair, this thing is not comfortable," Leo said.

"I'm fine here."

"Please, you have no natural cushions," Leo insisted.

"We'll switch if it gets too bad."

"Ah, you are stubborn . . ."

Leo ran to the kitchen and came back with two full coffee mugs and a bowl of chocolates. Then sat and dealt the cards. After a while, as anticipated, the wooden chair began biting into Elise's flesh. She pushed it aside and sat directly on the floor, still refusing to switch places.

In a couple of hours, they grew bored with the cards and switched to tic-tac-toe. Elise kept losing and started to squeak and squirm. Then she gave up and laid flat down on the floor. He looked at her and their eyes met. She wearily stuck her tongue out. There were chocolate stains on her face. She was extremely childish at times and Leo had a hard time reconciling her behavior with her age. Even a thirty-year-old woman would be considered infantile if she did what Elise was often doing. She was like this for as long as he'd known her, but in the past, there'd been no such massive dissonance between her apparent and her true ages. Leo shook his head as if physically trying to shake off the thought, but said nothing.

When he looked at her again, she was fast asleep. He kneeled, lifted her from the floor, and moved her to his bed. He then covered her, returned to the armchair, put his headphones on, chose a tape from his collection, and played it. He realized that this was the first time ever for her to spend the night at his place. Her dad wouldn't allow it. They stayed till late, often well after midnight, but then he walked her back home. The father was always on guard duty and gave him menacing looks when he accompanied her all the way to the apartment door. Leo wondered how she'd managed to get away without a curfew. Other girls did not. He never asked her. Yeah, literally another lifetime. Whatever was happening now was amazing.

Soon, he too was fast asleep.

BABETTE

Leo woke up at dawn with the morning light invading his space. He kept his eyes shut, but the light and his aching neck conspired against his desire to continue sleeping. He rose from the armchair, flexed, and raked his fingers through his hair. The fingers caught in it and he flinched. A feat impossible to pull off at eighty-one!

Elise was still in his bed, her chest barely moving as she breathed. The body paint was gone. Leo remembered that she painted his face; he licked his finger and rubbed his cheek. There were no traces of color. He then tilted his head and scratched his neck. He expected her to have vanished by morning, the way he found himself at home after being somewhere else the night before. He couldn't think of a single instance where this didn't happen. Well, not quite, it actually did occur once—when they were in Köennendorf. But there he was awake all night, wasn't he? However Elise slept, she was frozen and exhausted, and she was still there too, when dawn broke. Just like now. Perhaps she was different in some way.

He yawned and quietly slipped out of the room. The fragrance of something fresh out of the oven was taking over the hallway's airspace. A paper bag full of crispy hot croissants was lying on the kitchen table. He took one out and sank his teeth in it. The coffee maker was empty. Didn't this thing refill itself? *Whatever* . . . Leo was still half asleep. He unscrewed the top, filled the tank with water, then slid the filter in. He tried to remember where they kept the grinder and the coffee, but too much time had passed since. Leo started rummaging through the eye level cabinets, and it didn't take long to find what he was looking for.

He completed the ritual of old, thinking about what was more satisfying to use: this simple device or the expensive machines he had later in life. The advantage of this maker was that he could take it with him to the living room or to his own and just keep refilling until it ran dry. Yeah, the coffee inside was eventually getting cold, but nobody really cared in those days. Steve was mixing it with booze from the flask he was often carrying. His friend hadn't been abusing alcohol; he'd been a bit of a showoff at school and carried it to impress the girls. He'd been seeking the bad boy vibe.

Leo didn't bother with clean cups. The mugs from the night before were still in his room. He took the maker instead, just like in the very old days. He threw a few croissants on a plate, bit again into the one he'd started eating, and headed back to his room. He knocked lightly on the door, then pushed the lever down with his elbow. The latch clicked and the door leaf moved just enough to produce a narrow gap. Leo was about to elbow it further in when he noticed that it was not his room; it was Babette's. *Ah, yeah, I knocked.* He wanted to apologize to his great-grandmother—in case he had disturbed her—and stuck his head inside.

The curtains were drawn shut, but the morning light still found a way in via the loosely woven fabric. The balcony door was closed, and the air in the room was still. There were no specks of dust floating over from one tiny beam of light into another. Babette's bed was made. Her books were neatly stacked on the table adjacent to her rocking chair. The wick of the tiny oil lamp beneath the crucifix was cold. That was unusual. His great-grandmother was a devout believer and kept the lamp burning at all times.

"Is Babette not in?" his mother's voice asked from behind him.

"Nuh-uh . . ." He shook head, muffled by the croissant in his mouth.

"This is unusual for her."

Leo parted his jaws and let the croissant fall into the plate he held in his hand. "She might have gone out. You know . . ."

"Nah, that's unlikely. It's too early in the morning, and her friends all drifted away, she was the last—"

Annette did not complete her sentence. She rushed past him into the room and came to a stop in the middle, right beneath the ceiling pendant, and swiped the room with her gaze. Leo noticed tears bubbling up, then overflowing and rolling down her face.

"She's drifted away, hasn't she?" Leo felt his heart sinking.

His mom nodded and sobbed. "That's how they all went . . ."

"How exactly?"

"You see them less and less until one day you realize that they are gone, their space deserted . . . Damn, I'm gonna miss her!" She angrily swung her head.

Leo sat on the small shoe rack in the hallway and swore. He'd fucked this one up! He'd missed the chance to tell Babette stories from his life, which she would have most certainly wanted to hear. Was she convinced that his queer daughter was also a good human being and mother, or had she left with doubts? The opportunity to say "Thanks!" had gone! His great-grandmother had practically raised him. Annette was still in med school when Leo was born. Richard was busy too with his career. Babette would come each morning and ring the bell of the small apartment his parents were renting. Richard and Annette would give him a kiss and run out. He had no recollection of these days, as he was still a toddler, but both his parents praised unreservedly his great-grandmother for her help. The first memories of Babette were of him sitting on a swing in the park and her armed with a spoon, literally shoveling food into his mouth as he swung closer. He spat out the food when the swing reversed direction. Then the cycle repeated, and the memory faded.

Leo looked down and sighed. When he started school, Babette was the one to lead him there in the mornings and bring him home in the afternoons until he learned the route and began going by himself. She prepared his meals, then helped him with homework. She stayed until Richard or Annette showed up. Then she quietly went home. He'd been so engulfed by Elise since he arrived here that he barely considered anything and anyone else. Remorse took possession of his mind.

Annette shut the door on her way out.

"Wait!" Leo shouted and sprang up. He offloaded the stuff from his hands onto the rack, knocked, and opened the door. The space appeared ready to break loose from this reality and drift away, following its inhabitant. He tried to etch the scene forever in his mind, adding also the person it belonged to. He pictured his great-grandmom in her rocker, with Ginger on her lap, and let his tears run unrestrained. He closed the door, then knocked, and opened it again. Maybe there was still hope!

"It is over," Annette said wearily and lit another cigarette. She helped herself to coffee from the maker she'd taken to the living room and sat on the couch. Leo lifted the plate from the rack, reluctant to shut the door. Then he remembered Elise, closed it, then quickly opened it again. It revealed his room—the cards scattered on the small table, the empty mugs, the bed sheet on the floor. Only, Elise had vanished too. *Not forever! Not like Grandmom! It will be too much!* Cold sweat secreted from his glands.

The doorbell chimed once. Leo went, plate in hand, and looked through the peep hole. It was her. Leo's panic eased. He opened the front door, but the girl was no longer there. He checked the stairs and the elevator, then retreated into the apartment and kicked the door closed. His obsession with his sweetheart robbed his great-grandmother of his attention. He should wean off Elise and diversify his days, explore more. That wasn't going to bring Babette back, but he still had his mom and Vivian and Nick. And Richard.

"Mom, when did Marcus drift away, do you remember?" he called her.

"That was sometime after I showed up. A few months, maybe half a year by my estimate," she replied from the living room. "Why?"

"I wonder what's causing the drift . . ."

Leo went to his room, put the plate he was still holding on his desk, tore a clean sheet from his sketch pad, lifted a pencil, and drew a horizontal line in the middle. Then placed four large dots on it, changed the pencil, and drew four vertical arrows. The first and the third—over the dots, pointing at each one, the second and the fourth—below the dots, pointing away. He labeled them: Mom, Marcus, Me, Babette. He looked at this simple chart, trying to find a correlation, but the data points were too few. He needed more. He had to talk to Richard and finally get to the damn library; he might find clues and information there. Elise Sinclair would have to wait!

THE LIBRARY

Leo spent the rest of the day in the company of his mom, remembering Babette. Annette retold old stories and some more—Babette working as a teacher in some godforsaken village in Bukovina, struggling with the local dialect and how Babette had caught her smoking a cigarette at fifteen and had scolded her while not divulging the information to Vivian or Nick. Or how she had shown up to check on him in the rented apartment using her own key while his parents were busy banging. They had tried to be discreet and quiet, but so had she—the efforts had collided, resulting in some mild embarrassment. He went to the door a few times, knocked quietly and checked the room, but it stayed his. They popped open bottles of wine, drowning their grief. At the end, when the night had become dominant, they staggered to their rooms.

Then the morning came and settled. Leo was determined to get some work done. He was missing his smart devices and the internet; this place was so far behind, as all tech he came across was analogue or not connected, like the flat-screen TV. His dad mentioned computers, but Leo was yet to see one. There was a notepad in his drawer. He took it out and made a copy of his chart.

The apartment was quiet. His mother was either in her room still sleeping or out walking Sylvester, the dog. Leo realized he hadn't sighted either one of his cats recently. Did they also drift away? He switched the color of his multi-pen and added the animals to his chart. What kept Sylvester here? Leo turned the page and wrote the question down. He drank his coffee and stepped out.

Good intentions notwithstanding, he had no real idea what to do. The last visit to a library was when he was still studying at university; he spent time there preparing for his master's thesis. Then the internet made inroads and all information searching moved online. Realistically, he lacked the skill to use a physical repository. All he could think of were online documentaries depicting people in white gloves handling fragments of ancient scrolls and thick leather-bound books. He should have asked his dad to come along. Or his mom.

Elise was also too much of a distraction. When she was around, he had a hard time thinking of anything else. All he wanted was to kiss her and make love. If he let that continue unchecked, he might become an addict and that would be very bad for her too; her personality would no longer matter. He had almost gone there once with someone else, and it didn't end well.

Why was it different in his other life? He'd had girlfriends, and they studied, worked, and fucked. Work came first. Here, there was no imperative, no deadlines, and no need to earn a buck, so procrastination became the norm. He spent decades self-motivating after his marriage to Bea fell apart, and he wished so much that he could share some of his interests for once. Annette became passive and disinterested after she retired from the psychiatric ward. Richard—Leo didn't know, they weren't talking much. Steve was first and foremost a motoring enthusiast.

The sound of pounding footsteps cut his introspection short. Then the runner pulled his shirt. He braked hard and the runner slammed into him. It wasn't difficult to guess who that was. Leo pivoted on his heels and met her gaze. Elise stretched her mouth sideways and produced a smile. She was again wearing a wide-brimmed hat, a smaller one this time and not made of straw. The hat had tilted to one side and was making a last-ditch effort to stay on her head.

She pushed it back with both hands and said, "Hi! Where to?"

"City library."

"Great! Let's go!" She stood at attention and extended her arm in expectation of him taking it.

Leo kept his hands in his pockets. "Listen, Liz. I want to search for some info, try to make sense of things. With you around it is very hard to concentrate, almost impossible. All I can think of is you . . . and sex . . . maybe we shall slow down a bit."

Her mouth unstretched and formed a tiny "o". She looked down then up again and said in a trembling but clear voice, "Okay. Lizzy come, Lizzy go!" She pivoted and marched away with wide resolute steps. Leo couldn't help cracking a laugh. *Ah, this girl, woman, granny, er, old girl.* She made it so easy to forget her age. Not just her appearance but also her mannerisms and attitude. She was carrying the innocence that the vagaries of life had extinguished in people like himself. She lacked the cynicism of those who'd actually lived. But wasn't her voice kind of sad this time? Leo could not deny that he was glad to see her and felt culpable for sending her away. She'd spent so much time alone. She said that it was bad; she even cried. He surrendered to his emotions and chased after her.

"Lizzy, wait!"

She continued to walk. He caught up with her, grabbed her arm, and said, "Please, don't Lizzy go!"

She stopped but did not turn.

He let go of her arm. "I didn't mean to hurt you."

"You did not."

"Then why are you acting this way? Like I did . . . ah, wait! You are lying, aren't you?"

She considered her answer, then said, "I am," and sighed.

"Sorry!"

Leo took her right hand and gently made her turn around. She offered no resistance but continued to study the condition of the pavers under her feet. He pushed her chin up and hesitantly brought their faces closer. Elise remained still. Unsure if that was the right thing to do, he let their lips touch briefly. She squeezed her eyes shut as if expecting to be pricked by a needle in the butt, yet she didn't push him away. Leo gained some confidence and locked lips with hers. She hesitated at first, then wrapped her arms around his waist and tasted him with the tip of her tongue. It took only a blink to reconcile.

"I didn't want to be clingy. I apologize," Elise declared while they were walking leisurely toward the library, arm in arm.

"I don't think of it this way; it feels good to have you around. It could be seen as clingy indeed, but I honestly don't mind it. I actually love it!" He spilled his emotions, "But aside from not being able to concentrate on anything, I am also afraid."

"Afraid? Of what?"

"Experience, I suppose. At university I met another girl . . . Olivia was her name. I fell in love with her too." He glanced at her. "Sorry, these things happen. And she, with me, or so I believed. But then we took it too fast, maybe also too far. We were all over each other all the time. We were doing it under the blanket with other people present, in elevators, on building sites at night . . . it was wild. But then I became possessive, controlling. I even smacked her once. Well, she was very drunk, and it was to bring her back to her senses, but still. She felt used and abused. I guess . . . Anyway, it didn't end well. We split and she began dating someone else in the class. It felt like rubbing salt in a wound while they lasted."

Elise was looking straight ahead, her mouth ajar. He saw the tip of her tongue roll along her upper lip.

"This is what makes me apprehensive, that something like that may come between us." Leo drew the story to an end.

They walked past a sex toy shop. Unlike the old world, the store window wasn't painted black and covered with bright posters hinting at the merchandise inside. It was crystal clear, with all the dildos, ropes, chains, and butt plugs on full display. The posters were not subtle either. The models were openly showing how the products were to be used. He concluded that there were either no children or no religious morality in this realm; perhaps neither one. He nodded in its direction and said, "We shall come visit this place, shan't we?"

Elise glanced at the store. "Sure, why not, I like sex toys." She continued, "I understand your concerns. But think—why did you behave that way?"

"I was afraid of losing her to someone else. Ironically, this is exactly what happened in the end, isn't it?" Leo chuckled. "In retrospect, it was not her, but rather the pleasure and the thrill she provided, that I didn't want to lose. It was lust, not love."

They arrived at the library. The spectacular baroque structure was a former royal residence. Initially the rooms of the palace held the books, but as the collection grew larger, the city administration built a modern-for-its-time extension with climate-controlled underground vaults and research facilities. The books were moved to the new storage space and the palace rooms painstakingly restored to their glory days.

The grand white marble staircase leading to the entrance was flanked by two cobblestone ramps for the royal coaches. Leo and Elise took the ramp. Leo pushed the ornate door, but it didn't move. He peeped through the glazing out of habit then corrected the direction of the force he was applying. It was a public building; all doors had to open outward, he recalled. The door yielded, and the couple went inside.

The interior was impressive with its richness in detail and color. Leo began doubting his hypothesis about this world existing only in his mind. There was simply too much of it. The ceiling frescoes, the twisted columns, the intricate cartouches, the ornate fabrics—there was no way for him to have stored them all in this brain.

The main level was split into three halls. When Leo was alive, the library hosted exhibitions, book signings, and other events. In the hall on their left, they spotted a podium with a white grand piano and period chairs scattered in front, as if the concertgoers had just left. Leo tried to sense a presence, however failed to pick anything.

Elise was looking up at the ceiling frescoes with her mouth open. "Stunning! I should have come here earlier." She moved her gaze down to the tapestries on the walls and began absorbing their beauty.

Leo frowned. The hall on the right was as opulent as everything else in this building and he didn't mind that. What drew his ire was the row of vending machines lining the far wall. He drilled down his memories, trying to confirm their existence in the real world but found nothing definitive. "Do you remember these?" He pointed them to Elise.

"Ew! Abominations! No, I don't think so."

Somebody had to. Otherwise, they would not be there. Also, what was the purpose of a vending machine in a world with no money? Leo approached to check if they demanded payment. There were no banknote slits or coin slots. Just like the one in Köennendorf. One of the abominations was dispensing lollipops. He dialed the code and pushed the button; the machine grunted and fulfilled the request.

"Thank you!" Elise said when he handed her the candy.

"You are welcome! Anyway, this is what worries me." Leo returned to the original conversation, "That I may do something stupid and drive you away, and that would be worse than physically losing you as it happened back then."

"What? Oh . . ." Elise waved at him to come closer. She breathed warm air on his cheek, kissed him gently, and whispered in his ear, "You are old and wise now," then continued in her normal voice, "I am sure you won't do anything to drive me away. But if you feel that you are getting too much of me, we can make a plan. Even split up . . ." The last words came out with observable difficulty.

"No, no!" Leo protested keenly. "I'd rather learn to do things *with* you. It is lonely without your face around. You see, there's no one else here"—he raised his palms—"and I wonder how you coped all those years—" Leo stopped midsentence. That was an insensitive thing to say and made his problem look petty.

Elise looked down at the polished marble floor, then took a deep breath and pulled his shirt. "Come, I'll show you." She led him to the improvised concert stage, pushed the hat and the lollipop in his hands, climbed on the podium, and sat on the stool in front of the piano. She opened the lid, massaged her fingers, and hit the keys. It was a false start. She rubbed and wiggled her fingers again and gave the instrument another try. This time, the music flowed.

Leo could not recognize the piece. It did not sound classical, so maybe it was by a contemporary composer. But he knew one thing: it sounded sad. Maybe he was reading too much, but it was as if her past loneliness was singing a song. He had no idea that she played the piano and played it so well.

The music reduced to a whisper, then echoed out. Elise lifted both hands then turned to face him and rested them on her knees. "I also learned Swedish and created dreamworld."

Leo felt that clapping would be corny. He stared down, then said, "Sorry, I did it twice today, didn't I"—referring to hurting her feelings—"just like back then."

"Back then you didn't do anything to me. You probably mean Olivia."

It sounded like he had just made a third strike in one day. How could he be so clumsy with his words?

Elise tried to reassure him and smiled. "Don't worry, shit happens." She continued in a serious tone, "Did she talk to you about these issues, before breaking up?"

Leo tried to remember, then shook his head. "No. It was weird. One day she stopped talking to me completely. Just like that—out of the blue. Not calling, not answering my calls. At school she looked away and didn't say a word. I felt like a mop left out to dry."

"This is very childish. She was what, twentyish?"

Leo nodded.

"Well, child indeed, no matter what we think of ourselves at that age. Still, she could have picked someone outside your circle. I suppose it is not that hard for a pretty girl. I tend to agree with your assessment; she probably did want to rub it in. But why? Maybe she did have feelings for you, expectations, which you betrayed. Anyway, our story is different. I am not giving up on you just because you reminded me of shitty times for a moment. The way I feel for you, my love," she blushed, "it won't be genuine if I did. Yes, the loneliness was carving me up hollow but also showed me that I could fly." She winked at the last sentence and smiled again.

"How?" Leo asked apprehensively.

She brushed the floor with her gaze. "I tried to kill myself. I jumped from the roof of Allianz Building."

Allianz Building used to be the tallest building in the city in the eighties. Poor girl . . . But she learned to fly?

Leo climbed on the podium, kneeled in front of her, placed his palms over her hands, and kissed her knees. Then he got up, sighed, and struck a random key with his index finger.

"So, you will teach me to play the piano, won't you?" he asked and laughed awkwardly.

"Mmm!" Elise nodded, then stood up.

I must conquer my fear! Leo told himself. He pulled out the notebook he was carrying from where it was tucked in his trousers under his shirt and showed her his diagram. "Do you know how drifting works? There must be a connection."

"Let me see . . . no, I can't think of any, but that doesn't mean that none exists."

MARGOT

It was decided: they would force some separation between them. Thus, the reunions would be even more rewarding. The endeavor, however, turned out to be a game of cat and mouse with the city. They would stay away from each other for a couple of days, sometimes a whole week, then the city would fold space to cross their paths. She would find herself standing at his door and he would open hers. They would then turn slowly and walk away only to open another door and bump into each other.

Elise began giving Leo piano lessons. She took him to the same place where she herself went to learn. Years ago, when she was trying to figure out what to do with her afterlife, she passed by an apartment building a few blocks away from hers. To the side of the main entrance, she saw a weathered brass plaque reading: PROFESSIONAL TUTOR PIANO LESSONS AND VOCAL COACH, FLOOR 4, APT. B. She always wanted to play a clavier. Not violin or cello, as strings didn't excite her—unlike her cat—but this was a different story altogether. She enjoyed the tactile sensation that pressing the piano keys induced; the sound they made was somewhat secondary. She pestered her parents, but the instrument she got from them was a recorder. A real piano was too expensive, and the toy piano her grandparents had gifted her didn't count. She was a kid, and kids had short wish spans.

Back then, Elise climbed the stairs and buzzed the door. She was still hoping for a response, a miracle of some sort. When nobody answered she turned the knob. The door was unlocked. She pushed it open—it screeched—and she went cautiously in. *"Hello! Anybody here?"* she remembered calling. The foyer had a coat hanger and a shoe rack underneath, but there were neither coats nor shoes. There were two doors, both open. On the left there was a galley kitchen; straight ahead was the vestibule.

The piano was there. In the corner she saw a double bass. She walked to it and plucked a string. Then she turned and looked around. On the left an open French door led to an old-fashioned living room. The space was taken by a large and heavy dining set—a table with legs like those of an elephant and eight upholstered chairs with tall backrests. The set was complemented by an equally imposing walnut-veneered display buffet.

Behind the glass she saw richly decorated tea sets, crystal glasses, and porcelain figurines—a ballerina, horses, two cute kids, Hansel and

Grethel probably. Elise squatted, opened one of the solid doors of the lower section, and glanced at the objects residing there. Tablecloths and other items were neatly stacked on the shelves. She smelled mothballs.

She shut the cabinet door and rose. Planters stood on both sides of the window, in front of heavy velvet curtains. The plants in them looked alive. The wall opposite the cabinet was bare; only a crucifix and a vintage indoor weather station were breaking the monotony of its plane.

On the other side of the vestibule was a closed door. Her curiosity drew her to it. She pushed the lever and peeked inside. It looked like the master bedroom. The apartment occupants were obviously fond of large pieces of furniture—the room featured a humongous bed, flanked by two large nightstands with ornate bedside lamps atop. In the corner there was an old TV set: a wooden box with a sage screen on four thin legs. It was decorated with a lace runner and an empty vase. Her grandparents were adherents to the style. To her right stood a large wardrobe.

She closed the door carefully and faced the vestibule. Something had changed while she was exploring. At the corner sat a large armchair and a disproportionately small side table. When she came in, the table was empty but now it was occupied by a petite teapot, a cup, a plate with cookies, and a sugar bowl with a tiny spoon stuck in it. She guessed that this meant that she was welcome. She didn't want to offend the invisible hosts, so sat in the armchair and washed a cookie down with some tea. Then another change caught her attention—the piano itself. The keyboard lid was open, and the sheet holder was at work, propping an open folder up. The first page read: "Please take a seat!"

Elise instinctively looked around, then followed the instructions and sat on the stool. Each white key had a small sticker with its note letter and octave. She read most then looked up again. The page in the folder had changed; it now displayed hand-drawn lines with large notes, each note labeled as the respective key.

In the next months and years, her invisible teacher would write remarks and instructions on the pages of this folder. When she was done playing a piece and turned the page, she would always find comments on her performance, words of encouragement, and critique. The critiques became harsher as she advanced, but this didn't deter her. She loved coming to this flat and conversing with her tutors—she noted two distinct handwritings—in this strange way. Sometimes, she thought that she even felt their presence. She brought a pencil and tried to write back, but the tutors made no comment in reply. So, she stuck to playing music for hours on end, switching off her thoughts and immersing herself in the sound. Until she met someone and was no longer lonely.

She had not visited her teachers for years. *Has anything changed?* she wondered as she rang the bell with Leo in tow. No answer again, so, they went in uninvited. The place looked largely the same.

"Hello! It's me, Elise Sinclair!" she greeted the stillness. They waited in silence for a while.

"Perhaps they've drifted away," Leo suggested when there was no response. "Or maybe not, the place is still here."

"As in?"

Leo explained how his great-grandmother's room had disappeared after she'd drifted.

Elise remembered Leo's deep bow in the art supplies store, and repeated it, sincerely apologizing for her long absence. However, the hosts apparently remained unmoved, and so, she took it upon herself to teach her friend.

Leo was a keen learner. They spent hours training almost every day in this "time capsule," as he called the place. At the beginning, Elise was mostly crying, brought to tears by Leo's clumsiness at the keyboard, but sometimes the tears acted as a substitute for laughter. She didn't want to make him feel inferior by laughing at his mistakes. It was easy to look down on people. She often blundered too in her early days, yet never saw an LOL on the comments page.

When the lesson for the day was over, they would sometimes linger. Elise would deliver a reward for her student on the large bed in the adjacent room and he would recompense her for the teaching effort. They would cuddle for a while, then carefully remake the bed and tidy up after themselves before leaving. They imagined their hosts to be a polite elderly couple, and they didn't want to be brats.

She also lent a hand with his research by asking questions and seeking answers from all the people she could see. The notebook pages were getting fuller, but the research still lacked critical mass. There was no breakthrough.

Leo began learning the guitar in secret; he wanted to surprise Elise one day. He also met more friends. None of them could see Elise and Leo was unable to change that, which resulted in another question being added to his list. However, his grandparents saw her! Leo hypothesized that it was related to them dying first, but then he remembered his dad—Richard passed many years after her, yet he almost called her "monkey." What remained as a possibility was that Leo had emotional connections to everyone that saw her.

Steve had rekindled with a former girlfriend of his, Margot Stein, who had joined the club recently. Leo knew her too, and back then he was keen on dating her, but that time Steve got there first. In life, the three had met at a cocktail party, organized by some company Steve's father was associated with, and Margot was working for. Margot was four years older—not Leo's usual first choice—yet there was something in her that he found attractive. Her large bust was certainly a contributing factor; however, she also had a personality, which he liked. She was calm and reassuring. She could converse with confidence on a variety of subjects and cook a tasty meal while doing so. She knew what she wanted in contrast to the younger girls. And she had her own place where they could party almost any time.

Steve also knew what he wanted and moved fast, while Leo was still waiting for the stars to align. Steve just asked her out, she accepted and that was it. They split two years later. She wanted to settle but Steve was not yet ready, and they parted ways amicably; she married within a year at the age of twenty-eight. Leo met her once after that, on the street and she was expecting.

That was his last memory of her, and when Steve said that he was bringing her along to their gathering at the old tavern, Leo wondered whether he would see her pregnant. When she sailed to his station, she was to him, but not to Steve. Leo had no idea when Margot and his friend saw each other for the last time in the old world, obviously not during her pregnancy. When Margot approached to greet, Leo patted her tummy, which made Margot and Steve question his soberness. Perhaps from their perspective he was waving hand in front of her for some odd reason. But he felt its mass!

"Margot, I am not alone," Leo said.

"Oh, your wife died too?" Margot assumed.

"No, maybe, I don't know, I had two . . . I am here with Elise, my first girlfriend."

"Oh, the one who was killed in a car crash?"

"The hit and run, yes," Leo confirmed. "But you two can't see each other; it may feel weird." He turned to Elise. "She remembers your story. Can you see her?"

Elise shook her head. "No. I don't think indirect memories work."

"But Dad saw you."

"He was your father, much closer to you. Maybe she would see me too one day and I, her. Say hi from me," Elise said, then flashed her middle finger in the direction of Margot.

"Elise says 'Hi,'" Leo passed on the greeting, pretending to be oblivious to the gesture.

"Is she there?" Margot asked while nodding to his left, where Elise indeed stood. Leo blushed; maybe Margot saw. Like his dad.

"Yes."

"Hi, Liz! Nice, er, not meeting you!" thundered Margot.

Elise had stuck her thumbs in her ears, waving her fanned out fingers. Leo stepped on her toe. She curled the fingers and looked at him questioningly.

"Did you hear?" he said.

"Hear what?"

"Margot greeted you too." Then he snapped, "Why are you doing this crap?"

"I don't like her. Also, I'm checking whether I am being seen. You know, just in case."

"What you are doing is rude, and Steve and I can see you!"

Elise instantly turned red; she did get carried away indeed. Again. Steve's laugh rumbled.

"What's so funny?" Margot asked.

"Leo and Lizzy are having a discussion," he said, sparing her the details.

"Some things never change, even after death." Margot sighed theatrically. "Are we staying here or going somewhere where we can sit?"

Leo pulled open the heavy wooden door and the company headed down to the tavern they used to frequent more than six decades ago. It no longer existed in the other world, as the building had been demolished, but Steve found it in this one shortly after his arrival and had become a regular since. Elise was a patron, too, on a couple of occasions, the owners turning a blind eye on underage pupils for as long as nobody wore a school uniform.

"Why don't you like her?" Leo asked, as she had no reason given the two had never met.

"Look at her boobs!"

Now both men guffawed in unison. Elise poked them in the ribs.

"Now what?" Margot asked. "She must be very funny."

"Can I tell her?" Leo inquired.

"Whatever, go ahead," Elise agreed grudgingly.

"Elise said she didn't like you—"

"Why?" Margot cut him short, looking tense.

"Because you possess impressive boobs!"

Now it was Margot's turn to crack a laugh. Then she stopped. "How does she know?"

Leo and Steve looked at Elise.

"What? Was she offended? I'm sorry!"

"How do you know she has big boobs?" both men spoke at the same time.

Elise rolled her eyes. "Steve hasn't missed a chance to mention them. He always lamented not meeting, let alone touching, another pair like hers."

"So, you can't see her?" mumbled Leo.

"No, dummy! I tricked you. But I wish I could."

The quantity of spirits they consumed grew proportionally to the hour. Margot and Steve were reminiscing about their days together and the stupid things they did. Leo was relaying and Elise was absorbing every word as she usually did when listening to stories from the other world.

Leo was aware of most except the intimate ones. He was surprised by the revelation that Margot was the first woman to fellate Steve. Leo always thought that his friend was ahead of him in such matters. Steve was wise enough in his days on Earth not to brag about his sexcapades, but now it didn't matter, and they were talking about themselves. At one point, Margot stood up unsteadily and excused herself to the ladies' room. Steve offered to show her there in person, and they sank into the dimly lit corridor.

"Restroom my ass!" Leo laughed.

"You can't blame people for getting raunchy. It is in our genes."

"Which we probably no longer possess. We are not expected to procreate in this realm, so why bang?"

Elise looked at him and retorted, "Are you saying that we shall have no sex drive?"

"Nah!" he clarified without a lick of hesitation. "I am making the point that having sex is predicated on the instinct to procreate, but as you said, we are ghosts. I don't understand how I can even be in love with you here. Yet, here I am."

"Love is hormonal only in the other world. Here, to be honest, I don't know. I intend to take it to the fullest for as long as it lasts." She placed her hand over his. "You with me on that?"

He nodded. "Sure, old girl."

Steve and Margot emerged from the corridor and approached the table. Steve conducted himself as if nothing had happened, but Margot was glowing. She parked herself in front of Leo, placed her hands on his shoulders, and bent over. Her breasts bounced invitingly right in front of Leo's face. Margot clumsily kissed his cheek, then stepped closer, sat unceremoniously on his lap, and found his lips. Her tongue protruded deep into his mouth.

Leo felt awkward. Elise was right next to him, and Margot was Steve's companion. He tried to wriggle free.

Margot rubbed her cheek against his and whispered in his ear, "I want you!"

"Not now, Margot, Steve's here. And Elise." He held her wrists and gently pushed her away from his face.

"I want an orgy!" she announced, then reached for the bottle and drank straight from it. Leo was trying to send a message with his eyes to his friend to intervene. Margot dropped the bottle on the floor, embraced Leo, and began sobbing.

"Margot's drunk." Leo turned to Elise. "Tell Steve to come get her. If I address him directly, she may hear."

Steve rose, came behind Margot, and tried to make her stand. Margot clutched Leo even harder, her weeping intensifying. Steve kneeled, and Leo slowly transferred the crying woman's embrace to his friend.

"What is it, Margot?" Steve managed to get her up.

She hugged him and hid her face in his chest, her long hair dropping to the sides of her head like a curtain. Then she snorted loudly, lifted her head, and said, "Sorry, guys!" She freed herself from Steve's arms, sat in her chair, lit a cigarette, and spoke, "May I ask for permission to offload?"

Elise was observing Steve after she conveyed the message—to her he didn't move at all. "Aren't you going to act?" she asked. Steve remained silent and still. Elise leaned over the table and pinched him.

He turned sharply, "Ouch! What?"

"Leo asked you to do something!"

He looked puzzled. "Asked me what?"

"To get Margot."

"But I already did. She is seeking permission to talk. I guess about something that's burdening her . . ."

"Ah, OK, I didn't see it . . ."

"How could you?" asked Steve.

Margot poured herself more wine, sipped from the glass, and continued in a resigned voice, "I killed my boy . . . Jonas, the younger one. I was involved in a crash, and he was on the front seat, not wearing a seat belt." She burst into tears again.

"Margot's boy died like you," Leo told Elise. "And she blames herself."

"In a car crash?"

"Yep."

"Why is she blaming herself?"

Leo lifted hand, telling her to wait.

"I should have put him on the back seat and made him wear the damn thing! But he begged me, and I let him have it his way." She lifted her gaze and looked at the men imploringly, "Can you help me find him? Please!"

"What do you mean?" Steve asked. "Isn't he with you?"

She slowly moved her head from side to side. "No, he's not . . . and neither is his room at my place. I mean the room is there, but it is bare, unoccupied."

Steve looked straight ahead into the space in front of him, motionless, and Leo was not much different—a statue, with hanging shoulders and hands clutched between his legs, staring at the floor.

"What is it?" Elise asked.

Leo sprang back to life. "Maybe you could help!" He briefed her on the story.

Elise listened intently, then got up and began walking back and forth while holding her chin pensively. Then she announced, "I must talk to my granddad. I don't myself have answers, but maybe he would. He found me . . ."

"Where?" Margot jumped up. Leo was repeating Elise's words as soon as she spoke them.

"She asked where your grandad found you," Leo relayed.

"At home. In bed. One morning I woke up and he was in my room, sitting on a chair and looking at me. That was the first thing I remember from this world."

"But didn't your granddad pass after you?" Leo asked, recalling the story.

"Precisely. That is why I want to talk to him," she said. "C'mon, let's go."

"Why don't we wait here?" Steve suggested. We won't be able to see or hear him anyway."

"No, let's go with her," Margot insisted. She rose then staggered and sat back. Then she grabbed Steve's arm and stood up again, "Which way?"

"Liz, is now a good time? It is probably well past midnight," Leo asked as they were climbing the stairs up to street level.

"I wouldn't be concerned about this." Elise pushed the heavy door.

Leo squinted, momentarily blinded by the sun. Where did the time go? Leo held the door open for Margot and Steve, but nobody was coming out. He looked down the stairs. They were empty. Leo turned around. Elise had disappeared too.

Leo let go of the door and swore. He sat on the pavement, stretched his legs, and lit a cigarette.

DISCO BALL

Leo was downstairs in the dungeon a moment earlier. It was late night or early morning. Had time rewound or skipped forward? He looked at the sky—the sun was high, must be around noon, but which noon? Yesterday or tomorrow? He squinted at the bright disk and drew from the cigarette. *What am I doing here?* He knew he would have a recall, but the jumps were getting on his nerves. What was the deal with these jumps anyway? Shortcuts in the simulator's circuitry or—for some reason—planned events.

"Am I that late?" a familiar voice asked. Leo looked up. Elise stood in front of him, wearing a knee-length, yellow dress and white plat-form shoes. She reminded him of a doll his daughter had—same dress, same antique gold hair. He'd picked the shoes for her in the clothing store they went to recently, but the dress was something she had chosen herself.

"Nah," Leo responded.

"Then why are you sitting on the pavement like a beggar? Only thing you are missing is a hat or a tin can."

"Maybe I got tired." Leo got up wearily.

"Tired from what?"

"From your being late."

"So, I was late."

"How would I know?" Leo snapped.

Elise looked at him with bemusement.

"It is so bewildering . . . time in this place, I mean," he complained.

"Did something happen?"

"I jumped again, and I have no idea why I'm here."

"Ah, that's why you are so grumpy. Come here." Elise beckoned him.

He leaned toward her. She placed her arms around his neck and kissed him slowly. He instantly felt better. She always had a soothing influence on him. When they were still teens and something made him restless or angry, Elise would come and cuddle up with him and he would relax, as if she were draining out all negative emotions. She made him feel confident and carefree again. Nobody else, ever, was able to precipitate the same feelings of tranquility and peace. Elise was demanding in her own way, but not much, and this trait of hers made her so precious to him.

"Well, now you are crying," Elise said. "You are in some weird mood today."

Leo touched his face and wiped the tears with his palms.

"Yeah, seems I am indeed. Anyway . . . why are we here?"

Before she could answer, the roar of the sports car engine tore through the quietness that surrounded them. Leo looked in the direction the sound came from to see the Lamborghini pulling to a stop. The engine went silent, and Steve emerged and waved. Elise's dress matched the color of the car, noted Leo. "*What a coincidence! Also, how does Steve have a car here?*"

Leo must have spoken his thoughts, because Elise said, "This is his dreamworld."

"Can I have mine?"

"I suppose so. For as long as it doesn't include people."

"Ah, shame!" Leo rolled his eyes.

"Why, who do you want to be in it?" Elise asked.

"You!"

"Am I not here now?"

"I want you to be everywhere," Leo said enthusiastically.

"Ah, you are becoming a kid." She smiled. "Be careful what you wish for."

"What's up!" greeted Steve as he came close.

"Not my dick. I was just—"

"What?" Steve prompted him to continue.

"Fuck! I don't fucking remember!" Leo wailed. "I have a hole in my head! Why do we jump?"

"Pure entertainment," Steve said unflinchingly and pulled the tavern's door open.

"Huh?"

"Existence here is uneventful, if you think. Jumps add flavor. I am grateful that they exist!"

"That's no real explanation," scoffed Leo.

"Well, then give me the real one." Steve pushed the swing door and let his friends enter first.

The place had changed somewhat. There was a disco ball above the dance area. A small podium had appeared next to it with musical instruments—a drum set, a keyboard, and two amplifiers with built-in loudspeakers. The amplifiers were on, playing music at low volume. It seemed the dungeon had now a live band.

"Disco ball!" Leo's eyes sparkled. It had mirrors! He was excited by the prospect of finally getting a good reflection and perhaps even seeing his face. He grabbed a chair and dragged it to the spot below the ball. Then he climbed on top and stretched his neck, trying to discern some image in the mirror tiles. The ball was spinning. He could see practically nothing, as the reflections moved too fast.

"Hey, Steve!" Leo called. "Will you please find the switch for this thing and turn it off?"

"Why are you so fired up by a disco ball?" asked his friend, while following the electrical lead from the ball's ceiling mount. "There!" he said and unplugged the cord from the receptacle. The ball stopped revolving.

"Mirrors!" Leo answered.

"Which would be of absolutely no use if your face is what you want to see," Steve replied.

"How do you know?"

"My car has no rearview mirrors. And the reflections in the chrome parts are distorted. You can't see your face here."

Leo felt somebody pulling on his shirt. "What is it, Lizzy?" he asked without looking.

"I have to say something too. Come down."

He stepped onto the floor. She removed her shoes, placed them neatly at her feet, and took his place up on the chair. *What's with the ritual?* wondered Leo. Standing on the chair, she towered over him, so maybe that was her goal.

Elise placed her hands on his shoulders, bent forward bringing her face very close to his, looked him in the eyes, and said, "I have to ask again, what do you expect to see in the mirror?"

Leo had no ready answer. What was he expecting to see in the mirror indeed? She had a point when she posed the same question previously. "I don't know," he said quietly and lowered his gaze.

"What if you see your true self and get shape locked? I've no idea if that is what would happen, just speculating . . . but it could happen, no? So—"

Leo silenced her with a kiss. Then effortlessly lifted her up by the waist and gently landed her on the floor. Either she wasn't heavy, or he had grown stronger.

"I get it, Liz."

Elise flexed her knees reaching for her shoes.

"Oh, and you should stop doing this."

She looked up. "Stop doing what?"

"Pulling me by the shirt; it is childish. And drop the yellow dress."

"Why?" she asked again.

"Same reason," he answered, and dragged the chair back to the table he'd taken it from. He wanted to help her appear more mature, but the dissonance was perplexing. She was over eighty now, yet looked around seventeen and realistically, dressed and acted in accord with that. He plopped into a chair by the only primed table in the hall and continued his musings—would she still climb on chairs and pull shirts if she was in her aged body? The probability was low.

Steve plugged the disco ball back and joined him.

Elise stayed in the dance area for a while. She swayed slowly with the rhythm of the song playing from the speakers with her eyes closed, then opened them abruptly and swung them around as if startled. She then walked to the table, dropped the shoes on the floor, and sat.

"Cheers!" Leo lifted his perspiring mug. "To another day in Neverland!"

"Cheers!" the others responded.

Leo took a few gulps and returned the mug to the table. "I still don't know if this place is real or a dream," he complained. "I can't stop thinking about it."

"I told you once that if you were dreaming you wouldn't kill your nephew, what about this?" Elise reminded him.

"Peter was a biker, a careless one at times. The risk for him was elevated."

"Did he die in a crash?" asked Steve.

Leo affirmed with a nod. "A robocar cut him off on the highway, and he lost control."

"What's a robocar?" Elise asked.

"Self-driving cars. They are all over the place now. In some jurisdictions, they are the only vehicles allowed on the roads."

"I've seen them in movies, but I wasn't sure how real they were."

"Well, they were still experimental when I died," Steve said.

"That was thirty years ago, mate," Leo said. "They were everywhere when I followed your lead."

Steve chuckled and nibbled on a chip.

"I like them," Leo said. "I don't have to worry about driving home under the influence and driving at all for that matter. When I grew old, driving brought anxiety: delayed reactions, poor eyesight, the lot."

"I would have hated to be forced to use one," Steve opined. "If I don't control the beast, it is not the same."

"Of course it isn't. But you can still drive your sports car on the highway and in many other places. Also, how many times did you drive your Porsche drunk? You had a Porsche, not a Lambo in the other world, right? You didn't let people touch it with a feather, let alone risk smashing it."

"I had my license suspended!" Steve said, his tone containing pride.

Leo raised his eyebrows. "For drunk driving? I bet you weren't in the Porsche."

"No," admitted Steve. "I had an old Opel for everyday use, and I got drunk with colleagues . . ."

"You could have called a taxi or walked, this city is, er, was compact. You've always been a petrol head, farting exhaust fumes. You might have liked it in the States."

Elise had gone to the dance area with a glass and a bottle of white wine. She was dancing alone with her arms crossed on her chest. Leo felt at fault—he forgot that she was there—and was about to rush to her, but Steve acted first. A track from their youth had just started, playing "Rainbow Eyes."

Steve asked Elise for a dance. She put her glass and the bottle on the podium and extended her hand. Leo remembered how he invited Wasilla, the girl from his class he had a crush on before he met Elise, to dance to this same song. She'd accepted and they'd stomped awkwardly for a while, then she ran back to her spot amongst the other girls. They were like sworn enemies in those days—strictly separated, boys on the right, girls on the left. Then things changed, of course. In some cultures, segregation was still enforced. Dumb. His gaze moved to his friends. What if Steve had scored this girl first? His friend was a rash person, and more self-confident in those days. Had Elise become Steve's girlfriend, Leo would have been spared the anguish brough by her untimely death. But he wouldn't exchange his days with her for painlessness, no!

Elise seemed to be getting aroused, he could tell. What if she sought sex? She had been in a relationship with Steve for years. That was fine. People in the old world were driven by instincts, their selfish genes. Males wanted exclusive access to females to ensure the continuation of their own genetic line. More women, better the odds. Caring for someone else's child was unacceptable, hence the rivalry and jealousy. Women had their own motivation—they wanted their own offspring on top of others. But this world was very different. No births as far as he knew, no competition for resources. The selfish gene was screwed. However, a residual of selfishness nevertheless remained. Leo wouldn't do anything to prevent Elise from seeing his friend, if she wished it, but wouldn't encourage it either. He kind of did this in the past, even mentioned a threesome, but at the time he'd been overly emotional.

A threesome. The thought gave him goose bumps. What if she wanted a threesome? Leo pictured her with both him and Steve, naked. Nah, he wasn't ready. He wouldn't mind being in a threesome with Elise and another woman. That was unfair, he admitted, but he couldn't change the way he felt. Not yet.

"Hey, come!" Elise dragged him out of his thoughts. He liked the song that had just started playing but loathed dancing. He compromised for his girls though, and they compromised for him too. He imagined his awkward movements from those days and shivered.

"Hey, hey, hey! Look who's here!" Steve laughed. "Hang on . . ." he added and transformed.

Leo looked at his now-teenaged friend and volunteered a guess. "I did it, didn't I?"

"You did what?" Elise asked.

"Transformed, apparently."

"You both are still the same. Ah, wait . . ." She had figured it out. "You are normally seeing each other as, how much, er, fifty-year-olds, right?"

Both men nodded.

"And you transformed into teens, or I would have seen a change otherwise. Well, welcome to the club!" Elise spread her arms. "Now that we are all in that unstable age, shall we have fun and do something stupid?"

"I can't pee in elevators or on rooftops here," said Leo. "And smoking and getting drunk doesn't count."

"Is that all you did back then?" Elise asked, pouting slightly.

"OK, you take the lead then. What stupid thing did you do as a teen?"

"I fell in love with you!" Elise said, then straddled his lap and gave him a long fiery kiss, her tongue probing and tracing his lips.

"And that, you reckon, was stupid?" he said when she allowed him to speak. She was obviously teasing, and he decided to play along.

"No, but dying a virgin was," she whispered in his ear and bit it lightly.

Her nipples were erect under the soft fabric. A faint layer of sweat had polished her skin. Leo could feel her heart pounding and panicked—maybe she did want a threesome! He gulped.

"Steve's alone," he whispered back.

Elise kissed him again and abandoned his lap. "You are right."

But Steve was already gone.

"I sent him away," Leo mumbled.

"No, we both did!" Elise said and shed her yellow dress.

SHE HAS QUESTIONS

Elise emitted a deep sigh and relaxed her muscles. Her feet rested on the tabletop, savoring the aftershocks of the explosion that had taken place a few loud heartbeats ago in the area just south of her abdomen. Leo slowly pulled out of the moist, welcoming cavity. She groaned and started swaying her legs, then stopped, reached between them, glided her index finger inside and swirled it. Then removed it and growled.

Leo had noticed and ran his hands up her thighs. Then he pinched his fingers, licked them, and reached down, but she unexpectedly drew her legs together. "No!"

He stepped away and sat on the bench. She closed her eyes and began swaying her legs again, then grabbed and squeezed her breasts. She could carry on doing it for hours. *Is this normal, or have I become a sex addict?* she wished to know.

She flipped her eyes open, "Leo . . ." He was dangling a strawberry dipped in whipped cream a lick away from her mouth. She bounced her head and sank teeth into the juicy fruit. It tore in half. Leo helped himself to the remaining piece, then picked another strawberry from the bowl next to him, sprayed it with cream, and placed it in her mouth. She munched it with no hurry. *These strawberries are good*, she thought, *not lemons in disguise.*

Leo smiled cheekily, outstretched the arm holding the canister and began to turn her unassuming hills into snowy mountain peaks. She giggled. He put the canister aside, bent over her, and began scooping the "snow" with his tongue. She moaned and slammed her knees into one another when the action reached the nipple. Leo diligently removed all traces of the soft white substance. Satisfied with a job well done so far, he took a short break, dropped another strawberry into Elise's mouth, moved to the other side of the table, and repeated. She shivered and gasped again. At the end he sat on the edge, delivered a strawberry, and asked, "How do you feel about Steve?"

Elise bounced the fruit inside her mouth for a while, then chewed it quickly, swallowed, and said, "Steve . . . we spent a lot of time together. He's intelligent and can be fun. I like him." She paused for a moment with eyes trained on the ceiling. "My feelings for you are much more intense, but I'd be lying if I say that I don't have desire for him too." She looked at him trying to catch his gaze. "You aren't upset, are you?"

Leo turned his head from side to side in slow motion and fed her a strawberry. Elise took her time then looked back at the ceiling and continued, as if thinking aloud, "He still turns me on. When we were dancing, I felt impulse, maybe for a threesome." She laid her gaze on him again and smiled. "You planted it in my head, remember?"

"Yeah, I did," he said with a nervous chuckle. "But I am not sure if I can do it. I played the scene in my head, and oddly, I think I'd be OK with a man we've just met than with an ancient friend. Anyway, I also said that you two can spend time together—"

"Don't worry about that! We were on and off for thirty years. You are the person I want to be with now. Call Steve old news if you don't mind being a bit cynical." She paused then looked at him and demanded, "Give me a banana!"

Leo reached for the banana in the fruit bowl.

"No, not this one." Elise giggled.

He looked down to gauge his ready state, then smiled and shook his head.

"Aw! A small banana then?"

"Really? What's wrong with waiting for a few minutes?"

Elise resumed swinging her legs, then rolled, sat on the tabletop and spread them right into his face. "Am I a nymphomaniac?"

"Who's asking? You or your mumu?" Leo nodded at her.

"What? Ah . . ." Elise switched to a less aggressive pose.

"I don't know," Leo replied honestly. "You're certainly greedy, but you're talking about a medical condition, and I am not qualified to answer. If you dare, you could ask Annette. But why should it matter in this realm?"

"I want to be normal."

"You *are* normal!" Leo wanted to alleviate her fears.

"What was sex like in the other world? Like this?"

Of course, she had no idea. "Experiences vary wildly. I can talk only about myself."

"I don't expect you to generalize."

"Well, when I was young, it was similar, a bit less intense I'd say; took me longer to recharge." He smiled, recalling snapshots of these days. "With age, one slows down, eventually to a complete halt. A lot depends on the partners too."

"How were yours?" Elise had crossed her arms on her thighs, her forehead now almost touching his.

"Varying . . . it was pretty good with Olivia and Beatrice."

"Elizabeth?"

Leo looked down. He didn't want to badmouth his wife, but the truth was that it was not great. Not even good. At the beginning she made an effort to meet him where he stood, but after Abigail was born, she gradually transformed into a soulless sex doll, and he gave up. He felt no satisfaction. It was as if he were abusing her. She refused to acknowledge the problem, let alone offer an explanation. He was puzzled, because she was intelligent and educated, and this attitude was unbefitting. In a way, it was advantageous that he was twenty-one years older—his libido had already considerably diminished.

As if reading his mind, Elise asked, "Did you masturbate?"

"Most people do. Why?" He tried to ascertain how much she sensed.

She reproduced his downward gaze from a moment ago. "I did that a lot . . . And I still do."

"Would you do it now?" Leo tried to lighten the mood.

"You pervert!" She laughed and paused. "Well, only if you do it too!"

"OK, challenge accepted! Who goes first?"

She rolled her eyes and reached between her legs. He followed suit. Elise was more relaxed; she closed her eyes and breathed slowly, her pinched fingers reaching deep, trying to locate the magic spot. When she found it, she accelerated the pace, moaning and panting. She was wet both on the inside and out; the tavern's air was so hot— was the ventilation broken?

Leo had never touched himself in company before; it was always a private deed. Looking at her though, hearing the noises, gave him courage and he pushed his continence aside. He abandoned the bench, stood up, and faced Elise. She glanced at him through half-closed eyes, licked her lips, and started rolling her fingers and swaying. Leo wrapped his hand around his dick at the root and began pumping, slowly at first. The nerves of the corona fired up. He took a prolonged breath, held it for a second, then exhaled. His hand kept gliding steadily back and forth, squeezing lightly the glans and raising the pleasurable tension inside him with each pass.

Wow! This is fun! He crossed gazes with Elise and smiled. She sped up the pace and so did he. The contest continued, nerve endings firing at each stroke and roll, keeping all thoughts at bay. Until she shivered with clenched teeth, and he shut his eyes and squirted a warm stream her way. Then they looked into each other's eyes and laughed.

"Wow!" Leo exclaimed. He returned to the bench and kissed her hand.

Elise spread the emission on her abdomen, licked her palm, leaned forward, and blew air into his hair. "It is hot!"

"What? Competitive masturbation?"

"That too!" Elise giggled and slipped on the floor. "I need some water!" She fanned with her hand, looked around, pulled the chiller jug, and peeked inside. A lone block of ice was floating on the surface. Elise scooped it up, put it in her mouth, then poured the icy water over herself and moaned.

Leo rose, collected the plates, canisters, and bowls and took them to the restaurant's kitchen. Luckily, they didn't have to mop the floor—all spilled fluids had by now evaporated. When he returned, Elise was holding her yellow dress in her outstretched arms, rocking slowly from side to side, as another ballad was playing through the loudspeakers. Leo came from behind, outstretched his own arms, and guided her to put the garment on. He then crouched, took a shoe, and maneuvered her foot into it. He closed the clasp, then repeated.

"Don't gents prefer undressing their ladies?" Elise said lazily, and leaned on him when he got up.

"This is a perk a particular gentleman is often being denied." Leo winked and pushed her toward the exit.

"Ah, really?"

"I think we shall apologize to Steve for tonight," Leo said, changing the subject. He held the door for her.

"*Tack*," she said in Swedish, then continued in a language he could understand. "He knows these things are involuntary, and he does them too. But fine, we'll do so. Anyway, when was the last time you when to a club?"

"What club?"

"Music, you know, disco, techno, bang, bang." She gave him two mild punches with her fists.

"Ah, yeah. Last century? Something like that, I think it was in '95."

"Not surprised. You hate dancing."

"Well, that too. You knew, eh?"

"Of course, it was stamped on your forehead!" Elise smiled. "However, I appreciate your sacrifice."

"You are welcome!"

"Will you take me to one again?" Elise asked.

"To a techno club?"

"Mmm." She nodded. "Something not as ancient as my memories and my dance moves. Something new."

"I don't mind making an ass of myself for you, even less so here, where there's nobody to bear witness, but I don't think I can. I'm lacking in recall when it comes to these. It was so long ago—I remember practically nothing."

"Don't underestimate this world. If it leads us to a club regardless, you may reconsider your hypothesis of it being all in your mind."

Unlikely, thought Leo. He was actually closer to concluding that he was plugged into a machine, generating interactive visions. As for the techno clubs, they had changed over the years. The new ones, he'd seen them only on a screen—in movies and in documentaries—but he believed that his mind would still be able to put on a show good enough for Elise, if she were somehow real. She wouldn't know the difference. Maybe she was an AI! Modern VRs could do it, just that none was this immersive as far as he knew. His mood swung wildly into despair—he wanted Elise to be real! He almost started crying.

The sun was absent from the sky, and the moon would have been the brightest source of light if not for the streetlamps. Most buildings around them contained homes. The windows were predominantly dark, with the occasional pane behind which somebody or something was still awake. Sometimes the curtains weren't drawn, and he could see inside. Mostly wardrobes, some with suitcases or other stuff stashed on top. Juliette balconies like his own were more revealing—couches and coffee tables, wall units, planters. But no people. Not even shadows. Leo looked down. Yes, he and Elise were casting shadows.

"You are quiet," Leo broke the silence.

"So are you. Anything wrong with that?"

"No, nothing wrong." Leo moved his arm over her shoulders and reduced the distance between them. She wrapped hers around his waist, and they continued their silent stroll through the city, just as they had done in their youth some sixty odd years in the past.

Back in those days, they would see and hear the last trams, the nightly delivery vans, the cleaning trucks, the taxis, ambulances, police cruisers, and private cars. The city was not like New York, but was never fast asleep either—there was always something crawling, eating, moving, breathing, pooping . . . This world was quiet. He could hear leaves flapping up in the tree crowns and the whistling of the wind and that was all. Oddly, he couldn't escape the expectation of something—truck, tram or car—driving by.

Elise wanted him to take her to a club. He'd dreaded going to them when she was alive, but he'd done it, nevertheless. He knew that he had to compromise. She asked for very little. She liked dressing up for these occasions. She alternated between a pair of tight leather pants, a black leather skirt, and an animal print one—leopard or cheetah, something like that. The tops were sequined, silk or lace blouses. Once she tried out a Madonna-style outfit. She would also wrap herself in scarves, colorful ones. He would then shake clumsily his body until the DJ played a ballad. These he found acceptable.

"Hey, listen!" Elise interrupted his thoughts.

Indeed, he could hear muffled beat coming from afar. They were in a part of town, which used to be industrial—warehouses and factories, taking supplies and sending wares from the docks along the riverbank—but later morphed, as many others of its kind, into a trendy place with fine eateries, upmarket offices with views, and expensive residential lofts.

As they proceeded deeper into the zone, the beat became louder, eventually leading them to a building on the edge of the river—a prewar red brick warehouse. The windows were tinted, however, streaks of light, albeit faded, could still be seen delivering lashes to the glass. Leo tilted his head up and frowned—he was hoping for the realm to pass, but Elise's desire was likely strong. Or was it a need of some kind? He didn't know.

Elise livened up at the sight. She pulled his shirt. "See! I think we've found one."

"You did it again!" Leo jabbed.

She looked at him. "I did what?"

"Pulled my shirt. I told you, it is childish."

"Sorry!" She dismissed his complaint with a wave of her hand. "Let's check it out."

Well, they were here anyway, why not indeed. Not that they were going in, as they had to be dressed for the occasion. Or maybe not, as the possibility of bouncers sending them away was practically nil.

Leo dragged his feet behind Elise. She ran to the giant metal door and tried to pull it open. The door did not move. She started knocking, then after receiving no response—banging, quite worked up. Leo put his hands into his pockets and leaned against a tree trunk, silently begging management to keep the door shut. Elise stepped away from the door and inspected the façade for other doors, or possible ingress points.

She spotted a large crate under a window. "Come!" she beckoned him.

Leo shook head. "It's not gonna let us in. Not tonight, anyway."

"Why?"

"There's a dress code. From what I remember, ravers were expected to wear unconventional attire—leather collars, straps, chains—not regular clothes."

"Ah!" She seemed disappointed but recovered quickly. "OK, then let's go home and brainstorm!"

"Now?"

"Yes!"

"No."

NOISE

They returned eight days later, probably almost to the minute, if there were clocks to measure with precision the passage of time. Elise disappeared for a week without explanation, but when she gleefully invaded his space again, he asked no questions—the disappearance was a welcome reprieve from the impending boom-boom.

Elise ran and pulled the heavy metal door. This time it swung open, and a blast of light and sound hit them in the face. Leo raised his hand and shielded his eyes from the powerful spotlight pointed straight at him. He could make out Elise's silhouette, but the light was too bright for anything else. Nobody stopped them to check their attire or ask for passes. The door yielding meant that the gods had approved.

Leo started feeling uncomfortable wearing the wacky outfit now that he was brightly lit. Being clad in nothing else but plastic bags and combat boots was in line with the expectations for the place. There was that intermittent feeling that they were not alone, but even in the crowded old world, people wore weird clothes and enjoyed themselves. He was at it again, unable to relax.

Elise was dressed as silly as he, however, in stark contrast, she was enjoying it to no end. True, it was her idea to use the bags; he contributed the suspenders and the boots. In the morning, she arrived with a stack of thick plastic bags of different sizes and various prints and dumped them on the floor. Then she guesstimated a few, cut the bottom of the chosen one open, stepped inside, and pulled it up. Further, she made cuts into another to turn it into a tank top, though found it tickled, and so settled for a friction fit. The outfit was wacky, but they were not going to a cocktail party, so he agreed. For him she created shorts—three bags, one for the rise and two for the legs, held together with sticky tape. Leo added the suspenders after the shorts kept slipping down when he walked.

The pair proceeded past the spotlight illuminating the entrance. The music was so loud that he could feel the beat in his chest. The space was faintly lit overall; however, the strobe lights were throwing bright flashes at every major beat, and lasers were tirelessly drawing abstract patterns on the walls and floor. He could see only their lone shadows, yet he had the feeling that the place was packed. The feeling turned into fright when somebody slapped him on the back. Elise was in front of him, already immersed in the rhythm. Leo turned sharply to confront his assailant and was in a way disappointed that it was just old Steve. His friend's mouth was moving, the words barely audible. Leo went closer.

"I am with a friend!" Steve shouted, but since he appeared to be alone, Leo deduced that the companion was someone he didn't know.

"Say, 'Hi!'" Leo shouted back, then inspected his friend's attire. Steve wore leather boots, so they seemed to be on the same footwear wavelength tonight. He also sported leather shorts and leather straps crisscrossed his chest. He had donned a yellow hard hat to complete the ensemble. There was something Village People-esque in this outfit. The construction helmet would certainly be a problem if Steve tried to dance. To prove him right, Steve began shaking his head; the hat promptly tumbled to the floor. He bent down to catch it, put it back on, and switched to moving only his arms and body while trying to keep his head still.

Elise pulled Leo's suspenders. The clasp lost its grip on the bag. "Sorry!" she shouted and reattached it, then waved her hand at their friend. "Ain't you coming?" she asked, pointing at the dance floor. Leo followed her and began rocking, trying to be less aware of himself. Maybe if he smoked a joint or something that would help. "Going for a drink! Do you want something?" Leo yelled in Elise's ear.

"Coming with ya!"

They gestured at Steve of their intention. He showed two fingers in response and turned to whoever was with him.

"Steve's with company," Leo said, when the music became less loud.

"Who? You know her?"

"No, I can't see."

"You are such a stump!" Elise laughed. "Relax and just move— body, limbs, whatever . . . judging by the music, everybody does their own thing." She began illustrating her point by jumping and waving her hands. It suited her.

"I need a drink to do so, or a joint. Is there marijuana in this world?"

"Mmm," she confirmed. "But we always got it from a dispensary in town. Funny, the dispensary appeared much later. For a long time, there was only tobacco."

The bar was empty but also felt busy. Plastic cups and beer cans littered the place. Leo approached the counter and checked a few cans—all were already popped. He went behind it and pulled a six-pack from the cooler. He detached a can and tossed it to Elise. She hastily raised her hand to catch it. The sudden motion tore her top at the seams. She seemed to lack the instinct of most women to cover her breasts and instead went for the can of beer, letting the plastic strip depart.

"Oops! Sorry!" Leo said.

She looked at the former garment, shrugged indifferently, and pulled the tab. "Cheers!"

Leo took a gulp from his own can and then said, "There!" Behind her at the far corner of the hall was a row of vending machines. One of them had a hemp leaf painted on the front. The others were displaying images of cigarettes and chewing gum. When they approached, they saw that the machine was dispensing small bags of weed and rolling paper.

"Thank you!" He bowed to the invisible caretaker and indicated to Elise to take some; his hands were full holding the drinks. "Can you roll two joints?"

"Sure." Elise put the weed on the nearby table, unsealed the paper, and quickly rolled four. "Who do you think Steve is with?"

"Beats me!" Leo shrugged, offloaded the cans, and picked up a joint.

"Must be a new arrival; otherwise, I would know."

"You still may. He didn't mention names." He lit the joint with a match from the squashed box someone had abandoned on the table and took a drag.

"Whatever . . ." She followed suit, then came closer and suggestively shook her now bare breasts.

Leo's mind relaxed. He looked at his almost naked friend; she was not the little Lizzy he once knew. She was a frankly fascinating medley of young, middle aged, and old, wrapped in fresh sexy skin. He suppressed the thought of her true age, fearful that his stimulated brain would start to paint pictures that he didn't want to see right now.

Elise stuck the two extra joints behind her ears, took the weed and her drink in one hand, and raised the other above her head. "Let's go." She headed for the dance floor, seductively moving her hips as she walked.

He lifted the remaining beers and followed.

Steve had put his hat away and was rocking his head up and down and stomping with his eyes closed. Leo patted him on the arm and handed him the beer. He was getting high, but his interest had not yet dulled. He kept his gaze fixated on the pack. Steve detached two cans and swung his hand to the right, obscuring it from view. Leo quickly stepped to the side, trying to keep the cans in sight, but it was too late—one can had gone.

Steve caught the motion. "What?"

"Trying to see what happened to the beer!" Leo shouted. "Who's with you?"

"Dr. Schultz. You don't know him."

Not indeed, as the name didn't ring a bell. The joint was almost gone. Leo took a deep draft and exhaled slowly, enjoying the light-headedness this action introduced, then saw the bottom of his beer can. He dropped the butt inside the empty container and threw it in the nearby rubbish bin, where it joined many others of its kind. Leo lurched to one side, hiccupped once, then turned and joined Elise in the middle of the floor. He could see much better in the dark now!

After a while each strobe light flash became too bright to bear. He fixed his gaze on Elise's bare chest. *What an exhibitionist!* He felt a movement in his loins and wondered if the bag would hold or burst like hers, probably greatly overestimating the power of his dick. Somebody handed him another joint and more beer. Leo's head became even lighter, lighter than air, almost pulling his body up. *Is the weed in this world that potent or did somebody mess up the programming?* Everything around him turned into one big pulsating blur. He managed to find a chair and sat, before passing out.

When he regained consciousness, he was as usual back at home, staring at the ceiling. Leo got up, went to his desk, pulled out the designated notebook, and marked the arrival of the new day. Then he paged back and forth, wondering if his timekeeping would be able to detect a jump.

PEEPING PETE

The restaurant Elise chose was classy. Located on the ground floor of Grand Hotel, it was known for its gourmet dishes and was frequented by local celebrities and members of the business elite. In this realm it was as well appointed as it was in the other world, only deserted. The spaghetti she threw quickly those few months ago had given start to something of a tradition—going to eateries and taking a shot at preparing their signature dishes. The couple attempted to pull Steve into the game, but his partake remained limited to the critique—yummy or yucky.

"You are really quite an exhibitionist," Leo noted when Elise slipped out of the little red dress she was wearing and suspended it on a wire hanger she took from the open locker. "Even the panties? Do you have to cook completely au naturelle?"

"Mmm." She growled. "I respect my clothes even when I get them for nothing. Besides," she paused, "I'll be wearing this!" She pulled a yellow apron from the locker and put it on.

Leo leaned against the wall while she gathered products from the restaurant's pantry, holding a sheet of paper she had scribbled something on. Her appearance was certainly provocative.

"Let's see for how long you will be able to hold off! I bet you'd be all over me before the dish is done." Elise threw a smiley glance at him while carrying her loot stashed in a cardboard box.

"Don't count on it! I have many decades of training of holding it inside my pants!" Leo laughed. "No, seriously, why do you do it?"

She dropped the box on the counter. "Well, I'm trying to make it more—how shall I put it—entertaining. And I like to be naked!" she added unapologetically.

"Easy to say when you are in the never-aging body of an attractive teenage girl. What about those who are old?" He closed his eyes for a moment and shape-shifted, albeit not all the way to max. "You know, like this? Or simply born unattractive? Remember Fat Louise and Flatpack from my class?"

Elise stopped sorting the products, faced him, and looked in his eyes. "I know what you mean. But can we change the predicament of such people?"

He had to agree.

"Besides, nobody's gonna see me except you, and I don't mind you. I actually enjoy it when you are looking at me, especially when you steal a glance or two. You always liked nice things, so, I guess you being drawn to my appearance is an unspoken compliment. Especially considering that I can't see my face; I don't even remember what it looked like."

"It is oval, with a small mouth with juicy lips, little nose, and big eyes."

"And small boobs," she added after checking under the apron.

"You keep obsessing about your mammary glands. Your boobs aren't small; they are average size, I'd say. But even if they were small, it wouldn't matter, not to me. It is like men's infatuation with big dicks. I guess size matters, but that much?"

She stood silent, which introduced some uncertainty to his stance.

"Anyway, cup size aside, there are still people who can see you. Your relatives, my mom, Steve . . ."

"Seems you worry more about yourself than my reputation, whatever that might become if they saw me without clothes. Steve got used to this long time ago, and as to the others, it is not like that."

Leo raised his eyebrows. "Like what?"

"This place protects you, even against embarrassment. Many years ago, I was still only with Grandma and Grandpa Sinclair. I was masturbating in my room when Grandma came in suddenly. Imagine the scene—me, butt naked with fingers up you know where, and a very conservative lady. I'm guessing they didn't even fully undress when they made Dad. Anyway, I literally froze. But she looked at me totally unfazed and asked why I was covered up to the eyes with the blanket. Was I cold or trying to hide from the bogeyman?"

Leo pictured the scene in his mind and burst into laughter.

"Stop it!" Elise slapped him on the arm. "I tried it again with her. I went naked to her room, and she did not react. I grew bolder and tried it with Granddad, and to enhance the possible embarrassment I drew circles around my tits with lipstick."

Leo guffawed again. "And? Did he see you?"

"No, he saw nothing."

"Maybe he lost his speech seeing you like that? Or chose to not say anything," Leo speculated.

"I doubt it. They are both fuddy-duddies. Whenever they were around, they would tell me my skirts were too short, and I dressed like a whore."

"Did they use that word?"

"No, they'd say, 'You look like an easy girl, dear, and that is not good for you, what would people think?' Too bad my parents were almost the same!"

Leo felt that something she claimed was off. His mother saw her naked, her father too, up there in the mountain when they crossed paths, and he came out of the closet. "And you are sure that they saw no skin?"

"Yea, why?" She threw mushrooms in a pot and placed it on the stove.

"Nothing . . ." He released the image of the aged himself. "Want me to help?"

"Yeah!" she said slowly and stretched her mouth into a sinister smile. "But you will have to change too!"

"OK." Leo grinned in response. It would be harder to keep cool, but he knew he could do it. He found another apron in the locker and put it on. Then he returned to the kitchen and glanced at the sheet of paper with the recipe. It didn't ring a bell; he couldn't remember having a dish like this. "Where did you get it?" He waved the sheet.

"Grandma. She has a notebook with old recipes at their place. I copied it from there, as she wouldn't let me take the book."

He decided to wait and see, as maybe he would recognize it once done.

"The mushrooms are ready; can you slice them please?" Elise asked. "And put them in this bowl." She was sautéing chicken pieces in a large wok.

She miscalculated in a way—when she finally pulled the tray from the oven, they exchanged a brief kiss, and Leo left the kitchen to set up a table for two in the restaurant's courtyard. Elise tossed some greens into a bowl, sprinkled dressing on top, carefully cut her creation into squares, and moved two of them onto plates. She loaded them on a serving tray and headed out.

Leo picked a table under the shadow of the vines growing in the yard. There wasn't much to do. The table lacked only the silverware. "What wine? Red or white?" he asked Elise when they crossed paths.

"I don't know, maybe white?"

"OK." He made a turn. The whites were in a large display cooler adjacent to the bar. The labels bore no vintage year. Not that it ever made any difference to him, as he was not a wine connoisseur. Leo chose a random bottle and tossed it in the ice. When he returned, Elise was sitting in a chair and her red dress was back on.

"Sorry, it is my first try," she apologized, pointing at the not very sightly slices on the plates.

"No worries!" Leo pulled a carnation from the small vase in the center of the table and embedded it into her hair. Then he poured wine and sat. Elise was beautiful, particularly so with her cheeks borrowing some of the color of her dress, likely motivated by her concern about the food. Would he love her so much if she wasn't such a flower? No, probably not; she was right about him. It was unfair, he knew. Fat Louise had not been a bad girl. She was actually very smart and not even fat; she simply had the bones of an ox, large breasts, and a big round face that somehow made her appear overweight. But what could she do? Flatpack bore no guilt for being very tall and colorless, with no bust to speak of. Shame on him—he didn't even remember her name! He met a girl at the university; she was an angel—gentle and intelligent and very attractive from the waist up. But her legs were short and chubby. Nature was not fair, and neither was he. At least he didn't exploit her feelings toward him and apologized for not being able to reciprocate.

"Cheers! I lost you again," Elise said softly.

"Cheers!" Leo lifted his glass. "What's this dish called?"

"The recipe is titled 'Creamy Chicken Bake.'"

"Never heard of it." Leo cut a piece and put it in his mouth. "Mm." He nodded in approval. "Not bad at all!" The dish featured a layer of baguette slices, soggy as opposed to crisp, and the salt was a few grains in excess, but it was her first try after all, and ultimately unimportant. The taste was promising, and they'd had fun making it.

Elise took a bite too. She chewed slowly, like a food critic ready to write her first impressions down. "Not bad indeed. Not that I would know what it was supposed to be like anyway."

"What do you mean? You forgot the taste?"

"No, I never had it before. Grandma never cooked it for us."

"So, you didn't know the recipe?" Leo nudged his eyebrows upward.

"No."

But if she didn't know the recipe and had never tried the dish before and he was on the same boat, whose memory was that? Leo felt that this was important. He had to share it with his dad! He saw the bottom of his glass, jumped, and grabbed Elise's hand.

"Sorry, Liz, we need to find Father!" He gave her no more than a second to get up and maneuver out of her chair and ran with her toward the exit. When they entered the dining hall, Leo hesitated. *Is the exit to the left or right?* He hurried up again, pushed the swing door he saw in front of him, and they found themselves in a dark corridor. *Wrong way*, thought Leo, *it was not like that before*. They should be in the hotel's lobby. He was certain of that.

"What is it? Why the rush?" Elise finally succeeded in asking.

He turned to her. "The recipe! I don't remember it or ever tasting this creamy bake of yours! It could have not originated in myself!"

Leo pulled her after him back through the swinging door, seeking to reacquire his bearings, however, the door did not open to the dining hall. They were no longer in the restaurant but in what looked like an office building. He realized that the space was folding, so he pivoted and proceeded along the dark corridor. He made a few turns and ended up at a fire door leading to the street. Leo pushed it open and waited for a second to allow his eyes to adjust to the bright light. "Aha, I know!" he mumbled and turned left.

"Where are we?" Elise asked, almost running after him.

"Father owned a country home. It's close, two streets down," Leo explained.

"OK, but slow down a bit! My legs are not that long!" She had pulled the already short dress up almost to her hips trying to keep his pace. "And look at yourself!"

"Sorry!" Leo reduced his stride, then looked down and touched his buttocks. His face turned bright red—he was still wearing nothing but the apron and his shoes. "Ah, shit! It was your idea!"

"Think before you act!" Elise snapped. "I took time to change, you see!"

Leo halted. Should they go back, when Richard's country home was just around the corner? Hell, he'd raid his dad's closet for some clothes if this place didn't intervene in the meantime.

It did not. When Leo pushed the garden gate open, he was still naked under the apron. "Dad!" he called. "Are you here?"

Richard emerged from the tool shed and frowned, then moved his gaze to Elise. She raised her shoulders and rolled eyes.

"Sorry, where can I check for clothes?" Leo asked.

Richard nodded at the house and removed his gloves. Leo ran inside.

"What's with him? Why is he so worked up?" the older man asked. "And why is he dressed like that?"

"We cooked a meal . . . something my grandmother had in her cookbook. He said he had no recollection of such dish and dragged me here." Elise did not elaborate further, and Leo's father did not ask.

They climbed the few steps and entered the house. Leo descended the stairs from the second floor wearing sweatpants and a white tee. Richard's study was on this floor, and he directed them to go in there.

"Hi, Uncle!" Peter, Leo's nephew, emerged from the living room, likely on account of the commotion.

"Hi, Pete!" Leo greeted.

"May I ask who's that cute girl?" Peter said. "She ain't Abi, that's for sure!"

The others were lost for words for the silence ran unabated for a while.

"What girl?" Leo asked. Elise should be invisible to Peter.

"This one here." Peter pointed at her. "In the red dress."

"Er, my wife . . ."

"Your wife? You mean Elizabeth? She's dead?"

"No . . . she's Liz too, but . . .", stuttered Leo. "This here is Elise Sinclair, my first girlfriend."

"Ah, I see . . . ma'am!" Peter offered his hand. "I am Peter Hackensack."

Elise was still shocked. *What is Leo doing, and most importantly, how is he manifesting these people so I can see them?* First, it had been his father, then Nick and Vivian, and now his nephew. Nobody else she knew of had ever caused another person to be seen. She shook his hand hesitantly or rather let him move her hand up and down.

"Geez, you must be really close!" Richard said when his own surprise cleared. "If you pulled that off for Jess, that would be good; it's awkward with invisibles around."

"May I call you Liz?" Peter asked.

She nodded and tried to catch up with Leo in his father's study, but Richard slammed the door, almost hitting her in the face. She hastily retreated.

"Perhaps we shall leave them to talk?" Leo's nephew suggested and politely pointed at the sofa in the open space. "May I tempt you with a drink? Coffee, tea, or alcohol?"

She nodded again and sat down. Peter headed for the kitchen, whistling. In a short while he returned with a tray with two cups of espresso and two wide glasses with amber liquid swirling inside.

"Here we go!" He served the drinks. "Some Cognac too, if you want! At least this is what it says on the label. And is the same in taste." He smirked, sat on the armchair next to her, and lifted his glass "Cheers!"

153

"Thanks!" Elise said quietly while trying to read him. He was somewhat different from both Steve and Leo, more assertive perhaps. And more muscular. She had become accustomed to seeing skinny teens, as Leo and Steve rarely transformed into their more mature selves, but even then, this guy had a more athletic build.

"Are you always this quiet?" Peter asked.

"You are not supposed to be seeing me," Elise said.

"Well, I am not." He chuckled. "We haven't been out on a date yet, have we?"

Elise smiled and hinted at her true age. "I could be your grandmother."

"Really!" Peter said, leaning forward. "Show me! Pull that neat trick!"

Did he really not know? "I can't, I died young. You yourself—have you tried projecting past the age you passed at?"

"I haven't projected at any age yet. To be honest, I'm not interested at all. I like myself the way I am!"

"You are cocky," Elise noted.

He sighed and checked the view. "Yes, I am often told. Apologies!"

She realized this was who he was, and that she shouldn't judge. After all, she had her own traits that others disapproved of, but which she was comfortable with.

"Are you dating Uncle Leo?" Peter asked, then waved away briskly. "Sorry, too personal, you don't have to answer!"

She nodded almost undetectably and moved the corner of her mouth in a half smile. Then she sipped from her glass.

"Uncle!" Peter jumped to his feet. "*Ahem,* I had forgotten this look!"

Elise looked over her shoulder. Leo was standing by the French door, older, sporting longer hair and a short beard. His facial expression was tense. His eyes flicked from Peter to her and back.

"Care for a drink?" Peter asked.

"Maybe some other time," Leo said, then turned to Elise. "Shall we go?"

She hummed and got up, somewhat hesitantly. She hadn't touched her coffee yet!

Peter closed the front door behind them, then followed Elise with his gaze—she noticed—and whistled again.

The couple returned to the door they came in through. It belonged to what appeared to be a warehouse and could only be opened from the inside. Leo led the way through the main entrance, likely in hopes of finding the corridor and letting space fold again. They walked past offices, some with their doors open. The man next to her—what made him so attractive? The beard? The long hair? No, Peter was clean shaven, and his hair was short, yet he also stirred desire. The muscles? Nah, Leo had no six pack. The mature look? The sturdier built? Too much thinking . . . Elise grabbed Leo's hand, pulled him inside the nearest room, jumped on him, and started kissing and trying to disrobe him. "Shut up!" she ordered even before he spoke a single word. "I want this version of you!"

He immobilized her with some force. "I'd lose the bet if I succumbed."

"I don't care, I withdraw. You win! Pick your prize!" The little red dress landed on the floor followed by Leo's borrowed shirt.

Peter peeped through the window and wondered how he knew where to look. He had eyes only for her—lying flat on the desk with legs spread wide and a tearful expression on her face, her hands rolled into fists and nipples so firm, probably in this instant capable of punching holes. He adjusted his trousers at his crotch, clenched his teeth and took a deep breath.

LITTLE LIZZY SPUN HIM DIZZY

Leo scanned the room again, then the tubes and bottles and the toys on the long shelf, then tried reading the titles of the books, stacked at its end. When she led him here, she found her way with confidence. Curiosity took the upper hand. "Liz, may I ask you something?"

"Mmm, yep."

"It's not your first time here, is it?"

"Your eye is keen," Elise said. "No, it is not. Do you wanna hear?"

Leo declined politely. "Maybe some other time." What she was doing, what she did in the past, was a very private affair. He didn't want her to bare her soul and regret it later.

She, however, ignored the hint and started speaking, "When I woke up here, the only other person I could see was my grandfather. No one else. I was asleep for four years, just like Snow White, and look who turned up to be my prince . . ." She scoffed, then looked at him. "I missed you horribly. I wanted to be back with you. I wanted you to be hugging me, touching, kissing, licking, sucking, be inside of me. I no longer feared falling pregnant, and shit, I didn't care . . ." She took a deep breath then continued, "I needed damn physical contact! But you were not around. So, I was fantasizing. And masturbating. A lot. You know how horny teens can be. I wonder why this place is not installing some sort of sex-drive dampener into residents like me. It is not fair . . . Anyway, then I came across the sex shop. I tried every toy in it in every pose I could think of on any contraption I could sit in." She paused and reached for a cigarette. "I performed fellatio on mannequins. I wonder why they don't come with dicks. I had to strap dildos to their hips." She giggled and saluted the life-size plastic doll in the far corner of the room.

"I did anal too . . . with a vibrator." The memory made her chuckle. "A bit tricky when you are on your own, but I must say I liked it. Different sensation . . . probably because it was on my terms. I mean, that's why I liked it . . . anyway, I went completely crazy. I stopped wearing clothes and began pleasuring myself on park benches and on store counters. I started drinking quite heavily too. The weird part is that when nobody can see you, you want to be seen. You become desperate for someone to shout, 'Look at her!'"

Leo frowned. "So, you made up the story about this world not revealing you to others without your consent, didn't you?"

She blushed. "Yeah. By omission. It doesn't always work. Granddad saw me later, I guess, because I no longer felt embarrassment from being naked and playing with myself. Or he had accepted that neither thing was a sin. He just looked away and coughed. Now I'm trying to respect their sensibilities, even though they do seem changed—happy, relaxed, er, satisfied?"

Leo crawled closer and kissed her breasts.

Elise pushed his head against her chest and continued, "I think this is when I became addicted."

Leo sat and raised his eyebrows.

She quickly added explanation, "To wanting to be seen. And to sex as well. What is wrong with it? It can bring a great deal of pleasure. We've fucked this up as well in the real world!" She balled her fists. "Violence, abuse, hurt, injuries, ridicule, name calling, ostracizing, shame, denial! Why do we do all that to sex instead of simply enjoying it?" Then she looked at him and giggled. "I am not advocating for a worldwide orgy, don't get me wrong. What I am saying is—"

"I know what you are saying." Leo placed his hand over hers. "We humans are, sadly, still very primitive and dumb."

"Thanks!" She pulled her hand from under his and placed it on top. He stacked his free hand over hers. A short competition ensued, then she spoke again, "This is also when I tried to die for a second time. I should have shared my demons with Granddad . . . probably . . . I don't know . . . talking about sex was taboo. I told you what he compared me to for my short skirts. They attended church service almost every Sunday and were shocked, I mean he and later, Grandma, to find neither Jesus nor Satan here and the doors of their church were locked. He could see his parents, though, and other people I had no recollection of. It was different for him."

"When did he drift away?"

"Nah, they are still around," Elise replied. "But you only die twice, so here I am." Her face was beginning to lose its gloominess. "Then came Joleen, then Granddad Chris, then Grandma Tisch . . . The place got livelier, and I started building my dreamworld. And do other stuff. I learned the piano so I could show something to the old folks and get some praise. They liked it!" she said with pride, then added, "Hey, you've become a softie."

Leo looked down and chuckled. He was so immersed in her narration that he had indeed forgotten why they were here.

She extinguished her cigarette, jumped off the bed, and fetched a tube of lubricant. Then she climbed back, delivered a solid dose on her palms, and started applying it to his penis with slow motion, squeezing gently from time to time as her hand traveled along the shaft. When he was firmly back in business, Elise shifted so she was on all fours and said gently, "Come in, upper door."

Leo's blood was split equally between his face and his dick. Anal sex was such a taboo in his life! He was burning with desire yet embarrassed to his core by this. He hesitated, ready to abort.

"Get in, don't be shy. I am a very consenting, very old adult," Elise invited.

Leo clenched his teeth, added lubricant, and carefully went inside. And climaxed on the tenth stroke, a shockwave traveling from his groin up to his brain and erupting into colorful fireworks. For Elise, it was just the beginning. She hugged the pillow, tensed up, and panted, "Use a vibrator please. There's one on the stool."

Wow, that is intense! Leo was flabbergasted and absolutely fired up. He had recharged while still operating the toy, removed it, and replaced it with the real deal. His eyes were set on her for any sign of discomfort or pain, his movements discreet. To the point that Elise grabbed his buttock and rocked it. "Go faster!" she moaned. He lasted much longer this time, long enough to take her to the end.

She hissed, then bounced, arched backward, and wrapped her arm around her neck, twisting her body like a cat. Leo reached from behind, cupped his hands, and squeezed her breasts, all while rubbing into her with his chest. Then his hand traveled down toward her sweet spot, but the space was already occupied. Elise was panting and vigorously massaging herself. Her eyes were closed, tears of elation running down her cheeks, her mouth ajar. She wanted more and now. She turned, pushed him on his back, bent down, and drew his penis into her mouth, sucking aggressively, then reached between his legs and rubbed his ring. Leo twitched and moaned. The blood rushed down so fast that his eyesight darkened for a moment.

Elise rolled on her back and grunted "Come!" He complied. She was wet and slippery and Leo—hard as a rock. Each stroke made her moan. He swayed his pelvis left and right as he rocked, breathing through his teeth. The sensation never grew old; the exalted nerve endings celebrated every time. He pulled out, aimed at her chest and the stream met its target with a mild splash. He then scrambled down and ran his tongue over her vulvar slit, then drove it deeper and scooped up. She moaned loudly and rocked her hips while spreading the fluid over her breasts with both hands. Leo pulled the labia aside with fingers and aimed his tongue at the pea-sized bulge. Elise twitched and hissed again then let out a gleeful sigh, disheveled his hair, and finally relaxed. He planked over her and traced her lips with the tip of his tongue. She pulled his head down, and they kissed. He felt her hand reaching for his crotch.

"I need some time to recharge," he whispered in her ear, then lay flat next to her.

She turned on her side, propped up her head with her hand, and fondled his private part. "Looks like the bum turns you on, no?"

Leo's ears started burning again. "I must admit that it is indeed the case."

"That's OK. No reason to be ashamed; you are so very red." Elise smiled. "Like a cooked lobster!"

"Do *you* like it? I mean—in the bum?"

"I told you already—I do. But I like it in the pussy too."

Leo was confused by the reminder—he was aware that she did. He opened his mouth to ask for clarification, but she shushed him, straddled him facing away, and converted the reminder into action, noisily rocking and arching, until both exploded again almost in unison.

Elise then reclined over him, her back resting against his chest. She scooped his hands and made him hold her breasts. Leo dragged his palms over the hills a few times, then held them still. Minutes passed in silence. Leo felt the urge to move. He gently rolled Elise off him and onto the mattress. She sat up, yawned, and stared in his eyes over her shoulder. Then she faced him and said with a gentle smile, "How do you feel, Leo Hans?"

He sat up too. "That was intense!"

"Have you ever done bondage?"

"Bondage?" Leo tried to decipher if she wanted to go there or was just casually asking.

"You know, when partners tie—" Elise launched an explanation.

"I know what bondage is." Leo raised a hand, then took his time staying mute.

"Well?"

"Never. Why?" He looked at her with a combination of worry and keen interest.

Elise pulled all stops. "It can be fun. Come!" She jumped on the floor and pulled his hand.

"Don't tell me you enjoy pain too . . ." Leo mumbled, worried while being led out of the room and down the corridor.

"No. I tried it, though."

THE WHOLE PICTURE

Leo knew where to find her—the park at the bend of the river, by the water, behind the bushes in the secluded spot where anglers used to congregate and chance a catch with their feet in high rubber boots. She was sitting on the pebbles, arms wrapped around her legs, gaze lost in the cityscape across the lazy stream. She twitched and turned to look, when the pebbles crunched under his feet.

Leo sat quietly next to her and stretched his legs. After yesterday's performance, he felt like he had come of age again. And Elise too. She was no longer his cute teenaged girlfriend; she was a grown-up now. The perceptual constriction had been shattered for good.

Leo threw a pebble in the water and said, "Liz, do you realize what happened yesterday?"

"Are we breaking up, or from now on do you only want to do it in the bum?" she inquired in a businesslike manner.

"Neither one."

"Then I am all ears," she affirmed and produced her adorable wide smile.

"I saw the rest of you!"

"Good!" This time Elise threw a pebble. It bounced a few times on the water, then predictably sank. The river did not complain.

"What do you mean by that?" He'd expected her to ask this question, but somehow, he ended up doing it.

"That is what I was hoping to achieve." She turned toward him and looked him in the eyes. "I'm glad it worked, that I took a chance."

"You wanted me to say goodbye to my little Lizzy?" Leo smiled.

"Mmm," she confirmed. "I wanted you to see beyond your toy girlfriend."

"You were never a toy!"

"OK, sorry, the expression sounded good, so I used it. I wanted you to see what you probably called 'the rest' of me, that I was a mature person, stuck in a teen girl's body. Or worse." She smiled again. "I mean, eighteen is the oldest I can do, but I can also be a baby."

"Can you?" He had learned a thing or two about age projections and doubted the claim.

"OK, I can't go that far indeed, as one must have a memory, and babies don't, but you get the idea."

"Yes," Leo confirmed, "I do. And before you ask, I like what I saw!" He shifted closer and wrapped his arm around her waist.

"Thanks!" she said, receptive of his affection. "I gave you quite a performance, no? To be honest I was worried. I could have lost you, couldn't I?"

Leo nodded absentmindedly.

"Exactly! The fear, insecurities, mistrust, and prejudices of the old world. You were there for eighty years, which is a long time, and it's very difficult to shed the habits. I still see these in my grandparents, even my parents. You know that my dad is gay and has yet to come out completely, as Mother is still in the dark. I am infinitely glad that you did not fail." She sobbed out the last word.

Leo stretched out on the ground, looked straight up at the sky, and probed, "Did you plan it?"

"Mmm." She nodded.

"But why like that?"

"Mixing business with pleasure." She sent a smile his way. "How many other options did I have to make you see me older? Smoke cigarettes? We've been doing that since we were sixteen. Talk wise? Dress like a granny or a nun?"

"A nun would be nice." Leo could not help it.

"Get drunk and vomit?" Elise ignored his remark. "You hesitated long enough to tell me you were not in just for the thrill and that you cared. You should have seen your face though . . . ah, I love you!" She rolled, snuggled and rested her head on his chest.

Leo caressed her hair, thinking. Seemed she had devised a plan to take him past her visage and into her entire self and that plan involved kinky sex acts. His morals might have been too rigid for the kinks, or he might have been inconsiderate and rough. In either case, she would have lost the Leo she loved. The question she asked about losing him—that had to be it! But there was no way for her to know that the older him would never engage with a real teen. He would have done it in a flash back in their day if prompted as she did, but yesterday he had to forcefully remind himself that she was an adult—when he performed the anal penetration and had her tied up and hanging from the ceiling. Not an octogenarian—no, that would have been a line impossible to cross—just a mature consenting woman. This requirement became the hammer that fell on the perception shell. *Wow! What a lucky guess!* crossed his mind. Or she knew him far better than he thought.

"Do you know that in some cultures people get new names after their rites of passage?" Leo asked.

"No, I didn't." She sat upright, "Interesting! I like that!"

"Well, you can pick a new one." He smiled. "What shall I call you from now on?"

"Antoinette," Elise said, referring to her middle name.

"Not very original but will do. I think I am going to miss my little Lizzy, though. Just that tiny bit." Leo pinched his fingers and let out a noisy sigh.

"Ah, don't worry, she's still here." Elise stood up and did a pirouette. Her light skirt flew high. "After all, she's part of me!" she chirped.

It was Leo's turn to say, "Good!" He rose and lifted her in the air. She wrapped her limbs around him, squeezing tightly. They stood silent, motionless, consuming each other's warmth. Until Leo staggered and offloaded her to the nearby beaten-up table, emitting a loud puff. She let out a giggle and dangled her legs while trying to reach the ground with her toes.

"Do you think I shall change the way I dress?" Elise asked.

This was an interesting question. Leo would normally say that it was up to her, but he felt that she wanted him to become involved in her decision. Maybe she needed to be nudged one way or another. He liked her style choices: the colors matched, and the garments suited the occasions and her age. Her apparent age, that is. Ah, this is what she meant.

"No!"

"Why?"

"Because the only time you wore long skirts was in school, so how would that make you appear more mature?"

She burst into laughter. "Please, seriously! I don't know what exactly to do. What I wear is comfy and I like it, but it is a teenage style, no argument."

"Talk about clothing coming from you is strange," Leo said, suppressing with difficulty his guffaw.

"I could try to change that too!"

"Be yourself." He wasn't sure if he wanted her to change that particular habit. "I like it when people dress appropriately for their age, and in this case, it is your apparent age not your actual age. That's my fifty cents."

"Then you should try something more youthful too."

"Different people see me at different ages," Leo reminded her.

"Yeah, right, it slipped my mind."

Leo smiled. "But! We can costume play! Kind of like what we did that day in Old Town."

"Good idea!" She seemed excited by the proposal. Then reined in her enthusiasm and added calmly, "Thank you!"

***

The following day, Leo wore a Scottish kilt.

His mother guessed right. "It has to do with your chick, no?" she said when she saw him and inadvertently proved Elise's point that it was difficult for people to see more in her than an upper grade school-girl. Leo sat and reported a very heavily redacted version of the events from the previous two days. Annette kept nodding, then delivered her verdict, "Why do you think that movie villains are often ugly and grotesque?" To which Leo responded, "Thanks, Dad!" She meant that appearance was influential in the perception game.

Elise howled when they met later in the day.

"What's so funny?" Leo complained. "Kilts are worn by people of all ages. Shall I laugh my head off when you wear trousers?"

"It's not the skirt, it's your face," Elise explained. Leo blushed. Yes, he wore a kilt for the first time ever, in the traditional way, with no underwear, and was indeed feeling somewhat embarrassed. But he was also surprised that he found the garment comfy and liked the emancipation of his balls. Leo tried to relax and get used to his new attire.

Elise was still wearing one of her short skirts; however, her shirt carried the digits eight and zero, embroidered in multicolor silk thread on both the front and back.

"Liz, you've overdone it I'm afraid," he said calmly.

"What?"

"The shirt. I get it you are trying to remind people, me, that you are not what we perceive you as. Too bad being eighty is anything but fun; you are wrinkled, weak, your body hurts, and you are counted lucky if you are not very sick and still with half your mind."

She weighed his words, then took off the shirt and tossed it in the nearby rubbish bin. "I understand. I will think of something else."

Leo was well acquainted with her disregard for old-world public decency norms. He had moved from embarrassment to acceptance, even joy. Right now, he returned to embarrassment—seeing her topless excited a certain appendage of his under the kilt. He didn't want to sexualize her so much, but it was hard. Literally. With Elise, Leo felt as if he were eighteen all over again and his hormones raged once more.

"Can you think of this something else now?" he asked politely.

She looked up at him. "Why?"

Leo explained.

"OK," agreed Elise. "Let's go and find something. There are stores around."

"Would you dare walk topless on the streets in the old world?"

"No-o, er, unless it was in protest or to make a statement . . . No, I would not, I'm not a nut job! It's different there. I'd be arrested for indecent exposure, I suppose."

Right, he hadn't really expected a different answer.

"But I'd certainly be a proud nudist and go topless on the beach and be a member of a nudist club," she added.

Leo laughed.

"Why are you laughing? What's funny about nudists?"

"Their shoes."

"Huh?"

"Well, I have no problem with naked people, other than you that is," Leo joked, referring to the state of his appendage, "and I've been to nudist beaches and clubs myself, albeit not regularly. In the clubs, what I always found funny was people there wearing nothing but socks and sneakers. Had they been barefooted or wearing flip-flops or even boots, I wouldn't laugh, but socks and sneakers? Why?" He rolled his eyes.

Elise checked her feet. She was wearing sandals with no socks.

Leo followed her gaze and added, "And sandals *with* socks, these make me cringe. Beats me why."

The next turn revealed a pedestrian thoroughfare lined with shops and eateries. When they were in school, it had been a busy boulevard with cars and trams, until the city council voted vehicular traffic out and replanted the trees, which Leo remembered from an even earlier time. Leo scanned the storefronts looking for a fashion outlet.

Elise grabbed his hand and pulled him behind one of the large trees. "My grandparents!"

"Where?" Leo extended his neck and peeked from behind the trunk.

"Quick, give me your shirt!" She started to unbutton him. "There's nowhere to hide, too late!"

"I wonder what they would think of me?" He chuckled and passed her the shirt.

"Nothing, they wouldn't see you, dummy!" She hurriedly covered herself and tucked the shirt into her skirt. Then she stepped into the open and raised hand.

Leo could neither see her mouth moving nor hear anything. It was as if time had stopped for everybody else but himself. Or maybe the other way around—when he blinked, Elise was pushing the shirt back into his hand.

"That was close!" She exhaled noisily and looked behind her shoulder.

"You can keep the shirt."

"No, I'm good. I'm gonna pick something from that store." She pointed at a shop on the other side of the street.

Inside they went. Some garments were neatly stacked on shelves and display racks. Others were inattentively folded or simply piled on the racks. There were the obligatory posters promoting the merchandise and even the annoying background music, which in the absence of other sounds had also taken over the foreground. Leo took a crack at guessing the period the fashion inside the store belonged to. His memories were lacking data for a good determination though, as it could have been any time past the eighties when shoulder pads and pastel colors were not a thing. Clothing fashion is cyclical. Old becomes new again, but always with a twist, and, as he remembered, shoulder pads never made it back. Not in his lifetime. Oddly though, their conservative school uniforms were padded. He felt his left calf itching and tried to scratch it with his right foot.

"Ouch!" Elise cried out.

He dropped the shirt he was inspecting for period clues and looked down at his feet." What the . . ."

Elise was rubbing her forehead under the table. She looked up and made a puppy face.

"What are you up to now, my dear?" he teased her.

"I tried to look under your skirt."

"Ah, you are such a child sometimes. How can you expect to—"

"I can make myself look like one," she said.

"Absolutely not!" Leo barked.

"Oops, sorry. I just wanted to do what you boys usually do to girls; I wanted to see what it was like peeking under skirts."

Leo lifted the kilt all the way up. "There, happy now?"

She looked at him, her expression blank, as if she had not understood the source of his anger. "Take it easy," she said unapologetically. "Nothing lasts forever, so enjoy it while you can." She collected a few shirts in different colors and styles from the nearby rack and announced, "Going to the fitting room."

Leo did not register at first. By the time he did, she'd disappeared. Why would she go to the fitting room when she could have tried the garments here? She couldn't see much of herself anyway. His eyes were her reflection. Wait, fitting rooms should have mirrors. Maybe, just maybe . . .

He looked around, then saw them at the bottom of the store next to some screened area. He pulled the curtain of the first one—empty. No mirror either; no surprise there. Curtain up for the second— empty too. He turned, and there she was with the rest of her clothes gone.

"Ah, you are horny—"

"I am. I told you—nothing lasts forever, so enjoy the afterlife while you can." She stepped closer, placed her hands on his hips, and began to slowly pull his kilt up. Then she dropped it back. "But, fine, if you are not comfortable, we can confine our activities to a bedroom." She lifted a pale-green shirt from the pile on the floor and put it on.

Leo grabbed her arm, drew her toward him, and stuck his tongue into her mouth. Why would he abstain indeed? She responded by un- buckling his belt. The kilt slipped down on the floor. It was his first time having sex in a fashion store.

INTERFERENCE

Leo slowed down in a bid to extend the run, but Elise huffed, and he resumed, counting sheep. When he did that, he lasted somewhat longer, often just enough to bring her to a conclusion—to see the girl arch her spine, to feel the muscles of her body get tense, then shiver briefly before relaxing, to see the sobbing euphoria on her face turn into a goofy smile. He lifted her lower body in the air and swayed her legs. The pale-green shirt furrowed over her breasts. She buried her hands in the pile of fashion items strewn on the floor and twitched her open mouth.

Leo could hold no longer. It seemed the warm squirt nudged her over the threshold, and she tensed, squeezed her eyes shut and froze, mouth still ajar. Leo halted swaying and lingered inside—both enjoyed the sensation of being one—then abandoned the comfort of the warm cavity and carefully returned her to the floor. Elise smiled and brushed her hair from her face with both hands. Leo sat on his heels and slowly glided his gaze over her—from her spread legs to the top of her head, where intertwined antique gold strands pointed in random directions. He enjoyed observing her silently and holding the desire for physical contact back. She pulled a shirt from the pile and threw it at him. Leo caught it, rose to his feet, and noted, "We made quite a mess here, didn't we?"

Elise kneeled and started to collect the shirts from the floor. She tossed the heap at him and moved so she could pick up the garments that were underneath her. Leo began to fold the shirts and stack them neatly on the table.

"Move!" Elise bumped him with her hip and dropped the load she carried. "I'll do it faster."

Leo readily retreated and put his kilt on, thinking of their first intercourse in the attic of their old school. At the time, she had been dusting off her skirt with the palms of her hands. Now he was straightening his own with the same motion. Funny . . . skirts . . . Elise, done with the shirts, slipped back into hers and pecked him on the neck.

"How did it come that your grandparents were invisible to me? We've met in the past," Leo asked as they were leaving the store.

"Not with the Sinclairs. They lived in Edinburgh, and they exist in its clone now. They came to visit."

Leo was intrigued by the notion of long-distance travel. "How? Did they catch a flight or ride on Eurostar?"

"No, they did not. The same way we go to places: we either wake up there or space folds. Distance doesn't matter."

"Therefore, we can travel too, right?"

"Mmm." Elise nodded.

"Wanna go on a trip, say to LA?"

"Sure! Why not!" she said with excitement and tried to climb on his back. In a way, he was already on a trip, but to the past where he was in his teens again, with her being as she was back then. Almost. He was conflicted—she was a mature woman yesterday, but today she was her usual lighthearted self. She used the phrase "Nothing lasts forever" twice. "Enjoy the afterlife while you can," she also said. What did she mean? Was something happening he did not know about?

Elise pulled his sleeve and pointed with her finger. "Let's go there." It was a store selling apparel.

"So soon?" Leo giggled.

"OK, wait here then." She pushed him down on a bench and walked away.

Leo reached into his sporran for a cigarette. He lit one and glanced at the garments and the posters on the storefront window—the place was selling mostly formal stuff it seemed. *What is she up to now?* He obviously misinterpreted her intentions. She went inside alone. Unless she wanted to pleasure herself in a more formal way.

Elise looked different when she emerged. She was wearing a much longer mid-calf dress in flower print, a thin, braided leather belt, and black shoes. So, this is what she wanted to do. Leo felt ashamed by his presupposition. The dress was oversized, making her look like a little girl in her middle-aged aunt's clothes. Leo could not help but release a chuckle. He stood up, buried the cigarette in the sand of the ashtray, and took her hand. "Let's try again, shall we?"

He led her back inside. "What size do you wear?" Leo asked while scanning the store.

"Dunno," Elise said. "You know how things normally work here; I wonder why this is not happening now."

Leo speculated that it was because she had no clear vision for management to act upon. He had been bouncing the idea of trying on a skirt for a change last night. He dressed himself in drag in his mind, then in Scottish kilt, then in those things men on Fiji wore—he could not recall the name—and Greek fustanella too. In the morning, he found samples of the proper size neatly hanging in his wardrobe. He wasn't sure what style would make Elise appear older. Makeup would certainly achieve the desired effect, but she couldn't apply it by herself.

With her hand still in his, he dragged her to the shoe department and sat her on a bench. Then closed his eyes and ran a slideshow in his mind—something longer, yes, darker, maybe, depends, formal, yes.

"I have some ideas." He moved his gaze around. "There, there may be something . . ."

"OK." She slipped out of the large dress and followed him, holding the garment in her hand.

He stopped and pulled out a hanger with a red business suit. He had already picked a white silk shirt on their way. He tossed the garments to Elise. "Here, try these."

She looked good in red and white. *Was the memory of our first date the covert driving force behind this choice?* he wondered for a moment. He pulled out a light blue almost white dress. Light colors make objects appear larger. "Try this one too." The dress was longer and would look better with higher heels. Leo saw a mannequin with the roaring twenties style of dress in gold. This was way too formal, but she would look good in it too. He tried in vain to find the same style on the rails, then pulled down the big doll and undressed it unceremoniously. It was now time for some shoes.

Elise followed him back to the shoe department, carrying the stack of clothes he chose. She dropped them in a nearby armchair and traced his movements while standing still. He was picking pairs, inspecting them, then placing most back. He returned with the ones he kept and offloaded them at her feet.

"Try these."

Elise looked at the pile. "I don't like high heels, you know that."

"You want to appear grown up, right?"

She nodded.

"Well, not much choice here; we will have to fake it."

She raised her eyes. "By putting me on high heels?"

"Yes, that will make you taller. Child, grown-up, you get it?"

"Okay," she agreed begrudgingly, and started with a platform heels pair. She put them on, closed the clasps, and tried to walk. Leo suppressed a giggle—in this moment, she reminded him of himself when he once climbed on stilts and walked awkwardly and full of fear that he might trip and fall. But the stilts had been over half a meter tall, and the heels were about a fifth of that, yet she was still anxious and unstable. Weird phobia she had. She returned from her walk. "These, I'll go with these!"

"You like these the most?"

"Yeah, but I feel like I'm walking on stilts."

"You will learn. I get your fears, but being taller would add some age to your look. But if you are uncomfortable, then don't wear them."

"No, I will get used to it. All other women do it," Elise said.

"Why don't you try these?" Leo said, pointing at a pair of booties. "I think they would give you more support. And this." He stretched out a hand holding the golden dress he'd relieved from the mannequin. When she changed, he exclaimed, "This one's a keeper!"

"Fine, but isn't it too formal?"

"So what? You look great in it. Let's go outside so you can see for yourself." He grabbed the remaining garments. "You pick the shoes, all of them."

"We don't have to do that."

"Why? You wanted stuff that would make you look more mature, and I tried to help." Leo was somewhat offended by her refusal.

"Because I will find them in my wardrobe. We can simply leave them here," she explained.

"Mm, if you say so . . . But don't you want to have been doing shopping? I mean, carry the bags home for a change? Like in the old world?"

"No, it would be just dragging stuff. It is not the same. I'll take just this one, because I'm wearing it." She dropped the shoes on the counter.

He did the same with the clothes and they stepped out of the store. Then faced the glass door. Again, they could see their bodies reasonably well, but their faces were just dark flickering blobs.

Elise swiveled from side to side, checking her reflections, then nodded. "Looks good!"

"What's the occasion?" asked a voice they both knew.

"Pete!" Leo greeted. "What brings you here?" He hadn't thought of his nephew since they met the other day.

"I was bored at home, so I took a stroll. There's a tech bookstore nearby, and I want to check it for some bike stuff."

"Bikes sent you prematurely here," Leo pointed out.

"No, it was a fuckin' robocar. Anyway, what's with the outfits? Ma'am, you look fantastic!" Peter turned to Elise and bowed a bit.

"Thank you!" Elise blushed slightly. "We were shopping."

"Cool, but you are both dressed up. Are there parties here that I am unaware of?"

Leo decided to take advantage of the question. "We can have one. Pop in and pick some sharp clothes"—he pointed at the store behind him—"and we can go to any fancy restaurant we can think of." He didn't really want his nephew around, but, on the other hand, this place was poor on choices when it came to seeing others that some diversification should be welcomed. He turned to Elise. "Are you OK with this?"

She nodded. When Peter stepped inside the store, she whispered at Leo, "Will you please transform? As you did at your dad's the last time. Like, what, when you were forty?"

Leo closed his eyes.

"Wow, that's even better!" his nephew remarked as he exited the store. He had picked up a blue tuxedo with a bow tie. "Where to now?"

"Savoy Plaza," Leo said. He never went there on his own tab. He considered the place to be a waste of money frequented by rich jerks. Now there was no cost involved and no other jerks beside themselves. With no objections they were on their way.

Peter noticed Elise's unstable gait. "Ma'am!" He offered the support of his arm.

Elise declined with a shy smile. Leo felt an almost irresistible urge to kick his nephew in the butt. He had no idea that Peter was so presumptuous. In the past, they had nice chats, and Peter had been a cool kid. His sister, Penny, was the one considered pretentious. If Elise required assistance walking, she would have leaned on him, wouldn't she? He was somewhat sour at her not seeking his arm and continuing instead to wobble between himself and Peter.

"So, that bookstore you mentioned, what's the idea?" Elise asked after a prolonged silence.

Peter leaped at the opportunity. "I need some technical manuals, as I want to build a bike! I love bikes, and here there are none. The conclusion is, build one!"

"But how are you going to get parts?" Leo said.

"Well, the way we get clothes and food here—make them be God-sent. It already happened . . ."

"Jeez, has your dad converted you, by chance?" Leo asked, sounding annoyed. "Anyway, what appeared?"

"Parts. In the toolshed of the country house. I was thinking of my bike and wondering if I could get it here, and I had the idea of assembling one from parts. Then I found a set of tires and a chain in the shed. Then a pair of struts. But I never knew all the parts that went into it. If I find a maintenance manual, it lists everything. I bought several from that bookstore when I was still there."

"I've never ridden a motorbike," Elise said. "I wish I could try one."

"I will certainly give you a ride when I build mine!"

Leo slipped again into déjà vu. He knew it was brought on by the desire to be the one offering the thrill to the girl in the face of competition. He sighed quietly. It was very weird, being compelled to rival his own nephew over his own girlfriend, in the afterlife. He was not shy of engaging other men when they were vying for the affection of uncommitted ladies, but competitions were off the table once someone had prevailed. It did cost him the relationship he sought on a few occasions in his youth, yet he'd have to bend his personality to an unacceptable degree if he wanted it to be otherwise. He was not a motorhead, fast boats notwithstanding. If Elise wanted to ride on a motorbike, then Peter would be the person to deliver the excitement.

They reached their destination and sat around the table with the ice buckets holding still-sealed bottles of sparkling wine. When all three were in their chairs, the cork of the bottle closest to him popped and the liquid bubbled up and began to overflow. Leo grabbed it and poured wine into the crystal flutes.

"Cheers!" Peter lifted his. "To the Scotsman and his queen!"

Elise charmingly stretched her lips. "Sir!" They clinked glasses.

"I'm glad to be here," Peter said as if to himself, then louder: "Life can be so lonely in this place; me and a partial set of grandparents. I envy you!"

"What partial set are you referring to?" Leo asked.

"Jessica's dad is missing."

"Do you know why?" Elise asked.

"I can't be sure. But I wouldn't be able to see him even if he was around, as he died when I was a toddler. All I remember is mentions of him, not even photos."

Jessica's father had been an abusive alcoholic, long divorced from her mom. Leo was unaware of this person ever being a part of his stepmother's life. He looked at Elise. She was staring at Peter. Then she sighed and turned her gaze at the glass in her hand. She took a sip. "Yeah, existence here can be very lonely indeed."

Music started playing, a ballad. Peter jumped and promptly asked the only lady for a dance. She gracefully accepted, and it irked Leo again. Peter's game was clear and unashamed. Leo was confused, unsure what to do. Jealousy had never solved a thing in his past, but pretending to be above it created problems too.

Leo closed his eyes and glanced at the blank mirror in his mind. His visage reverted to default. He was not going to compete! He was too old for that.

"Uncle?"

He raised his eyebrows to Peter as his nephew returned to the table. "What? Is it not acceptable for old men to wear kilts?"

"No, but . . ." Peter stuttered. "Were we not . . . Ah, forget it!" He sat in his chair and reached for the glass.

Elise gave Leo a condemning look, sat, dragged her chair closer to the table, and began poking her salad with the silver fork.

"Pete, I think I know what you are up to," Leo began. "And I am not sure how to handle it." He sipped wine and continued, "I am pretty certain I read Elise—she likes you and she's trying to make up her mind, that's why she asked me to transform. She is also almost certainly commiserating; she spent an awful number of years on her own in this realm. She is very dear to me, and because of that I will not stand in the way of her desires."

It crossed his mind that perhaps he should have reserved this speech solely for Peter's ears, but he'd already spoken so there was no way to undo it. As if to substantiate his doubts, Elise rose from her chair and strode out of the dining hall. Both men froze for long enough to give her a good head start. Then both rushed after her, but she was nowhere to be found. Leo kicked the first door he saw in the dark corridor and entered his room. He dropped into his armchair, turned the music on, and lit a cigarette. Losing her would hurt.

REUNIFICATION

Leo and Elise remained incommunicado for several days. He spread out his drift charts and notes and tried to discover correlations, but his mind was inevitably circling back to her, and he spent more time chasing her image away than doing useful thinking. Sharing the burden with his dad under the circumstances was not an option. In the evening, he tossed and turned until he eventually fell asleep in the early hours of the morning.

When he awoke, he found himself in a bungalow on an ocean beach. The tide had receded; hermit crabs were making trails in the soaked sand. The bungalow was on stilts with a boardwalk leading to dry land. There were no other houses as far as he could see. Solar panels were providing power, the fridge was loaded, and, on the table, he found paper and a bag of weed. He rolled a joint and relaxed in a lounger. The marijuana calmed him down initially, then he started picturing intercourse between Elise and his nephew and his heart rate rose again. Why didn't she show up? Was she with Peter?

He fell asleep, waking up sometime in the afternoon. The tide had arrived. He sat on the platform's edge and soaked his feet before disrobing and jumping into the water, where he floated on his back. This made him feel calm and composed again—he was going to get over her, he had always succeeded in mending his broken heart.

Day three was pretty much the same: alone, on the deserted beach, with a fresh breeze carrying the aroma of the sea. He spent the time in and out of the water and in the lounger, drinking beer and wondering where it went. He understood why she liked undressing—the gentle touch of the warm wind on his bare skin felt good indeed. Where was she? Leo's mood turned gloomy once more.

On day four, the seaside vacation was over—he was back home. The doorbell chime sounded. Leo turned in bed to face the wall and ignored it; Annette would take care of it, or the visitor would just let herself in. Then he jumped up. *Her!* It may be her! He rushed to the door and looked through the peep hole. Elise stood there, holding something in her hands. Leo tried to decelerate his heartbeat. He took a deep breath, exhaled slowly, counted to ten and then opened the door.

"Hi!" greeted his visitor then checked him head to toe. "Why are you naked?"

Leo touched his crotch. "Ah, must have come from you." He made way for her to enter.

She stepped inside, turned at him, and lifted her hands. "Here, I made this for you to say 'sorry.'"

"What's that?"

"Cookies!"

"And you are apologizing for what?" Leo looked around the corner. The door of Annette's room was open but seemed that she was out. He proceeded in the direction of the kitchen.

"For Pete!" Elise sounded desperate.

"I meant what I said, Liz! There's nothing to apologize for. If you like the dude, so be it!" He looked up at the ceiling, trying to conceal a tear.

Elise left the parcel on the table, stretched out her arms and locked her hands behind his back. She hugged him tightly. "It was just lust, I admit. You both turn me on. You are both burning hot in your late thirties, I don't know why . . ."

I hope that it was good! Leo was tempted to belch out but was able to refrain. *They banged, so what.*

"Rest assured, nothing happened!" Elise said, as if hearing his thoughts.

Leo lifted her chin and pecked her on the lips. Then he handed her a coffee mug, sat, and began unpacking her gift. "Thank you!" He straightened the paper with his palms and pushed the plate toward Elise after helping himself to a cookie. "But you know, you can bang whomever you want. As long as you come back to me." He tried to inject maximum warmth into his smile. "Of course, same applies to me, right, or else it would be unfair."

"Deal, OK, but not with your nephew! That was so insensitive of me!"

I'm glad you realize it, thought Leo while munching. What he said instead was, "Mm, these are good!"

Elise sent the last bite of her cookie down with a sip of coffee and said, "Aren't you going to get dressed?"

"Look who's asking!" Leo chuckled and shook his head.

"Then I'll join you." She bared the bottom half of her body, then straddled his lap and proceeded to reveal the rest. "Will you do me a favor, please?" she whispered in his ear.

"Sure, what?"

"Age a bit. Sorry, it makes you so damn hot!"

Leo shrugged mentally and called the mirror, then joked, "And what would you do for me in return?"

She slowly slipped down and kneeled in front of him.

Leo smiled and said, "Not now, come back up here."

"Why?" She rose and resumed her position on his lap.

"Because I want to look you in the eyes." He kissed her with a pounding heart and caressed her cheeks as she accepted him inside.

Annette, upon arriving home, heard the sounds of passion, quietly shut the door, and thought of LaRen's chiseled body. Maybe the moment was ripe for a trip to new New York!

ANGST

Leo hit the last note of the piece he had been tormenting for over a week now and let the sound fade away as indicated on the sheet. Then he turned to his tutor.

"What is it, Lizzy?" he asked. "You are different today. And yesterday, and the day before . . . Quieter than usual, kind of gloomy. I'm certain that something's bothering you, yes?"

"No, there's nothing." She looked him in the eyes and winked unconvincingly.

"Don't give me that, please! Did you notice how many times you said that nothing lasts forever, etcetera? I know that, just wondering why you keep mentioning it."

Elise sighed. "I'm scared. I don't know how much time I have left."

Leo's body stiffened, his heart sank—nothing lasted forever she kept saying, and she was referring to herself! "What are you talking about? The drift? Why?" He fired his questions in a single breath. Now he was scared too.

"Yeah, the drift." She lowered her gaze. "I've been here for over sixty years. People drift away much sooner. Your granny's gone. Your cats too . . ."

That was true. Fluffy and Ginger disappeared around the time Babette drifted away. *There must have been a connection*, thought Leo.

"Something anchors us here for a while. Then one day the chain breaks and we drift away from the shore," Elise continued. "Maybe my day's coming . . ."

Leo made room for her on the large stool, seated her next to him, and tried to gather his thoughts. He hadn't made much progress on his investigations. Yes, the chart had grown bigger and more inclusive, but what tied it all together, he still did not know. He had to look at it again, but later, when he was alone. Richard could contribute too, and he would pay a visit, if not for Peter, who he was reluctant to see.

"I thought more and more of death as I grew older," he began. "I was wondering what form it was going to come in. There are so many choices . . ."

Elise laughed wearily.

Leo continued, "It can be depressing. Eventually I stopped thinking so much about it and let life go on."

"And?"

"And one day death came, and do you see who I found?" He turned, grinned, and looked her in the eyes.

She smiled back and buried her face in his chest. "I get your point, but my experience was different. I had to wait for sixty years to be reunited with you, and I don't want to wait another sixty, if there's an after-afterlife. I don't want to be alone again . . ." She shivered and cuddled up.

Leo exhaled slowly through his mouth. "On the flip side, you didn't have to bear with me for six decades."

There was a lot more that he could add to this statement. However, the moment wasn't right for a full disclosure. Yeah, he loved her dearly, but back then he had not even considered marrying her. He wanted more—more girls, more experiences, and she was just the beginning. He saw their relationship as a teen adventure, a romantic story unlikely to last. He didn't expect it to literally die in a crash; he anticipated one of them eventually breaking up with the other. But now—now it was different. He'd had his relationship adventures, and he was given a second chance at his first love. This time he didn't want their bond to break.

"What makes you think that I wouldn't?" Elise said.

"Nothing. Just that it doesn't happen very often, as it is the exception rather than the rule. When it comes to personal relationships, what starts as a fairy tale often turns into a nightmare. I admit, though, that this is a different world, so my observations may be invalid. I have no objections to being in love with you for decades to come!" He tried to steal a kiss, but she kept her head low.

"I may not have decades . . . I don't have decades . . ." Her voice trembled.

"You have been here for a long time indeed. Have you observed something that you can share? About the drifts?"

"I don't have anyone drifting away on me. They all arrived later, even Joleen. This is what makes me apprehensive; maybe my time is up. You said that your great-grandmother passed away just before we met. I died three years later . . ."

"Sixty years, you say," murmured Leo. He switched to a clear voice, "Please try not to think about this. It makes you miserable and could drive you insane. Even if you are correct and we can be here for about six decades, there is nothing that we can do to change that, that we know of. So, why spend whatever time we have left in fear and anticipation of the end? You yourself said it: enjoy what you have while you can. Right?" Her anxiety was contagious, as now his heart was riding low, perhaps at the bottom of his stomach. This is how it felt.

"Let's go to the hotel, shall we?" he proposed. "Do it while we can!"

"Precisely!"

***

The hotel was located across the street from the adult toy shop. Leo had a strong suspicion it'd been a brothel in the other life. Most rooms had shelves with adult paraphernalia—dildos, butt plugs, lubricants. Elise had expropriated a room on the top floor and had stashed some extra goods, including an expressionless full-size male mannequin she said she'd snatched from a nearby fashion store and had kept as a souvenir after it was no longer needed. Whenever they felt a penchant for something more elaborate, they climbed the stairs and improvised with the toys or consulted the books or visited the special room at the end of the corridor—the one with the contraptions and the ropes.

On their way, management decided to turn the rain tap on and by the time they reached the hotel, they were soaked. They removed their clothes, hung them on the bed frame, and jumped into it. Leo remembered Elise's fascination with his older self and changed.

"Thanks!" She pushed him face up on the bedsheet, jumped on top, and began rubbing her vulva on his abdomen while pinching his nipples. Behind her, his appendage became excited. She reached out blindly, held it at the base, then glided her palms up a few times, alternating hands. Then she crawled backward and tried to bring him into herself.

Leo grabbed her arms, pulled her down, and whispered in her ear, "I know it is not exactly the same, but . . . I did you in the bum, so it is only fair to return the favor."

She burst into laughter and rolled over to his side. "Ah, sweetie, you don't have to do that, you know?"

"But I want to. I want to experience it. I may not like it, but this is not the point. Trying it out is, and you are the only person I can do it comfortably with."

"Well, you did manage to get me distracted," she said with a smile. "Thanks again!"

"So, will you or I shall ask how you did it by yourself?" Blood rose to his face, but he remained determined.

"OK!" She jumped from the bed, raided the shelf and returned with a pair of cuffs, a lubricant tube, and a dildo harness. "We start with some foreplay! Come down, kneel on the carpet!"

Leo stepped on the floor and kneeled, as told. Elise climbed back on the tall bed took his hand, cuffed it, pulled his arm straight, and secured it to the frame. "It's going to be more fun like this!" she whispered, licked her lips, and moved to restrain his other hand. Then she returned to the floor, dragged her fingers up his groove, and leaned quietly against the wall, out of view.

Leo waited patiently, his heart beating loudly. When nothing happened, he twisted his neck to catch a glimpse of her. "Lizzy! What now?"

"Let the anticipation build up." She kneeled behind him, laid hands on his buttocks, and pulled them apart. Leo twitched and moaned.

"You are very tense. Relax. It is not going to hurt. Let the doctor do her job."

"I . . . The doctor is the problem . . ."

"How come?" Elise let go of his rear.

"I'm a man; I have a prostate gland."

"I know. Is it not the source of pleasure in this case?"

"I am an old man. I had prostate screenings, and the doctors were quite rough. So—"

"Ah, sorry, shall we stop then?" Elise clutched hands at her chest.

Leo twisted his neck again. "Climb up here! I want to whisper in your ear."

Elise followed the instruction, kneeled next to him, snuggled up, and rested her head on his arm.

"Proceed!" Leo said with a faint voice.

Elise brought her face so close that their noses touched. "Are you sure?"

"Yes!" Now their lips touched too.

Elise sat upright, ran her fingers over his spine, then reached down and rubbed his ring. Then she stepped on the floor, positioned herself behind him, split the cheeks, and vibrated her little tongue over the orifice, triggering a jolt of desire in her friend. She opened the tube and squeezed a solid dose in the crack, spread it, then gently glided her index finger in.

Leo took a deep, shaky breath. "You OK?" she asked alertly, while moving the finger slowly in an out.

"Yeah!" answered Leo through his clenched teeth.

Elise leaned, kissed each buttock, then drove her tongue as deep inside his anus as it would go. Leo squeezed his eyes and smiled. He had performed rimming on her many times, but it was her first venture into his zone. She reached between his legs, wrapped her palm around his dick, and started pumping slowly, while still working out her tongue. Leo became eager to embrace and kiss her, but his intention was in the way. And the cuffs. Elise paused to put the harness on, then squeezed a handful of lubricant in her palm. She dipped the dildo, rose on her knees, aimed, and carefully introduced the toy.

Leo pulled on the cuffs and moaned. Each thrust increased his arousal, almost to the point of going off, but then he plateaued. She kept going until he eventually shook his head. Elise pulled the dildo out and reached for his penis. She started pumping with long slow strokes, then accelerated. The nerve endings fired up again, and he shivered. She stepped to the side, held the glans in her loose fist, and applied short brisk strokes. That did it. Leo felt the wave of delight ripping his groin and then traveling through his body and buried face in the bed sheet, panting. Elise was also breathing heavily.

She let go of his dick and rested her head on his back. "Phew!" Then she removed the harness, climbed on the bed, and unlocked the cuffs. Leo grabbed her instantly, rolled and delivered a very passionate kiss, reaching deep with his tongue. She held his head, savoring his taste, and he hers.

"Thanks!"

"Did you like it?" Elise asked cautiously. "You didn't climax, not right away."

Leo chuckled and licked his lips. "I'd say—it is an acquired taste. But I did like it, definitely! We must go for it again!"

"Same here. It took me a while too. Anyway . . . I hope you aren't going to get jealous," Elise said.

"Why?"

"I let Stephen do me in the bum too," she disclosed. "After that, he didn't want anything else. He became quite rough too. You, you are different. You make me love you even more. You never take advantage, and you are open to new experiences. Steve—he was set in his ways, and he liked to watch me doing kinky things but never tried anything of the kind himself. Boring."

"No reason to be jealous, no."

"Great!" Elise chirped. "Let's do a classic now." She rolled backward and lay flat on the bed.

"Anal sex can be considered classic. If I'm not mistaken, it was openly practiced in ancient Greece," Leo said while wiggling his fingers down her abdomen.

Elise giggled. *Sex is like a drug*, he thought. He recalled memories of big fights with his first wife. They screamed and shouted and hurled insults at each other, then they called a truce and made amazing love. Then hostilities flared up again. No problem was ever solved, though, as the toxicity kept going up. The memory acted as a dampener—his hand came to a stop. He retracted it, pulled a cigarette from the pack on the stool, lit it, took a drag, and offered it to Elise. She shook her head, crawled, sat in the bed, and leaned against his back.

"Leo!" she looked over her shoulder. "May I ask of you something very personal?"

"Like what?"

"Will you show me your true self?"

Leo hesitated—the picture wasn't going to be pretty. She had no idea what being old was like. But she asked so nicely so why the hell not! He moved to the edge, put out the cigarette, took a deep breath, and pictured himself in the hotel the morning before he supposedly died.

"Ah!" Elise exclaimed.

He opened his eyes and looked at her. "Isn't it what you imagined?"

"You died with hair!" She declared very seriously.

Leo chuckled.

"I've seen old people, so it was pretty much what I expected. You are the first one I am seeing in the nude though." She ran her hand down his wrinkled forearm. "How does it feel?"

"You mean the touch?"

"No, being old."

"No difference here, but in the old world it was bad. Fatigue, pain, stiffness, and that is best case scenario. People develop all sorts of afflictions. The worst I think is when they lose their minds. We are meant to want to die at certain point."

"Yeah, I know, my great-great-grandmother had Alzheimer's. Mom said it was a nightmare."

"Is she here?" Leo asked, intrigued. Alzheimer's affected memory and this place made heavy use of memories; even at this very moment he was employing a memory of himself to fulfill Elise's request.

"No."

"Can I revert now?" Elise's hands traveling all over his body were stirring up a fresh wave of desire.

"Hang on for a bit longer please!" She looked fascinated. Her prodding, albeit gentle, contributed to the discomfort, as he felt like a freak show exhibit.

"I will never be like this!" Elise sighed.

"Do you really want so strongly to have been old?"

"Yes! Maybe not if I was unaware of this existence but knowing that there's another life . . ." Elise sat on his lap and met his gaze.

"What the!" Leo pulled back, startled. He regained his composure, lifted his hand, and touched her cheek. "What happened to your eyes?"

"What about them?"

Leo slowly brushed her hair back. "They are old," he said quietly. "Your face—it is still young, but your eyes . . ." He smiled gently and left the rest of his sentence up to her imagination.

"Aw!'" She blinked a few times. "I was trying to—"

"To do what?" He was almost certain that what she had attempted was a forbidden transformation.

"To make myself look old."

He released his aged image. "OK, but don't do that with others is my recommendation. It is spooky."

Elise stepped on the floor, walked to the window, and opened a gap in the curtains. The evening had arrived, the rain still pouring. She turned at him having switched back to her bubbly self. "Do you want to take a shower?"

"Huh?"

"I mean—let's go outside! It is still raining."

She ran downstairs and jumped out onto the street. He followed at a moderate pace until he heard her screaming in pain. Leo rushed out. Elise was down on the pavement, writhing while holding her right leg below the knee with both hands. A large, deep and obviously painful bruise was dripping blood.

"Shit! Let's go inside, I'll try to find some bandages." Leo squatted beside her and tried to help her up.

"Nah, I'll be OK, just watch!" she hissed, putting on a brave face. The raindrops were converging on the wound and washing the blood away. Soon the spot was clean, sporting a fresh layer of shiny pink skin. The skin began to change color and blend with the surrounding tissue until there was no trace of the bruise left. Elise jumped and climbed on his shoulders while he was digesting the observation. "I am the rider. You'll be the horse!"

Leo found his balance, grabbed her legs, and stood up. Touching her renewed his desire. She threw her hands up in the air, enjoying the warm downpour.

"Can you wash my hair while you are up there?" Leo asked.

She laughed and began rubbing his scalp, while he was traversing the distance between the nearest two trees.

Peter, in a nearby alley, took a short step back into the shadows cast by the building over him and grunted in disgust. What was this attractive young woman finding in the old jackass? The duo looked pathetic—she was a fresh flower, ripe for picking where the dude was frail, with wrinkled, pale skin and sagging flesh, yet hard. *Ew!* He spat on the side of the building, protruded his neck out of his hiding spot, and looked at his uncle and his uncle's lady friend again. She deserved better—he had to make a move!

JONAS

Leo leaned against the lamppost with hands in his pockets and a resigned expression on his face. The distant silhouettes were rapidly morphing into recognizable beings—Margot and Steve. The stretch of time between them leaving the tavern together and now was lost. The sun was shining; Margot was wearing a suit now and was sober. Must have been a few hours, maybe more. Non-linear time, they said. Were the jumps the manifestation?

"Did she talk with her granddad?" Margot called when they were within earshot.

"Did you talk to your granddad?" Leo asked Elise, who was standing next to him, holding a daffodil in her hand. Did he get it for her?

"I just told you!" she snapped, then softened the tone. "Ah, you jumped again."

"Yep, I am missing a few hours. I think!"

"OK, he said that he had to satisfy an urge to visit our place, space folded, he was up on our floor, he went to my room, and that was it. Not very helpful."

Steve and Margot had reached the spot where they stood, and Leo relayed Elise's words. Margot looked down, tears bubbling up in her eyes. Steve tried to comfort her, but she wriggled away. "Sorry, Stephen, it won't work! Let me shape up on my own." That was the Margot Leo knew and found attractive all those years ago.

"But he mentioned something about tombstones," added Elise.

"What about them?" Leo asked.

"He said that he went to the cemetery to see his grave and it wasn't there. But he saw graves of people who were yet to die. And when his close ones drifted away, he again went to the cemeteries where they were supposed to be buried and found their graves."

"So, if someone is not here, that person gets a grave, it seems. Let's go check that out!" He looked up at Margot.

"What are you talking about?" Margot asked, reminding him that nobody was relaying what Elise had said. "Check out what?"

"Let's go check out if my grandmother has a grave," he began and then explained why, "If your kid is not here—"

"I know where he was buried!" Margot interrupted. "Let's go there first!"

The tombstone was unimposing—small, like the child supposedly lying below it. Margot dropped to her knees and began sobbing. Steve shook lightly her shoulder. She slapped his wrist to push his hand off, but he squeezed and said, "Check the dates!"

JONAS SEBASTIAN MIERLING 2002–2081, read the letters carved in the granite block.

Margot moved her lips in silence then turned around with an unspoken question in her eyes.

"I don't know!" Steve protested, gesticulating, "Maybe he's not dead? When did he die?"

"2002, in August," Margot said with a glimmer of hope, "So, what is written here as the year he was born is the year he died. But why?"

"And perhaps reborn somewhere. You know, the reincarnation thing . . ." Leo said. "Let's check other graves! Richard was buried here, a couple of sectors away."

The tombstones they passed featured a mix of lifespans—some were strictly in the past and others just like that of Jonas had future termination dates. Unfortunately, this meant nothing, as the names did not ring a single bell. There was a fresh mound—the wooden cross listed the year of passing as 2049. In the absence of clocks of any kind and the temporal jumps, they had difficulty keeping track of time. However, Leo's estimate was in agreement with this recent grave—he'd been here for almost two years now. He had a notebook with tallies of the days. He realized that they should have reached his father's grave already. Leo studied their surroundings, looking for familiar landmarks but found none. Just as he expected, his father was, in a way, still alive.

"I'm lost," he admitted dryly. "By the way, do you know of someone who drifted away recently? I wonder if the grave would be fresh."

Steve and Margot shrugged. Elise was looking to the side with her hands clutched behind her back, seemingly oblivious to his question. Leo snapped his fingers a breath away from her face.

She turned at him. "Sorry, what?"

"You jumped?" Leo asked.

"No, just thinking." She shook her head. "So, what do we do now?"

"At least we know that Jonas is not here. If he was reborn, that is just a speculation. We can ask about these things the people we can see—"

"Is that Elise?" Margot asked, her index finger right on target.

Leo rolled his eyes.

Elise took the finger in her hand and shook it up and down with care, "That's right! Jeez, your boobs are really an impressive thing!"

Margot could not sustain her laughter. The hope of her kid being still alive albeit reborn had elevated her spirit and Elise's comic introduction was the cherry on the top. She embraced the apparently younger lady, "Well, I'm Margot." She turned to Steve. "Was this not supposed to happen? Like me, seeing her?"

Steve clicked his tongue and said, "Blame Leo, he does it all the time."

"As in?" Margot persisted.

"You are, what, number five?" Steve looked questioningly at Leo.

Leo nodded, placed his arm around Elise's shoulder, and drew her nearer. "There's no explanation, so please don't ask!"

"Who else saw you?" Margot politely addressed Elise.

"Leo's dad, his grandparents, his nephew, Pete, and now, you."

"So, only people close to him," Margot observed.

"Do you count?" The question felt like a snap, even though Elise spoke calmly.

"I had a crush on Margot once," Leo admitted and blushed.

"You had a crush on my boobs! Everybody does, including this jerk here!" She waved hand at Steve.

"No!" Leo stood firm. "I liked your personality. The boobs were a bonus I could do without. Look at her!" Leo nodded at Elise. "But truth be told, even if we started dating, it would have ended the same way as with Steve—I also wasn't ready to commit."

Elise wrinkled her nose and shook off his arm, though remained silent. They were past the cemetery gate and had moved onto the boulevard. Nobody was setting a direction, and they just walked. Margot held Steve's arm, and Elise was walking a few steps behind and studying the other woman.

"Stop surveying me," Margot said without turning. "I can feel your gaze."

"Sorry!" Elise apologized and hurried to catch up with her. "I don't see new people often."

Leo removed his hands from his pockets and snatched his girlfriend. Then asked, "Where is your husband now?"

"Tylo, you mean?"

"I am not aware of any other."

"I don't know. He may be here. He passed away in '38, but we haven't yet met. After Jonas died, our marriage eventually turned into an empty shell. We stayed together for Christian's sake, but that was all. Later, we moved to our own places and drifted, er, drifted way apart."

"This is interesting—even if you were once close, the bond may break and this place reflects that," Leo suggested.

"Seems to be the case, yes," agreed Margot. Then she turned to Elise. "Thank you plenty, dear! For the help finding Jonas, you know! Fantastic seeing you too. Next time we get together, it won't feel weird."

She hugged her again. She then grabbed Steve's arm, and they headed in the direction of his place.

"I don't know if her son is indeed alive, but at least she got hope, and hope is important," Leo said philosophically.

Elise made no comment.

"Seriously, I learned that in the other life. Part of getting old is diminished hope, you do know that your unused days count is getting lower and lower. Very disheartening. People go nuts and try to compensate in all sorts of ways. Carl became born-again, Father turned to New Age esotericism—plenty others to incredibly stupid conspiracism . . ."

"Like what?"

"Like Earth is flat and the moon landings were a hoax and reptilians ruling the world . . . Most people that I knew became angry, very angry and bitter. It was a pain to watch and live through. I lost friends. I lost hope! Do you still wish old age?"

"Certainly!" was the reply. "Now, tell me more about the reptilians."

Crap, Leo thought, but obliged.

BEATRICE

Leo was near climax when he heard a greeting:

"Er, hi Leo!"

He tilted his head up and looked straight into the enlarged eyes of Beatrice, his first wife.

"Hi, Bea," was all that he could say.

She pointed at him and said with a trembling voice, "Are you wanking, in the raw and in a public park? What kind of place is this?"

Leo shifted his gaze down. Elise was still hard at work, unaware of the other person's presence with his fingers still buried in her hair. Who beside her knew what Beatrice was seeing?

"Er, I am not by myself," he mumbled then said, "Lizzy, stop, we are not alone."

Elise looked up and withdrew his penis from her mouth, just as he reached climax. There was not enough room for embarrassment— there was simply too much of it. Leo resigned himself to his fate.

"What do you mean, you are not alone? And what just happened now?" Beatrice dipped fingers in the wet slimy spot on her blouse, head tilted to the side, her mouth ajar, her brows drawn together.

"I wonder what real sperm tastes like," Elise said.

"What does semen taste like?" Leo asked Beatrice.

"It's salty, why? Hey, idiot! What's wrong with you!"

"Salty," Leo relayed the answer to Elise.

"Interesting. Here it has no taste," Elise said, unperplexed.

It was time for Leo to get serious. "Lizzy, Bea's here!" he announced, then reached for his shirt and kilt. He discovered that the kilt was much easier to take off.

"Where?" Elise said sharply and turned instinctively to check the space behind her.

"You are wearing a kilt?" Beatrice's eyes widened.

"Bea was your first, right?" Elise asked. Leo's attention was split.

"Yeah." The answer worked for both.

"Since when?" Beatrice demanded, as if it were important.

"I see," Elise said. She wriggled up with hands on her head, careful not to bump into the other as if it were possible without seeing.

"Sorry, this place can be very confusing," Leo said, buttoning up his shirt. "People who had never met cannot see or hear each other. I said I was not alone. I was . . ." He turned to Elise and asked, "May I mention you by name? I am explaining the visibility rules to Bea. She's heard about you."

Elise nodded.

"I am here with Elise." He completed his sentence for Beatrice.

"Your school girlfriend?"

"Yep."

Elise kissed him on the cheek and whispered in his ear, "See you later."

"Sure, thanks, Liz" Leo said, grateful that she understood.

"Thank you too," Elise answered. She took her clothes in one hand and headed home, waving them as she walked.

Beatrice sat next to him on the bench. "Am I really dead?"

Leo shrugged. "How would I know? It can all be a dream of a co-matose mind. Or a simulation with my brain wired to some machine. But it is not bad here." He smiled and looked her in the eyes. The same beautiful green eyes he really missed but didn't want to admit even to himself.

"Ah!" Beatrice exclaimed and looked at the ground.

"How did you find me?" Leo asked, although he already kind of knew.

"Well, I died. I think . . . I think I had a stroke. And I woke up in my room. Mom was there. And Grandma. They told me I had passed. And I thought of you; I wanted to see you if you were here. I went out and ended up at this spot." She looked around and added, "By the way, this park is quite far from home, how—"

"This is how this place works. Space folds here. And time." Leo lit a cigarette and offered one to Beatrice. She accepted and drew in the smoke with zest. "How's Eric?" Leo asked.

"He's good. Business is doing well, got a major joint project with Taller & Rheubenhoit. And he's gonna be a dad."

"Eric? Father? Ha!" Leo exclaimed. Their son was not the sticking type.

"It has been two years since you died. He got involved with two girls. Well, women. They are in a polyamorous relationship. He got both pregnant and said that he was losing hair . . ."

"What's that have to do with his girlfriends?"

"He meant that he was getting old, and it was time to settle down," clarified Leo's ex.

"Jeez, only now? He's, what, fifty-five?" Leo chuckled. "Whatever . . . And your other kids?"

"Do you really care about them?"

Leo shook head slowly. "No, not at all. Just trying to be polite."

"Fuck you!"

"OK!" Leo immediately agreed. It was just like in the old days; she would say something that would anger him, and a stupid fight would then erupt. Or the other way around: he would banter and ignite her temper. Then they would take advantage of the double meaning of the swear word. Then fight again.

"Actually, I missed your silly jokes," lamented Beatrice.

Leo chuckled and threw the cigarette butt in the nearby ashtray. "Are all of your exes besides me still alive?"

"No, all of my ex-husbands are deceased."

And you picked me out of all . . . thought Leo.

"But you were the one I wanted to see," she added hurriedly.

"I'm honored!" Leo said sarcastically, then continued in a changed tone, "Sorry, old habits die hard."

Beatrice opened her mouth to respond, then seemed to change her mind and only sighed.

"Shall we take a stroll?" Leo suggested.

"Yes, why not?"

Leo stood up and extended a hand to assist her. Beatrice rose gracefully. Leo unashamedly checked her out head to toe. They last saw each other at the signing of the divorce agreement. She was thirty-two and still very attractive—a trait he observed again. He wondered what she really looked like now, but she was new, unlikely to be able to transform.

"Bea, is something not striking you as odd when you look at me?"

"Yes, in fact. Why do I see you so young? You must be in your eighties now."

"Because I was thirty-five when we met last. This is how things work here. You see others as you last remember them. With time we all learn to transform as it is called. That is, to shape-shift, project a different age. Look at me now."

Beatrice gasped.

"Yeah, this is your first ex as he looked when he died. OK, perhaps a bit earlier, I looked at myself while I combed on the day before I had the heart attack. And isn't this the guy you met?" Leo asked and shifted his visage many years deeper into the past. Beatrice's beautiful green eyes again widened in astonishment.

"No shit, you can do all that?" She was becoming her normal self—not very mindful of her language.

"I'm still acquiring the skill. I can't hold the shape without effort. But older residents can do it like breathing. It will come to you too."

"Wow, just wow!" She finished digesting the information and asked nervously, "Er, how do you see me now?"

"Young," Leo answered.

She produced no response, allowing an awkward run of silence.

"It is interesting. You are still a redhead," Leo finally said.

Beatrice raised her eyebrows, glancing at him.

"You are a natural blonde, but you were dyeing your hair red. I remember you as a redhead and this is what I see."

She squinted angrily. "What were you doing on the bench?"

"Can't you deduce?"

"I guess I can." She lowered her gaze. "But why in the park?"

"Because it is fun. Me and you, we've done it in the forest and on a paddle boat in the middle of a lake, and in other places, haven't we? Anyway, not that many people can see us. Even you, you saw only me. It should have been embarrassing, and truth be told, I was for a moment when the gun fired, but then you stop worrying about many things here. As Elise put it once, you want someone to scream, 'Look at them!' I mean, it can get lonely." He glanced at her. *Damn, she still tickles my fancy, after all she did.* "It could be worse for you, the loneliness that is; you are accustomed to so much attention."

"Did she see me?" Beatrice asked, seemingly ignoring his last words.

"No. How could she? You stand better odds of seeing her; you've seen her photos." Indeed, Leo had kept a small album with the few pictures taken in school featuring Elise. Her official photographs from the yearbooks, pictures from a school trip, and a couple he took with his father's Polaroid camera. Some were in color and others in monochrome. This album was always a point of contention. He was not pushing it in anyone's face, as it was something very private, but, for some reason he never learned, the other women in his life felt threatened—by a ghost which they wanted exorcised. But he never allowed this to happen.

"Has she changed?"

"Should that matter?" He tried to put an end to the interrogation.

"Sorry, I guess it shouldn't."

They walked in silence for a while, then Leo announced, "We have arrived."

Beatrice abandoned her downward stare. "That was fast!"

They were standing at the gate of the small gray house in the inner suburb, where she used to live.

"We've been walking for over an hour by my estimate."

"Time flies when I am with you." Beatrice turned at him and hesitantly placed hands on his arms. Then she grabbed and hugged him tightly. "I'm sorry, Leo! I'm so sorry!" Beatrice sobbed. "I was such a fool!"

Leo frowned without moving a single muscle on his face. Wasn't it a bit late for apologies? She never uttered an apology before, and she couldn't have known that they would meet in the afterlife.

Beatrice looked up trying to catch his gaze and continued in a steadier voice, "I saw you as a loser, that my son's dad was a nobody, a tiny cog in a big corporate machine. But I was wrong. I didn't get your lack of praise when everybody else was doing it. I failed to appreciate your personality, your warmth, and ability to love. You may rightfully say that it is too late, but now that I am given another chance to show humility and regret, there I go . . ." She took a deep breath and said, "I am truly sorry, Leo Hans."

That had some effect. Leo raised his arms and embraced her too. "No worries, Bea. I don't hate you. There was a time when I did, but it is in the other world and is long gone. We were young, you were, er, are a beautiful and sexy woman, and shit happens. And Otto helped Eric start his business. I would have not been able to."

Otto was Beatrice's fourth husband, a wealthy guy thirty years her senior. He'd thrown a bone at Eric, which proved to be big enough to help Eric make a breakthrough.

"Will I see you again?" Beatrice asked and let go of him.

Leo thought for a second. He felt no desire for revenge, and the fact that he let her find him and stay meant that he still harbored a soft spot. They'd had a run of happiness together before it all turned sour, but he tended to attach greater weight to the positive. "You will."

Beatrice was crying silently. Leo wiped her tears with a thumb, leaned closer, and repeated, "You will."

She read that as an invitation to exchange a kiss and stretched her neck, but Leo pulled back and said without emotion, "Greetings to your mom."

"Would you not come inside to meet her?"

"Some other time. Bye for now." Leo pushed the garden gate open, inviting her to leave the street. She took a step into the yard and held the gate, still trying to catch his gaze. Leo released his grip, turned around and walked away.

Beatrice sobbed. She would have hated him for this in the old days— how dare Leo turn his back on her! But now she felt nothing but regret. And an overwhelming desire for them to reunite.

POSTSCRIPT

"Why did you thank me when you left yesterday?" Leo asked.

"Are you dumb, or you want to hear it?"

"I guess I am dumb." Leo grinned.

"You didn't send me away," Elise said, her voice soft.

That's right, he didn't. "I fuckin' love you, stupid woman; why would I get rid of you?" Leo squeezed her tightly. "It was never easy for me to admit my feelings, say this openly, yet I am doing it for you. That must mean something."

She cuddled in his arms. "It does. A lot. But I can tell you still have feelings for her. You didn't send her away either." Then as if anticipating criticism, Elise wriggled free and waved her hands in denial. "Not that there's anything wrong with this; I am not indifferent to Steve either . . ."

"You can never become completely indifferent to people you've emotionally been involved with. Love, hate, lust . . ." Leo said.

"What is it with her?"

He took his time looking for the most honest answer. "The hatred's long gone. I am not sure if I should feel sorry for her. She apologized and that struck a chord. Good and bad memories cancel each other out. She's still hot, in my eyes that is, so maybe lust?" Leo speculated. "But I felt humiliated and betrayed during the breakup and that is hard to swipe aside. I tried to correct my mistakes with Olive . . ."

"Thanks again," Elise said.

"Stop thanking me for being honest. Accepting an unpleasant truth is harder than telling it. Besides, being able to be honest is so liberating. Your stint in the old world was short, so you didn't have to go through all its shit. It got so tiresome having to constantly weigh your words, worrying that something you say may make someone feel bad. I am not talking about being rude to people, calling them names. It is about lying to them so they can feel good. Or praising them for being born like that."

"Did you do this with Bea? Praise her for being attractive?"

"No, and she was displeased, I believe. Other men did it all the time, even before we started dating and got married. But she chose me, and I thought that she didn't want all that flattery. She was born beautiful, and I thought that she was against unearned praise. She could eat and not put on a sliver of weight, and other girls envied her for that alone. Her metabolism was pure magic. But I was wrong.

Maybe not in the beginning, however, things changed later." Leo's face morphed, became angry. "It is like being proud for being born in the States or some other popular place. It is a fucking chance, a numbers game, none of those dimwits with the flags have done anything to improve the nation, but they are 'proud' to be American or German or Russian or whatever!"

"Calm down, none of this matter now. Ghosts have no nationality," Elise said and caressed him.

"Are you sure?" Leo laughed, realizing how pointless his rant was. He took her hand, brought it to his lips, and kissed it. "Anyway, I have an idea."

"What?"

"I can try to hook her up with Steve. They know each other, there are no skeletons in their closets, Steve's alone and maybe lonely, and so is she."

"Where's Margot?"

"Margot had apparently met your equivalent—her first boyfriend—and left Steve to hang dry."

"Break is over, back to the instrument!" Elise ordered abruptly and rose to her feet.

Leo swiveled on the stool and got ready to continue playing the piano.

"Try from this bar. Slow at first, it is tricky." Elise pointed at a place in the sheet music in front of him.

"Sure, ma'am!" Leo read the notes and struck the keys. Then he stopped and said, "We shall go to Köennendorf. I don't know what season it is in now, but it surely can be fun."

"After what happened the last time?"

"Yes, why not. It was a thriller."

"I'll think about it," Elise said.

Leo turned back to the piano and started again. Then again stopped. "Did your dad come out?"

Elise glanced away. "No, not yet. I don't know if I should push him or not. He'd be way happier in the open, but Mom worries me. He's right about us—being able to shout out loud how we feel about each other. In a way making love in what's supposed to be public places is a reaction to the limited audience, don't you think so?"

Maybe she was right about this one. He wanted the whole world to know about the two of them, but the whole world here consisted of a bunch of relatives and close friends. When she was alive, she rode the tram on his lap or in his arms and they kissed, unperturbed by other people's gazes and attracting the ire of older folk. But that was OK; the other passengers were angry because they could see.

"Can we make love now?" Leo asked.

"Play!" Elise barked and rolled her hands into small fists.

Leo obeyed.

***

When later in the day he met with Steve, Leo asked, "Can you guess who's here?"

"Maybe," Steve replied.

"OK, then would you do it?"

"Depends." Steve continued the little game.

Leo chose not to engage and said, "Bea."

"Ah, the queen!" Steve said mockingly. "And what wind did blow Her Highness to our humble shores?"

"It is 'majesty.' She died."

"This is pretty obvious. People don't just pop in to check the joint out." Steve pouted.

"She mentioned it, but I forgot."

"So, you met, eh?"

"Don't ask how," Leo said and proceeded to present a slightly redacted version of the encounter. Steve threw a laughing fit, then said with envy, "Why don't these things happen to me?"

"'You alone?" Leo asked.

"Mmm." Steve nodded. "Margot is head over heels with her sweetheart and forgot about old Steve. Everybody else is still alive and kicking. But let them be for now; they will show up someday. No dead first loves or wives here."

"Then who's Dr. Schultz?" Leo remembered that Steve mentioned the name that night in the techno club.

"Ah, no one special." Steve waved a hand dismissingly. "A guy."

"A guy? I thought it was a gal."

"If it were would I bang . . ." Steve hit the brakes and changed the subject. "So, how's the missus?"

"She apologized. Her other hubbies are dead too, but she chose to connect with me for whatever reason."

"You are the only one who's not the product of an asshole. That in my book is a good motive," Steve declared seriously, then asked, "What did you see? Hot or not?"

"She was thirty-something. I think she was thirty-two when we met last. After that it was her mother talking to me. About Eric mostly.

So, yes Bea's still hot as far as I can see, but I don't care. You can have her if you want. I mean, you two can have a good time, without worrying about hurt feelings and egos. She seemed lonely too."

"Thanks, mate, that's generous. In honesty, if she's interested, I wouldn't run away. I envied you when you two started dating!"

"Wait, you wanted Lizzy, and you envied me for Bea? I always thought that I was the one behind on the chick score." Leo flinched.

"And Olive too," Steve added. "Yes, I envied you for them all. I always scored the second best."

"What about Helena, Angie, Elsie, Sophie . . ." Leo began listing Steve's girlfriends, "Your list is longer than my divorce settlement."

"Since when are you a numbers man? Quality, you always beat me on quality."

"Margot is a great woman," Leo said.

"Well, there are exceptions to every rule." Steve crossed his legs on the empty chair opposite his and took a sip from his beer. "Yeah, the girls really liked you, man, but you were so clueless. Even Margot wanted to be with you."

"Margot?" Leo raised his eyebrows.

"Mmm. I lied to her that you were in a relationship," confessed Steve.

"You bastard!" Leo laughed, dismissing the transgression.

"Whatever . . . I appreciate your offer, but I bet a testicle that Bea wants you back and she will fight." Steve sighed. "Take care of Lizzy, as she would have to fend off an invisible assailant. It doesn't matter that Bea can't see her too. What matters is that you can see Bea."

"Liz has nothing to fear."

"But how can she be sure?"

"Liz is not young either, and she can take care of herself."

However, Steve raised another point. "She practically grew up here and she was never in a competition with another woman. Bea is holding all the aces."

"Maybe more of a reason to get together, don't you think?" Leo asked. "Keep an eye on both."

"Even better option—you never see Bea again."

Leo hesitated.

"You see what I mean?" Steve asked. "She's already opened a bridge head."

"Nah." Leo shook his head. "You are being too extreme. Let's slow down and have some fun. What about Köennendorf? Could be summer there, could be winter. So, we will be in for a surprise."

"Sure, why not. I am not particularly busy." Steve sighed. "I will pick you up with the car."

"Where did you get it from?" Leo finally remembered to ask. "There are no other cars here beside yours."

"There are, just that you can't see them. Same as with people," Steve said. "And this one? This one I dreamt up. Just like dreamworld."

Ah, he knows about dreamworld. That's fine, thought Leo, before remarking, "You should update your dreams. This Aventador is circa 2012."

"But she's beautiful, isn't she? That's what matters!" Steve smiled. "I know she's kind of vintage."

"Gotcha!" Leo finished off his beer, got up, and gave his friend a mild pat. "See ya."

ANIMUS

"We are going to Köennendorf," Leo announced and briefly hugged Elise.

"I don't know, I'm still shaken." Elise twitched. "Is Bea coming?"

Leo shrugged. "Dunno, haven't told her yet." Then he turned to her and said, "Let's go and tell her together. This way, you will learn her answer on the spot."

"No, you go alone, there is nothing for me to do," Elise said in an unsteady voice.

"I know what's on your mind. You don't want to be clingy. But I don't want to be alone with her, so please come."

"OK," she agreed.

When they exited the last bend and reached the gate of the small suburban home set inside a lush garden, Leo pushed it open and held it for Elise to pass. Then he caught up with her and moved to lead the way on the narrow path to the single-story building with a glazed verandah.

"Hi, Leo!" Beatrice greeted. She was standing in the open door, wearing a deeply cut blouse, inviting gazes to her cleavage,

"Howzit, Bea." Leo felt the familiar pull on his shirt behind him. He didn't know how to react. What would Beatrice see if he turned to address Elise?

"Who is that?" Beatrice asked in a nervous voice and stood alert.

"Who's who?" Leo took a sudden step back and bumped into Elise. She tripped and landed on her rear.

"Ouch, be careful!" She scrambled back up and dusted off her skirt.

"I see her." Beatrice swung around and said sharply, "Come on in!"

"So can I," Elise said quietly, her eyes enlarged.

Leo moved his gaze from her to Beatrice's back then her again. "Stop!"

Beatrice halted and turned.

"What do you see?" Leo almost barked out the question.

Both women lifted their hands and pointed index fingers at each other. Now that he had confirmed his suspicion, he shrugged, as he had grown accustomed to this phenomenon. His thoughts shifted to the consequences—was this development a complication or a relief? When they stepped inside the living room, Leo made quick introductions, mumbling out the names. Beatrice seemed to be the one who recovered faster from the unanticipated encounter—she swirled elegantly as she left the room, exposing a great deal more of her toned legs. She then halted for a moment and glanced back.

Leo eyed the room, overlaying his memory of it. The pieces mostly fit. The old sofa with matching armchairs and the two otto-mans, the polished wall units, the wrought iron planters—all was here. Only the framed pictures of dead relatives were missing, prob-ably because in this world they were not dead.

Beatrice returned with her mother. Leo was far from thrilled to see his ex-mother-in-law, even though she was always reasonable in her demands of him and appeared to be disapproving of the divorce. She never openly admitted to the sentiment, though, having to at least pretend to support her daughter's decision, a necessity he could perfectly comprehend.

Ulrica rushed to greet him, and he rose from the sofa to recip-rocate.

"Can you believe this place exists? How long have you been dead for? Why didn't you call earlier? How's your mom?" She emptied her lungs, demonstrating their impressive capacity. She was always like that as Leo could recall, alternating between hours-long deafening si-lence and protracted monologues.

"I wouldn't have believed that this place existed even if someone told me that it did. How are *you* doing?"

"Mom, this is Leo's girlfriend," Beatrice said.

"Huh? Where?" Ulrica looked around.

"Right next to your former son-in-law," she clarified, pointing at Elise, who sat quietly with hands crossed in her lap.

"I'm not alone," Leo intervened. "Indeed, but you don't know Elise and you can't see her; neither is she able to see you."

"I didn't know her until moments ago myself. Mom might see her too."

Leo shook his head slowly. "Not necessarily. Richard saw her too and my nephew, but not my stepmother."

Ulrica had quietly withdrawn from the room during the exchange. Beatrice took the opportunity to perform another swirl. "Gonna fetch some drinks, will be right back", she said and stepped out.

"She's gorgeous!" Elise whispered in his ear when he sat back down. "Congrats!"

Leo scoffed.

"So, what now?"

"The same. We invite her to the trip," he answered in a quiet voice.

"There we are!" Beatrice returned with a serving tray in hand. She placed it on the table and pushed it toward her guests, "Here, help yourselves please! I'm not much of a hostess, as Leo already knows."

She sat in the armchair opposite the couple, took a glass herself, and crossed her legs.

Elise paid far more attention to Beatrice than the man in the room seemingly did. Beatrice was a delight to look at, so gracious in her movements and oozed sex appeal. Compared to the ex-wife, she felt like a chicken next to a swan. Knowing that she was seeing Beatrice through his eyes rushed her heartbeat.

Leo, though, looked unperturbed; he accepted the offering by simply saying "Thanks!" and leaned back.

"So, what brings you here?" Beatrice finally broke the awkward silence.

"You, of course," Leo answered.

"Certainly not just to say 'Hi.'" Beatrice sounded indignant.

"Well, actually kind of yes. We want to throw you a welcome party in Köennendorf."

"You two?" Beatrice pointed at them with her finger. Then she added hastily, "By the way, what are you seeing, sweetie?"

Elise sensed the worry in the other's voice and smiled. "Don't worry, you are hot! I see what Leo sees and the same applies to you. It is his memories of us we both see."

"That is a bit rude, don't you think—calling me hot? In the face, I mean; normally it happens behind my back."

"But you are!" Elise insisted. "If that offends you—"

Leo raised his hand. "Please!" After a short pause he continued, "You are both mature women regardless of your looks. Will you try to behave as such? No bickering, eh?"

Elise sighed and squeezed the cushion, trying to keep her mouth shut. Beatrice looked away and sipped from her glass. A faint amount of extra blood made it to the surface of her face, slightly altering its hue.

"Steve Haaspert's here and, well, I came up with this idea to go and spend a day or two in Köennendorf. We all have fond memories of the place. I went there on a school trip with Lizzy. We were already dating, and I sneaked into her chalet and almost got caught. With you it was before the, er, you know, the shit hit the fan; we were still in love. Steve is by himself right now and so appears to be you . . . Of course, this is if you want to . . ."

It took several seconds before Beatrice answered with determination, "Thanks, I'll come! How, er, how does this work here?"

"In different ways," Leo began. "You may wake up in another place or you may teleport. Space seems to bend. Stuff like that. But tomorrow we will try with Steve's car."

"Steve has a car? Here?"

"Yep, that's another thing about this world . . ." Elise's eye twitched. *Don't mention dreamworld, please!* She stepped on his toe under the table, "You can dream up things here." Her face turned red. "Steve dreamt it up. I want to try it too, but it takes time, like a decade or so."

Elise released slowly the breath she'd held for a while.

Beatrice didn't miss the interaction—the other woman hushed her ex and was thereafter relieved. She felt compelled to find out why but couldn't pick the right words with which to interrogate. What followed was more awkward silence; the conversation was dead, and nobody tried to revive it. Leo and Beatrice locked gazes, as if trying in vain to read each other's minds, then that was history too.

When both registered that Elise was no longer in attendance, Leo glanced at the empty spot and rose from the sofa. "I must leave now."

"Where did your girlfriend go?" Beatrice asked.

"Probably home, I told you—weird things happen here."

Beatrice immediately tried her luck. "Maybe she wanted to leave the two of us alone?"

"That is a certainty and also why I must go now." He tried to reach the door, but Beatrice blocked the path. She grabbed his arm and tried to pull him closer.

Leo raised his hand, "Bea, I still don't trust you", he said in a quiet yet firm voice.

She let go of his arm and moved to the side, tilting her head down. Her lips twitched.

"You are still coming, right?"

"Mmm." She nodded.

KÖENNENDORF

Steve scratched his head, thinking *Damn, I screwed up!* His Lamborghini was a two-seater and there were four of them. They had to come up with a plan or hope that management would somehow solve their transportation woes.

"Leo, get in!" he ordered.

Leo sat in the low sports car.

"Now you, Lizzy. You two are all over each other anyway." When she complied, Steve inspected the result and, satisfied, grunted, "OK, this will do. I take you two first, then I'll come back for Bea."

He went to the driver's side, slipped in the seat, turned the ignition on, and revved the engine. Elise frowned and stuck fingers in her ears. Steve paid no attention, revved the engine once more, lowered his door, and pulled carefully from the curb. Their destination was about an hour's drive away in the old world—a short stretch of freeway beyond city limits, followed by a panoramic mountain road with lots of sharp turns.

Steve made the pedal meet the metal as soon as they cleared the city streets and were onto the freeway, occasionally glancing at his friends with a smug expression on his face. Then he transitioned to the narrow winding road, and the ride became even more rough and uncomfortable. Steve was taking the tight turns at high speed—the centripetal force made his passengers lurch in the seat they shared.

"Your driving skills are impressive, mate, but we both are already well aware of this," Leo said as the next turn hurled him and Elise at the door. "Why . . . ugh . . . don't . . . ugh . . . you save the presentation for Beatrice?"

Steve mumbled something in response and entered another turn. The tires screeched, the passengers were tossed to the left, and the seat belt dug into Leo's flesh. He cursed, but the noise drowned his words. Elise said something in his ear, which made him laugh. When the car finally came to a halt in front of a hotel and Steve looked at them, he saw two kids in a tight embrace. "Perverts!" He chuckled.

"Less mass to throw around." Leo grunted and followed Elise out of the car.

"And?"

"What?" Leo made himself older and stuck his head back inside. "Did it work?"

"You've been here for over thirty years. Don't you already know?"

Steve shook his head. "Nope! Never tried it. Never came to mind."

"It did. Therefore, transformations are more shape-shifting than mental projection or the laws of physics won't apply."

"They don't," Steve reminded him. He gripped tightly the steering wheel, closed his eyes, and pictured himself in grade one. He braced for a jolt, but the change was inconspicuous—he found himself sitting on the edge of the seat. He let go of the wheel and rolled backward delivering an awkward kick to the underside of the console when his feet lost contact with the pedals. He cursed and his friend burst into laughter.

"I must remember not to shrink while driving," Steve announced in a high-pitched yet somber voice.

Leo guffawed again and banged his head in the doorframe. "Shit!"

Steve emerged from the car, stretched, pulled out a pack of cigarettes, and lit one. Then he exhaled slowly and chirped, "You deserved it!"

Leo was getting short of breath.

Elise walked to Steve, disheveled his hair, crouched down, and kissed his cheek. "You are cute like this. Why don't you keep the visage?"

Steve looked at both and smiled wearily. "Am I this funny?"

"No, ordinarily no, but you are hilarious now . . ." Leo finally managed to sustain his laughter. "Anyway, why did you stop here?"

Steve nodded in the direction of the marina. "They have sailboats; we can take a ride. I can pilot small ones."

"Small man—small boats!" teased Leo.

"Kiss my small ass!"

"You wish! See you later!" Leo took the bag he shared with Elise from the trunk, threw it over his shoulder, raised his hand straight up, and headed for the hotel. She looked at Steve again, giggled, and rushed to catch up with him.

Steve finished his cigarette and stuck the butt in the nearby sandbox. Then he returned to his car and slipped into the seat. His limbs were too short—he needed to arch forward to get hold of the steering wheel. He closed his eyes and tried to reset. Normally that happened effortlessly. He was puzzled why this time he had to be explicit. He popped eyes open—he was still a boy.

Steve changed tactics. He recalled his thirties, then his last days. He then screamed, "Leo!"

The couple halted and looked back. The chubby boy was standing by the open door, waving hands. "Come back!"

"What is it?"

"I'm stuck!" chirped Steve.

"The car broke down?"

"No, I'm stuck in this shape!"

Leo and Elise hooted with laughter again, but Steve cut them off. "Shut the fuck up! It is no fun! Not anymore!"

Leo snorted and stopped. "Sorry!" He turned to Elise. "What can we do?"

"I don't know. Me and you—we transformed back. Try changing to your teen self to see if that would work."

Steve imagined himself in his late thirties instead. If he also got stuck, at least it would be at an age at which both Elise and Leo would be able to confirm the change. "Well, do I have a moustache?"

His friends shook their heads and spoke over each other.

"Negative!" "Steve, try again!"

Steve remained a boy.

Leo frowned. "This place is cursed!"

"Why?" Steve asked.

"Because!" Leo gave him a brief narration of their ordeal.

"Guys, don't be so negative. This is not a permanent affliction. Steve will reset eventually, maybe soon," Elise implored. She then addressed Leo, "I had a gut feeling that something might again go wrong. But," she paused, "this town is a resort. People came here to be away from their daily grinds for a while. We have no chores, so, maybe throwing us curved balls is how this town is trying to be entertaining, no?"

"Maybe." Steve realized that her proposition wasn't meritless. Leo seemed to be in agreement—he mooed.

"But now, who's going to fetch Beatrice?" Steve asked. "I am way too short to drive."

Leo said, "I'm gonna go."

"I'll come with you!" Elise said quickly.

"This is a two-seater, as you already know. And Steve would need a chaperone," he added with a wink.

Steve tried to kick him but misjudged the distance and lurched backward instead.

Elise retreated. She lifted the bag and extended her hand. "Come, Steve, let's go." Steve sneered, reached into his pocket, and lit another cigarette.

Leo took his place behind the wheel. "Anything I shall know?"

"Just be gentle on the gas. Ah, and you can drive on auto." Steve leaned over him and flipped a switch.

Leo adjusted the seat, lowered the door, started the engine, and drove off.

Steve closed his eyes and tried to revert again. Annoyed by the failure, he dragged his feet behind Elise with a scowl on his face. His shoes were also smaller and his clothes too. *Laws of physics, my ass.* He noticed the bag Elise was carrying and nodded at it. "What's inside?"

"Spare clothes, mostly. You heard the story already, so we decided to take some precautions."

"I see." He stuck fingers in his pocket and exhaled a cloud of blue smoke.

She turned and looked at him. "It is indeed weird to look at a kid smoking."

"Yeah, we are a freak show, Sis!" Steve grunted as his discomfort with his present shape grew.

⁎⁎

"Where's Steve?" Beatrice asked when Leo presented himself at her door.

"He's too short to drive." Leo inspected his ex from head to toe. He couldn't recall her dressing like she was now in their shared days. She looked as if she had just materialized out of the centerfold of a fashion magazine: stilettos, a gray denim mini-skirt and a crop-top, exposing her belly button, which was decorated with a diamond stud. Only the makeup was missing, but she didn't need it anyway.

"Impressive," he congratulated her without emotion.

"Why is Steve too short?" She ignored the compliment.

"Climb into the car. I will tell you on the way."

Beatrice sat, stretched her legs as far as she could in the confined space, then retracted them and buckled up. She tapped fingers on the console and sighed. Leo glanced at her and strained a few facial muscles into a faint smile.

"So, what happened?"

Leo informed her of the events.

"Can you imagine this place?" Beatrice said after a long pause.

"This is a lame attempt at small talk. Better tell me what's on your mind."

She looked down at the wide-brimmed hat resting on her lap. "A lot, but I don't think that I can talk about it."

Leo remained silent for a while. "Is your father here?" he asked when the solemn mood became too thick.

"Thank God, no!" Beatrice shivered and turned her gaze at the landscape outside.

"Sorry, I know the memory causes pain, but I am trying to figure out who is allowed here and who is not. Your father was a brute, my aunt Miriam was a drug addict, Jessica's dad was a drunk . . . none of them are here."

"I'm here."

"Don't be cheap!" Leo snapped.

"Sorry!"

Leo glanced at her. "Don't dwell on the past."

She looked around.

Leo rubbed his nose and rested his hand on the center console, eyes firmly set on the road. Beatrice moved hers on top and applied a mild press. He considered for a moment how to respond, then said, "Don't send me that far back in time, please."

Beatrice swallowed hard and withdrew. Leo gripped the steering wheel with both hands and kept them there until they arrived in the resort town.

**

Elise had glued her nose to the large glass pane of the foyer window, staring at the deserted road. She tensed when the yellow car made its appearance and came to a halt. When Beatrice opened the door and set foot on the ground, Elise's mood took a dive. She looked at the other woman and thought of a commercial: a tall, seductive female emerging from glamorous sports car. She felt small and insignificant again wearing her canvas shoes and oversized shirt.

Steve raised his head from behind the reception desk. "Greetings, sunshine!" he shouted enthusiastically and jumped over the counter with key cards in his hand. He was his usual self both in dimensions and demeanor.

"Steve!" Beatrice produced the obligatory excited smile and spread her arms, "I heard you shrank!"

"That was temporary," he said with relief in his tone. "Here!" He tossed a key card to Leo and turned again at the new arrival.

Leo looked at the card and summoned Elise with a nod. She lifted their bag with both hands and walked to him, occasionally glancing at Beatrice. They entered the waiting elevator. Leo pushed a button, and the short ride began.

The room the card unlocked was disappointing. It was at the end of the corridor, overlooking the service yard of the hotel. The window refused to open, the furniture was worn, and the velvet drapes had bald spots. The bed was large though and looked clean.

"This place doesn't like us very much!" Leo tried to crack a joke. "Probably the worst room in the whole hotel. Do you want me to try to get something better?"

Elise dropped face down on the mattress and let her shoes slip off. "No, room's good," she answered, her face buried in the bed sheets. She pulled a pillow and covered her head with it.

Leo helped himself to a bottle of apple juice from the minibar, drank, and tickled Elise's feet. She turned, sat on the edge, and gave him a grumpy look. Then she reached for the bottle, took a gulp, and handed it immediately back.

"Okay, do you wanna tell me something?" Leo asked.

Elise remained silent for a long, tense moment. "Not really, no." She grimaced at him and added, "I'm fine!"

"No, you are not. It is probably Bea . . ."

"Yes, it is her but let me deal with it on my own!" Elise pulled the small bottle from his hand again.

Leo walked to the minibar and opened another. "You know, her father's not here."

Elise lifted her gaze, perplexed.

"I mean, like Aunt Miriam and my stepmother's dad. There seems to be a link."

"Like what?"

Leo raised his hand palm out. "Can you think of someone who's dead but not here?"

She took a gulp then shook head. "No. What's the link?"

Leo ignored the question. "I must ask Steve."

"About the link?"

"No, about missing dead people."

"What dead people?" Steve asked from the door.

"How did you get in?!" Elise gasped.

"The door was open, I—"

"Then you shall knock!" she retorted.

"Wow, you are a meanie! How out of character," Steve complained. "Anyway, let's go on the boat. I picked one and Her Highness's waiting. And what about dead relations?"

"'Majesty,'" Leo corrected him again.

DIP OUT

Leo repeated the question on their way out. Steve listed two names. The owners seemed to fit the profile Leo had drawn up in his mind.

"Here." Steve directed them to one of the moored mini yachts without his intervention being necessary—Beatrice was standing on the jetty, making the choice of boat quite clear. She was much better at challenging men than he remembered, and she was already a force to be reckoned with when they'd started dating. He stepped in the cockpit first and held out a hand for Elise, then his ex-wife. Elise jumped inside without trouble, dropped the bag, and went exploring.

Beatrice's choice of stiletto slippers proved to be an issue the very moment she set foot on the deck. The boat listed just enough for her to lose balance, and she ended up in Leo's arms; her hat flew off and landed on the cockpit floor. She lingered for a while then wriggled out, "Oops, sorry!"

"You OK?" Leo let go and gestured awkwardly. *She smelled good, she felt good.*

"Thanks to you," Beatrice said, smiling. She lifted her hat and proceeded to the starboard bench.

Steve jumped in the cockpit last with a rope in his hand. "Mate, go release the bow line," he instructed his friend, and began hoisting the main sail. "When I tell you, that is . . ."

Leo threw his shirt on the bench and moved to the front. Released from its captivity, the yacht floated cautiously past its colleagues until it reached deeper waters, where its captain set it completely free. Elise emerged from the hatch, shed her clothes, and threw them in her bag. She lifted the straw hat and let the pair of sunglasses hiding underneath slip down and come to a rest at the root of her nose. She reinstalled the hat, kneeled on the bench, bent and tried to reach the water with hand. Gravity overpowered friction and the hat fell off.

She grasped at it in vain, then stood erect and turned to Steve. "Would you turn around, please?"

Steve heeded her request. When they approached the floating garment, its owner removed the sunglasses, resumed her previous position and tried to grab it, but her arms were too short. Steve was trying not to look in her direction, but on the other side was Beatrice.

Elise kneeled upright, placed hands on her hips and appeared to consider whether to initiate another attempt. She looked around for something to extend her arms with, then stepped on the floor and stuck head in the hatch. Disappointed, she climbed onto the deck and tottered to the bow.

Beatrice followed Elise with her gaze, trying to figure out the other woman's game. She could see the appeal Elise's appearance would generate in the male population and wondered how to beat it without looking cheap. Elise's movements barefoot and, without clothes on, were so natural and clean. She herself would struggle au naturelle. Was it how Leo saw the other—she said something about seeing through Leo's eyes?

She moved close to Steve and nodded at Elise. "What's with her?"

"What do you mean?"

"Why did she disrobe?"

"Ah, she's our resident nudist." Steve laughed. "She does it all the time."

"Aren't you getting aroused?"

"Hah, hah, always!"

"What about Leo?"

"I don't think that he can take his out of her." He chuckled again and winked.

Well, why not . . . She shed off her swimsuit and stashed it in her beach satchel. When she saw the bulge of Steve's crotch, she smiled. "Don't worry, I'd be offended if it didn't happen!" She moved closer, breathed in his ear, and slipped her hand inside his shorts. Steve grinned cheekily. Beatrice abruptly pulled her hand out and slapped the back of his head. "You wish!"

Steve appeared unperturbed. "I do, actually!"

"Mmm." Beatrice smiled seductively, leaned against the cabin wall, and crossed her legs on the bench. Steve returned to steering the boat.

Elise jumped into the cockpit and cast a glance at the other woman under the cover of her sunglasses. She climbed on the bench and looked at the shore. Beatrice was tough competition, very tough. Elise smacked herself mentally—she should not have tried to compete using animalistic sex appeal.

She brought her knees close to her chest and wrapped arms around her legs. She felt like a puppy, which had just been reprimanded by her master. Beatrice was that master. Elise sighed, then reached for the cooler and popped a can. Leo plopped on the bench at her feet and extracted another.

"Why are you all so gloomy? Didn't we come here to have fun?" Steve said. "Anyway, we are dropping anchor now. Leo?"

The boat had reached roughly the center of the lake. The floating garment was barely visible and largely forgotten. The anchor sank into the depths and rested on the rocky bottom. Hordes of fish swam away from the disturbance. Leo bared all and dove in.

"Care for a swim?" Steve proposed to Beatrice.

"Er, I can't. I can't swim."

"You can't? Did they not teach you how to swim at school? Well, you don't have to worry about drowning in this world. Do you wanna try?"

Beatrice hesitated, then firmly declined. "No, not here. Maybe in shallow water."

Elise took off her sunglasses, sat on the deck, and slipped in the water. When she resurfaced, she heard Steve saying, "Suit yourself," then fabric shuffling, then a splash. She frowned and swam toward Leo. When she reached him, she turned and glanced at the lonely figure on the boat. Beatrice had climbed on the cabin's roof and was looking at the mountain peaks, steading herself with the mast.

Elise sighed. Her adversary would look like a renaissance nude painting if not for the hat—a masterfully sculpted body haloed by her long red hair. Botticelli! The scene evoked that painting *The Birth of Venus*. She dipped her head in the water and released air bubbles through her nose. She then let herself float face up and soon bumped into something.

"Do you know that here you can see underwater?" she asked after ascertaining the nature of the obstacle.

"I could see underwater in the old world too," Leo said.

"I know. I mean here you can see clearly without a mask."

"Really?" Leo charged his lungs and dove.

She gasped when he surfaced between her legs and held on to them, then flapped with her hands when his lips made contact with the skin of her inner thighs. When his tongue tickled her vulva, she took a deep breath and held it, so that she would stay afloat.

"Are you sure you don't want to try?" came a call from below Beatrice.

She stiffened in surprise then relaxed. Steve was grinning at her from the water. Maybe if she flirted for a while with him, Leo would pull his head out of his girlfriend's vagina and notice her too! "OK. What do we do?"

"First you come in the water. Come, sit on the deck, and I will help you."

Beatrice followed the instructions and soaked her feet. "Oh, not cold at all."

"No, the surface is warm; it gets much colder in the deep, but we are not going there. Now, come down here."

Beatrice lowered herself as much as her arms allowed, then had a sudden change of heart and tried to reverse, but her palms slipped. Her head bounced off the hull, and she splashed in with a shriek. Steve reacted instantly and seized her. The water closed over them and gushed into the frenzied woman's gaping mouth, converting her scream into a desperate gurgle.

She clutched Steve with all limbs and convulsively breathed in as they continued their downward travel. Steve thrust up with the full force of his legs and cursed in pain—his heels hit a firm surface. Beatrice became heavy in his arms. She sensed the change and set her feet down. She let go of him, staggered, kneeled, and started coughing violently, trying to expel the water she had inhaled an instant ago.

Steve kneeled next to her and patted her back repeatedly.

"Whe . . . Where are we?" Beatrice wheezed between bouts of coughing.

The man looked around—they were in a meadow, surrounded by pine trees. The white caps of the mountains peeked down over the treetops.

"Not in the water for sure," Steve stated the obvious.

"But . . . how?"

"We were teleported."

"What?" Beatrice asked and spat.

"This place . . . it is not letting anyone get badly injured or killed. Maybe it sensed that you would drown and teleported you to safety, and since we were in an embrace, I followed. Do you know that you can fly here?"

Beatrice could breathe almost normally now. She sat back, wrung out her long hair, and tied it in a loose knot. "What are you talking about?"

"Stuff . . . I mean I was frightened too." He sat on the grass and stretched his legs.

"And now? How do we get back?" Beatrice turned her head surveying the landscape. The lake was not in view.

"We use the peaks as a landmark." Steve pointed at the distant white caps. "Moving away from them should take us back to the water. By the looks of it, we will have to walk for a while. Can you do that?"

Beatrice nodded.

Steve jumped and pulled her up. "This way. The lake must be down there." She took a cautious step, followed by another. The grass was soft. She relaxed and grabbed Steve's hand.

Soon they were between the trees. Beatrice grew fascinated by the massive trunks around her. At least two people were needed to circle most of them, sometimes more. The real forest was much younger, though she had no way of knowing. She was a city dweller in her lifetime, going out in the mountains on a few occasions in her distant youth—all school outings. She grew up in a poor household where vacations were not on the list. During summers she stayed home, playing in the garden when she was young and getting bored to her core when she grew older. Her friends from that time often traveled with their parents and life was dull, particularly for an otherwise popular girl. She started working during school breaks to help make ends meet and make some cash for herself and went on her first proper vacation with Leo, but it was on the Spanish coast. True, she'd gone to the woods with Leo once. Her memory of the forest, however, was completely blank.

She let go of Steve's hand and approached a tree. The pine aroma was unexpectedly pleasant. She touched the bark and drove her hands down the rough surface. This triggered a sense of tranquility and peace. She went to another, much smaller tree and hugged it. She remembered the derogatory "tree hugger" reference for nature activists and laughed—hugging trees actually felt good.

Her neck itched; the kind of itch indicating an observer. She turned sharply. Steve was the one looking, "Bea, let's go, shall we?"

Beatrice nodded and they continued their walk amongst the trees. There was no path to follow; the sun was obscured by the crowns making it hard to maintain bearing. She wondered why she was not getting thirsty after all this walking and why her feet did not hurt, since she wore no shoes.

Her mind shifted to fairy tales—walking through this ancient forest was so reminiscent of one. Then she noticed Steve's dangling dick and giggled silently. Penises looked funny when not erect, like sausage links suspended between the legs, but walking while rigid would probably be uncomfortable. Why didn't God make them fully retractable? Thinking of erect, she realized that she had not had proper intercourse in ages. Her last husband, Otto—the prick never touched her once, even before the accident, which left him wheelchair bound. Was he dysfunctional? He liked to watch, though. He made her perform for him with the damn doll. But truth be told, she was not attracted to him. She married him so she could piss off number three—Otto was much wealthier and influential than Christian. Then the menopause came.

She stole another glance from Steve; the man was concentrating on finding their way. She liked him—back in the day and now—but never considered him for anything beyond being best friends with Leo. But Leo was with his little girlfriend. Beatrice pictured Elise as she was kneeling on the bench, then brushed the thought aside and weighed Steve's rear.

Not bad, she thought. She felt desire bubbling up. She knew that he was ready because he had proved that on the boat. Her nipples stiffened, and she felt the temperature rising between her thighs. They were in a lush forest, walking as nature had them on strangely soft and aromatic pine needles. Elise liked walking, as nature had her . . .

"Stephen!" she called.

Steve stopped and turned around, looking past her. "Yes?"

"Er, I changed my mind."

"About what?"

"About . . . Will you look at me?"

Steve looked straight into her eyes, not a whisker up or down.

She sighed, took the few steps required to close the distance between them, lowered head onto his chest, and hesitantly touched his penis. It seemed to twitch. She closed her eyes, her heartbeat increased. Steve was standing still, but she felt his desire in her hand. She squatted, popped his dick into her mouth, and rolled her tongue around the glans. It expanded fast.

"Oy, oy, oy!" Steve stood on his toes, then relaxed and sighed. "Ah!"

Beatrice looked up, grabbed his hands, and pulled him down. "About that." Steve seemed conflicted, but his reaction was a lustful one and she didn't care about romances right now; it was her body that wanted him. She stood on her knees and kissed him on the mouth. His tongue rolled in; he tasted good, manly. Steve's hands were running over her flanks and back, then he squeezed her buttocks, his erect member seeking entry inside her.

Beatrice pivoted, stood on all fours, and closed her eyes in anticipation. Steve glided in with ease and moaned then slapped her behind. She reached and grabbed his hand. He gently freed it and lifted both arms above his head, rocking from the waist down as if performing a crude erotic dance. His movements inside her were a pleasure she had not experienced for so long. The strokes merged into a stream of delight flowing throughout her body. She released her vocal cords from the decades of self-imposed control. The measured huffs turned into loud moans. She grimaced and arched her spine, tears bubbling from her eyes.

His dick felt so short. She wanted it to go right through her. And she wanted to kiss the pussy of the little one. Beatrice's body began to shiver, her head dropped, she bit the pine needles and dug her fingers into the soft soil. Steve grabbed her by the waist and increased the speed and thrust. Beatrice squeezed her eyes, her heart racing, her breathing fast and loud. Steve slapped her rear again, but this time she didn't mind, as long as he kept dancing.

She felt rumbling in her groin, then a volcanic eruption. She issued a loud moan and arched again. Steve pulled out and ejaculated. She sat on her heels and felt a warm streak traveling down and through her backside split. She shivered and clutched her hands at her chest.

Steve moved to her side and glanced at her with a shy question in his eyes.

INFIDELITY

Leo scrambled onto the deck with considerable effort. Elise swam to the stern and climbed the short ladder.

"Why didn't you tell me?" Leo asked, brow furrowed.

"You didn't ask!" Elise laughed and quashed his anger with a kiss. "I wonder what happened to Steve and Beatrice?" She checked the other side of the boat.

"They didn't drown, for sure."

"Maybe they dove?" She kneeled again on the bench, bent over, and tried to make out human figures in the deep.

Leo dragged his gaze over her wet skin. Water droplets sparkled like incrusted gemstones under the playful sunrays, some of them rolling and merging and then departing for a brief trip to the floor. Her provocative pose triggered his deprecated instinct to procreate, and a memory of a Muslim friend of his explaining why women had to cover head to toe and were not allowed to stand in front of men—they were allegedly too hard to resist. *C'mon*, he thought, *it is not that difficult to look away*. His gaze moved to the shore, then he searched around for his shorts, begging his dick to behave. Then he glanced at her again, and his heart pounded.

Elise looked over her shoulder. Her gaze traversed from his face down to his crotch.

"What are you waiting for?" Her voice was soft and so inviting. She turned her head toward the shore and took a deep slow breath.

The hell, they were not in a mosque and butt naked and both willing. Maybe they should do it in a mosque! Leo glided his hands down her flanks in a slow, probing motion. Goose bumps popped on the surface of her skin, but her pose remained unchanged. Leo bent and ran his tongue up her spine; his hands traveled and fondled her breasts. The nipples had already been standing to attention. When he touched them and rolled them with his pinched fingers, she shivered and sighed.

Leo kissed her back below the shoulder blades and squeezed gently her breasts, then glided his hands down to her abdomen. She huffed quietly and tilted her head up, water from her wet hair draining down onto her skin. Leo pulled his scooped fingers up and fondled her breasts again, then kneeled and separated her buttocks. Elise gasped. He ran his tongue from her vulva all the way up to the beginning of the split, then returned and vibrated the tip over her ring. Her body twitched, and she arched her spine in anticipation. He performed one long run of his tongue along her groove, rose to his feet, and found his way inside her. She breathed in noisily and grasped the edge of the boat's hull. Leo swung slowly, allowing the sparkles to fade away and a demand for more to rise.

He ran his hands over her hips, then held her waist, pulled almost all the way out, and halted there. Elise emitted a short high-pitched moan and waited, then began to rock, subtly at first. The boat was too big to follow immediately. By the time it did, and splashes of water could be heard, Elise let go of the hull's edge and the tearful expression on her face, arched back and grabbed Leo's head, panting . . . Leo remained still for a while. The slippery warmth alone eventually triggered him, and he came. She felt the squirt and glowed. He kissed her neck, then her cheek, when she turned her head. She smiled, "Yeah. It never gets old, not when you are in love."

Leo pulled out, sat on the bench, scooped her with his arm, and tried to pull her closer. She resisted giggling, looked down at him, and asked, "Can you pilot this thing?"

Leo let go of her. "Not as well as Steve, but I will manage."

She sat back on her heels, returning her gaze to the shore where it remained for a long while. Her entire body swayed with the boat, her arms held straight, hands clutching and squeezing the bench backrest. She was restless again—he could tell. As he nudged his mouth open to emit a soothing word, she turned, slipped down on the bench, and announced softly. "Bea scares me."

"Why?"

"She's very attractive, even more than I expected, and she is not dumb."

"Well, she is attractive indeed, but so are you. You two are simply different." Leo tugged her nearer, successfully this time.

Elise cuddled up and continued, "I tried to compete with her today."

"How? What did you do?"

"You didn't notice?"

"Nope."

"I tried to play seductress, but she smashed me flat. Like a fly."

"You mean by her getting naked too?"

Elise nodded and gazed down, blushing.

Leo didn't speak immediately. "I didn't know that it was a contest nor who started it. It could easily have been her. She's competitive and likes showing off. Flaunting her body is entirely her style."

Leo paused. How best to tell her that there was nothing to worry about. Beatrice using her feminine charm was also annoying. And stupid. She knew of his propensity to root for the underdog, which in this case was Elise. Maybe he shall talk to both.

"How is she now?" Elise asked before he could speak again.

"She seems changed. No longer condescending. Remorseful. She apologized."

"Are you buying it?"

Leo did not hesitate. "Yes."

"Why?"

"Are there any bad ghosts here? I have yet to see one. She must've truly owned her sins to be allowed in."

"Now you sound like a preacher, but I see your point." Elise sighed.

"Come here, sit." Leo directed her to his lap. She moved over, straddled him, held his hands, and started rubbing his palms with her thumbs.

"Remember when you said that Steve was old news? That can be said about Bea too, old news, half of them bad."

She tried to laugh.

Leo continued, "May I share a lesson I learned in the previous life?"

"Mmm." Elise nodded.

"You shall never compete over a person."

"Why?"

"Because you may lose yourself. I mean just think what we do when we compete over someone. Is it really doing our best or something else?"

Elise offered no answer.

"Well, it is something else. We try to be what we think the other person wants us to be. We masquerade. And if we win the competition, we must keep doing it or else. An act with no end." He paused for a second. "There is one exception though . . ."

Elise stopped fidgeting, "Yes?"

"It is when we are competing with ourselves, like—can I do the shit I'm already doing better? But in this case, it does not apply. So please be yourself. And have more confidence in me. You surely remember the first techno club we went to—"

"Yes, what about it?" she asked in a worried voice, her body twitching just a bit.

"I saw Steve's advances and I was happy when you turned him down. My ego was exhilarated! I can certainly do the same for you!" Leo smiled confidently.

Tears filled Elise's eyes, ready to overflow. She dropped her head and bumped it into his shoulder, leaving him perplexed. Why was she so touched by his admission, when it was nothing special? It is not that hard to do simple shit for the people you love. He was not interested in Beatrice, as that train departed a long time ago and eventually turned into a wreck. Would he have sex with her again? Yes, that was the one thing that went right between them until the very end. Could he refrain? If Lizzy were like the other Liz, he would not want to, but she gave him all he wished for and even more in this department. And they were doing other things together, and had long conversations or none at all, and he was content either way.

Elise lifted her head and looked straight into his eyes, as if resigned to whatever might come next. "I didn't." The tears were running unrestrained now. "You passed out and we fucked . . ." She wobbled backward and sank to the cockpit floor, still holding his hands. Then she let go.

"Oh!" Leo momentarily lost control of his lower jaw, letting it drop a bit, but recovered quickly. "Well, we were high. Maybe you mistook him for me?" he joked. "OK, you didn't." He sighed dramatically, then said, "But so what? I said it was OK, didn't I?" His eyes darted around. He bit his lips, trying to think. His ego was hurt, but he had to hide that for her sake! "Liz!" he called and stroked her hair. Silence. "Liz!"

She did not respond, just rolled to the side, wrapped her arms tightly around her knees and hid her face, her shoulders shaking as she sobbed.

He joined her on the floor, spread his legs, and began servicing himself.

Elise looked at his crotch with wet eyes, pouted, and furrowed her eyebrows. "What are you doing?"

"Wanking!"

"Why?"

"To distract you!"

She laughed wearily, squeezed herself as close to him as possible, and took over the job. By the time the canon fired, Elise seemed to have mostly calmed down. The bizarre distraction he created had worked! She rested her palms down on her knees, dropped her gaze, and remained still as if performing a religious ritual.

Leo reached into the bag, lit a cigarette, inhaled, then passed it on. "Time to go back onshore, I guess." He took another drag from the cigarette she held for him and stood up. His sailing skills were not up to par. He managed to get to the marina, but for the final stretch he lowered the sails, jumped in the water, line in his hand, and swam to the outermost vacant jetty, where he pulled the boat.

"You should get sailing lessons from Steve," Elise said and disembarked.

"I like motorboats," Leo answered. "But they seem to be as rare here as cars."

"You can dream up one!"

"Can you do it for me? You are already a pro!"

"I don't think so. The dreams are personal."

"Then I must get some books. Remember what Pete said?"

"I must tell you something else." Elise held his arm.

Leo stopped and turned toward her. If he were a cat, his ears would be aimed squarely at her mouth, waiting eagerly for the words to emerge.

"Pete has been asking me out. I mean, he's been showing up on the street or at the door, bringing flowers and small gifts."

She did not say that she had accepted, and it was uncool to ask.

"But don't worry, I kept my promise! I said no!"

"You never promised anything," Leo said, looking at her in confusion.

"It was implied!"

He hugged her and they proceeded to their worn-out hotel room. Leo glanced at the parking lot. The yellow car was still there; maybe that applied to Beatrice and Steve too.

AMICABILITY

Back in the forest, Steve spread his arms and panted. "Wow! You are truly a beast!" He was shocked by Beatrice's sudden pull of all stops. If she did this with Leo, the heartache she caused later was a fair price to pay.

"I haven't had a decent fuck in thirty years! I've forgotten what it felt like to be a woman, to experience orgasms. I realized I had a chance," she said.

"A strong one, I must admit!" Steve chuckled and fondled her thighs. "Isn't it amazing how soft the pine needles are?"

Beatrice leaned forward, spread her palms on the ground, and tried to extract some more sparkle from his softening appendage. When this failed, she arched back with a fistful of needles, rubbed them in her palm, and sprinkled his chest, smiling. "Yes, indeed."

"Thanks!" Steve said.

"You are welcome! A word of caution though—on my side it was just lust, so if you are expecting more, I cannot deliver." Then she corrected herself, "I may not be able to deliver."

"What, you don't like me at all? Not even a tiny bit?" Steve asked with a cheeky smile in his eyes.

Beatrice laughed. "Well, I do, but love?"

"Who's talking about love? We are ancient adults, museum pieces; love is for the young and immature."

"Is it?" She dismounted him and rolled to his side. "What now?"

The day was approaching retirement. The sun was gone, and the patches of sky visible between the foliage carried a strong orange tint.

"If we fall asleep, this place will usually take us back home, but this isn't guaranteed. Anyway, we will not die here, as our second time is yet to come."

"You know, I am getting cold," Beatrice said and moved closer to him. "What second time are you talking about?"

Steve sighed. He wasn't in the mood to discuss the drift. He never was, as the thought of disappearing into the unknown made him anxious. But he nevertheless obliged.

"I see. And how long does existence last in this world?" she asked.

"Difficult to tell. I can't put a number on it. Why?"

It was Beatrice's turn to sigh. "I am truly sorry for what I did to Leo, and I want to be with him again . . ."

"Well, that would not be easy, and, if you think you are not up to a good start."

Her body stiffened. "What do you mean?"

"We just had sex, didn't we?"

"He'd understand. He and I are not married, and he has his sweetheart . . ."

Steve refrained from disclosing that Leo practically offered her to him.

"Anyway, I thought that I may be able to wait out. I don't want to wedge myself between them." She pulled her legs underneath her and continued angrily, "Ah, the little one drives me nuts! All her cuteness and childish mannerisms! Flaunting her skinny ass!"

Steve spoke gravely. "The one you call little is older than you."

"Exactly. Can't she act more mature?"

"Maybe she can't."

The silence became thick and the forest dark.

"Tell me, how did you live, and how did you die?"

Beatrice did not respond immediately. Then her bitter laughter filled the forest. "I got murdered!"

"What!" Steve jerked upright and tried to make out her features in the twilight.

"I got killed by my own son!" Her laughter subsided, and her words came out with extreme sadness.

"Eric?" Steve asked in horror.

"No, not him. Eric is a gentle soul." Beatrice's next words were almost a screech. "That brat Jansen! The asshole had gambling debts and came to beg for money. Again! One point two million euros down the fucking drain! We argued, I said 'no more,' he turned blue with rage, and hit me. With a statuette. That was it." Beatrice took deep breaths. "Otto, my last hubby, he was old. A few million were my share of his estate when he died. Jansen knew. His father had already cut him out, so he kept coming to me to pay his debts and living expenses. And Otto, he was weird too. For eighteen years of marriage, he didn't touch me once. He ordered me to masturbate in front of him and make love to a doll while he watched. Or else no cash for me! Ah, I was so dumb! And greedy! I sold myself, no? Anyway, since you asked, my life was no pleasure cruise. My father beat me up, and my husbands mistreated me as well." She gulped. "Except Leo. Damn! I humiliated him . . . Maybe it was karma . . . The years with him were my best. But I was always a trophy wife. I felt like that, even with your friend, he looked so proud and smug!"

Steve had already sensed her need to drop some emotional weight off her chest and was intrigued by her story. "Please, continue," he said calmly, when the silence stretched for too long

"Leonardo and Christian paraded me around, showered me with expensive gifts, then beat me up to a pulp. Then they sent me overseas to recover." Beatrice began sobbing. "After Leonardo, I thought that I could handle a bully, and Christian appeared civilized. But he was even worse. Do you . . . you don't know what it is like? Do you? Fuck!" She started sobbing uncontrollably.

Steve moved closer and put his arm around her shoulders. She leaned on him and continued to cry quietly in the dark. He detected a change in her skin—it felt thin and wrinkled. He took hold of her hand; it belonged to someone old. She had transformed! He was unconvinced that he wanted to see her now and was grateful that the moon was new, and the forest canopy was too thick to let the starlight through.

Beatrice regained her composure. "Anyway, this is my cross to bear. Sorry to have bothered you . . ." She snorted once and seemed to rub her nose with her hand, but it was too dark to tell for sure. "Promise me one thing though—you will never ever tell them any of this. I don't want their pity, or anybody's for that matter. Not even yours! Thank you for listening. And we can fuck again if you want. On one condition."

"What?"

"We don't hide!"

"Good with me!" Steve agreed promptly, envisioning his friends' public places escapades. Then a doubt crawled into his mind as to what she meant. He took a mental note to resolve the ambiguity.

"Sex always made me forget my troubles for the moment. Even when I was with that doll. Making love to a doll . . . Heh! I turned it into art. Otto loved it! Weird—it made me proud." She chuckled. "Perhaps sex was my substitute for drugs and alcohol. I should have done something about this while still alive, not wait until I died," lamented Beatrice. "So, I must catch up now! Are you ready?" Her voice became excited, she reached for his penis and squeezed it in her hand.

"Bea . . ." he wondered whether to tell her that she had transformed.

"What?"

"It's OK!" Steve was again immensely grateful that the night was so dark.

*
**

In the morning, Steve caught his breath, opened one eye, looked to his right, then breathed out the air with relief. Beatrice had reverted—she was the proverbial sleeping beauty in this instant, and he did not want to look away. Unlike last night, when he did not want to look at all. They were still in the forest though and still naked. Steve saw shimmering reflections of the sun between the tree trunks. Must have been the lake.

He gently shook Beatrice's shoulder. "Sleeping beauty, time to rise."

Beatrice took her time. She rolled onto her back and stretched with her eyes still shut, then revealed them, one by one. She sat up and slowly looked around. "Wow! It was all real!" she exclaimed.

"In a way—yes, and I hope that you have no regrets."

She placed her hand over his and smiled. "No regrets, no."

"Good! Then let's hit the road now. The lake seems to be down there." He pointed at the flashes. "For now!" He helped her get up.

"For now?"

"Yeah, did you not notice that this place morphs? By noon the lake may be gone."

"Ah, this world is really weird, no?"

The chat continued all the way to the hotel, revolving mainly about the many peculiarities of the realm and its surprising choice to remain static and let them find the place. When they entered, Elise was standing on a chair in the middle of the lobby, next to a table, on which were jars of paint and Leo was hard at work with his brush, placing what seemed to be finishing touches to the artwork on her skin.

"You really like your body paint," Steve quipped.

"Yes! I am a savage; it turns me on!" Elise grinned and shuffled her fingers.

"Welcome back, I hope you enjoyed the night," Leo said without turning his head to look at them.

"Weren't you worried?" Beatrice asked indignantly, then gasped and rushed to the waiting elevator, waiving the need for an answer.

"What are you up to?" Steve said and scratched his groin.

"Did you catch papillon d'amour?" Elise winked.

"What?" He looked down instinctively, then giggled. "Maybe, remains to be seen."

"Lucky you!" She laughed again, then turned to Leo. "Hey, my wings are getting tired, aren't you going to be done soon?"

"I'm doing your boobs now, can't you feel? You can fold the wings." Leo added a few more strokes, stood back, checked his work from a distance, and said, "There! Done. Just let it dry out for a few minutes."

"I asked what's up?" Steve repeated.

"It was meant for last night. Like masquerade ball . . . We prepared costumes—"

"Yea, we made costumes for you and Beatrice too; they are in the room. Wanna check them out?" Elise interrupted excitedly. Then, as if afraid that her enthusiasm was excessive, she changed her tone to be more subdued. "You know, existence here can be uneventful, that was the point."

The elevator bell dinged, and the doors opened, revealing an angry and still-*au naturelle* Beatrice. "Fuck! I can't get into the room! Where's my bag?" She cursed again and swiped the lobby with her gaze.

Elise jumped from the chair, took what appeared to be a burlap sack with both ends cut open, pulled it up and fastened it around her waist with a wide leather belt.

"Come!" she grabbed Beatrice's hand and pushed her back in the elevator. "I have something made for you to wear. I'm afraid you don't have much choice now, even if you don't like it."

"But why?" Beatrice mumbled.

The elevator arrived on the desired floor and split its doors open. "Because . . ."

Beatrice's dress was made of peacock feathers with large, leg revealing cuts and a black mesh top. She slipped into it and looked around for a mirror, forgetting that there would be none.

Elise stepped back and nodded approvingly. "Yeah, you do look good!" She then reached inside the bag again and produced a pair of stilettos. "Here, you know how to wear these." She then sighed, clutched her hands behind her back, and looked down at her feet. "Bea," she began with a shaky voice, "I want to tell you something . . ."

Beatrice looked at her. "Yeah? Me too!"

"Well . . . go ahead then."

"Stop trying to charm the dudes with your childish mannerisms!" she barked.

Elise cowered. "I am not! Seems mannerisms go with the body."

"Then age up! Steve said that it is something everybody here eventually gets to be able to do."

Elise turned head from side to side. "I'm afraid that *I* can't."

"What do you mean you can't?" Beatrice squinted.

Elise sat on the edge of the bed, spread her legs, and pushed the burlap skirt down. "I can't," she said again. "You must have lived the age; you must have a memory of it. I died barely eighteen. This is how old I can go. Funny—I am actually older than you, but this body," she knocked on her chest, "sets the rules. Mannerisms and shit. If I had acting talent, I might have been able to do better, but I don't."

"Ah!" Beatrice mumbled. "I didn't know this."

"Well, now you do. And what I wanted to tell you was that I am not going to compete with you over Leo. I will let him decide who he wants to be with. Me, you, both, or neither. I waited for Leo for over sixty years. I am shit scared to lose him now, and he knows what I went through in the beginning, but I don't want him to be with me out of pity. Things are different now. I can go back to Steve or to my dreamworld . . ." Elise looked down, her cheeks changing color to a shade of red.

Beatrice stood silent for a while. "I think that he really loved you," she said calmly. "He always kept this little photo album close to him. The one with your pics. I was jealous, but he said there was no way that he would part with it. He was pissed that I was being resentful of a dead girl. Maybe I was prescient that you two would meet again one day and put me firmly in the backseat."

"You seem to think too much about yourself and your feelings," Elise noted.

Beatrice pulled the lone chair from its spot by the wall, also sat and nodded. "I guess that you are right. I was selfish and I still am. I realized that Leo was the guy I wanted to be with, when my second marriage fell apart. He had not yet remarried, but I was too afraid to go back and ask for forgiveness. I thought I would hand him an advantage. Not even pride, it was fear. And I cannot ignore your determination to overcome your own fear and be so generous. But I felt so fucking lonely . . ." Beatrice gazed away.

"You don't know loneliness, Bea." Elise frowned.

Beatrice nudged her eyebrows higher.

"I was alone in this world for decades. With my grandparents and nobody else. But it is not about me now . . ."

"How's sex with Leo?" Beatrice asked out of the blue.

"Great, why?"

"I slept with Steve last night. He's a bit rough."

"Yeah, and he only wants to do me in the bum," Elise agreed.

"You did anal sex?"

"Yeah, and with Leo too, but Leo's different. Always gentle and try- ing to be even."

"What do you mean by 'even'?"

"Well, he's trying to give me as much pleasure as I give him. In any possible way."

"Yeah, that was Leo." Beatrice sighed then became animated. "Can you show me?"

"Show you what?"

"You know, how to do anal. I've never tried it."

Elise was at a loss. Where did this abrupt change come from? "Now?" she asked, dumbfounded.

Beatrice nodded keenly.

"I would need a dildo and lubricant . . ." Elise mumbled. "I don't have either one here. Unless we call the boys? No . . . Sorry, I can't . . .".

Beatrice squatted while staring incessantly at Elise's face, lifted Elise's hand, fanned the fingers, and drew them one by one into her mouth.

Elise felt the tickles of desire. The woman in front of her was gorgeous, but she pushed the lust aside and said softly, "No, Bea, not now."

Beatrice kissed her palm and let go of the hand. "Sorry. I must confess that you turn me on. I thought it was my being jealous of you, but last night with Steve, I was with him, but I was thinking of you." She returned to the chair. "I am a narcissist." She laughed. "And you remind me of myself."

Beatrice seemed to slip into a daydream—a still smile, her eyes focused on some indistinct point on the wall. Elise looked at the red- head and suddenly felt relieved, being capable of breathing again without anxiety. She should celebrate! She checked the minibar for sparkling wine, popped the small bottle open, and rose on her toes when the wine started spilling on the floor. She glued her lips to the bottle's neck, slurped in the liquid, glanced at Beatrice, and swore through the bubbles, "Ah, crap, I'm getting pissed!"

"What now?" Beatrice returned to the present.

"You transformed!"

"And?"

"You are blonde and still curvier, with bigger boobs than me! How old are you now?"

Beatrice gleamed. She ignored the question and said, "We took too long. Let's go back!"

Elise raided the bag again, took out more clothes, and followed the triumphant Beatrice. In the elevator, Beatrice looked at her, grinned, and pinched her cheeks. *If that made her happy, so be it,* thought Elise.

"Mmm, you are so sweet!" Beatrice chirped, clearly exalted by her current appearance.

Elise looked away and rolled her eyes. The elevator door opened, and they stepped out onto a street. Beatrice hurriedly retreated into the cabin and tried to pull Elise, but her fingers glided over the other's bare skin. The elevator descended two more floors then came to a stop.

When the doors opened again, Beatrice saw the familiar interior of the nearby shopping mall. So, this is what it was like to live here. She stepped out and walked slowly toward the exit, past storefront windows displaying wares. At each one she faced the glass and checked her reflection. She made out her body in the feather dress, but the face was just a dark blob. The hair—the color of her hair—was also imperceptible. All she could see was that the hair was long.

Beatrice reached the food court and dropped into a chair. In front of her was a serving of french fries and a fizzy drink. Her stomach gurgled. She pulled a chip from the pack and chewed it, then another. The empty expanse was suffocating. She got up, ran back to the elevator, and began hitting the button with her palm; she wanted to go back!

The machine remained indifferent to her plea. Beatrice's throat tightened. She leaned against the brushed-steel door feeling lonely and sad. Was she falling in love with a girl? She was terrified by the thought, but she could not lie to herself—she did like Elise, she wanted to be with her! That was crazy! A day ago, she loathed her, but now . . . what had changed? Beatrice was utterly confused; she slumped to the floor and buried face in her palms. She was shaken by the intensity of her emotions, yet content. It was so weird. Did she feel . . . alive?

She missed the *ding.* When the elevator doors parted, she tumbled into the cabin, and the back of her head met the floor with a thud. When she looked up, her heart melted at the sight of three stupid faces with stretched mouths.

Beatrice also smiled. She didn't love just the little one—she loved them all! She moved her gaze to the area beneath Elise's burlap skirt. "You have no underwear."

Elise grinned. "Neither have you!"

THE PROPOSAL

Elise crawled and hovered over Leo on her palms and knees. Leo tried to nudge her further up so his lips could reach her nipples, but she dug into the soft yet sturdy grass. He stretched his neck instead, they exchanged a brief kiss, and he resumed his pose, staring at the sky. She silently pierced him with her gaze for a while. Then she said, "Tell me more about your wives."

"You already know number one; what is there to tell?"

"Your side of the story for a starter."

"Well, Beatrice was a PA and I was a junior designer—"

"What's a PA?"

"Personal assistant, or secretary as the term was when you were alive. Of the boss. She was a honeypot for males, as you might have deduced, and the rumor was that the boss was banging her, but it didn't stop colleagues from asking her out on a date, bringing flowers and shit. I was dating Dulcinea then . . ."

"Dulcinea?" Elise enlarged her eyes. "Like in *Don Quixote?*"

"Yeah, she was pissed by everybody asking the same moronic question!" retorted Leo.

"Okay, sorry!" Elise giggled.

"Some parents are really dumb, condemning their kids to ridicule and asinine jokes with their poor choice of names. Anyway, I always hated standing in a queue. Dulcie was a gentle soul, and I cared about no other. We often gathered for drinks after work. Beatrice was there too with her entourage. We went to the old pub on Barrent Street, you know it. With time, she moved closer to my spot at the table, we started talking there, then at work. We became friends. I broke up with Dulcie, the relationship was short-lived, and I told Bea. She then suggested a date. It was great, and I'd dare say the same as what we have now. She fell pregnant by accident—the condom tore—so we decided to marry and have the kid. We moved to my place. Mom made room for us and went to live with her boyfriend. We had a great run. Then I went to South Africa in '95. She stayed behind on account of Eric, as he was still very young. I was flying home every couple of months for a week. It was lovely, this time, but in retrospect, this was perhaps when the seeds of separation were sown. Aren't you getting tired?"

She was still hovering over him, eating up his words.

"Yeah, I think I am." Elise spread his legs as far apart as she could and nestled between them. "Please, proceed."

"She wasn't happy when I told her I had an offer to work overseas, but I was eager to experience the world, and it was a promotion I couldn't get at home. Maybe I should have stayed with them." Leo sighed, sat up, and tried to reach her lips, but his body failed to flex to the required degree. He returned to horizontal and resumed his monologue, "When Eric turned two, they came to stay with me, but she was restless, and they flew back home after six months. Then I got a job offer from Toyota and this was when we had our first big fight; it was before I had accepted. She accused me of being selfish and only interested in my career, then she called me a loser; it was a mess. The next day she called to apologize and gave me the nod. Thus, we ended up in Japan. Eric was older, and she joined me. They both did." Leo paused. She saw him nibbling on his lips.

"You are noticing where you went wrong, aren't you?"

"Mmm." He moved his head in confirmation. "Perhaps. Would you have come if you were in her shoes?"

"I don't know. To a country so different and so far away, with a small kid . . . I think that I would!"

Leo remained silent so she had to prod him to continue. Literally, as she stuck her index finger in his thigh. "Talk!"

"She was a stay-at-home mom, obviously. I tried to be there for her, but with the Japanese work culture that was hard. She was lonely and she was picking fights. I could understand and I offered to resign so we could go back home, but she then changed her tune. We went to a couple of company functions, and she became the star, as you might expect. That curvaceous, green-eyed, European redhead; she was what many of them dreamt about. She was the embodiment of their favorite anime heroine, only without the katana. I was junior staff, but we got invitations to events alongside top brass. She was surrounded by admirers, and she started leaving me behind. I told her about my discomfort, but she attributed it to my being jealous and selfish. The colleagues began talking too—in English, so I could understand—that I didn't deserve a woman of this rank, that I was too ugly and insignificant for her."

The strain in his voice was palpable, Elise could tell, but he soldiered on, "I refused to attend the next function, and she went on her own! She called the office and asked for a car, and she got it! She left me home with Eric. I tried to reason . . . unsuccessfully. I hid from her future invitations, but the boss's assistant made direct arrangements.

She even went to a resort with them, the bosses, I mean. It was utterly humiliating. I had no choice but to resign and we returned home."

Elise caressed his thigh, still listening intently with her mouth ajar.

"She went back to work, but I stayed unemployed for a while. I turned my back on BMW and then Toyota. She began working late, which was atypical. When I asked, she said that she was chasing a promotion, and it was her turn to advance her career. In honesty I didn't buy it, but I didn't want to appear jealous too, you know, after what happened with Olive. I found a job as a graphics artist for a local website, though the pay was way less than before."

Elise sensed the pain the memories brought along. "Thanks, you can stop now," she said softly.

"No, it's OK. She wielded the *loser* word again, quite often in fact. She did get a promotion, to a deputy head of the PR department."

Elise made a quizzical face, prompting him to expand.

"Public relations. I knew already that she was seeing someone else. She was 'working' overnight, not answering her cell, er, mobile phone, and she started traveling on business trips. She didn't seem to care much about Eric anymore. I confronted her, and the next day she called to say that she was moving back to her mom's. She didn't even bother to collect her stuff." Leo paused again. "Funny though . . ." He breathed in.

"What's funny?"

"Funny, that last fight—before the day she left—we didn't make up in bed. We didn't fuck."

"I don't follow."

"Well, now that I think of it, when we had the fights, we also made love afterward, and our disagreements felt petty for a while." He waved his hand. "Anyway, it was lust, which is pretty obvious."

"Some people turn to alcohol to drown the ache; don't you agree that sex is better? I suppose you didn't take up drinking?"

Leo chuckled. "No, no, and you have a point. But I smoked like a blast furnace chimney stack. So that was it with Bea. She filed for divorce, got custody of Eric, and dumped him on Ulrica, remarried— her boss's son, I was told. I went back to Japan and tried my luck as manga artist with a friend I made during my first stay; Shinji was his name. But the endeavor failed, as competition is too fierce. I got a job as a CGI specialist. I loved computers, as you know." He smiled. "Then got fired and I went to the States."

"Why not back home?"

"Bea. I was afraid that we may cross paths, and too many people there knew the story. Pride, you see; she was the queen, and I was the one who fell from grace. I visited from time to time to be with Eric for a while. I was on my own for many years. It is hard for immigrants without large diaspora to meet someone they like and be liked. It was hard for me at least."

"What's a diaspora?" Elise asked.

"People of same nationality living in another country."

"Ah, OK, sorry."

"It is fine to ask if you don't know. I met Elizabeth at her step-brother's birthday party. She had flown in from the East Coast. She was getting her PhD at Johns Hopkins. Ha! She was also thirty-two! What a coincidence I never thought of before."

"What is the coincidence?"

"Bea was thirty-two when we signed the divorce papers. I liked Liz at first sight, and as I knew that she would not stay for long, I asked her out that same evening, and we had a date. She went back to school, but we stayed in touch. She completed her dissertation and was awarded her degree and returned to Campbell. I was working for Pixar, and she got a job nearby. She was in biotech. We shared a car-pool. She was twenty years younger, by the way. I still don't know what I was thinking when I asked her out on a date, and I wonder why she accepted. We got romantically involved, and having such a young girlfriend is a big deal for men past their prime, as I was no exception.

"This time it was she who proposed. I thought that she would grow tired with me and seek a younger chap, and I was quite surprised. We tied the knot, and she fell pregnant with Abigail. Things get boring from here on. We raised Abi together, and after the pandemic I worked from home, so I was able to do a lot more. Liz was building her career, and Abi was playing in the crib next to my desk. Abi was a great girl and still is, I hope. So much fun to be with. She had a cute doll. I mean this one was her favorite. She never took the others out of their boxes."

Elise failed to immediately notice that he went silent, absorbed in her own thoughts. When she did, she asked. "Was she pretty?"

"Who, Elizabeth, Abi, or the doll?"

"Elizabeth."

"She was no Beatrice, but she was attractive too, yes. Her problem I think was that most men found her intimidating. She was a doctor of science, and she was bossy too at times. She needed someone to accept her for who she was—an educated and ambitious woman—

and I became that man. That said, one of my sins is that I am a visual person and gravitate toward good-looking women, which I admit was unfair to the ones less fortunate."

"Thank you!" Elise teased self-deprecatingly.

"You are good-looking, get over it!"

"I suppose I am. It fits your profile. Truth is, it still matters to me. Especially now that you are here and one day I will have to compete with yet another of your exes."

"Well, you wanted to hear about them."

"Yes, I did, so please continue."

"What next?"

"Your sex life. Was it good?"

"With Bea—quite intense. She was bringing soft porn to watch and loved trying new positions. But when I discovered that she was fooling around, I could not ignore the humiliation, and I lost the drive. We were doing it only to calm ourselves down after a fight."

"I understand," Elise said. "And Liz?"

"With her it was, er, disappointing in comparison. We had some exciting moments, but overall, it was bland. Eventually we grew older, I developed erectile disfunction, which I had no incentive to address, and that settled it."

"You don't seem to have it now!" Elise noted cheerfully.

"No." Leo stayed on subject. "My hypothesis is that she was either asexual or carried some significant trauma deep inside her, but it is hard to maintain a sexless marriage in one's prime, and she forced herself to have sex for our sake."

"Did you not inquire?" Elise asked, dropping the cheer from her voice. She realized her remark had been in poor taste.

"I did, but she always denied that there was a problem. She's very intelligent, and this steadfastness was way out of character. That is why I lean toward the trauma option."

"Poor woman . . ."

"Assuming I am right."

"No, even if she was asexual, which I assume is what we called 'frigid' in my days on Earth, she was unable to experience the pleasure, yet she had to pretend. My dad still pretends at home to be straight, and he is not happy, believe me. Neither is Mom."

"How would you know what she could or could not experience? Pronouncements can only come from a pro or herself. And the truth is that I wouldn't care if it wasn't affecting me personally. This is what we are—always selfish."

Elise puffed her cheek and pouted, taken aback by the sudden sharpness in his voice. She was not a pro indeed. She had no education to speak of. Suddenly she felt inadequate, but that only raised her curiosity, and she prodded him again.

Leo continued, "Have I told you that Abi's queer?"

"Lesbian, you mean?"

"Yeah. She married another gal, Susi. They have a kid from, can you believe this, Eric!"

"That's not right!"

"It is, actually. Susan was the one who got impregnated, not Abi."

"Ah, I see, that's OK then. At least as far as incest goes, but is still weird."

She started playing with his dick—fondling, pulling it lightly with a pinch, then letting go while observing with amusement its transformation. She did that often, always causing his appendage to swell and harden. Then depending on her mood, she might take it into her mouth and propel him to ecstasy or use it as the fuel for her own. Leo quite naturally liked this simple foreplay, subject to so much ridicule in the old world. He wondered why exactly things sexual were labeled "dirty," regardless of context. His personal, informal favorite was that celibate priests were envious of lay people and demonized sex. While plausible, of course, he knew that there was far more to it.

Elise mounted him, allowed him to find her, and began slowly swaying her hips, looking at him with languid eyes and a shy smile. He rested his head on the soft grass and gazed at the sky, her sky, his hands barely touching her thighs. Caressing her skin felt good—the smoothness, the warmth . . . The signals from his groin were getting stronger. She was moving as if dancing to a lingering love song, with the lyrics driving her to tears of elation, her hands in tight embrace with his own. Leo drew out his blink, then shut his eyes completely, filtering the visual stimuli out and leaving just the sense of touch on.

"Leo . . ." her voice was quiet and soft.

"Mm?"

"Would you . . . marry me?"

Leo's eyelids flipped open as he tilted his head forward, his eyebrows almost squashing his forehead into nonexistence. She was still dancing, her eyes closed. She accelerated the rhythm as his penis shrank. Eventually the fit became too loose, at which point she finally opened her eyes and blushed. "Sorry, that was dumb of me." She looked away and bit her upper lip.

Leo propped himself up on his elbows, looked at her and tried to put her proposal into context, but he could find none. Why would one want to get married in this place? There was no purpose to it. Seemed that previously married people who made it all the way through were still together, like his father and his stepmom or Elise's parents. But who knew what else they were doing, like her dad and Uncle Boris for example, and there was also certainly no societal pressure or economic imperative. Traditional marriage had become obsolete in the old world too, in its progressive parts.

"Hey!" Leo called her softly. She peeked at him shyly. He smiled and asked politely, "Would you explain?"

"I, I know that it would not be the real deal but just another game we play. There's nothing in this realm to make it even remotely similar to marriages in the old world . . . what would we fight over? What would we struggle with? No kids to raise. No worries to rob us of our sleep . . . just that . . . I have this stupid wish to go through the rites, be dressed in white, move into our own place . . . you know, all that jazz." She paused for a breath, then again turned her gaze away. "That was stupid . . . forget it."

Leo tugged her shoulders softly. She brushed his cheek as she came down and rested her head, still unwilling to meet his eyes. Leo stroked gently her hair, considering, then twisted his neck and landed a kiss somewhere behind her ear. "Okay! I will marry you."

It took her several seconds to digest his words. When that happened, she released a quiet "Thank you!" and snuggled into him.

"Don't worry," Leo added. "We will certainly find something to fight over."

THE ANNOUNCEMENT

The decision was news. The news had to be disseminated amongst the narrow circle of relatives and friends. Leo pushed his fiancée into her room, shut the "portal" and asked, "OK, who do we start with?"

"Parents, I suppose. Mine, since we are here. Now, let's dress up!"

"Classic or crazy?"

Elise thought for a moment. "Classic this time." She pressed her palms against her eyes and pictured clothes. Before she opened the magic wardrobe again, she turned around and added, "But we shall get creative for the day and not just by thinking."

"OK."

She pulled the doors open and bit on her lip, "This? No, mm . . ." She pulled out a hanger. "This one will raise to the occasion." She removed the short sequined dress from the hanger and slipped it on. The sequins sparkled in the colors of the rainbow as she moved. After the dress, the wardrobe parted with a pair of silver platform shoes.

"Platforms?" Leo noted.

"Yes, I learned to walk on them." Elise crouched and fastened the clasps, then returned to a standing position. Leo couldn't move his eyes away from her; there were those moments when she looked so amazingly beautiful.

She looked at him and smiled. "You approve?" Then without waiting for the answer, she walked to her nightstand and removed a pair of crystal earrings and a tube of lipstick from the drawer. "Can you help with these?" She shoved them into his hand. "I can't see myself, you know . . ."

Leo fastened the earrings and put some lipstick on her. "You've worn makeup and earrings before. How did you do it then?"

"Mother, but I can't use her help now, can I?"

"Yeah, true."

"You are still naked, if I may point out."

"Aw, yes!" Leo giggled and went to the wardrobe. His Scottish outfit was there.

"Why did you laugh?"

"I pictured us as we are, you all dressed up and me butt naked, delivering wedding invitations. It would be very original indeed!"

"Then why don't we just go?"

"Are you serious?"

"Yeah, why not!" She delivered a gleaming smile. "Going for weird is something I like."

"Uh, no!" Leo promptly covered himself with clothes and sat on the bed to put the socks on. Then he transformed into his long-haired self.

"Maybe you shall stay true," Elise said softly.

"But I am old in most other people's eyes, and you look so young. Wouldn't it be weird? Creepy, even?"

"I want them to accept us as we are. Would you transform each time we visit someone, or someone visits us?"

Leo switched to his real self, trying to make her understand.

She approached and locked lips with him, pushed her tongue inside his mouth, checked the taste, then retracted it briskly. "I don't care what you look like! Do you wanna fuck? Like now and in this state of yours?" She pulled her dress up.

Leo grabbed her arms. "But the others do care. And I . . . I feel like a creep when I picture my true self next to you, Lizzy. Please understand!"

Elise sighed and dropped the dress back. "OK." A tear rolled down from her eye. She snorted and removed it with her finger. "It's good I don't wear eye makeup, or it would be ruined." She smiled wearily. "Damn it, man, I wish so much to have aged as you!" She snorted again and wiped her other eye.

Leo held her in his arms and kept pecking her lips and cheeks until she'd reacquired her enthusiasm.

"OK, old man, let's go!" She marched out of the room.

First stop was Elise's parents. Elise knocked on the living room door, but there was no answer. She stuck head inside, surveyed the space, then shrugged. "Empty, no one here. In fact, I don't feel presence at all. Hell knows where they went. We'll try later. Off to Ann now."

Annette was walking her dog as usual. She threw a suspicious glance at them. "What are you up to now?"

"You still pissed about the body paint? That was ages ago," Leo said.

Annette laughed. "No, no! But it is much better now, you must admit, like—you in your thirties. Yeah, I've forgotten this look. So, what's up?"

"We are getting married!"

Annette looked around for a bench, then hiccupped. "Seriously?"

Leo pulled Elise closer and confirmed with aplomb. "Yes!"

"I can explain, Ann. Leo's doing me a favor."

"No need. You do whatever you want to do. Just that there are no priests here, the churches are all hollow, so, how are you going to solemnize it?"

"With you and my parents and relatives and friends," Elise said. "Perhaps somebody would agree to play the priest. I don't care about any god's blessing; it is rubbish anyway." She stopped and looked up at Leo. He nodded—he didn't care either.

"You are a blasphemer," Annette said squeezing her lips together. "What if this God you deny sent you here?" Leo knew his mother wasn't religious, but she remained uncertain whether a deity of any kind may exist.

"This conversation is getting off topic," Leo intervened. "However, I was a blasphemer my whole life and I am here, am I not? Therefore, if God exists, he/she/they/it is not petty and vindictive, is he/she/they/it? As I would expect from a hyperintelligent and hyper-loving being."

Annette thought, gasped through her nose, and shrugged. "Congrats, then!" With the dismissal of the concern, she opened her arms for a hug. Sylvester barked and wagged his tail.

"And I don't hate Beatrice," Leo said, chancing a guess at the nature of his mother's thoughts.

"Shall I tell Nick and Viv?" Annette inquired.

"Nope, we will do it. This world is small."

And so, they did. Vivian sobbed for half an hour with no explanation. Nick had a good laugh, kissed both, and gave them a basket with fresh eggs from his hens.

"What are we supposed to do with these?" Leo asked.

"They are fresh," was all Nick said and sent them on their way to Richard.

When they rang, Peter answered the door. "What are these?" He nodded at the egg lot.

"White eggs, can't you see?" Leo snapped.

Peter did not respond immediately; he inspected Elise head to toe, then turned back to his uncle. "Er, you are bringing a gift?"

"No, my grandfather gifted them to us."

"Why?"

"I don't know. Some sort of ancient fertility symbol perhaps? You know, eggs. Or maybe just to eat, that makes most sense."

"Who cooks here?" Peter mocked.

"We do!" Elise said and proceeded to the living room where her future father-in-law was waiting.

"Why would Nicholas gift you eggs?" Richard asked when Leo joined his bride-to-be in the room.

"Geez, why so much talk about a dozen of eggs?" Leo rolled his eyes. "Nick has hens, hens lay eggs, perhaps he's stuffed."

His father raised his eyebrows. "Nick has hens?"

Leo resigned himself to the nonsense. He sat quietly next to Elise and placed the basket on the coffee table. "Call Jessica, please."

His dad shouted, "Jess!"

Jessica stepped into the room and exclaimed, "Oh!"

"Do you see her?" Leo asked in low voice while looking straight ahead.

"Yes . . ." his stepmother said after a moment's hesitation. "Who . . . who is she? I don't remember . . ."

"Just as I thought," murmured Leo, then said in clear voice, "This is Elise, my fiancée! And my first girlfriend."

Richard rumbled, laughing just like Nick. If he now pulled a basket of fresh eggs from under a blanket or something, Leo wouldn't be surprised.

"You started a new game it seems." The older man chuckled. "Aren't you a bit too old for that?"

"And what? Just fuck and that's all?" Leo retorted. His father looked at him suspiciously after the last remark but made no comment. "Call it whatever you want. Yes, it is a game in this world, but so what? You are invited to participate, so, will you?"

"It isn't entirely a game for me," Elise said. "I know that it is not the same as in the other world, but I'm trying to experience things I couldn't, and Leo has been kind to indulge me. I would appreciate it if you joined him, but if you refuse, that's also fine. Things like that happen in the other life too, right?"

"We will be there," Jessica said. "Apologies for Rich, men are not particularly sensitive creatures."

Elise got up and bowed. "Thank you, ma'am!"

"Come with me; let the men talk." Jessica waved her over. "How old are you, dear?"

Elise squeezed herself past Leo and joined his stepmom. "Eighty-two," he overheard her saying.

Richard sighed. "OK, I get it now. Besides, I was never a father-in-law in any real sense to any of your wives. Perhaps this is a chance for me to experience that too. Count me in! When will the wedding take place?"

"Thanks, Dad. And I still don't know. We decided on getting, er, married just today. I'll let you know. Eggs?" He pointed at the basket. "They come in peace."

Peter remained in the hallway the entire time, listening and biting his fingernails, trying to come up with a plan. He had to do something before the old fart and the girl moved to the next level in their stupid game. Marriage his ass, they were all dead, but the idea wasn't that bad! What if he proposed too? If she wanted to experience things, marrying him instead would also do. And he would experience some good old-fashioned sex with an almost real girl, as he was getting tired of masturbation and primitive sex dolls.

He felt an itch in his right hand. He looked at it, and it seemed translucent for a moment. Then the itch jumped to his left. He scratched it and thought, *What the fuck!*

※

When they arrived at Steve's, he crawled from underneath his car and wiped his oily hands with a rag, "What's up?"

"We are getting married," chirped Elise with a grin.

"Whoa!" exclaimed Steve. "I didn't think of that!"

"Like what, marrying her?" Leo asked.

"Yeah!" Steve confirmed with a somewhat strained voice and coughed, "*Ahem*, if that were so, when you arrived, she'd been bound by a vow to stay with me! OK, let's do it! I suppose I'd be your best man?"

"Can you be the priest?"

"I can be both." Steve chuckled. "I'm multitalented."

"Deal!"

Elise kissed Steve on the cheek. He pulled her boldly into his arms, and his tongue entered her mouth and lingered there.

Leo pointed at himself. "Me too." Contrary to his expectation, Steve complied. Leo had to push him away with considerable force, so passionate was his friend's kiss.

※

Beatrice sat on the edge of the sofa, her heart beating fast after being told the news. Her emotions were entangled. She was jealous, and she was glad. She raised her hands. "Well, I wish you happiness and glee!"

"Come on, Bea, wishes mean nothing, and we are well aware that it is a game. Just be yourself and be around, will ya? Do you want to be the maid of honor?"

"Liz?"

"Er, maybe not, sorry . . ." Elise appeared to be considering something. "Can we come back on this?"

"Yeah, of course!"

"Leo, can we go?" Elise seemed unsettled.

"Will you please explain?"

"Please, come, I will tell all soon. I am unsure, well, er, you know the person I'm gonna take you to . . ."

"Go, jerk, I know what you are thinking." Beatrice waved him away.

⁂

They were back in their district. Elise was walking fast and cursing the shoes, "That's why I dislike high heels!" Leo followed with wide strides. Elise opened a door, went to an apartment on the ground floor and pushed the door handle down. Then she stepped to the side and invited him in with a wave of her hand. He moved closer and peeked inside. Another girl in her late teens stood there with hands tightly knotted in front of her. Brown hair, brown eyes, slightly darker complexion.

"Wasilla?" Leo mumbled.

"Leo? Hi!"

Leo looked at Elise, oozing a lack of understanding.

"Shall we go inside?" Elise asked.

They sat around the table.

"Wasilla died age thirty-nine, during surgery. She can give you the details if you are interested. I brought you here because she is my friend, and well, we are, we . . ." she was lost for words. She reached for her purse and retrieved a cigarette, which she lit nervously and took a long drag from.

"Let me guess—you were intimate?"

Elise shook her head quickly and took another drag. "We *still* are . . ." She looked away, then back at him.

"Ah!" Leo tilted his head up and held his breath for a moment. "Okay."

"Is that all?" Elise finally broke the tense silence.

"What else do you expect me to say?" Leo stood up, walked out of the room, and slammed the apartment door behind him.

"Leo, wait! Please!" Elise jumped and rushed after him. "Leo!" When she crossed the threshold, he was gone. She returned to the room, sat, and nibbled her lip. She screwed up big this time. She should have told him about Wasilla right at the start, even before they fucked in the old school. And let him decide if he was okay with sharing her with someone else. But it was so harrowing. He might have freaked out and left, or he might have demanded from her to pick a favorite. To pick Wass . . . She quivered.

Wasilla came behind Elise, laid her hands on her shoulders, bowed, and rubbed her cheek against Elise's.

"Don't cry baby, it will be OK," she whispered gently in Elise's ear, and kissed her. Elise did exactly the opposite of what she was told—she started crying.

The horrible sensation of betrayal permeated Leo's mind. He walked aimlessly along the streets—the only direction was away from her. He stood in the middle of a bridge and looked down into the muddy waters of the river. The waters were never like this before, not in this realm. Was the river god angry like him or confused like him or simply washing dirty laundry? Leo wanted to spit in the water but spat on the railing instead and watched the saliva slowly disappear.

What were they? Spitting, fucking ghosts? Why did he have feelings? Couldn't he be just dead? If this world existed only in his imagination, why did he inflict this pain on himself? He was no masochist. Maybe it was not him dreaming but something outside him. Or maybe Bea's betrayal kept his mind confined, and it ran a variation of past events. He wanted to vent out, to seek consolation and advice, but who from? His mom? Beatrice? Stephen? Did Steve know? Why did Elise keep it secret? All she had to do was tell him that she was bisexual, and she also had a girlfriend. The world had changed, he had changed . . . the world had changed . . . but she didn't know, that's it!

No, he didn't have to seek excuses for her. This is what love does—try to justify bad deeds, rationalize unbecoming behavior.

Leo continued walking, staring at the ground, his mind abuzz. He could not make decisions now, whether to forgive her, whether to reunite or not. When the pattern on the sidewalk changed, he lifted his gaze. He was standing at the city airport's departures hall. He pushed the revolving door and went inside. What was this world trying to convey? That he needed an escape? Leo scanned the vastness of the hall, read the information displays—all flights were delayed, as if it could be otherwise. Computers, there must be computers! But he was not in the mood. He rested his forehead against the glazing and looked at the tarmac—no jets were anywhere in sight. Leo dragged his feet to an escalator and headed up to the business lounge.

He wanted to stretch and relax. He crashed on the large sofa and looked straight up. The tall ceiling seemed so low, almost crushing. He turned to the side and closed his eyes.

THE ASSAULT

Elise was staring blankly past her girlfriend's face. She was imagining a little ant crawling on the wall, lost, trying to find its way home. From the ant's perspective, the world consisted of an endless expanse of shallow white hills. It felt the same to her now—no direction to follow, no landmark to get bearings from. What was best? Find him and seek forgiveness, or wait and hope that he would eventually break and crawl back to her? She shivered—it was all her fault, how could she bet on someone's weakness exposed by love! Perhaps other people did it, Beatrice was probably such a person, but not her!

She stood up resolutely. "I'm gonna find him and apologize!"

"As you wish," Wasilla said softly. "Probably that would be the best."

"Come with me!"

"Why? I will only complicate it."

"Come. I love you too. I need you by my side. If he refuses to share, I already betrayed his trust, and I'm not going to lose yours, sell you out, just so I can have him back. Makes sense, right?"

"OK, I will come, but I'm still unconvinced that I shall be present when you two talk."

"We'll worry about that later," Elise said. "Let's first find him. I know that it would be hard. I can't sense him anymore. I don't know where Leo might be . . . Ah. And let me get rid of these shoes!"

Elise unclasped her platform shoes and kicked them to the side. Then impatiently pushed Wasilla out of the apartment and onto the sidewalk.

Peter followed her with his gaze from his hideout across the street. Elise stopped and looked back as if she felt his presence. Maybe she did! Peter swiftly withdrew behind the concrete column and breathed in nervously. Elise resumed her walk.

Have they broken up? wondered Peter. He saw them entering the building, still jolly, then his uncle walking out looking upset. Now his chick, also sad and in a hurry. What was inside that caused all that? Maybe he should make a move now? He stepped back and thought of a shortcut to catch up with her. But with no idea where she was going, all he could do was to follow at a distance and hide behind the trees. He saw how she sank into another building—was that his uncle's place?—and he positioned himself nearby, ready to greet her when she came back out.

"I know Leo's not here, I can't sense him, but . . . can you?" Elise asked when Annette answered the door and let her, them, in.

"No. What happened?"

"I screwed up. Big time." Elise could hardly sustain bursting into tears. Her throat was tight, and she had no idea if confessing to Annette was right.

"How?" Annette pushed a pack of cigarettes and her lighter across the table.

Elise pushed them back. "I don't know if I should tell you before I talk to him, maybe not." She got up and prepared to leave. "Please, Ann, if you sense him or see him, please ask him to let me in so we can talk."

So, the game was over before it even started, thought Annette. Another heartbreak for her son. Annette showed Elise out and wondered why the girl lingered at the door as if making way for someone else.

"Liz!" she called out sharply.

Elise froze.

"You are not alone, are you?"

Elise shook head and looked down. "No, I am not."

"Can Leo see him?"

"Yes, and it is her, not him. Wasilla, a girl from his class." Elise turned to face her. "But you obviously don't remember her. I should have told him . . ." She turned head from side to side in regret and sighed deeply. "Well, now you know."

It was not as bad as Annette thought, considering the prevailing mindset at the time Elise died. Being bisexual and that. It was easier to admit to an affair with another man than come out as queer. Still bad, though, as broken trust is very hard to mend. She sighed. "OK, I will try to help. But only to find him. After that, you are on your own."

"Thanks, Ann!" Elise bowed deeply and ran down the stairs.

Where did she pick this habit from? She's not Japanese, wondered Annette.

Peter jumped out from behind the wall as soon as Elise set foot onto the sidewalk, "Hi!"

Elise gasped and took a step back, startled. She tripped on the low threshold behind her. Peter leaped and caught her fall. Wasilla did the same. Elise looked at her, then him. Each time she moved her sight to one of them, the other disappeared.

"What happened?" Wasilla asked.

"Who happened is the correct question." Elise turned to Peter. "Hi!"

"How's the preparations going?"

"Wedding's off." She looked away.

"Oh, but why? Did something happen? You two broke up?"

Elise gathered some nerve and said calmly, "We had a miscommunication."

"Tell me, I may be able to understand. And lend a hand in mending broken parts, er, hearts."

"I'd rather not. See you." Elise took Wasilla's hand and squeezed herself between Peter and the wall.

"May I walk with you?" He chased after them.

Elise clicked her tongue. "Pete, as usual the answer is no. Please leave me alone. Go away and find someone else to stalk." Damn, that was a bad thing to say! "Sorry, don't stalk anybody, just get an afterlife, OK? Go build your bike!"

"I am getting there. I promised I would take you for a ride!"

Elise accelerated her pace, but so did Peter.

"Why is my uncle so special? Yeah, I understand that you were school sweethearts, but you already experienced him, right? Don't you want a change? Someone from a different generation, so you can learn new things, new ways to see the world?"

"Who happened?" Wasilla pulled Elise's hand.

"Leo's nephew, the one I was telling you about," Elise answered briefly and turned her attention back to Peter. "Your uncle is special because I love him!"

"Love?" Peter laughed with derision. "What is love? Hormones gone wild. What hormones do you have here? None. So how is that love?"

"That's the gist of it—I have no raging hormones, yet being with him makes me feel happy and serene. It doesn't matter what age he is displaying—a boy or a granddad—I want him, period! With you it is only lust. I grant you that, you are an attractive specimen, but I fucked up things twice, so I would be out of my mind to do that again!"

"You fucked up things how?"

"None of your business, now go!" Her face was turning red, her lips trembled.

Peter grabbed her arm, pulled her closer, and kissed her on the mouth. Elise tried to push him away, but he was strong.

Wasilla saw the strange convulsion her friend's body was going through and tried to intervene but was almost paralyzed—her movement was painfully slow, her hand taking ages to advance a tiny bit. Only her thoughts were racing. She was like a creature caught in fast-setting amber.

Peter dragged Elise to the nearby apartment lobby, pushed her against the wall, and continued to kiss her. Elise tried to scream until he gagged her with his hand. "Everything here is about lust. Don't you realize that?" He drove his hand up her dress and squeezed her inner thigh. "What do you feel now?" He pulled down her panties and dragged his fingers over her labia. "Desire, that's what you feel, I bet!" Elise's eyes were enlarged, and terror ran through her. *Where is Wass, where is Leo?!* She didn't want this man, so why was he still here? He should be sent away.

She tried to wriggle out, but he overpowered her. He pushed her, and she hit her head hard against the wall. Her mind felt dizzy, her body weak. Peter grabbed her hair, tilted her head, and drove his tongue deep into her mouth that was gasping for air. She tried to push it out, then sank her teeth into it. He cursed and smacked her hard with the back of his hand. Her head bounced off the wall again, cushioned only by her dense hair. Elise almost lost consciousness—everything became a painful blur. He pulled her dress up, tore her panties, and unzipped his jeans.

Leo woke up and sat upright—where was he? Ah, the business lounge. Something was going on. Something was wrong! His heart was pounding—Elise! Something was happening to her! He jumped and ran for the exit of the airport.

In the glass of the revolving door, he saw a reflection of a scene—a girl in a silver dress pulled over her head, pinned against a wall, and with a man trying to force himself into her. He leaped without thinking, and the glass shattered, turning into hundreds of small shards. Leo landed on his side, ignored the pain from the many cuts, grabbed the other man's shirt, and pulled hard. The shirt tore. The other man was jolted, and he turned to look.

"Uncle!" A vile smile appeared on Peter's face. He let go of Elise and she collapsed to the floor.

"Scumbag!" Leo thrust forward with his fist but met no resistance. He lost balance and fell across Elise's legs.

Wasilla ran inside the lobby through the glassless door leaf, gazed down, and kicked Leo hard in the ribs. "What are you doing, you dirty asshole!" She looked at Elise's bruised face and her naked body, grabbed his hair, and started pulling it with force, screaming, "What did you do to her, rotten piece of shit! What did you do to her! Why!"

Leo curled up on the floor and tried to protect his head from the vicious kicks.

"Wass!" wheezed Elise, "it wasn't him . . ." She tried to scramble on her feet. "It wasn't him; he saved me . . ." She descended in a bout of cough.

Wasilla registered and stopped kicking. She jumped over Leo, kneeled, and hugged Elise.

"It was Peter, his stepbrother's son." Elise continued to wheeze.

"Same shit! I hate them!" Wasilla hissed, making a giant effort to not drive her heel into Leo's skull. Her body flickered, turning translucent then opaque again.

Leo coughed too and lumbered up. Then he kneeled and reached to pull Elise's dress down. Wasilla hugged the other woman tightly and prepared to pounce on him.

"Cover her up!" he ordered with a firm voice. Then he sat on the terrazzo floor and asked, "What happened here? Where did that asshole go?"

"Peter forced himself on me. He was waiting by your place, started pestering me again, and when I told him to take a hike, he attacked . . ."

Leo shook his head in disbelief. He always liked Peter. He had been bothered by Peter's advances, but his nephew had been alone, looking for company. But going this far?

"And Wasilla? I guess she saw nothing . . . except me, that is. She doesn't know him."

Wasilla nodded, then added, "Sorry, Leo, I didn't think of that, and after the way you left . . . I thought you were angry, taking revenge."

"Holy cow, Wass, was I ever violent?"

"People change."

"True. Lizzy, can you walk? Let's get out of here."

"I am getting better, yes, we can walk."

"Mount the horse!" Leo squatted with hands touching the floor. "I will carry you."

"No need!"

"Come, woman, you are barefoot."

Elise climbed on his shoulders and wrapped her arms around his head. She rode in silence until they arrived at Wasilla's place.

"Thank you!" She hugged him, not willing to let go, but eventually released her hold. "Will you come inside?"

"Do I have to? Like, do you need consolation after the attack? Because if you want to talk about what happened between us, I'd rather do it some other time."

She dropped his hand.

"OK. We'll find each other if it is meant to be so." She turned around and walked into the building, followed by her girlfriend.

Leo squeezed his lips, shook his head, and headed home. Now he also had Peter to deal with.

GONE

Leo punched the doorbell button at his father's. This time, Jessica answered the door.

"Is Pete in? We need to talk."

"No. Did something happen?"

"We need to have a talk, that's all."

"Are you jealous of him?"

Leo thought for a second. Maybe this was the best way to avoid further questions. He nodded.

"Come in."

Leo didn't want to appear elusive and followed her into the kitchen. Jessica filled two coffee mugs and placed them on the table, then gestured at him to sit down.

"Pete's very lonely and he died young. He's missing his life back there, his fiancée, his work, his bikes. I hope you understand."

Leo sat motionless, only his eye twitched.

"He likes her a lot, he talks about her all the time, how lucky you are, you know, boy talk." Jessica sipped her coffee. "So, don't come on him so hard. I can see that you are angry."

She has no idea! He tried to stay calm. "He's been bothering her, if I may put it that way . . ."

"Ah. But isn't what you boys do when you like a girl?"

"Jess, we are not boys, and neither is she a girl. But that is beside the point—no, normal men don't bother women. When they ask them out and are turned down, they can take no for answer."

"I was young once, and boys, er, men could be quite persistent in their courting. I can attest firsthand."

"A few times, yes, but he's been more than persistent. He's been stalking her." Leo's heartbeat accelerated. Maybe it was time for him to go.

"That's not possible. He's a good boy and you know that. You like him, no?"

Leo quickly finished his coffee and rose. "Where's Father?"

She shrugged.

Leo closed his eyes and tried to sense Richard but failed. "OK, tell Pete that I want the two of us to have a talk. I'll pop in soon."

He strolled out of the home. Next stop was Steve.

"Really? Fuck man, this guy is a shitbag! And you said you liked him!" Steve delivered two beers to the table and sat down. "And what now?"

"Well, there's no police here to file a charge with. So, I don't know. I can't kill him." Leo laughed bitterly. "Only option is to try talk some sense into him. Have you got any other ideas?"

Steve thought, sighed, and leaned back in his chair. "Nope. The only thing coming to mind is me and you ganging up on him and keep beating him up until he stops. But here this shit is mostly for exercise, as we heal extremely fast. This place, I think, is supposed to be violence free; you can't smash a fly."

"Have you tried?"

"What, smashing a fly? No, there aren't any that I can see or hear."

"Then how do you know that the place is violence free? Pete tried to rape Elise and almost succeeded, and this place did nothing to stop him!"

"It woke you up and folded so you could intervene in time."

Leo looked down. "True, but she'd remember the experience."

"She remembers being run over by a speeding car, and you remember dying from a heart attack. Same here. Nasty stuff, but we all had to get over it." Steve drank from the beer. "I know someone who got killed by their own son and they must exist with this fact. They are trying to look on the bright side and not dwell on pain."

A faint buzz sounded in Leo's ears, then subsided. "Well, I am sorry for them. I see your point, thanks!"

"How's the wedding plan going? Will this put it on hold?"

"Affirmative. I'm not in the mood to see any of the other Hackensacks right now. If I see the brat, whatever is running through my veins now would boil and with Father and his wife, I will have to give explanations as to why Peter was disinvited. Lie or tell the truth? It gets messy, no?"

"It does. OK, then we can think of another outing, something to improve the mood."

No matter how reluctant Leo was to meet with the other Hackensacks, he still had to confront Peter. But he pushed it for the next day and went home. He browsed his music collection, searching for something to calm him down—Vangelis would do—then sat in his armchair and rolled a joint. Elise was also on his mind. He still felt cheated. She had not been alone for thirty-two years, as she claimed, since Wasilla died roughly forty years ago—ten years less. Unless they met after Steve's arrival for some reason, but how likely was that?

Did Steve know? Leo was afraid to ask. He was tired, and the music carried him to sleep.

⁂

"Hi, Dad! Pete here?" Leo repeated yesterday's question.

"No, I don't think that he was home last night. He was here yesterday morning though. What's up?"

"I told your wife already; did she not share?"

"She said something in fact. Like you're jealous of him and your Elise."

Leo sighed. "He's been stalking her, Dad. That's not jealousy!"

"Ah, Jess didn't put it this way."

"Anyway, I want to make him stop. Lizzy doesn't want to be bothered by him anymore. I'd rather tell him this myself, so will you please try to arrange something when he shows up. I don't know, maybe take him by the hand and think of me?"

"OK," his father said.

Leo rose and headed for the door.

"Bye, Leo!" chirped his stepmom from the kitchen. What the heck was she doing in the kitchen all the time anyway? When he and Lizzy cooked, they went to restaurants and made use of the facilities there. He debated going to meet her. He descended the stairs and walked out of the building. On the street he looked left and right, undecided which way to go. He had to explore the airport for tech and contemplate life without Elise, even though he was hoping that it would not come to this.

Leo chose a direction and began advancing slowly with his hands in his pockets. He was lonely and demotivated. Even walking was a chore. There was no imperative of any kind in this world. There was no need to eat, no need to drink, no need to do anything at all. He found meaning in the relationship with his first girlfriend, the experiences they shared, in giving small things and receiving. He was ready to forgive. What stopped him, however, was fear. He was afraid that he would forgive her only so he wouldn't be alone.

He reached the middle of a bridge and again leaned against the railing and looked down. The river was clear, no trace of mud. Whirlpools were forming then collapsing. Leo rested his head on his forearms and closed his eyes. He imagined himself falling in the water, then he heard a splash. He raised his head and looked around alarmed. There was nothing and no one. The river continued to flow lazily. He resumed his pose and shut eyes again. It was dark now. His consciousness slipped away.

**

A knocking on a door brought him out of his stupor. Leo opened his eyes. He was at home, in his armchair, wearing earphones. The music was no longer playing. The door opened.

"Your dad's here," his mother said.

"Ah." *He probably brought Peter.* Leo ensured that his attire was neat and dragged his feet in the direction of the living room. He was yet to fully awake. His father was standing in the middle of the room, alone.

"What, where's Pete?" Leo tried to concentrate. It felt like a hangover, but he had no recollection of drinking last night. He remembered looking at the river from a bridge and that was all. Perhaps he jumped and whatever happened after that was still to come.

"I came to ask the same question. He's not been home for three nights in a row."

"So? I go to places for many days."

"I get it, but you have friends, you go with them, and he's alone."

Maybe it was time to reveal what really happened. "Mom, bring us some drinks please. Anything will do." Leo then turned to his dad. "Please take a seat." He followed suit. "I don't know how to put it mildly, but . . . Pete tried to rape Elise."

Richard squinted and furrowed his eyebrows.

"I thrust to hit hard, and he disappeared. It happened so fast. I can't tell what exactly occurred, but you know how this place works. Perhaps space warped and he ended up in Kinshasa or hell knows where."

Leo looked at his father. He imagined a mechanical brain inside his dad's skull with cogs spinning fast, crunching the information he had just divulged but producing no meaningful output and causing the body that the brain controlled to cease up—so still and expressionless was Richard, yet red-faced. When he finally moved his mouth, it was just for a short exclamation, "Huh?"

Leo sipped his beer and waited patiently for his father to finish digesting the news.

"I need to talk to her!" Richard stated in a resolute tone. "To your, what is she now, fiancée?"

"Why? What difference would it make?"

"To make sure that it is not all made up!"

"Ah, for fuck's sake, Dad, why would I come up with such an egregious claim? Besides, she would be conspiring with me if it were a hoax."

Richard murmured. "Shit, that's bad!"

Leo looked at him, surprised. He'd never heard his father curse.

"I have a gut feeling . . ." Richard began with painful hesitation. "You know, I am a scientist, and gut feelings don't count, but for lack of better word . . . or shall I say—I have a hypothesis, that . . ."

Leo prompted softly, as he could sense the mental angst. "Yes, Dad?"

"You know how not all people make it here, right?"

Leo was beginning to guess his father's hypothesis, but let the older man present it himself.

"Well, maybe . . . maybe Pete was expelled." Richard leaned forward and buried his face in his palms. "Rape is a serious offense, you see, and who knows . . . this is another first for me, but you have a propensity to cause shocks. Like making people see . . . fuck, how am I going to tell Jess?"

"I will come with you."

"Not the best idea. She's biased, she always was, regardless of her kind talk. Fuck, Son!" Richard looked desperate.

"You know, there was a sort of eyewitness . . ." Leo began.

Richard lifted head with hope. "Who? Do I know them?"

"I'm not sure . . . no, it is unlikely. She was a classmate of mine in school. I had a crush on her, but that was it. You were also not around, you know, since it was years after the divorce."

"What's her name?"

"Wasilla."

"Wasilla Buhari?"

"Mm, maybe . . . I forgot her surname. How could you know?"

"Tarek Buhari, we worked together at the institute. He had a daughter; I knew her. He used to bring her and her brothers with him to the lab when they were kids. Later, she visited from time to time to learn on the computer. Take me to her! Please!"

Leo wasn't yet ready to talk to Elise, so he hoped that she wasn't there. But as soon as they entered the old apartment building, she popped like a champagne cork from Wasilla's place and ran toward him, then braked hard, lowered her gaze, and said quietly, "Hi, Leo, Richard, please come in."

Wasilla was sitting on an ottoman and smoking. When she saw them, she rose swiftly, and her eyebrows nudged upward. "Mr. Hackensack?"

"Wass? It is you, right? Tarek's kid?" Richard's eyes sparkled. He stepped forward and hugged her. "It is you! Hi, where's your dad?"

"He's not here," Wasilla said coldly.

Richard mumbled, "I see . . ."

"What is it?" Elise pulled Leo's sleeve and whispered close to his ear.

"Pete's gone. Father thinks that he was expelled."

"Expelled?"

"Dad, talk to Wass. I'll have a conversation with Elise." Leo pulled her in the hallway and said quietly, "He thinks that Pete was expelled from this realm because of the rape attempt."

"Ah, you told him."

"I had to. I tried to stick to 'stalking Peter,' but my dad came in worried about him, and I told him the truth. Now he needs help breaking the news to my stepmom, and Wasilla is a witness. Of a sort. Her father, they were colleagues, and Richard remembered her, which is why he can see. By the way, where's her dad, indeed?"

"He was very strict. Religiously, that is. They are Christians from Lebanon. He used to punish them, Wass and her two brothers, very harshly for what he saw as lack of faith, blasphemy, and shit. He made them kneel on dry peas—quite cruel, don't you think? He drove her younger brother to suicide. Walid's here though, with their mom. So, my guess would be that Tarek didn't make it for those reasons. And Pete . . ." She leaned against the wall and looked down. "I don't remember clearly. I remember him kissing me and tearing my underwear, then I bit his tongue. He smacked me, I hit the wall, and things got fizzy from this point. Next thing I remember is Wass kicking you."

"Peter has not been seen since the attack. I tried to hit him, and he disappeared before I could land the punch. Father's worried about my stepmother; I mentioned Wass as a potential witness, and he figured that he remembered her and asked to meet with her."

She raised her head, "Leo?"

"Mmm?"

"I am so sorry . . . I . . ."

He didn't know what to say.

"I . . ." She seemed desperate for words.

Leo peeked into the room. His father was standing up. Richard adjusted his trousers and looked at his son. Wasilla also rose.

"We are going to talk to your stepmom," Richard announced as he closed the distance.

Wasilla donned a pair of black shoes and shaped her hair into a ponytail.

"Give me a sec, gonna change now," Elise said and was about to head for the bedroom, but Wasilla blocked the hallway with stretched arm. "I believe that you have something else to do," she said, looking straight into Leo's eyes.

Leo moved his gaze to the side. She was trying to force a conversation between himself and Elise, he got that, but he was still conflicted.

"Son, you stay here," Richard said quietly but firmly as he let Wasilla exit first.

Leo pulled a pack of cigarettes from his pocket, removed one, then pushed it back in. He grabbed Elise's hand, led her to the sofa in the living room where he sat and motioned for her to do the same. The latch clicked behind them when Richard closed the door.

Elise met his eyes. Silent tears were running down her face. Leo let go of her hand, looked down, and said in trembling voice, "Please, Lizzy, don't ever lie to me again. Ever! Neither for good nor for bad. All you had to do was tell the truth."

"Can you forgive me?"

"I already have . . ."

"I only gathered enough courage after you told me that Abigail was queer. Only Wass and you know. And yes, I lied about the time I was alone. But twenty-one years is also an eternity when there's no one to share your existence with."

"When did you figure it out? You know—not being quite straight."

"I liked girls in school, but I still didn't know the attraction was sexual. It was, you know, bad . . . so, here, after I died." She moved closer.

"Abi also went though some self-reflection. But it was easier for her. Queer people were out of the closets for a long time when she realized who she was. However, her mother wasn't happy."

"Did she reject her?"

"No, but her mood always turned gloomy when she was reminded of her daughter's sexual orientation. She never said anything though."

"And you?"

"I don't care who people love, not whom and how they fuck for as long as it is consensual."

"Including me?"

Leo nodded. "There is just one thing . . ."

"What is it?" Elise questioned nervously.

"I can't play the marriage game anymore. That would be asking too much."

"I understand." Elise moved even closer. Leo laid his arm on her shoulders. She hugged him with both hands and snuggled tightly. "Thank you! I promise—no more secrets and lies!"

He resisted the attraction of her lips until she suddenly rose to her feet and then straddled his lap. The kiss was incredibly sweet and lasted very long. Elise pulled his shirt up and threw it on the floor. Leo did the same with hers and soon they became one.

After returning home, Wasilla removed her shoes and placed them diligently on the shoe rack. She heard the panting in the living room, quietly walked to the open door, and peeked inside. The scene made her smile. She leaned against the doorframe and stood there watching. Then she caught Leo's glance. Did he beckon? She suddenly felt emboldened, walked in, dropped on her knees, and locked lips with Elise.

TRINITY

Wasilla was moving objects around in her quest for perfection—she was somewhat obsessive when it came to, mostly order, because the world she was existing in now was nicely set to be self-cleaning—when Elise entered the room and announced wearily, "I told Mom and Dad about me."

"And?" Wasilla put the vase she was holding in her hand back on the shelf and sat down, ready to listen.

"Father came out of the closet too." She sighed deeply. "It was bad." Elise kicked her shoes in the corner and threw her purse on the couch. Wasilla glanced at her with disapproval but remained silent. She began pulling the shoes closer with her foot, staying seated on the ottoman.

"Really bad! Mother didn't seem to mind me at first. She said that she'd always be my mom and that emboldened Dad. He looked at me, I gave him the nod, he confessed, and Mom went mad. She started screaming, throwing stuff, accused him of corrupting me in youth and passing down bad genes. She jettisoned us out eventually, you know, the local way, as we found ourselves on the street. We tried to go back but were unable to reach our floor. She locked us out." She paused. "I think that Leo's coming."

"I'll take that!" Wasilla grabbed the shoes and the purse and ran in the hallway.

"Sorry!" Elise called after her.

"Hi, Wass!" Leo stood at the door.

It took Wasilla a micro-eternity to realize that she was in the way. "Ah, sorry!" She moved aside and let him in.

He took a few steps, then halted and looked at her. "Can we talk? Just the two of us, that's it."

Wasilla hesitated for a moment, then said quietly, "Yes."

"Lizzy, I'll steal Wass for a while!" Leo took Wasilla's hand and led her out. They walked in silence, until he selected the words to use. "How do you feel about me and Elise? She got what she wanted yesterday, but is it the same for you?"

"I don't know." Wasilla was counting the pavers on the sidewalk. "I gravitate toward not wanting to share her, but I understand that she loves both of us and . . . well, I knew about you. I grew accustomed."

"I had a crush on you at school all those years ago." Leo chuckled with unease. "You probably didn't know."

"I guessed it actually." Wasilla smiled. "But by the time I was already aware that I preferred girls."

"Ah, I see, so you are not bisexual like her, right?"

"No, I don't think so."

"That's OK, my younger kid is a lesbian too. Maybe I was too old when she was conceived, and something clicked wrong." He halted and blushed with a terrified look on his face, "Shit! That sounded bad, apologies!"

"Do you love her? Your daughter?"

"Yes. Her being queer is of no consequence to me and how I feel about her. I don't give a damn about who people like and fuck, as I keep clarifying, for as long as it is consensual."

"There shouldn't be any pedophiles here if that is what you mean."

"Yeah . . ." Leo looked at her. "I kind of feel the same about Lizzy and you." He laughed awkwardly again. "If you were also bisexual, there was a chance for polyamorous relationship."

"We can be friends, no?" Wasilla took his hand.

"It is not that simple. Yes, we can be friends, but I was already in love with you once, a fleeting one indeed, but what I see is you from those days and it still stirs emotions." He withdrew his hand. "You see, even simple touch generates some electricity." He rubbed the hand she touched. "Anyway, what happened at the Hackensacks?"

"I couldn't see your stepmom. Apparently, she cried a lot. Your dad said that she would come to accept what happened, but she would need time. We can only hope that he's right."

"Speaking of her . . ." Leo had raised his head. "She's coming."

"Where?" Wasilla looked up too, alarmed, then relaxed. "Well, it doesn't matter, right?"

Jessica approached Leo and crossed gaze with his. Leo anticipated an explosion, so narrow were her lips and eyes, but she took a deep breath and said, "My apologies, Leo!"

"It's OK, Jess, I can understand. By the way, I am with the girl you could not see yesterday."

"Yes, I know that." Jessica pointed with her head.

Leo glanced at Wasilla. Her mouth was agape, and her eyes were enlarged.

"I don't know how you do it, but the point is, it happened again," Jessica said. "As for Pete, it is hard to believe that he would do something like that." Her voice trembled and she swallowed a sob. "But things happen, not all of them good. I admit that I am biased, as you are only my stepson . . ."

"I understand, Jess" Leo reminded her and took her hand. "I am sorry too. Loneliness and isolation can change people."

Jessica sobbed. "You know, you and your girl are still welcome!" She turned ready to walk away.

"What about her?" Leo asked, pointing at Wasilla.

Jessica looked back, weighed his companion, and said, "Her too!" Then she quickly marched away.

"How did you do that?" Wasilla asked, still undoubtedly flabbergasted.

"No idea, absolutely none!"

"Wow! This is happening for the first time to me. I wonder who else you may make me see?" Her demeanor changed from amazement to disgust. "I hope not my father!"

"Vent out!" Leo encouraged her.

"Have you ever seen me wearing a short skirt?"

Leo looked at her. "You are wearing one now. Or it doesn't count, because it is a dress?"

"No, I mean before, when we were alive."

"Ah." He accessed his memory banks. "No, I don't. Even in PE class you never wore shorts, always full tracksuit."

"That was because of him. He used permanent marker to draw lines on my thighs to force me to keep them under clothes."

Leo gasped. "That's abuse!"

"Yeah, but who cared back then!"

"Very true." He sighed. This time he took her hand into his. "You weren't Muslim, yes?"

"No, but we came from a Muslim country, and the influence is strong. He abused and beat my brothers too. Anyway, it was pretty fucked up. He was a respected scientist, but at home he was a tyrant. I ran away when I turned twenty-one. He prearranged a marriage for me, which you can guess how well it would go with a lesbian. I couldn't come out, so I went to France, because I spoke the language. Then when he passed, I came back and rented this place. I missed Mom, I missed Jaques and Walid. Walid was already dead though . . ." She wrapped her arm around his and drew him closer.

"Jaques is still alive—he should be almost ninety now—but Mom and Walid are here, in the old place two streets down. They remember Lizzy—she and Walid were in the same dance class. It is nice to visit them with her. You know what? Mom cooks." She looked up at him, then down again. "Maybe you can make them see you when we visit—you know, the three of us."

Leo swore silently, calling himself dumb fuck—how had he forgotten that relationships were not just about sex? He'd always feared making this mistake, but it happened anyway.

"Thank you!"

"What for?" Wasilla asked. "If someone should be thankful, that should be me, as you let me talk about my miserable life. Maybe it was a blessing that I didn't live long. And you showed understanding and made up with Elise."

"What about the three of us moving together? To a place of our own. I'm sure we can find something here. You are not allergic to cats, I hope?"

Wasilla stopped and looked straight ahead, obviously digesting the idea. "OK! Let's go tell Liz!" She pulled him around her, and they faced the opposite direction. The realm was kind enough to spare them the long walk.

ANN'S INDISCRETION

"I need to talk to Ann," Elise said as she entered the loft.

Leo twisted his neck and looked at her questioningly.

She caught his gaze. "About Mom!"

"It is that bad?"

"Mmm." Elise nodded. "She kicked Dad out—told him to pack and go. She's sobbing all the time, barks at me, and spends hours looking at one point. Sometimes I can see through her."

"You can see what's bothering her? Isn't that obvious?" Wasilla rose from her chair and went to greet Elise with a peck.

"No, I can physically see through her. Like objects behind her. She becomes translucent, then solid again. I've never witnessed such things before."

"Seems serious, let's go!" He descended from the stepladder and put the screwdriver in his toolbox.

The doorbell chimed. Elise turned and pushed the handle down. The door opened silently, with no more angry squeaks. Leo's mom was standing on the steel platform; Sylvester was panting at her feet.

"I sensed that I was needed, no?" Annette followed her dog inside and let the leash loose. Sylvester sniffed Elise, then ran to Wasilla and finally—to Leo. He took the leash in his hand.

"Wass, let's make room for them to talk. Just hold this guy for me while I change."

"No, you don't have to go anywhere!" Elise protested. "You are already in the loop! Wass can't see your mother anyway."

"It's not about you; it's about the doctor here." Leo nodded at his mom. "She would need to ask intimate questions about Ruth. I think . . ."

"So, it is your mother . . . yes, Leo's right," Annette confirmed. "They better take a stroll."

Leo followed the happy, tail-wagging animal out. Wasilla followed Leo.

Annette inspected the space. "It is taking shape, I see. I miss my son, but it is fine; he's always on call. As am I. So, tell me, what is going on?" She checked the folding chair for dust then sat and retrieved her pack of cigarettes from her bag. She lit one and let the smoke out.

Elise leaned against the future kitchen island. "I am bisexual, as you already know," she paused, "and Dad is gay." She expected the older woman to gasp, underestimating Annette's professionalism; the doctor listened intently.

Elise proceeded to tell the whole story.

"Looks bad indeed," Annette said after careful consideration. "Seems your father was the only man she knew. Intimately, that is. She's also the traditional type—strict separation of gender roles. She was a stay-at-home mom and always dressed you in skirts, right?"

Elise nodded.

"Your dad coming out as gay ... this has shattered her entire world. Both worlds, actually. Everything is now a lie in her mind—her relationship with him, the marriage, having children. Her kid is also nontraditional. I can't give you answers right now. I need to think, and I would like to talk to her. To complicate matters, in a way, my son took you away from her. Gonna be tough. I don't have access to resources here, no colleagues to consult with, no way to introduce her to new people. And I am rusty, very rusty. I haven't treated a patient for over thirty years. Can you imagine?" She chuckled and extinguished the cigarette in the makeshift ashtray. "All I can promise you, sweetie, is that I will do my best."

"That's all I need, Ann, that's all I need. And your son." Elise finally surrendered to her anxiety and let her tears roll.

"And your other friend."

"And her too, yes." Elise sobbed.

Annette approached, took Elise in her arms and began stroking the rebellious locks.

⁕

Leo opened the door and assessed the situation. It seemed that the ladies were done talking. He let Sylvester run to his owner and showed Wasilla in. At the door, she almost went through his mother, but at the last moment Annette turned around and went back to the big empty carton in the middle of the room—she had forgotten her smokes.

Why can't she remember Wass? They'd been in the same damn class for nine years, and Tarek was his father's colleague. But then Annette and his dad have already been divorced, so, yeah, it made some sense. But why did his charm work for Jessica, but not for his mom?

Annette spun slowly around as if she had lost something, then crouched and lifted an item from the floor. "There." She showed the object in her hand. It was an earring. She reinstalled it on her ear and said, "Leo, can you walk me home?" She then shifted her sight to Elise. "It is not about you or your mom, sweetie, it is about me."

Leo pivoted on his heels and again opened the door.

"Say bye to the invisible one." His mother smiled and left the loft. On the street, she locked arms with her son and spoke in a serious voice, "Leo, I must tell you something."

"OK, whatever it is let's make it official!" joked Leo.

"Your sister's not dead."

"I kind of knew," Leo said calmly. "Where is she?"

"How did you . . . figure it out?" Annette seemed taken by surprise; her eyebrows nudged upward.

"We never visited her grave. How's that for a start?"

His mom looked down. "True. Anyway, do you want the truth?"

"Isn't that why you asked me to walk you home?"

"Geez, you are just like your father!"

"OK, sorry Mom, his habit is annoying. Go ahead." Leo pulled chewing gum from his pocket and inserted the strip into his mouth; he had no idea his pocket had contained it.

"Richard and I went to Woodstock in '69. You know, the famous festival? It was the sexual revolution, and we were revolutionaries."

Annette pulled Sylvester's leash to stop him from going around a tree and continued, "I had sex . . . both of us had sex, a lot of it, but not with each other. For what I can tell, you may have a dozen half sisters and brothers out there. Anyway, we came back, and I discovered that I was pregnant a few months later. Rich was OK with it. He said he would recognize the kid as his." She paused again.

When the pause stretched for too long, Leo said. "And?"

"The problem was that the baby was Black. There was this sexy specimen, LaRen, LaRen Johnson is his name, who I was with several times, and he was certainly the father, as he was the only Black guy I slept with. We were able to contact him via a common acquaintance, and to our surprise, he said that he would take her. He changed her name to Shannon."

"Shana, Shannon . . . Close enough," Leo said thoughtfully.

"Yes. It was heartbreaking, but I gave her up. I granted LaRen the wish for me to stay out of Shannon's life. Sadly, LaRen died in Vietnam in '75, just before the war ended. But he is here! He said that his parents took care of Shannon, and she went to university and became a lawyer and married, and you know, the standard fare—husband, kids . . . She's still alive it seems, but LaRen didn't have any recent arrivals to bring him news."

"Were you dead too?" asked Leo.

"As in?" Annette mumbled.

"Was she told that her mom had died?"

"I never asked . . ." She gazed down. "Perhaps I didn't want to know."

"Then why did you lie to me? Not that it matters now, just curious."

"Too much evidence of the pregnancy—eyewitnesses, photos. And the so-called morals of the time—you might have been shamed and bullied for having an out-of-wedlock half-sister of color. Kind of why Lizzy's father held out. Hearing their story made me realize that I had to come clean too and tell you the truth about Shana."

They walked without speaking for a while.

"Anyway, that is it, the secret. Or maybe not—LaRen and I are now seeing each other and Richard and me and Jessica and LaRen . . ."

"OK," Leo said simply. Then realized that there was a problem and asked, "How can Jessica see him though?"

"She was also there. This is where your father and she met."

A suspicion grew in Leo's mind. "Did they have an affair?"

"Yes," Annette confirmed. "That's why Richard and I divorced at the end." She quickly waved her hands. "But it wasn't just your dad, so don't give him all the blame."

Leo kissed his mother on the cheek. "Hey, Mom, I guessed as much. Can you make the connection so we can meet with this LaRen? Like I did with Lizzy and Dad?"

"I doubt it. The connection you and Elise share is unusually strong. I don't know of anyone doing that before."

"I made Jessica see Wasilla, and I only had a crush on Wass for maybe a year in school. True, I can't make you see Wass so far. But isn't it worth trying? Besides, the girls, er, the ladies have never been to New York."

"OK, we can do it, but now trying to help, what was her name . . . Elise's mom, is more important."

"Her name is Ruth. Sure! Thank you for confiding!" Leo opened the door and called the elevator. Sylvester wanted to return outdoors, but Annette pulled him into the cabin and the duo ascended.

Leo headed back thinking about the secret he had just learned. He was intrigued, but far from shaken or hurt. That LaRen guy banging Jessica! He could not sustain his laughter, and it echoed around shamelessly, disturbing the quietness of this world. Jessica was always so modest and righteous, not at all like his mom. Old Annette was a free spirit, and didn't abide by many rules. He was not surprised that she'd participated in the summers of love.

But Richard? Richard was an orphan, raised in a convent after his parents' untimely passings in the war. He rejected religion but he was always serious, stiff, and very traditional in most other matters. Leo could not imagine his father in a rainbow shirt and barefoot, stomping in the Woodstock dirt. But it was refreshing to know that appearances were misleading in a positive way. He entered the old warehouse and ran upstairs to the loft.

ABODE

Leo heard the roar of the engine reverberating throughout the always quiet, formerly industrial neighborhood, then went on the terrace to witness the grand arrival of his ex-wife and Steve. Beatrice stepped out of the sports car with grace, despite the low seat. When the door went up, she pivoted on her rear and put on display her long slim legs, shifted outward, found her balance, and effortlessly extracted the rest of her physique from the vehicle.

Leo chuckled. "Did you practice it?" he called.

"Of course!" She laughed in response and flashed a leg again, while adjusting the sparkling mermaid dress she was wearing.

Steve emerged from the vehicle far less gracefully, waved with hand, pulled up his trousers, and rushed to move the barn door on the ground floor for Beatrice but slowed down his pace after noticing that it was already open. He turned around and pressed the button of the key fob. The Lamborghini closed its wings and beeped.

Leo went inside to greet them, as they climbed the two flights of steel stairs and entered the loft.

"Wow! You did all of this?" Beatrice scanned the interior, looking truly amazed. "You two alone?"

"The three of us, in fact. There's also Wasilla, but you can't see her," Leo clarified.

"But I can!" Steve hugged the dark-eyed woman and sought her lips. "So, how did we miss each other? When did you die?"

Wasilla blushed as she avoided the intimacy with a sharp turn of her head. "Sorry!" She moved her arms behind her back and clasped her hands.

Steve flinched, then said, "Oh!" He lifted his finger, smiled, leaned and whispered something into Wasilla's ear. Her eyes grew large then she laughed and gave him a high five.

Leo moved his attention back to his ex-wife, but she was no longer in front of him. He turned. Bea and Elise were standing arm in arm below the large canvas hanging on the wall, displaying one of his art installations. It featured geckos and other animals, some copulating. Art critics would probably search for deeper meaning, if they could. He just enjoyed painting lizards and monkeys. When he looked around, he was the only one without a companion, as Steve was chatting keenly with Wasilla.

They had more dead friends coming. The place could get quite crowded by the standards of this world. Leo smiled at the thought and poured himself a drink.

"Why can't Leo make me see this Wass?" Beatrice lamented loudly. She was unhappy. She often dreamed of Elise, and the news of a rival wasn't welcome. But she tried to keep her disappointment hidden. "It is always awkward having invisibles around. I'm constantly on edge, worried that I might bump into someone."

"You won't, as it never happens, and you will grow used to that." Elise smiled. "You are yet to fully decompose."

"So, tell me who is she? And mind you, this is just small talk."

"Why the warning?" Elise asked. "What if it is big talk?"

"Shit, I gave it away, didn't I?"

Elise flicked her eyebrows, gazes crossed.

"Ah, never mind! So, tell me, who is she?"

"A girl from school. We weren't friends back in the day, but she was in Leo's class."

"Oh, what was her name again?"

"Wass. Wasilla, that is."

Beatrice searched her records for a match. "No, doesn't ring a bell. I don't think that Leo ever mentioned her."

"We met here. It was a long time ago, one day on the street. We recognized each other, we started chatting, then we became close."

"And the juicy part?" Beatrice dipped her knees, keen to hear the details.

"Do you like gossiping?" Elise asked abruptly.

Beatrice was taken aback. Just before uttering no, she changed her mind and came clean. "Sometimes. Apologies, I was being un-becoming."

"It came naturally. She made the first move as you did a while ago, but that is because I often procrastinate and wait for the stars to align. Satisfied?"

"Yeah, sorry," Beatrice mumbled.

"Now it is my turn to ask questions!"

"Sure, go ahead." Beatrice did feel embarrassed by the way she had interrogated the other woman.

"What is it like to fall pregnant and bear a child?"

Beatrice looked at her interlocutor with raised eyebrows.

"I want to know. Not that I can have a child here, but I am never-theless curious. I tried asking my grandmothers and my mom, but they were always elusive, unwilling to talk. Is it such a big deal and perhaps so bad that nobody wants to share?"

"Well, I think that people perceive it differently. I always worried that my boobs would drop, and I would get scars and stretchmarks."

"Did you?"

She spotted a door nearby and pushed it open. Behind it was a bedroom. Beatrice ushered the puzzled Elise in. "I will show you." She struggled with the zipper a bit, then exposed her breasts. "Look." She inflated her chest and waited a few seconds. "And now."

"I see."

Beatrice then lifted the skirt. "This is me roughly before I fell pregnant with Eric . . ." she paused, "and this is me shortly after he was born."

"So? Your boobs are much larger, you have put on weight, and the skin on your stomach is sagging, but that is to be expected, no?"

"What about the stretch marks? Here." Beatrice pointed to her lower abdomen and her thighs.

Elise approached and touched the skin, "No, I can't see any. Can you move forward in time?"

Beatrice got tired of holding her dress, wriggled out of it, and laid it on the bed. She closed her eyes briefly. "Now I am in Japan. Eric was three and the stretch marks had faded, but they never fully went away."

Elise shook her head. "No, I can't see any."

"Well, maybe it is this place." Beatrice pulled her panties up and reached for the dress.

"Wait!" Elise lifted her hand. "Can you show yourself pregnant? I want so much to see."

Beatrice shut eyes again and her stomach popped, and her breasts grew large.

"Wow! This look turns me on," Elise said. "I wonder why? Your ankles are swollen though."

"That's part of being pregnant. Extra weight, swollen ankles, cravings for strange food. In Africa, pregnant women ate clay, you know? And I binged on gherkins. Can I revert now?"

"Please, a few more moments." Elise stepped back and looked at Beatrice with adoration in her eyes. "I really like the way you look! I wish I could take photos; I would make a poster for my wall." She moved closer. "Can I touch?"

Beatrice nodded. Elise glided her hand over Bea's tummy, then bowed and put her ear on it. Beatrice felt butterflies in her loins. She was tempted to stroke the other's hair, but lifted her hands in the air instead, as far away as possible. "I doubt that you will hear any heartbeat, as it is just an illusion."

Elise kissed her tummy, sparkling another bout of desire. "I know, I know," she said with sadness in her voice. "Thank you, you may revert now."

"Hey, it is not that great! You also get cramps, the baby kicks quite painfully at times, many women become very fat, and giving birth may hurt a lot. Don't idealize it!"

"Many things cause hurt in the other world, I know, but many other things can bring joy too. And a sense of accomplishment, impossible here. I remember how happy I was when I overcame some obstacle, when I was alive. Performing my first split in dance class despite the pain, learning to swim despite the fear . . ." Elise looked up at Beatrice and smiled. "Like when I was challenged for stupid things like not wearing a bra and I stood my ground. Here, the split is painless, and I can't drown. It felt jolly when I gave my first concert, and Leo claims that I'm good, but the public was my old folks, and they had no one to compare me to. So even being average would do, and they were my relatives, and I was a mess before . . ."

Beatrice had put her dress back on and had sat on the bed. "But this place is beautiful." She pointed with her hands. "You made it so yourselves. You didn't just wish it into existence, right?"

"Beautiful compared to what? Pictures in old magazines . . ."

"No, no," Beatrice waved hands. "Magazines just gave you inspiration! You know how this world works. It makes existence easy, yet you got your hands dirty, and you created something cool from scratch! Was that not so? Stop being so self-deprecating! Finding the will to do all that and following up is an accomplishment in itself! Finding the will to learn to play music without the prospect of a prize! What instrument do you play, by the way? My guess is the piano." Beatrice had spotted the piano in the big room.

"Mmm."

"Then please play it for us now!" Beatrice pleaded with her hands.

"No, I'm not that good, no matter what Leo says."

"Irrelevant. I don't think that anybody else can play."

"Leo can. He also learned to play the guitar, and he plays with Wass sometimes."

"I didn't know that. Did he come learned?"

"No, I taught him. The piano, not the guitar."

"Then you are still more skilled! Come!" Beatrice grabbed Elise's hand, led her outside, then called, "Attention everyone!"

The company had grown larger, as the other zombies had arrived and were conversing with whomever they could see. Some guests looked frozen, usually a sign of addressing the invisible ones. Beatrice could see a couple faces—all Leo's friends, but she knew that there were more and realized the complication—not all would be able to enjoy the performance. But she persisted anyway. "How many people can you see?" she asked Elise.

"One, two, you . . . seven, why?"

"That's good! Seven is a lucky number." She giggled.

"Bullshit! But I will play, OK."

"For those, who are not blind and deaf to Lizzy here, she will play the piano!"

"Wow, you are a splendid announcer! Did you do that when alive?"

"For a while, yes, for my second husband's pageant show."

Elise sat on the stool, then stood up again and tried to walk away. Beatrice blocked her path and held her hand. The others started clapping. Steve whistled loudly with his fingers, then shouted out, "Por favor!" Only Leo seemed nervous and without enthusiasm. Beatrice found this strange. He was unlikely to be jealous for not being the star, so it must be something else. Elise returned to the stool, cracked her knuckles, opened the lid, and hit the keys. She played "Für Elise." Leo's facial expression returned to calm. Beatrice hummed. Perhaps she should just ask him why.

When Elise was finished, Leo disappeared inside the hallway and returned dragging his keyboard. He whispered something in Elise's ear and then sank in the hallway again. When he reappeared, he was pushing a large loudspeaker on casters with an amplifier box on top. He quickly set them up. "Now the party can start!" He winked at his girlfriend.

"Why don't you fetch your guitar?" Elise asked.

Leo's ears turned red, but he nevertheless fetched the instrument and plugged it in. The tiny crowd began chanting, "Go, go, go!" The pair commenced playing an unknown but entertaining tune, reminiscent of Rick Wakeman. Steve went behind the kitchen counter and started mixing and distributing drinks. The loft saw a lot of transformations—apparently nobody wanted to appear old. The air in the large room became hot. Beatrice wished that she could change into her tight leather pants and leather bra, the kind she dressed during the days she danced in clubs with friends. Her formal evening gown no longer felt apt. She went back to the bedroom, opened the closet, and looked inside. It belonged to a woman, so maybe some garment would fit.

"What are you doing here?"

Beatrice turned back sharply and dropped her purse. The roughly twenty-year-old girl with long dark hair was unknown to her. "And you are?" she asked condescendingly.

"I'm Wass, and you?"

Beatrice recoiled and tumbled onto the bed.

RECONCILIATION

Simon sat upright and turned his head when he heard the approaching steps. His daughter, clad only in lederhosen, took the space next to him on the bench and looked up at the third floor of the building across the street.

"I haven't tried yet today." He answered the unspoken question. He liked her lederhosen—he and Boris wore lederhosen often. And Tyrolean hats. And nothing else.

Elise lifted her feet on the bench and began sucking on her thumb, her gaze fixated on the building entrance.

"What are you doing?" her dad asked with notable disapproval.

She pulled her thumb out and glanced at it. "Ah, nothing, I do that sometimes while thinking."

"You are not a baby; this is a silly habit."

"Some people say that we make a full cycle; in old age we become babies again. I'm eighty-three, so it is about time."

"I'm a hundred and ten, and I don't suck anything!"

Elise weighed him with a wry smile. "Are you sure?"

Simon's face turned bright red, but he succeeded in containing the bubbling emotion; he just waved his hand dismissingly.

"OK, let's go!" Elise jumped onto the ground and looked back at her dad. A young woman in a 1960 green psychedelic minidress and high boots was standing silently behind him. "Mom?"

Ruth walked to the front and said a bit harshly to her husband, "Move!"

Simon shifted to the left, staring at his wife in disbelief. Her appearance sent him almost a century into the past. For all the time in this realm, she never bothered projecting any age, always staying true, so he kept seeing the same tired face he left behind when he passed. He was indifferent to this, more interested in Boris and the gang. But he had married a pretty one.

"Yes, I know what you are thinking," Ruth said. "Ann told me I should do it and try to reconnect with ancient friends and crushes. So, I am giving her advice a try."

"And?" Elise asked, leaning forward.

"Come here." Ruth patted the bench.

Elise took the few required steps and sat.

Ruth elbowed her lightly. "I'm still gathering courage. I remember a couple of guys who might have had a crush on me. Somebody may be around. Ann said that my fear is probably what is keeping them away, that I'm afraid to face them. She's right about my being anxious—I was always shy, and it never crossed my mind that they would see the young me, but still . . . now I am changing, getting used to thinking that I appear young, and do feel young when I transform. In a way, I understand you much better now, why you still at times act immature despite your true age. The body you wear makes it so, right?"

"That is my conclusion, yes," Elise confirmed. "I am glad that you are getting better!" She warmly hugged her mom.

"Shall we go upstairs?" Ruth suggested and rose to her feet.

"Me too?" Simon asked with a trembling voice.

"You too," Ruth smiled. "I accept you for who you are, for who you both are. You are not bisexual by any chance? We used to have sex, didn't we?"

Simon shrugged with a guilty expression. He wished he was. Long time ago, he wished to be straight. But her changed appearance—it struck a chord. It seemed to have awoken emotions from decades ago. It made having sex with her palatable and—by association—their two kids. Perhaps her narrow hips and unusually short hair, at the time, had played a role. But then she'd aged, both aged, and it became impossible for him to whip himself into action. Their life became sexless, at least as far as she was concerned. Perhaps this is what made her so cranky and bitter; almost certainly this was it! Oddly, she never asked him why their lovemaking died.

"You know, what threw me into rage when you came out of the closet wasn't so much your being gay, but the realization that I had to endure celibacy while you were making love with Boris all this time. It is unfair, isn't it? We are selfish creatures, and from my perspective you only took care of yourself." Ruth looked calm, simply stating facts. She opened the door and let them in.

Simon considered his response. "You are right. I am most amazed that you can say it without going mad, to be honest."

"It took me many months and professional help to get to this point. Praise Annette!" Ruth glanced up at the ceiling.

Simon continued, "It would have been different if we were able to talk openly about these issues, but you know how things were. If you were queer yourself, would you admit it in those days? Seriously, Rue? Being gay was a crime!"

"I know, Si." Ruth sighed. "I know. I don't blame you anymore. You can come back home if you want. Boris is welcome too, or you can stay with him. I already spoke to Mom and Dad. I don't know if your parents are aware . . ."

Simon nodded. His parents admitted to arranging the marriage to Ruth when they sensed that he was attracted to boys. To Boris, they were childhood friends, and their families were friendly too. Boris also eventually married traditionally and had two kids, as well, but divorced his wife and, in the noughties, came clean and started sharing his life with another man. Simon felt guilty leaving Ruth to hang high and dry for so long. "Listen, Lizzy, why don't you . . ." He turned around but Elise was no longer in the room. "Liz!" he called out.

"I believe she left," his wife said.

Simon rose from his chair and approached her. "Listen, I am not sure if it would work, but we can try . . . you know . . . as when we made the kids."

Ruth's gaze met with the floor and remained there. Her breathing became shallower and her face—red. She lifted her hand and ran it down his chest then pulled it and rolled it into a fist. Simon noticed her nibbling on her lips and realized that he had to make the first move but was also worried, doubting his ability to give her what she desired.

"Stay young please! And . . . I may need some help," he said as he embraced her, found the zipper of the dress, and slowly pulled it down. The dress joined Ruth's gaze on the floor, followed by her bra and more underwear.

"Close your eyes," Simon urged her quietly. Just in case she disobeyed, he moved behind her and transformed. His shirt joined her dress. He stepped in front of her again. "Now you may look."

Ruth glanced up and smiled, hesitantly raised her hands, and caressed his chest. His heart was racing, mostly due to worry, but he nevertheless unfastened his belt and let his trousers drop. He bent a bit and pecked her cheek—seemed she was trembling. She then suddenly dropped down on her knees, pulled his undies down and drew his penis into her mouth.

Simon froze at first, but then relaxed and gained some confidence—his good wife's use of her tongue triggered a literally palpable desire. She had never fellated him before. That therapist of hers had to be good—Rue was surprisingly proficient! All he had to do was think of young Boris Haseloff. And the pleasure he might manage to provide for her. That last thought was stimulating!

"Rue, I must confess that I am thinking of someone else . . ."

She looked up, then pulled him down to the floor. "That's OK, as long as you stay this way!" Then she switched her pose, reminding him of how they made the kids back in those days. He found something very sexy in her still wearing the white boots.

Elise could hear the panting from within her room. She was hoping that what was taking place on the other side of the door would not result in another disappointment for her embattled mom. She opened the wardrobe and stepped into her dreamworld, or else she might startle them if they sensed that they were not alone. One of her corny unicorns approached and sniffed her. She made it sit, discarded her clothes on the grass, and climbed on the back of the animal, wrapping her arms around its neck and pushing it with her heels. The unicorn got up, unsure what to do next.

She gave it another mild kick. It chose a random direction and trotted, seemingly pleased that finally somebody was riding on its back. She released her grip and stood upright, absorbing as much as possible of the gentle wind with her skin. She adored the sensation. She stretched her arms as if to embrace the airflow and kicked again. The animal accelerated the pace. Elise tried to flush out her worries and enjoy the ride. She wondered if men could appreciate a naked ride with their dangling stuff. The bouncing of her own breasts triggered her sometimes; perhaps it was the same for them. What would it be for very "gifted" women, like Margot?

The unicorn reached the shore of a small lake. It stopped and leaned to drink. Elise lost her balance and made a splash in the shallow water. The animal was startled and ran away. Elise felt happy—she was with the people she loved, her mom's condition had dramatically improved, and her parents had reconciled and even trying to be intimate. She swam to the deeper part, dived and inhaled the water, suppressing the urge to cough. That was another perk here—no way to drown but breathing kind of like a fish required some self-control.

The bottom of the lake was unimpressive—rocks, algae, and brown slime. She glided at an arm's length and waved her hands. Hundreds of small, bioluminescent crabs abandoned their holes and ran in random directions. The algae turned red, and the rocks began to sparkle when she brushed away the mud with the palm of her hand. She heard a booming splash, rolled over, and looked up. Leo grabbed her, twisted his body, and pushed off the bottom with both legs.

Before she could signal that she was all right, he reached the surface, held her head above the water, and swam toward the shore.

Elise took air in and gurgled, "Cool off, I'm OK!" Then she forced the remaining water out.

Leo halted his panicked swim and released his grip on her arms. She floated. "What went into your head?"

"I saw you diving, and you didn't surface for quite some time. I assumed that something happened to you."

"You can't drown here. Worst case is you getting sent back ashore if you panic and lose control."

They walked out. Leo's clothes were dripping. He took them off and spread them on a large rock. "You can't blame me. It's eons of instinct kicking in."

"What about think before you act? But thanks, anyway! Now, tell me, what brought you here?"

"You. Why otherwise would the storage door downstairs open to your old room?" Leo sat on the grass.

"I must've wished you here somehow," Elise said thoughtfully and joined him. "Maybe to say thanks to your mom?" Then she remembered her earlier thoughts. "Leo, would you like to ride a unicorn?"

"Say thanks to Mother? Does that mean that your mom has improved?"

"Remarkably! She made up with Dad. But tell me, would you ride a unicorn?"

"There are no unicorns."

"There are, here, I dreamt them up. But a horse will do too."

"Yeah, why not?"

"Naked? Now?"

"You are pushing it!"

"Please!" She insisted.

"I am not always in the mood to do what you ask of me!"

"But you do things you hate without my asking you to. How does that stack up?"

"Like what?"

"Going to night clubs, for example. You hate dancing, no? Yet you still come. Why? So, you can wait for me to get high and want to suck dick?"

"Well, that too, but you enjoy dancing. And I enjoy making small gestures like enduring a night of loud noise for you."

"But you don't have to do it anymore, now that Wasilla is around."

"Not indeed, however there is something in it for me too—I feel content looking at you two—"

"Dancing naked on a pole?" Elise interrupted him, giggling.

Leo got up, collected his clothes in one hand, and set out in the direction of the wardrobe.

"Hey, wait!" She jumped and ran after him.

"You reduce everything down to carnal pleasure!" He continued to walk.

"Because this is the only thing that ultimately matters!"

"Really? Do you really believe that?" He stopped abruptly and faced her. "I have been spending more time with Wass lately than with you! And she is lesbian! Do you know why that is?"

Elise bumped into him and took a step back. What Leo said was true—he and Wasilla had been working on his boat together, studying books, and going through his charts and notes. She even saw them kissing, albeit on the cheek.

"Wass likes you a lot indeed, and you obviously like her too, yet you two don't fuck." She resigned herself to the facts. "You two give each other things that I cannot offer, is that so?"

Leo nodded, then pulled her into his embrace. "I don't blame you; we all have a limited set of traits; no person is universal. She shares my interests in machines to a degree and in trying to figure out this world. She's very organized and helps me categorize my work and sees patterns where I can't. Me and you—we both like art. You and Wass—I don't know what it is, but you two certainly share something that I don't have."

"Me and Wass . . . now that you mention it, I don't know either." She sighed. "When we met, I was so happy that I was no longer alone. She is warm and calm. She is like an older sister, taking care of a younger one. Poor choice of words, I know, as it makes our relationship look like incest."

When they stepped out of the wardrobe, Elise threw the lederhosen on the bed and shut the doors behind them. Leo pulled his pants, zipped up, and donned his shirt. Elise opened the wardrobe again and produced a dress.

Leo raised his eyebrows when she put it on. "What's next, a *niqab*?"

"What is that?"

"A cover many Muslim women wear to conceal their faces. The outfit you chose—it is like, what was this thing called, *abaya*, just that the color's wrong."

"Aw, that's interesting, what does it look like?"

Leo shut the doors and tried to picture a niqab; when he checked a moment later, the wardrobe contained no such thing. "Seems I can't visualize it well." He looked around for a piece of cloth, but beside the curtains and the bed sheets, there was nothing else.

"Anyway, why did you pick this look?"

"Because I don't want you to think of sex every time you see me."

"That won't change a thing, so be yourself. Our sex life is so good that it overshadows everything else. I expressed concerns in this regard a long time ago, if you recall. We share interests—that is, me and you—but the prospect of making love to you is hard to brush aside. The piano lessons—why is my progress so slow . . ."

"You are doing well there, so don't underestimate yourself." She removed her garment and reached for the lederhosen.

"Hang on a sec!" Leo stepped back and checked her head to toe. "Turn to the side please."

She complied and asked. "What?"

Leo looked at her intently, then waved his hand in dismissal of his thoughts. "Nothing really. For a moment it appeared as if your tummy had grown."

She looked down and touched her tummy with both hands. It was warm; however it didn't feel enlarged. She donned the lederhosen and placed her index finger over her mouth. The place was quiet. She went to the door and cautiously opened it just a bit, then completely, and said, "Come, we are home."

Leo closed the bedroom door behind him and headed for the steel staircase leading to the loft.

"Can we take a stroll?" Elise asked. "Just the two of us."

"Sure!"

"What you said was not flattering and I want to change it, but I don't know how. I am not going to become smarter or get better at math if we abstain from sex. I dreamt up cuddly bears and white unicorns, neither even remotely original. I am only vaguely interested in tech and not at all in motorboats. Art, yes—music, paintings, sculptures, poetry . . ."

She paused. Leo looked at her and caught her biting her lip as she looked away. She was taking deep breaths but exhaling slowly and quietly, so as to not turn them into audible sighs. Leo opened his mouth to encourage her to continue, when she said, "I want to be a mom . . ."

Leo closed his mouth unsure what to say. Her wish was normal. The world they existed in was not. Elise grabbed his hand and somewhat apprehensively said, "This is who I am!"

Leo stopped and leaned against the trunk of the willow, one of the many lining the narrow riverwalk. He caressed the hand holding his. "There is nothing wrong with who you are, Lizzy. I am not perfect either. What I wanted to say was that I was happy having both you and Wass in my afterlife. I like observing both of you expressing your feelings toward each other—the glances, the kisses, the way you two hold hands. The kindness these two old women can exude. Perhaps me and Wass . . . I mean you have both of us in a certain way and me and her, we have each other differently."

"You mean that I fuck both of you and because you can't, you two talk?"

"If you want to express it in this manner, so be it, but yes, this is what I meant."

"OK, let's do it then!"

"Do what?"

She didn't answer, just rose on her toes and kissed him, then disrobed.

GRAVIDA

Beatrice sank her teeth in the apple and was about to turn the ancient TV set on when a shadow was cast, and somebody knocked on the frosted glass of the front door. She chewed the bite quickly, swallowed, and shouted, "Come in!"

The door screeched open, and the visitor stepped into the room.

"You again!" Beatrice grimaced.

"Sorry, I will go away!" Elise pivoted and faced the door.

"Cool off, I was kidding! When do you want me to start from today?"

"Third trimester."

"Dressed or not?"

"Not."

"Jeez, Liz, you know that you turn me on. Here . . ." Beatrice pushed the apple into Elise's hand and began removing her clothes. "Particularly when you touch me and caress. It is torture."

"You sound so dramatic. If it is really that bad, I won't bother you anymore. What about some coffee and we can perhaps take a stroll?" She looked at the apple and took a bite.

"No, go ahead. I am being too dramatic. I'm exaggerating. But aren't you yourself a bit obsessed?" Beatrice walked to Elise and bumped her with her protruding tummy. Elise sat on the ottoman behind her, stopped chewing, and pushed her ear against the bare skin, as if expecting to hear a heartbeat.

"I am seeking inspiration. I am aware that I wouldn't be able to experience it myself, but . . . can you keep a secret?" Elise looked up while rubbing her cheek lightly at Beatrice.

"Maybe. What is it?"

"At least for a while . . . I want to make a sculpture of, well, something like you. Leo built us a home and a motorboat. Mind you, he did not dream them up; he built them with his hands. We—me and Wass—helped, and it was actually fun to get dirty. And sticky . . ." She showed her molars and shook imaginary goo off her hands. "But the initiative was his. I want to create something with my hands too. At the lake . . . when I looked at you standing on the boat, you reminded me of Botticelli, his Venus . . ."

"Ah, the goddess of love!" Beatrice chuckled. "OK then, I am totally with you!"

"So, I am trying to memorize the feel of the shape . . ."

"Have you done sculpting before?" Beatrice fought off the heat raised by the other, running her palm up her inner thigh.

"No. Will you please lie on the sofa, and I will make some sketches." Elise put the half-eaten fruit on the table and pulled a sketch pad from the large bag. "I tried from memory, but I didn't get anywhere."

"Do you have a studio?"

"I found one, yes. It is in a nearby warehouse, a few streets from ours. It certainly belonged to a real artist in the other life. I just want to make a clay sculpture. I can't go further than that. Anyway, since I saw you as pregnant, that maternal instinct kicked in so badly that it is indeed on the verge of turning into an obsession. Why is this happening?" Elise almost started crying. "This world is some-times so cruel!"

"It can be far worse in the other one," Beatrice said coldly.

"I know. But can I vent my frustrations just a bit?" Elise started lay-ing wobbly lines in her pad. "You bitch about getting horny when I touch you, no?" She smiled.

"What about moving to this studio of yours?" Beatrice had long become bored from her home, and she didn't know how to travel yet, nor did she want to set foot in any of the luxury residences she lived in while alive.

"Er, if that's OK with you . . ."

"Of course it is! Let's go, please lead the way!" She got up from the sofa and headed straight for the door.

"Er . . . This is what I usually do," Elise said hesitantly.

"What?"

"Going naked around."

"It is contagious." Beatrice giggled and made a playful twist. "It does feel good indeed!" She then stretched like a cat and slipped into a pair of moccasins. "And I am projecting, so, even of somebody saw, they would not see the wrinkled me, right?" She put on a cowboy hat. "How's that?"

"Like a *Playboy* centerfold. You can drop the pregnant look though, if you want. You said that it was heavy." Elise pulled the front door open and let Beatrice go first.

Beatrice made a few dance moves shaking her stomach. "Nah, it is not heavy here. It is not the real stuff." She hesitated before leaving the garden and stepping out onto the street, but then made a decisive move forward and stretched again. "Wow, it does feel liberating!"

"What feels liberating?"

"Being in the nude on the bloody street! This is my first time, to be honest. Pulling stops takes time, as I had eighty years of baggage to deal with. In the old world, this is a lewd act. It still feels very awkward though, being in the city, not like that in the forest or on the beach." She looked down and glided her hands over her breasts. If Elise would only accept her advance . . . But no, friendship first.

Elise glanced at her and started talking. "This is not the old world. The weather's mild, everything is clean, and you can feel good about yourself because you can transform and there's no one to judge you. There's not a soul to see you too, besides the few who wouldn't mind, so, an indecent exposure charge would make no sense. Adam and Eve were naked in the Garden of Eden and were not ashamed. This existence here—what is it? From so many angles, it is like the Garden of Eden, isn't it? We are never left to go hungry or thirsty, we get to be with the people we love for a while, we suffer no diseases, we cannot be injured, we can shape-shift, and we experience pleasure without negative effects. Well, there's loneliness and boredom too, but these are things we can deal with, right? I learned to play music, now I am trying to get my hands dirty with clay. If you don't have anything in store, you will eventually figure something out. This place is like . . . OK, there are things for you to do, but it is up to you to find them. And if you don't want to, you just race through time until it is your turn to drift away."

"No one to judge me? There's plenty of dead people to cross paths with!"

"Like whom? Leo, Steve, your mom? What would be the big deal?"

What about my father? Beatrice shivered.

The studio was not very big. Unfinished clay prototypes piled up in one corner. There was a sofa and a chaise. Stairs led to a loft, which was used as an office and a storage space for sketches and supplies. Elise pointed at the chaise. "This is where you can sit. Do you want something to drink?" She left the bag on the floor and started climbing the stairs.

Beatrice swept the space with her green eyes. She'd never been to a sculptor's place. It looked rough and inelegant, yet cozy. She saw a bronze female nude, went to it, and knocked on the metal. It sounded hollow. The face was blank, like the faces of clothing store mannequins. But at least there was a head. The decapitated dolls in some outlets always creeped her out.

"Bea, do you want coffee or tea?" Elise called from the loft.

"No, I'm good!" she shouted back. "Do you know who the artist was?"

"Nope, too much work to find out. I never tried to find out who my piano teachers were, as it felt wrong to search their apartment for clues. I try to be respectful and not trash the place, as maybe the owner is around but, well, invisible to us."

Behind Beatrice was a large, covered bin. She lifted the lid and peeked inside. It contained wet clay. She was tempted to leave deep imprints with her hands and spread clay over her body, but instead, she dropped the lid back and returned to the sofa, where Elise had sat with a mug in her hand.

Looking at the "little one" again, Beatrice could not help feeling that there was a change in her friend. "Can you stand up please?" she asked.

Elise left the mug on the wooden crate serving as a table and rose to her feet. Beatrice studied her slowly. "Lift your dress."

"You want me to work au naturelle?"

"I think you've put on weight."

"I have been here for a very long time, and I haven't changed one bit. I once shaved my hair and the next day it was back to this." She pointed at her head. "Luckily, I groomed myself before I died. For my birthday party, you know, Mom took me to a salon." The memory seemed to stir emotion.

"You were slimmer! Can you go about four months back?"

"That's way too precise."

"OK, whatever, just not very close to now." Beatrice was sure. "Yes, you have definitely put on weight. Your tummy's larger and your boobs too! Look at me." She transformed. "This is me in summer of '94 . . ." She shifted shape again. "And this is around New Year, some six months earlier. Did you notice difference?"

Elise nodded. "You mean I changed? As if I am expecting?"

"Mmm. You should see a gynecologist."

"Bullshit! it is impossible to get pregnant here!" Elise did not sound confident. She sat again and touched her breasts. "Or I might be, this world . . . it is unpredictable."

Beatrice sensed the anxiety and joined her on the sofa. "Relax! There is nothing to fear. Isn't that what you wanted to live through?"

"Yes, but . . . I am terrified! Scared that I may give a birth and scared that I may give a puff . . . You know, I read about women showing all signs of being pregnant because they wanted it so much. You said that I was obsessing! Maybe I am one of them!" She shivered.

"But such a case may not be that bad. What if it is in a way real, though, like, what if there *is* a baby? It will be the only one in this world! Who will it be able to see? How will it exist? This is not a place for babies, no!" Elise started to tremble with droplets of sweat emerging on her temples.

Beatrice wrapped the frightened woman in her embrace and began stroking her unruly hair. "Try to calm down, Liz," was all she could muster. She understood the fear. She was terrified when her period was late, and the test came in positive. She was on edge for eight months after that, then came postpartum depression. "Hey!" She shook Elise gently. "Let's go tell Leo and Wass. You'll need their support whatever the case may be. And Leo's mom, she is a doctor." Beatrice shed the bulge, looked around and added, "I must think of some clothes!"

"You already did," Elise said wearily.

"Ah!" Beatrice looked down, surprised. "How do you know that I like this outfit?"

"I don't, you do."

"But didn't I need a closet or something?"

"Everything is an illusion here." Elise rose and straightened the creases on her dress. "No, you don't. Closets make it easier and more predictable, that's all. You felt a strong urge to cover, didn't you?" Suddenly, she appeared very tired; her shoulders slumped, and she dragged her feet in the direction of the door.

"So many years and I still discover things!" Beatrice was fascinated and a complete opposite in terms of mood.

"Brace for more." Elise opened the door and stood by it, waiting for her friend. "Is that normal?"

"What are you talking about?"

"Desiring a child and being scared shitless at the same time."

"You shall ask the one and only Ms. Ann!"

"Why are you mocking her? She's good." Elise pouted.

"I am not. It is a statement of fact. Are you aware of any other doctor that you can see and talk to?" Beatrice was walking fast, wondering why the space was not folding, or maybe folding the wrong way. The studio should have been much closer to the trio's pad by her estimate. Elise's pace was unsteady—she was slowing down and falling behind, then catching up running. When she caught up again, Beatrice stopped and looked at her friend. Her face was white, drained of blood, her lips were turning blue, and her breathing was fast and shallow. Leo's mother was their best bet, but Beatrice had no idea how to get there. She closed her eyes tightly and shouted in her mind *"Ann!"* while imagining her former husband's former home. She wished that she had a joint or a cigarette, but she had no bag, purse, or even a pocket in her skirt to store them. She heard retching and looked at Elise again. Elise had leaned over the railing of the riverwalk, vomiting in the water. Beatrice felt cold sweat rising quickly, the strong pounding in her chest. She walked to Elise, grabbed her shoulders, spun her, and looked her in the eyes.

"Liz, toughen up for fuck's sake, girl." Beatrice put effort into keeping her voice calm. "You are scaring me too. Why can't we get to your place? You are not doing something, are you?"

"She probably is," a female voice sounded from behind Beatrice. "What is the problem now?"

Beatrice sighed noisily with relief—Annette had breached the fort!

"You both look frightened, but Lizzy here takes the lead. What's going on?"

"I think that she is pregnant," Beatrice said.

The doctor raised her eyebrows but did not dismiss the statement outright. She inquired calmly, "What makes you think so?"

"She has put on weight, her breasts are enlarged, and she just threw up."

"Liz, climb on this bench and remove your clothes," Annette commanded. "No periods here, so I can't use that as an indicator," murmured the doc, while inspecting the patient.

"Liz, do what you did for me—go a few months back in time," said Beatrice.

Elise shifted her shape.

"That's smart! Adapting to local conditions, I see." Annette smiled. "I agree that Lizzy is fatter now and the breasts are tender, there's some spotting too, but being pregnant? I don't know. Can this even happen in his world?" Annette pulled a pack of cigarettes and offered it to everyone. "A perk in the afterlife—medicinal purposes tobacco." She chuckled again. "Lizzy, it is obvious to me that you are terrified of being pregnant, no?"

Elise nodded. "What if I do give birth?"

"Unlikely, I believe."

"Yeah, but it cannot be ruled out. Leo made people see each other, and that was unheard of too." Elise seemed to be slipping back into panic despite the nicotine—the cigarette was shaking in her hand.

"Then you better prepare, we all will be here for you!" Annette tried to reassure her.

"I don't worry about myself. I worry about your potential grand-child! With no other kids around, it would be hell!"

"Wrong!" Beatrice barked, drawing puzzled gazes. "We can trans-form, can't we? We can be kids if we want to, right? So, there's the solution!"

"You have adapted well!" Annette said respectfully.

Elise squatted, grabbed her head, and started crying silently.

"You are going to burn your hair, bitch!" Beatrice snatched the cig-arette from Elise's hand and threw it in the water. "Come, Lizzy, now you can let us walk you home; don't make space bend away." She helped her get up and handed her the clothes.

Annette pouted lightly. "Ah, was it what she was doing? I did have trouble finding you indeed!"

Beatrice nodded. "Mmm, I think so."

ANTON

"Gonna spend some time with Mom," Elise announced in the morning, and sank into her room.

Wasilla was seated on the sofa, playing Solitaire. Leo poured himself some coffee and dropped next to her. "Hey, Sis, aren't you bored?" He sighed and continued without waiting for the answer, "I am. I lost the will to do anything lately. Other than trying out more elaborate ways of inserting my member into something or having something inserted into me, that is. I still have projects, just that I keep procrastinating. It was fun to work with you on the house and the boat, but these are all done now. Don't you have any wishes? Like something you would want me to make for you, which I would enjoy making?"

"Has Lizzy no such wishes?"

"I'm asking you. Lizzy—she's up to something, haven't you noticed? Quietly disappearing, becoming unreachable . . ."

Wasilla laid the cards she held in her hand on the table. "Now that you mention it, yes. When you showed up, she used to disappear too, but she told me where she was going and what she was doing. Maybe she needs time on her own? Now that she might be pregnant. Time to reflect, get used to the possibility of bringing a child in this weird world." Wasilla paused. "But then don't we do the same?"

Leo smiled and leaned on her. "No, Sis, we all always announce what we are up to; it had become second nature. She just blew the trumpet, didn't she? When one of you sneaks out, I notice."

Wasilla scanned her recent memories for evidence to the contrary but drew a blank.

"Would you throw the cards for me?" Leo sat upright and took a sip.

"Nobody plays these games here, as you know."

"We can start, there is no law against it. At some point, I thought that people went to fortune tellers seeking only positive prognostications, hope. But later it dawned on me that predictability was more like it, knowing what's to come. Our existence here is comfortable and secure, but still unpredictable. Not in a bad way. Perhaps the only secret of consequence is when the drift will take place and where it will take us to. But now with Lizzy expecting, I am also edgy."

"How's your research going?" Elise appeared all dressed up. She'd chosen a loose dress even though her change was hardly noticeable. She was balancing on elevated platforms and carried a purse.

"Wow, so atypical," Leo murmured, then asked in a louder voice. "Do you want a ride on the boat?"

"Spy op?" Wasilla whispered, giggling.

Leo used her head to prop himself up. "Perhaps."

"No, I will take a shortcut," Elise replied and left the loft. They could hear her descending the metal stairs until the door shut closed.

He sat back. "I procrastinate. Maybe I don't want to know. I'm writing a program to analyze the data, but its completion always slips away."

"Where are your notes?"

"In my room. Why?"

"I also have bacon in this project, haven't I? I collected data for you, and I helped you organize it. I would like to know what happens too, and I understand your lack of will. So, let's try together, shall we?" Wasilla rose from the couch and headed for his room. Leo put his mug on the table and leisurely stretched on his back. She sensed his failure to follow and looked at him. "Up, Bro! Unless you want to vegetate . . ."

Leo collected himself and joined her. The binders with his notes and charts were neatly lined on the shelf. In contrast, the large desk was littered with pages torn from a notebook, containing scribbles and occasional doodles. In the corner sat the computer Leo succeeded in keeping after multiple visits to the store he found it in. The machine was an iMac—a G4 model circa 2003, with a sentimental value; he'd owned one of these. They found it in an antiques store, amongst old china, patinated silverware, and vintage clocks. It was on display alongside the other items and would rightfully be considered antique in the old world. Leo had not believed his eyes when he'd spotted it and immediately, and pointlessly, began praying that the machine was in working order. It was.

Leo "purchased" it promptly and brought it home, but the machine was gone the next morning. Leo found the store again and again took his trophy home only to find it missing when he opened his eyes. He'd called a meeting. "You two have been here for much longer than me. Any ideas how I get to keep the thing?"

"Why?" Wasilla giggled. "So you could watch porn?"

Leo furrowed his eyebrows. "Who needs porn videos with you two around?"

She giggled again. "Yeah, good point! Back to topic—I don't know. I have never had a desire to keep objects, even in the previous life. Or . . . wait a second . . ." She thought for a moment. "When I was little, I was fascinated by trains and cars, but being a girl, I got dolls and strollers instead. I had my brother and his toys indeed, though, he was selfish and didn't want to share. I wanted my own toy car, and I got so obsessed that I started dreaming of possessing one. I wanted to keep it just as you do now, I guess, and I clutched it in my dream—"

"I don't see the point," Leo complained.

"Well, I started dreaming of waking up with the toy; in a way, I kept it. It was a dream within a dream indeed, but isn't this world a dream? At least this is what you suspect, and people dreamt up things, right? Lizzy, Steve. Even you—how do you think you got all the materials for the house and the boat?"

"OK, I get it, but I can't force myself into a specific dream and then hug the computer and hope it stays."

"May I suggest something?" Elise chimed in. "We fetch it again and we keep vigil."

Two pairs of eyes had turned at her quizzingly.

"We don't fall asleep for a while. Also, we can try hiding it in dreamworld, if this doesn't work."

The vigil worked.

Back in the present, Wasilla looked at the shelf and his desk with disapproval. It was obvious to her that the binders were untouched. Leo's propensity to leave things lying around was evident below and to the left.

"Shall I tidy up your desk?"

Leo, aware of her habits, said, "Sorry, Wass, but let me be me. I know what's in your head. I can find my way in my chaos most of the time."

"OK, no problem." Wasilla sighed silently, then abruptly changed the tone, "Leo!"

He jerked. "What!"

"Thank you!"

"What for? I didn't let you tidy up."

"No, not for that. For being a friend. I mean . . . I joked about the porn, but truth is, it must be hard on you watching me and keeping your hands away."

Leo chuckled. "Man, why do you think I call you 'sis'?"

"No idea, to be frank."

"Because I conditioned myself into thinking of you as my sister. That was my simple way to cope. But even if you weren't queer, I would still not try to touch against your will. It is a simple expression of respect."

"I've seen so many men ignoring that." Wasilla recalled memories from her other life. "They didn't take body language and even a vocal no for an answer. When I was working as a stripper, their drooling faces . . . They were so repulsive, yet there were those who waited for me at the staff entrance and asked me out. Some turned violent. Luckily, the club had bouncers. I also started wearing disguises."

"Yeah, the old world is pretty shitty. Why did you work as a stripper, by the way? You are smart. Wasn't there something else for you to do?"

"When I ran away from home, I had no money, and I wasn't thinking quite straight. I met a woman, Sharlize; she was kind, and she was lesbian too. She gave me a roof over my head and, well, we became intimate. She was making a living as a waitress in this club, the owner saw me and offered me good pay to strip. So, I went after the money. I decided to stay the course until I saved enough. Years later, the owner was outed as gay. He's smart: he turned his establishment into a queer club."

"'He *is* smart' you said. Does this mean that he's here?"

"Yes. Too bad you two can't meet. Steve, too."

"What has Steve to do with it?"

Wasilla blushed.

"Spill it out," Leo said. "What has been kept a secret?"

"I can't."

"No, no, no, you can! Or else I will tickle you to death!" Leo laughed and raised his hands, wiggling fingers. Wasilla tried to escape, giggling, but he blocked the door.

"Did he ask for whatever it is to not be divulged?"

Wasilla looked up at the ceiling, trying to remember. "No, I don't think so, but he's your best friend, so how does it come you don't know?"

"Maybe I do." Leo paused. "Ah—it is bad that Steve can't meet a gay man. Your secret is that Steve is bisexual?"

She nodded. "So, you *do* know."

"I found out here. He has a friend, Joseph Schultz. I can't see him, but the point is, he was dressing in classic gay nightclub attire when Joseph was around and that made me think, and eventually, I asked. We've been together, haven't you noticed that? His outfits, I mean."

"I paid no attention, no. To me it was normal, knowing who he was. Also, I can see Joseph; I met him in the old life in a gay club where he was bartending. He's older than us, he was born in . . . maybe '58? Nice guy."

"Bartending? Wasn't he a doctor?"

"Yes, but he was involved in a scandal—he had a relationship with a younger man and when the other guy's parents found out, they accused him of brainwashing their son. He lost his license as a result and his job too. He recovered later but he had a rough patch." Wasilla picked the last loose notebook page and tapped the stack of paper on the desk. She placed it near the edge and exclaimed, "Oh!"

Leo laughed. "Yes, Sis, you were unable to resist after all. You were doing it while talking. Thanks, nevertheless!"

"I'm sorry!"

"No worries! I will rectify the problem fast." Leo reached for the binders and placed them on the desk. "When I finish my program, we'll input the data from these and graph it."

Wasilla took a binder from the stack and paged through it. "Do you know what's inside? Seems you never touched them after me."

Leo gazed down and shook head. "No, I never checked your work."

"Each binder contains data from a single family. You always look at the whole when seeking answers and that is processing too much information; crucial bits may get lost in noise. What about breaking things down into chunks? If we see a pattern in one family tree, we can then cross-reference with others."

"You are wise. I was a CGI specialist for the most of my career, not a statistician."

"Neither am I. It is just the way I think." She found the binder of her own family and opened it with a frown, for her father's name was mentioned in the notes. "Let's start. Mine or yours?"

"Yours."

"OK." Wasilla detached and unfolded the large chart and spread it on the desk. Both trained their eyes on the lines, dots, and labeled arrows in silence.

"We only have markers for arrivals and departures, not lifetimes," Leo murmured. "What if?" He quickly pulled a ruler and orange pencil from the drawer and leaned over the chart. "Go ahead, give me birth dates."

"Mom is '42. Walid—1970. Grandmother—'23 or '24, I don't remember precisely. Granddad was 1911. You know what else we are missing? The living ones."

"Right. But we are also missing the ones that are not here, like your dad."

"We have no way of knowing if he made it here."

"It should not matter; we can be almost certain that he didn't. Your paternal grandmother is in this chart though, you said you saw her, right?"

"Yeah. Isn't it strange that, more often, it is a male relative that is missing? My father, his father, my uncles, your ex-wife's dad. As if this place prefers women."

"Let's try to stay focused, Wass. When I get sidetracked by such thoughts, I end up far away."

"Sure."

Both looked at the updated chart.

"Let's update mine too, that would give us more data to work with," Leo said imploringly.

"OK, but look—people were also born while others were here."

"So? This is normal, it happens all the time."

"Damn, I can't put my finger on it!" Wasilla cursed uncharacteristically and nibbled on her lip. "OK, update your chart. Gonna bring some coffee."

She returned with two mugs and looked at the graphs again. "See here, this is when my great-grandfather drifted." She pointed at a spot. "I was born after his death; I don't remember him at all. But my great-grandmother is still around. She was alive when I was born."

Leo pulled his chart, "Same here—Grandfather Marcus and Babette!" He quickly checked his other relatives. "But what is the connection?"

"When did your great-grandmother drift away?"

"After I died, why?"

"And your great-grandfather?"

"After mother died, I was told." Leo narrowed his eyes and scanned the chart. "And Nick and Viv."

"Who's George?" Wasilla pointed at another labeled arrow.

"My uncle."

"Does he remember your great-granddad?"

"Remember? I don't know. Probably not, I think that he met my aunt after Marcus passed away."

Wasilla shuffled the papers and moved her chart to the bed. "Maya passed, Christelle and Nabil were born, Nabil died, drifted, then Christelle," she murmured.

"I think I see a pattern," Leo said while still looking intensely at his own chart. "There!"

Wasilla came closer and began staring silently and sipping coffee from her mug.

"Can you see it?" Leo asked, pointing. "These . . ."

She turned around and glanced again at her family tree diagram.

Elise leaned silently against the door frame. She was happy seeing her two lovers absorbed in shared thoughts. At times, that made her feel sidelined, but she knew that she was not the center of their little universe. She was often getting double the attention, and she easily brushed the sentiment aside.

"So . . ." Wasilla started slowly, "you think that people seem to drift away after . . ." She turned around and her gaze crossed with that of Elise. "Ah, hi Lizzy! How's your mom?"

"Confused perhaps. Conflicted in her emotions," Elise answered. "Me too."

"Why?"

"Anton's here. Big bro. I was wondering why I was so drawn to Mom's this morning . . ."

"Oh!" both her friends exclaimed.

"He must be, how old . . . eighty-seven, eighty-eight?" Leo speculated. "Not a bad lifespan."

"No, hence the contradiction. Shall we mourn him or rejoice?"

"Rejoice of course!" Wasilla said.

"Yes, but I can't," Elise complained. "I don't know why. Neither can Mom."

"Maybe it is just a leftover from the other world? You know, somebody dear had departed, that sort of thing?" Leo tried to explain. "We had no knowledge of this place. Everything was based on hope for those who believed in the afterlife, but deep inside they had their doubts. For the rest, people like us, dead was final, no? So, reason enough to feel sad."

"Anyway, what were you two doing?" Elise absentmindedly shook off her shoes.

"Trying to decipher the drift."

"Ah, the local death." Elise said with sadness in her voice. She pivoted and headed for the big room. She felt somebody's piercing eyes on her neck and glanced back—Wasilla had followed her, carrying two empty coffee mugs and the orphaned pair of footwear.

Leo carefully folded the two charts and put them back in their binders. He pulled Elise's and updated it somewhat reluctantly, then folded it back and returned the binder to the shelf.

Why was Elise so gloomy? Leo thought, leaving the room. It was contagious, as his heart felt heavy too.

PRELUDE

It was Beatrice's idea to throw a welcoming party for the new arrival. However, she was not amongst the attendees gathered in the loft. It was a private affair, only relatives of the recently deceased and of course, the deceased himself.

"Lizzy pregnant! Here? Seems that it is true!" Anton looked at his sister in amazement and took a sip from his glass. Then he placed it on the table and leaned backward, balancing his chair on two legs. "Lizzy, stand up please, I wanna have a good look at you. It is so hard to believe! My little sister going to be a mother in the afterlife!"

Elise got up and turned sideways to display her enlarged tummy. "It is not real," she said. "Everything is an illusion. I guess I wanted so much to be a mom, and this place granted me that wish to the extent it could." She transformed. "You see? It is gone!"

"Wow!" Anton landed the chair on all four and drank some more. "Can you go all the way to the end too? Like, needing a wheelbarrow to move your belly around."

"No." Elise scoffed and looked down. "I don't understand it at all. It is not supposed to happen; we cannot take a shape we don't remember. I was never pregnant, so why am I morphing now? It is scary."

Leo took her hand under the table when she sat. "This realm is unpredictable, but this is not bad—it keeps us entertained, surprised. Lizzy being pregnant is perhaps part of that."

"Yeah, I am trying to enjoy it!" Her spirits lifted. "You should see . . ." She giggled and stopped.

"See what?" her brother asked.

"Nothing actually, it is not for your eyes."

"See what?" Anton continued to insist with a laugh. "What is not for my eyes?"

"The way they make love I suppose," Ruth chimed in from the corner.

"Mom!"

"What? Don't I know you well enough?" Ruth chuckled.

"Damn!" Elise gave up. "You do!"

"Well, you asked me if that was OK, didn't you?"

Elise blushed and the other people around the table laughed. Anton threw a surprised look at his mom, given how that type of talk was atypical of her. But she passed three decades ago—she had plenty of time to change. And his father being gay! And this world! Anton felt overwhelmed and reached for his glass.

"So, are we set to live forever, then? And where's God?" He snorted.

Leo scoffed. "God is nowhere to be found as usual. And no, we don't get to live forever, at least not here. I thought that there was nothing after death in the old world, but I was wrong. Maybe we do exist forever, maybe not, it would be stupid to claim otherwise."

"Makes sense. So, what exactly happens here then?"

"We drift away. We disappear after a while."

"After how much while?" Anton sat on the edge of his chair.

"Your sis is still here," Leo answered. "So, it is a while. I'm trying to figure out what's causing it, though. It is not like a classic lifespan—purely elapsed time. The drift always takes place about six months after a related new arrival. Time is not linear here, and there are no calendars or clocks. These six months are what it felt like, what those we asked estimated."

"Eighty-four years then," Anton said thoughtfully.

"Could be far more or far less. Seems like people who died in the wars had shorter stints in this realm—"

"Can't we talk about something else? You just died. Are you in a hurry to cross another river Styx?" Elise intervened in the conversation, but her brother ignored her.

"You mean those who died young?" Anton asked.

"Perhaps, I need to study the phenomenon more!" Leo added hastily, while the eyes of the others shifted to Elise. "Anyway, I wanted to ask what happened on Earth in the last few years. Is a Trump still the US president?"

"Anton, you were always a jerk!" Elise's voice sounded angry at first, but then she calmed down. "But if my time is drawing near, I must accept. However, it is normal to be afraid, so don't judge too hard when I go bipolar."

"Oy, oy, oy!" Anton looked at his little sister, surprised. "What did I do?"

Leo started speaking fast, "Well, as I said, I don't think it is time alone; it is if still-living people remember you. Looks like when the last person who knew someone dies, the other drifts away soon afterward. There are outliers in the data and the data is very sparse, so I can't be sure. The point is, for as long as someone close and not yet dead remembers you, your existence here is assured. You had kids, no?"

Elise rose abruptly and rushed to the kitchen sink, where she began retching. Wasilla and Leo jumped and ran after her.

"I'm OK! Must be the 'baby.'" She made air quotes and bent over the sink again.

*
**

Leo turned the tap on and looked at the drain. The water swirls somehow drew him in, as he soon felt disoriented and dizzy. He grabbed the edge of the countertop and pulled his sight away from the hypnotizing whirlpool with difficulty. The room was dark, and the guests were gone. Elise was standing next to him, naked and larger still. He had jumped. "What were we doing?" Leo asked.

"I threw up again. It tickled . . . Did you just jump?"

"Yep. I was at the first party with your brother. Were there more?"

"It will come to you, don't try to force it. You know how it works. Come, let's go back, I feel better now." She took his hand and led the way. As they made it around the corner into the hallway, she turned abruptly and pinned him to the brick wall with her stomach. Leo carefully enveloped her with his arms, his heart rate increasing. He was certain—something happened in the interim and he began feverishly trying to unlock his memories.

"How many months?"

"What months?" Elise was missing context.

"Since the party."

"About four."

"So, you should be on the final stretch now, no?"

"I can't transform anymore."

"As in shape-shift?"

"Yeah, I stay inflated." She took a step back. "Like that." She pointed at herself.

"Isn't this what you wanted?" Leo took her hands into his and kissed them one by one.

"I don't know what I want anymore . . . but I appreciate the surprises."

Her appearance took him decades into the past, to the time of the expectant Beatrice. He didn't count on a naked pregnant woman to be a turn on, but to his amazement he was wrong. It acted as an aphrodisiac. Perhaps because the instinct to produce offspring was so ingrained. But they were all deceased now, so why would zombies want to breed? There was a generous supply, some nine billion souls. But then Elise appeared to be heavily pregnant. His head began to spin again. *Not another jump, please, no!* Leo felt Elise's tongue reaching deep inside his mouth. He opened his eyes wide and extended his. His hand swept her hair away from her face. He kept kissing her smooth skin while going down on his knees. Once there, he ran his tongue over her tummy. He stopped at the belly button for a moment, then finished in one brisk stroke. The aphrodisiac kicked in. His hand crawled up her inner thigh, and his fingers glided over her vulva, then he split the labia with his thumb. Elise moaned and pushed his head down.

He resisted with a kiss and scanned the dimly lit hallway. Behind her, he spotted the silhouette of the armchair decorating the space. He rose slowly, led her in silence, sat and gently tugged her down. Elise turned around and straddled his lap. Leo ran his hands down her flanks then reached for the front. She felt warmer than usual. Her breasts had become big and soft. Her nipples were erect. They were also wet and somewhat sticky, but he didn't mind. She rocked her hips slowly a few times, rubbing her sensitive petals against his eager appendage then rose slightly and let it slide in. Leo quivered and huffed. The sensation rippled throughout his body. He offered the support of his hands and leaned back. They were now one. The experience was always enchanting. He cherished this woman in all her forms, and he was so happy to have her by his side or be inside her or whatever. He didn't want to go off fast, he wanted to stay joined with her and let the pulsing delight gather strength.

Her swaying became faster and her panting louder. Leo clenched his teeth and took a deep breath. Then he freed his hands and hugged her tummy. His cheek touched her back. She continued to rock her hips, emitting soft moans. Leo held her bulged stomach, then reached for the breasts. Elise grabbed his hands and rubbed his palms against her chest. She rocked faster, her tummy bouncing at each swing, her moans getting louder. Leo swayed too, high voltage pulses running from his groin all the way to his brain. He missed the moment when her muscles contracted, and a jolt traversed her frame. He sensed that her body was no longer tense, but Elise continued to roll her hips until his whipped-up receptors combined their signals into a single jolt and brought his extasy about. The eruption lasted unusually long. Jolly tears rolled down his face; that didn't happen often. She slowly reduced the amplitude of her swaying down to nothing and leaned on his chest, catching her breath.

Leo wiped the tears, kissed her neck and let his heart rate normalize. Then asked quietly, "Have you started to lactate? Your tits are wet."

"You are still not back, I see." She rose, turned around, and straddled him again, balancing on his knees. "Do you wanna try?"

"Mm . . ." Leo hesitated.

"Here!" She squeezed her breast a bit, dipped her index finger, and then put it in his mouth. "How's that?"

"I don't know. It has no taste, but I don't remember what it was like in the other life anyway. Holy shit! Something kicked!" Leo looked at her tummy with surprise.

"Yes. It started after I lost the ability to shape-shift. There's a heartbeat too! Two in fact."

"Twins? Get up!" Leo leaned and glued his ear to her stomach, but all he could hear was the pounding of his own heart. He tried recovering his memories one more time still to no avail. "Am I the father?" he asked, his voice shaking.

"All I can say is that I have not had sex with another male ghost since that night with Steve at the techno club. Also, you know that—"

"This was a stupid question, yes," interrupted Leo. They had checked his bodily fluid many months ago under a microscope, and by old world standards, he was sterile. She never had periods either. No woman that they knew here had.

"You must be the new Virgin Mary." Leo smiled and bowed his head down. "May I have your holy blessing?"

"Blasphemer!" She slapped him lightly and reshaped her mouth into a crescent. "Yes, you can!"

The door at the bottom of the hallway opened. Leo turned his head. The silhouette of a woman appeared in the frame, lit by the moonlight from behind.

"Where's Lizzy?" the woman asked.

"Bea?" *What is she doing here?* Leo wondered and looked back at Elise. All he found was empty space—she had disappeared. He jumped and hid his genitalia with hands, then remembered that it was his ex-wife looking. She had seen it all.

"What the heck are you doing here?" he asked sharply. "And why are you also naked?"

"Fuck, did you lose your mind?"

"Yes."

"Ah, I see. We're having a naked party at your place. And again, where's Elise?"

"She was here just now." Leo turned his gaze around, his brows up. "What do you remember?"

"Not much. I was standing next to her by the kitchen sink . . . before that I was in the past, with her brother, you weren't there, only family . . ."

Beatrice approached and placed her palm on his cheek. "Shall I tell you now or you'd rather wait for your memories to come back?"

"Tell me what exactly?"

"What transpired during these four months. Ouch!" Beatrice jerked forward.

"Bea, my nemesis of old . . ." Elise emerged from behind with the expression of a drunk villain on her face, wiggling fingers and barely containing her grin.

"What is going on!" Leo ran out of patience. "Tell me now!"

Both women gasped and froze, unaccustomed to him being this harsh. Music was seeping into the hallway through the narrow gap in the door.

"This is a farewell party—" Elise said quietly.

Leo's throat twisted in a tight knot. "For whom?" He managed to squeeze the two tortured words out of his mouth, almost sure of the answer.

"My drift has begun," Elise completed her sentence.

Leo lowered his frame in the armchair, overwhelmed by the avalanche of memories her words unleashed. He took her hand and pushed it against his forehead, staring at the floor. His tears returned, this time, charged with great sadness.

Without making a sound, Elise slowly freed the hand he held and wrapped her arms around his head. He rested it on her tummy. Whatever was inside her kicked again.

"Sorry!" Leo looked up into her eyes. "I remember now."

FLASHBACK

Anton had come to visit when Leo was alone. He'd drank several beers and made small talk before finally spilling the beans. "Listen, I must tell you something that may concern Sisi. When you said that people disappear when all who knew them die . . . I might have been the last."

Leo was not immediately spooked. "Well, this is just a hypothesis and, er, don't you have cousins? What about your kids?"

"C'mon, I am just two years older, my son was born in '92. We have a cousin, on our mother's side, but, well, I don't know . . ." Anton paused and looked inside his beer bottle as if expecting to find something else than what passed here for beer.

"Spit it out, what is it?"

"She has a disability. She's like a five-year-old, so I don't know what she will remember. She was six when Lizzy died."

"Is she still alive?"

"Yes, oddly so. Well, she was alive when I passed, that's what I wanted to say."

"I get it. Anyone else?" Leo leaned back and crossed hands; his face became expressionless.

Anton shook his head. "There are some relatives in Scotland, but we hardly ever met. No, I don't think so. Do classmates count?"

"Well, obviously yes—me, Steve . . . you can't see him, though."

"Ah yes, but you two are dead. What about the living ones?"

"Emotional connection. This is what my father keeps saying. He thinks that knowing someone is not enough, but having feelings also counts. His context is seeing; he reckons that I made people see Lizzy because we were in love. Maybe I can keep her here . . ." Leo finished in a quiet voice and sat straight again.

"Are you saying that one must also be loved by someone on the other side? Not barely be personally known?"

Leo nodded. "Probably. Look at the people around you. They are loved ones, aren't they? If not directly by you, then by someone you love. Father may be on the money too if we extend his hypothesis to apply to the drift. Damn, that's disheartening." Leo looked away from Anton, trying to conceal the moisture in his eyes.

"All you have is conjecture! So, man up, will you?" Anton said somewhat angrily.

"Conjecture it is indeed, but that doesn't mean that it is wrong, only that we don't know for sure," Leo retorted. "And the thought of losing her again is depressing to put it mildly." He fidgeted with the lighter, then took out a cigarette and lit it. He inhaled deeply, trying to calm down. "What is killing me is the helplessness, the inability to change a fucking bit of what's to come."

"Try to be more optimistic," Anton said.

"Oh yeah, that's great advice!" Leo said with sarcasm. "As if that's gonna change something!"

"Why are you acting like that? As if her disappearance is preordained?"

"Because it is! Listen, Anton, I get your point. Everything turns to dust eventually, just that with your sister—it is always a fleeting moment. Well, er, I've had shorter relationships, but with her—we clicked, we didn't want to break up; we were pulled away by circumstance . . ."

The door swung open. Elise entered and asked with a shaky voice, "What's going on?"

The two men turned their eyes at her.

"Nothing! Just having a manly chat with your brother. Why?"

"I felt urge to come back, as if something bad took place, you know, as if you were hurt."

"I am whole, as you can see." Leo stood up and laughed.

"No, I'm not talking about being physically wounded. You know that it is not a big deal here; wounds heal fast. You were," she searched for the right word, "heartbroken . . ."

Leo walked to her and wrapped his arms around her wide body. "I was, for a moment." He hesitated then preempted the question. "We remembered your end, and that always makes me sad; I guess Anton is as well. Sorry for sending you a bad vibe."

"What are you talking about?" Anton also rose.

Elise gently freed herself from Leo's hold, walked to the armchair, and sat, "We're all empaths here. To a varying degree, of course, but all possess the trait. Maybe even more than that—this is how we find each other; this is how we signal each other to get lost." She chuckled. "Leo, get me a glass please. I hate drinking from the bottle."

Leo fetched the glass she requested, full of orange juice, then sat back. Anton did the same slowly, reaching first with his hand.

"You are new, so the trait is still dormant." She took the glass. "Hey, I . . . Ah, never mind."

Leo flashed a smile.

She continued, "If the desire is strong, it attracts the person as a magnet or it repels. You can literally teleport. This is on the extreme end. Normally space bends to shorten the trip or lead away."

"Amazing!" Anton exclaimed and glanced at Leo with approval.

"Yes, indeed. Did Leo tell you that he killed you?"

"Now, that's creepy!" Anton said. "How?"

"He thinks that this realm is just a fantasy of his and he's on life support somewhere."

"Nah, I am not a fantasy!" Anton protested.

"I no longer think so. If that were the case, I would be crazy to—" Leo stopped short. If he was hallucinating, why would he want her to leave and inflict such anguish on himself? That argument killed the proposition.

Elise rose with a huff and walked to the kitchen sink with the empty glass in hand. She rinsed it briefly and placed it upside down to dry.

"I am glad you've changed your mind. I was wondering why you would want me pregnant." She smiled. "Anyway, have you seen Joleen?"

"How can a cat be alive for over six decades?" Anton asked.

"She's not alive. She's a ghost, just like us, but I love her. She's cute, and she purrs and meows and does cat stuff like a real one. So?"

Leo thought for a moment. "Now that you are asking, no."

"OK, maybe she's roaming outside." Elise returned to the table and pushed Leo with her tummy. "Whatever's inside is moving. Why can't we find an ultrasound machine?"

Leo bit his lip. He recalled Fluffy and Ginger—they drifted away with Leo's great-grandmother. Where the heck was Joleen! He put his ear to Elise's stomach and tried to detect sounds, but his heartbeat was again overpowering. *Why do we have hearts here*—his thoughts shifted—*or do we not?* He could identify a pulse, however, short of vivisection, there was no way to confirm that it was produced by a heart. So many things to research and discover in this world!

Elise stepped back and Leo's head lurched in the space vacated by her belly.

"You seem to enjoy treating me as a pillow lately." She sounded annoyed.

Leo chuckled and leaned back. "You have become so soft!"

*
**

Joleen showed up the next day, but then disappeared again. The cat walked into Elise's room. Leo traced its movements with his gaze, then kept his eyes trained on the door. Then he grew impatient, walked inside and scanned the room. The animal was gone. Usually, she stretched on Elise's bed. Leo checked underneath it, then the other hiding spots. The only way out of the room was the door, and he didn't see the cat leaving.

Elise did the same a few days later—she went inside to pick clothes. Wasilla was the one to check on her first. "Did you see Lizzy leaving?"

"No." Leo joined her at the door frame. This time, Jolene was sleeping on the bed; their friend was missing. Leo opened the walk-in closet—in this home it was the portal to dreamworld—only to see a few garments.

"Do you think that . . ." Wasilla hesitated. "Er, is it the drift?"

Leo sighed and walked back to the big room.

Wasilla followed. "Do you?" she insisted, raising her voice a notch. "Did Anton not say that he was the last? This is what you told me!"

Leo cursed silently. Why did Anton mention it! Why did he himself share? "Last what?" He was not good at pretending; Wasilla read right through him.

"You know what! The last person who remembered her with fondness. Don't try to pull the wool over my eyes!"

Leo nodded and sat on the countertop; his shoulders slumped. "Looks like it."

It was Wasilla's turn to shed tears. She moved speedily and tried to hug him. Leo stepped on the floor and held her in his arms.

"But it is not proven, maybe just teleportation," he said. "Whatever the case, when she returns, we shan't be sobbing, OK?"

"Easier said than done, but sure, I'll do my best."

"Have you asked yourself why you mourn?"

"I never mourned Walid. I was angry with my father for driving my little brother to suicide. I was mad, full of resentment. When Mom passed, I missed her, but even though she wasn't particularly old, she was very sick, and it was in a way a relief."

"For whom?" Leo went to the coffee maker, poured a mug, and slid it across the countertop. He then helped himself to one and plopped on the couch.

"Everybody. But I still cried."

"About what?" Elise stepped out of her room.

Wasilla clenched her teeth.

"Walid," Leo lied.

***

For the next three weeks, Leo and Wasilla took turns keeping their friend under constant surveillance. Elise spent most of her time with them anyway and never shut the door of her room—none of them did. Until one day, when she did push her door closed. The move was unexpected. Leo failed to notice at first, then threw down the book he was reading, rushed to the door, and reached for the handle.

Then it occurred to him that, if she was inside, bursting into her room with no warning would be hard to justify. He paused and knocked. There was no response.

When she emerged almost a day later, Leo was torn between anguish and rabid curiosity–he was itching to ask where she had been.

"We are empaths in case you have forgotten, and your gloomy mood can be cut with a knife," Elise said after a few minutes of silence. "Care to elaborate?"

Leo looked at Wasilla, who was sitting at the table, head in hands, but she avoided his glance. They promised no lies to each other. However, this promise turned out to be very hard to keep. He couldn't help telling the occasional white lie, and he also lied by omission. Leo took a deep breath. "You were gone for a day."

"Oh!" Elise exclaimed, her eyes widening. "I had just a change of clothes." She pointed at herself. "Unless . . . is it the first time?"

Leo shook head slowly. Wasilla was rubbing her palms without uttering a word. Elise walked over and sat beside her.

"Looks like the drift, no?" She took Wasilla's hand. "Well, you two may be right after all. I can't think of anybody else left alive who would remember me in the prescribed way."

"I'm certain there were other boys with a crush on you, some of them may still be alive," Wasilla said.

"Perhaps. I remember a few—there was Jimmy from my class and even big Gunther—the bully. He always picked on me in front of other people, but once he asked me out. You see?" Her cheerful demeanor returned. "There is still hope!"

"Did you take him up on his offer?" Leo welcomed the change of topic.

"How could I?" She laughed. "I already had a mean boyfriend!"

She was going to leave a very large void in his existence, indeed. He tried to brush the dark thoughts aside and borrow from her optimism but, regrettably, without much success. When she disappeared again a few days later, he roared like a wounded beast.

Wasilla rushed to him in shock. "Geez, man, you scared the bejesus out of me! Don't scream like that!"

"Sorry!" was all he said. By that time, the friendly gray cat, Joleen, had already gone.

MIRIELLE

Elise pushed the door and marched to the center of the big room, where she stood with her hands on her hips. Leo trotted after her inside and closed the door.

"Please stop following me around!" She furrowed her eyebrows. "It is getting on my nerves!"

"But it is working!" Leo replied. "We didn't lose you even once since we started!"

"Yeah, but it is creepy, always being trailed, like, day and night. What if I had to poop?"

"Well, luckily you are under no imperative to perform a dump. But that aside, think of yourself as a super VIP, a president or something . . ."

"Do you think that it would work long term?"

Leo sighed and leaned against the kitchen island. "Don't you want to stay?"

"I do. But it feels weird. I went from having no one to spit at to being constantly watched, even when I sleep. I've started craving some me time." She sat heavily on the couch. Silence prevailed for a while, then she continued with eyes fixed on a point in the distance. "I am no longer afraid, though, not like before. When I drifted for a while, upon return, it felt as if I was in a good place, just that there were no memories of it, only lingering sensation . . ."

"Of what?"

"Of peace and tranquility. We thought that death was final, yet here we are. So, who's to say that drifting away is the end? We need change to feel alive, don't we? Maybe reincarnation is a thing, maybe we go back for another stint in the old world."

"That would be awful!" Leo objected. "The old world is awful! Too much stupidity, suffering, viciousness, and deceit! Reincarnating there would be a cruel and unusual punishment. I mean within the context of this existence. Besides, if it were a thing, would it not make sense to remember more than one lifetime once we get here?"

"Yeah . . ." She gave a slow nod. "Ugh, I feel like dipping in a pool; this thing is heavy." Elise pointed at her tummy and bent forward, seeking balance to stand up. Leo pushed himself away from the island and sprang to her assistance. Elise grabbed his arm and rose slowly. "And I want to suck dick," she completed her sentence in an unexpected way and reached for his crotch.

"Seriously?" Leo wrinkled his forehead.

"Yeah, why not? There may be no sex where I am going, so I shall enjoy it while I can." She sat back on the couch, lifted his kilt and pushed the hem into his hands. Her palm glided over his dick as if trying to make it rise without touching. Then she moved the hand behind it and fondled his scrotum, then the penis itself. "You see, I love giving you pleasure," she said while observing the transformation, "I haven't told you before, but I have climaxed while doing that. True, with a little help from a finger. Or a tongue . . ." She smiled and kissed the glans, then held the penis at the root with both hands and drew it in her mouth.

Leo twitched; his muscles tensed. He loved giving her pleasure too and he had also been there. He wanted to be there now! Elise moved her head leisurely, taking the penis deep inside her oral cavity, then pulling it out. Each time her lips tickled the corona, he shivered, as sparks flew abound. She vibrated her tongue over the tip, then dragged it along the shaft. Leo felt a charge building up; he inhaled deeply and clutched the kilt. Would the sensation be the same if they didn't love each other? He quivered as she pulled it back into her mouth. He started rocking his hips in sync, his heart pounding. In and out, in and out. A pull, a roll of the tongue and out and in . . . Leo panted; his eyebrows furrowed. The charge inside him reached a crucial level and gleefully spilled out.

Elise looked up and met his gaze with a joyful twinkle in her eyes. Leo smiled. She sucked on the glans, then slowly withdrew the appendage from her mouth. Her cheeks were bright pink and the expression on her face—content.

She licked the tip, traced her lips and said quietly, "We humans are full of contradictions."

Leo let go of the kilt, squatted, reached and flipped her locks out of her face. "Yeah, I know."

"Sorry for stating the obvious." She smiled, and they kissed. "Now, let's . . ." she began rising to her feet. "Ouch!" Elise returned to sitting position, "Something is happening!"

Leo looked down. "I think your water broke."

"Ah! OK."

"Relax." Leo pushed a throw pillow behind her and shouted, "Wass! Wasilla!"

"What is it?" Wasilla's sleepy façade adorned her door frame.

"It started . . ."

"The drift?" Wasilla gasped and popped her eyes open wide, then registered Elise's presence and relaxed. "Or the birth, I suppose?"

"Lizzy's water broke. Keep an eye on her; I will try to find Mother." He maneuvered around the table and ran outside. A minute later the boat's engine gurgled then cut through the eerie silence with a high-pitched roar.

"Hi, Wass!" Elise greeted her with a smile. "What do we do now?"

Wasilla shrugged. "Don't know, I had no kids."

"Very reassuring!" Elise laughed. "Come here, sit." She patted the cushion next to her. Wasilla did not wait for another prompt. She joined her friend and looked at her with a mix of excitement and worry.

"Hey, you are staring! Tone it down, please."

"Sorry!" Wasilla downcast her gaze, leaving only Elise's legs in sight. "Does it hurt?"

"No, not at the moment." Elise reached for Wasilla's ear and gently pulled her face closer until their lips met.

Leo crossed paths with his mother halfway between her place and the dock. Dr. Charles was walking next to her. Leo nudged his brow up in an unspoken question.

"Don't you remember?" his mom asked.

"Remember what?"

"I'm, or rather, I was, an OB/GYN," Dr. Charles clarified.

"Ah, no, I didn't know, I had no idea what kind of doc you were, sorry!" Leo coughed in his hand.

"So, what made you broadcast?" Annette asked.

"Lizzy's water broke, so—"

"Interesting!" Charles interrupted. "A birth, here! I don't know what to expect!"

"What? Like she gives birth to a monster of some sort?" Leo replied indignantly.

"No, no!" Charles protested energetically, then immediately contradicted himself, "Ah, it could be that; it is a first as far as I know, but unlikely, it is probably pseudocyesis—"

"I told you I detected a double heartbeat," Annette said.

"Ah, yeah, twins then . . ."

"Mom, the good doctor here doesn't seem to be in full control."

Dr. Charles stared at him. "Leo, this is how I talk. I guess that's why your mom forgot my specialization until now. And I am very excited indeed but rest assured that I can handle a birth."

"Sorry, no offense meant," Leo mumbled. "You know that you can't see her, right?"

"Your mother will be my eyes and hands. She's trained."

Leo pushed the barn door open and led them inside the warehouse. The sunlight drew a path on the concrete floor from the door straight to the metal stairs leading to the loft. His father greeted them from a distance. Jessica stood beside him. Steve, Beatrice, and Margot were occupying space near the stairs, Steve with hands behind his back.

When he heard the trio coming, he turned and gleamed, "How's it, man! I brought Dr. Schultz! But then your mom is here, I see . . ."

"How the fuck did you all know?" Leo widened his eyes.

"I told you," Annette said. "You broadcasted. Or maybe Lizzy, not so sure now."

"Her parents are upstairs." Richard nodded in the direction of the loft.

Elongated shadows disturbed the path of light, as more dead friends filed in. *Crap, I must have done it!* He had no idea that broadcasting was a thing. Come to think of it, this was indeed a big event in this world: the possible birth of a baby, a state of being that was not known to exist here. With all these people, certainly more than he could see, the event was turning into a spectacle. Who knew how Elise was going to perceive it; he better rein them in. His dad and Jessica were already climbing.

"All listen up!" Leo raised his voice. "Please stay here and be quiet! Respect Lizzy's privacy!" She was under constant surveillance for the past few months, already on the brink, no need for extra eyes. "Or I will try to send you away! You know how things work here, right?"

When Leo and his companions entered the loft, they were greeted by the tense faces of Elise's parents, Wasilla, and Anton. "What? Where's Lizzy?"

"She drifted away!" Wasilla said tearfully. "I . . . I came to open the door, and I let my eyes go off her only for a second . . ."

Leo's legs wobbled. He bit hard on his lip, trying to contain a scream. There was nothing that he could do. He sensed Wasilla's desire to be consoled and beckoned her. Wasilla rushed to him, clutched him with both arms, and started crying. So much about the spectacle.

"There are people outside; let me tell them to go home," Leo whispered in her ear. Wasilla released her hold and stepped aside, still sobbing. Leo took a few steps toward the door. His vision blurred and he lurched forward, his knees bending under the weight of his body. Leo grabbed the handle, pushed it down, and gripped the door edge trying to stay erect.

⁎⁎

"It's a girl!" Wasilla's voice was distant and muffled. "Hey, man up, did you always faint?"

He took a few deep breaths. "No, I jumped." Leo checked his balance and let go of the door.

"Ah, sorry, when were you?"

"When you let Lizzy drift away . . ."

"That was the day before, she came back a couple of hours ago and went into labor."

Leo realized that something was amiss. "Where's the baby?" He turned around and surveyed the room. Ruth was holding the newborn, appearing shaken and lost. Elise was lying in her bed, sweating, and looking at him with a tired smile on her face. His mother was sitting on a chair with hands in her lap. When they crossed gazes, she gave him a thumbs-up. Next to her was Dr. Charles.

"Why are the babies not crying?" Leo asked Ruth, while trying to locate the other twin. "Are they alive?"

"She is alive," his mother said. "Congrats!"

"She? As in one?"

"Yes, I was wrong, I must have misheard. With a homemade stethoscope and the hearing of a shrink it is hard." His mother raised her shoulders apologetically.

Leo reached hesitantly, then withdrew his hand.

"You can hold her, no problem. She's asleep." Annette encouraged him.

Leo took the baby from Ruth. The tiny creature was warm and moved, as he held it. He sat beside Elise.

Elise stretched out her arms. "Let me have her, will you?"

"Sure!"

"Thanks!" Elise placed the little being on her chest and very gently touched the hair. "See, she isn't bald!"

"So what?" Leo didn't understand why that was important,

"Some babies are born bald, is not that so?" Elise replied.

"You were also born with hair," said Ruth and sat on the other chair.

"Everybody's so gloomy here. Can't you show some joy?" Leo scanned the mob. "Lizzy's back, the baby looks to be OK . . ."

"It is so confusing!" Elise's mother wailed and burst into tears. "What is she? Is she human? She did not cry, just started breathing! And look—the cord is gone; it turned to dust." She extended her arm, palm up, revealing the remnants.

"She's a mini ghost." Elise smiled and glided her fingertips over the little body, barely making contact. Then she folded her legs, pulled her gown up and covered the baby. "Maybe she's cold?"

"Ah, sorry!" Her mother sprang into action. "Here's a blanket!"

"She's so clean," Leo observed. "Shouldn't she have blood and stuff?"

"This is not Earth," his mother said. "She came out bloody, yes, but . . ."

"I get it, thanks!" Leo lifted his hand, then turned to Elise. "Well, what shall we call her?"

"Dunno." Elise shrugged. "Maybe . . ." She moved her eyes around the room. Her gaze stopped on her mother's face. "Ruth?" Then quickly added, "Or Antoinette, er, sorry, I meant Annette? Or both?"

"Mirielle," Wasilla said unexpectedly. All seeing eyes turned to her. "It means 'miraculous' in French," she explained. "And isn't she?"

"I like that!" Leo stretched his mouth into a wide smile.

The baby snorted and started sucking her tiny thumb.

"Agreed!" the baby's mother said.

DEPARTURE

Leo was observing Elise and Mirielle, his tiny new daughter, through his bloodshot eyes. He was not a starving werewolf; that was the cost of stealing thirty-five more days from the jaws of the drift. The relatives were pushing for a Golden Month celebration next week. Perhaps they shall have it, the baby's fine, Mom's still around . . .

"Ouch!" Elise squirmed. "She bites!"

"Bites? She has no teeth," Leo objected.

"I remember a story about some guy who checked if turtles indeed had no teeth. Well, that was confirmed to be the case but was no less painful nevertheless!" She squinted again.

"Sorry, Lizzy, there's no formula in this realm. We tried."

"Maybe she doesn't need food? Like us," Elise speculated.

"We . . . do get hungry, right?"

Elise sighed. "Yes. I survived many months without food, but back then I was depressed and had no appetite."

"You have plenty, can't we put some in a bottle?" Leo suggested.

"Ouch! Shit, do you wanna milk me? I am not a freakin' cow!"

"I was trying to make your life easier; that is what both my wives did—"

"Yes, I know, sorry, I reacted to the pain. But . . . I like feeding her this way."

"Suit yourself then."

Elise smiled playfully. "On reconsideration—you may milk me."

Leo laughed. "OK!"

"Are you happy?" Elise asked. "I mean having her?"

Leo nodded. "I never had a strong drive to spread my genes. Yet each kid made me happy—Eric, Abi, now Mirielle. Ah, the irony." He rolled his eyes.

"What irony? Ugh!"

"I didn't plan to have many children. One, two with a push. I wanted to give my offspring all I had, not have them all. Now I have fathered three, one in the afterlife! And I am happy for you—for your experience so far. You wanted it—the cramps, the vomiting, the swollen ankles, the whole deal—right?"

She hummed, also somewhat stretching her lips sideways.

The baby pushed the nipple away with her tongue and opened her eyes widely, staring nowhere.

"Now it is your turn!" Elise giggled and wiped her breast.

"Not hungry."

"I know. See, I can transform again." Her shape shifted slightly.

"Your boobs are smaller now," Leo commented with indifference. The baby cooed.

"Leo, I feel that I will drift away soon. I think that Mirielle is somehow extending my stay, but it won't last forever. It is almost a year since Anton died, and you know that the drift occurs after about six months." Elise caressed her little daughter. "Please take good care of her, you and Wass."

Leo gazed down, his eyes watering. Then he breathed in decisively and pushed the sorrow aside. "Needless to ask! But you are still here. Didn't you want me to suck?" Leo laughed then called, "Wass!"

"Well, have you ever milked a cow?" Elise dipped her finger in her milk, licked it, then licked her lips and smiled. What she told him was true—she enjoyed feeding Mirielle, despite the occasional hard pulls and the bites. The sensation traveled down to her groin and stirred a desire. Why was Leo lingering . . .

"Hey!" she called, "Here," she dipped her finger again and extended it to him. The touch made her shiver. She tried the other nipple—same result.

"Are you sure?" Seemed he had changed his mind. "Bea and Elizabeth . . . they were not keen. I spoke without thinking."

Elise rolled her eyes—so she was again the oddball out here. "Apparently, I am different. I . . . Breastfeeding, squirting milk—it gives me butterflies, it tuns me on . . ." She produced a guilty smile.

"OK then. But if it hurts, order me to stop."

"Don't worry, I already went through it with Wass."

"Tough competition!" Leo chuckled, stepped on the floor, turned, and whispered in her ear, "Get up, moo." He offered his hand.

Elise complied. Leo led her to his room and took the biggest of his sheep bells hanging from his bookshelf. She guessed his intention and giggled.

"Sorry, no cow bells; this one will have to do." Leo winked and tied the strap around her neck. The cold metal sent quivers down her body and nudged her level of arousal up.

"Now, step here, bend forward, stretch your arms and put your hands on the mattress." He pointed to a spot in front of his bed. "Closer, your legs must touch the frame. And keep them straight and a bit apart. Good, that's it!"

Wow, what is he up to? Elise thought and followed the instruction.

Leo joined her in her nakedness, grew his hair and his beard, stood behind her, and warmed her breasts in his cupped hands while running his tongue over her spine. When he started swirling his palms slowly with her nipples pinched between his fingers, she twitched, and the bell clanked. She took a deep breath as his touch rippled throughout her body.

Leo climbed on the bed, rolled on his back, and wriggled under her. She tilted her head down and flexed her elbows, aiming a nipple at his mouth. The clapper hit the bow. He squeezed the breast she offered. The milk squirted. He wiped the nipple with his tongue, sending delightful shivers down her spine. She blinked slowly and moaned but remained still. Then he repeated with the other; the shivers tickled her groin again. Leo traced circles over her areolas with his fingertips, then rolled her nipples with his thumbs, then squeezed the breasts; more liquid squirted out.

She arched her back and emitted another high-pitched moan. She felt moisture building up between her legs. The bell clanked, her muscles tensed, and her breathing paused for a moment. Leo pulled her closer, took a nipple in his mouth, rolled his tongue around it and then pulled it with his lips, then sucked on it. She gasped loudly and quivered. Her eyesight blurred. His hands traveled tirelessly over her back and flanks, then her rear and her thighs, while he vibrated his tongue over the tense protrusion, nibbled lightly and sucked more. Her body shivered. Another clank was heard.

Leo dragged his tongue flat over her breast and switched to the other, pulled the nipple into his mouth and repeated his routine. Each time his hands split her cheeks she felt the urge to be penetrated. As soon as the nipple felt the air, she scrambled up on the bed and drew his penis into her mouth. "Hey, I am not the moo!" she heard him saying between the strokes of the clapper. She pushed her rear in his face and rubbed her chest against his skin, then she felt his warm wet tongue reaching for her sweet spot. When he found it, the elation sent tears to her eyes.

She crawled forward, held Leo's dick upright, and started rubbing her breasts with it. She felt him separating her buttocks again, then his finger probed her ring; she gasped and arched her back. The urge to have him enter her returned. Her mouth hung open. Prodding her nipples with his excited member was setting small explosions off. Her body was shaking; the bell kept clanking. She directed Leo's climax to her cleavage, sat on his chest and spread the warm slimy fluid over her breasts, then tilted her head upward and drew air in her lungs. He reached from behind; his hands traveled up until they found the hills. Leo resumed pinching and rolling her nipples. She placed her palms on his hands and made him vigorously rub and shake her eager bulges until the sparks flying throughout her body finally set off the big bang. She wailed, bent forward and collapsed on her head in between his legs.

Leo waited patiently for her to move. She eventually rolled to the side, propped herself up on her elbow, and took a deep breath. He sat. They crossed gazes. Elise smiled and said quietly, "I never had a tit orgasm before Mirielle was born. I only got turned on. Funny how things work. Thanks!"

"But Wass had it, no?"

"Mmm. And she's better at sucking tits than you." Elise giggled and slapped him playfully with the back of her hand.

"But she lacks a certain body part that you enjoyed playing with again!" He rolled next to her and crossed his arms behind his head.

"Pervert!" Elise jumped and ran toward the room next door to be reunited with her baby. The bell clanked with glee.

He trailed her with his gaze until she disappeared into the hallway. He released the long-haired image of himself, the one she loved so much, slipped into the kilt, stood up and stretched, then put his shirt on. The baby did indeed seem to act as an anchor, as she was right that she was overdue to drift away. Leo sighed. Maybe he should shut the door and let his dread pour out. He acted bravely in her presence, but inside him his heart felt so small. He always kept a tissue beside him when he was on duty watching her. By morning it often was soaked. Wasilla was the same. They both explained the lack of sleep as an excuse for their red eyes, but he was almost certain that Elise knew. He slapped himself—he should be happy to still have her around.

The loft was strangely quiet. Leo could hear Mirielle's cooing through the open door and Wasilla's calming voice, but that was all. Leo's heart fell to his stomach! He sprang up, rushed to Wasilla's room and stuck his head inside. Wasilla lifted her eyes and looked at him. "Something wrong?"

Leo cursed and ran to the big room. The sunlight streamed through the windows, beams reflecting from inanimate objects—kitchen island, couch, dining table, the piano and its stool. Leo swallowed with great difficulty. He turned back. Wasilla stood by her door holding Mirielle; the baby was waving her hands, then she started crying. For the first time!

"I missed her in a flash," Leo said quietly.

Wasilla took a few steps forward and looked inside Elise's room. It was devoid of her presence. The bell was also silent. She bit her lip, brought the baby very close to her chest, and started rocking where she stood. Leo banged his head against the wall and sighed. Perhaps Lizzy would return?

∗∗

Elise did indeed and stayed for a while, nursing her little girl and going wild with her friends. They decided to make it the best time together in this realm. They took trips to the forest and around the world, threw many parties for their friends, always keeping her in sight. Elise hated being constantly surveilled; however, she endured it stoically for their sake, primarily for Mirielle, as she wanted to be a mom just for a bit longer.

Then she became translucent. Not by much at first—when she raised her hand against the sun, she could make out its disk not just scattered glow. Elise smiled. *So, this is how it is going to go down—fade away.* She was amused rather than afraid.

"Can you see through me?" she asked Leo.

"Sometimes."

"Ah!" She realized that he was referring to guessing her thoughts. "No, I mean it literally, like through glass."

Leo looked at her with incredulity. "No, I don't think so."

On that occasion, she left him alone. When her translucence increased, she pulled him outside, raised her hand, and said, "See?"

His eyebrows rose. "Mm, yeah."

Elise removed her blouse and climbed on the stone balustrade, casting a shadow over him.

"You remind me of . . ." He stumbled.

"Of what?" She spread her arms.

"A visual effect!"

"Bo-ring! I was looking for something more like 'goddess.'" She displayed her signature smile.

"Goddess." He scoffed. "You know that I am an atheist."

"After all that you have been through? After this world?" Elise threw her palms in the air and pivoted to face the river.

"Since when? When did it start?"

"Are you still an atheist?" she insisted.

"Yes, there is still no evidence of a god or gods. The existence of this realm proves nothing of the kind. We haven't shaken hands with Godfrey. Unless we are in hell, but somehow it doesn't feel like it."

Elise sighed and jumped on the sidewalk. He was so prosaic sometimes. She prepared to dive headfirst into her blouse.

"Hang on!" Leo raised his hand. "Don't move!" He crouched so her shadow could reach his eyes and looked up. Then he moved his head to the left and right. "Interesting!"

"What?"

"Your body is translucent but not your clothes. And . . . I must repeat it, but you look like alpha blend."

"What is that?"

"A visual effect where the foreground is partially or fully transparent. You are the foreground."

"Ah, yes!" Elise remembered his occupation in the other life. No wonder he called her that.

"The thing is, I see no flesh and bones," Leo continued.

"About three weeks."

"You are referring to what?" Leo seemed to have forgotten his question.

"To when I observed it for the first time. I am dissolving, and it is getting more intense."

Leo stepped closer, embraced her, and whispered in her ear, "I'd love you even if you turn into a jellyfish." His gaze flickered restlessly along the river shore.

*
**

"Wow!" Wasilla exclaimed a couple of weeks later. "I can see through you!"

Elise sighed. "You are not alone."

"It is scary!"

"Then stop looking!"

"But then you'll drift away."

"Don't you get it, Wass? Now I am dissolving, fading away!" Elise was suddenly overwhelmed with emotions. She sat and buried her face in the palms of her hands. She couldn't keep her tears in check; they started rolling down her cheeks and meeting her lap after a brief travel along her forearms. "I am dissolving! Maybe you all shall look away and let me leave!"

Leo kneeled in front of her and tried to catch her gaze, while tenderly stroking her now-long hair. It grew during the pregnancy to their shared dismay. The words he managed to force out were "If that is your wish . . ."

"Not yet!" Elise stood up resolutely and went to the crib. Mirielle looked up at her and smiled. "Not until she tells me to go." Elise lifted her daughter, hugged her, and began pacing back and forth across the room.

"French fries anyone?" Leo asked loudly.

"Sure, why not!"

*
**

After a while, Mirielle began crying each time her mom came into sight. By then Elise was indeed spooky—one could read a book through her even in low light. She noticed that if she pushed hard with her hand against a door, eventually it would sink in and pass through. If she held an object for long enough, it would merge with her.

One day, she woke up half embedded in the mattress of her bed. Her face contorted in terror. She pulled herself free, cursing, and rushed to the crib. Mirielle, startled by the bump, opened her eyes, laid them on her mom and began screaming. Elise dropped on her knees beside the crib and wailed. Leo burst into the room, surveyed the scene, joined her on the floor, and took her in his arms. Wasilla abandoned her chair, grabbed the baby and ran to the big room, trying to calm the little creature down.

Elise sobbed and wheezed. "It's time to go, Leo . . . it's time to go . . . please take good care of her. And Wass too, she's an angel. Fuck! I love you so much, all of you! But I don't want to become one with a damn concrete floor. I want to drift away as everybody else does. Please let me go!" She turned, wrapped her arms around his neck, and buried her head in his chest. "Strange, I can see your heart beating . . ."

"You can see my heart?"

"Well, not exactly. I see a pulsing glow and faint streams of light spreading throughout your body at each beat . . . Please, let me go!"

"We need to tell Wass. And Anton and your mom and dad."

"Okay."

*
**

On the next day she was no more. She said goodbye to all those present in the big room of their home and then asked them to look away. Only Ruth was sobbing openly. Leo looked mean and determined; Wasilla was strangely calm. When they turned back, Elise had

321

vanished. Mirielle wriggled in his arms and started crying and Leo realized that he was squeezing her too tightly. His baby daughter's mom had left for who knew how long, perhaps forever. He sat in the armchair and began to rock the baby gently. She soon relaxed and fell asleep with her tiny thumb in her mouth. Leo slumped backward and let her rest on his chest. He was tired from the vigils. The mood in the room was somber. Wasilla finally had let loose her emotions and was sobbing in Beatrice's arms. Steve's eyes were also moist. Simon and Ruth had embraced each other in the corner, her shoulders shaking. Leo couldn't see Simon's expression, but he had no doubt that her dad was sharing in the sorrow. Anton had buried face in his palms.

Leo closed his eyes and pictured Elise and her smile. He was hopeful that they would meet again. As before, on that day at their old school. Or anywhere else, the locale did not matter. His thoughts began slowing down and breaking into disconnected fragments until he felt somebody shaking his knee.

"Yes!" Leo jumped and sat upright. A young girl, maybe seven or eight, let go of his leg and stepped back, startled. He remembered that look! She used to transform occasionally into a child! Leo's eyes grew large! "Lizzy?"

"Leo?" The girl's eyes also became big and very round. Then she blinked a couple of times, lost the shocked look, and asked, "Er . . . Daddy?"

TO BE CONTINUED